TAD —
YOU ARE
FOLLOW YOUR DREAMS
& NEVER QUIT,

M000305363

Treasure
of
La Chiva

A Novel By
Steve Grumer

Treasure of La Chiva

Printed in the USA
www.stevegrumer.com

ISBN-13: 978-0-9845386-1-4 (pbk)
ISBN-10: 0984538615
ISBN 978-0-9845386-0-7 (eBook)
LCCN 2011903173

Cover Design by Michael Mallin

DEDICATION

This is dedicated to the ones I love. "All my relations."

CONTENTS

PREFACE

We were sitting on the deck of Captain Dan's sailing yacht, the *Toucan*, in the colorful waters over a coral reef in Placencia, Belize when Ellis Stevens began to share his amazing story about his adventure with an old treasure buried in Mexico. I knew at once that it had to be written. It took more than a year to gain his approval.

This book represents my best recollection of a few days in the summer of 2005 listening to my old friend share his secret experiences about a treasure buried in the 1880's on a mountain outside of Culiacan, one-third of the way down Mexico's west coast. We couldn't believe what we heard. It sounded like a Hollywood story but with more impact because of my familiarity with one of the players.

I was lucky to be on the catamaran when Ellis talked about his exciting experiences with Blaine Court and the Treasure of La Chiva. His years underground now made sense. I thank Captain Dan Powers for providing a forum for it all to happen safely.

If I told you it was true would you believe me?

STEVE GRUMER
Sausalito, CA
March 30, 2010

INTRODUCTION

I was hooked on his story when I first heard Blaine Court whisper the words "buried treasure." The rest of the sales pitch was a waste of his time, but I wasn't going to interrupt him. His words still echo in my mind.

Some things are true beyond trite, meaningful even if overworked, significant beyond cliché. This instant in time was unique. We were off to experience a dream. We were going to climb right up to the site of a buried treasure near Culiacan, Mexico.

Wouldn't it be wonderful to open a trap door that hasn't been opened since the early 1900's and find gold and silver coins, pieces of eight, jewels, artifacts and other valuables? How about boxes and piles of them?

Many young children dream of buried treasure. Is it a part of the archetype going back through books with characters such as the Hardy Boys, Long John Silver, and William "Captain" Kidd? I have read and re-read the passages where the amazing Count of Monte Cristo, Edmund Dantes, finds the treasure and exacts his revenge. What was Dumas enticing us to imagine? For him it was a cave, protected by water. The location here was slightly different. This cave was hidden high on a steep mountain face. It had protection provided by gravity and other forces.

It was hard to imagine experiencing it all at one time and in one place, old and forgotten. It was hidden in the 1880's and known to have only three visitors, the last being almost a century ago. It was our turn.

ELLIS STEVENS
Placencia, Belize
June 2, 2005

PROLOGUE
Northern California - 1982

The arrangements were made well in advance of the meeting. Almost four months had elapsed without any communication between the parties. The rules were set and deviation was not permitted. Unusual security precautions were always followed. The strictness of the guidelines bordered upon supreme paranoia. None of the members complained, for it would do no good. That was obvious to all concerned.

The project had taken many years, and a secret treasure of incredible quality and quantity was about to be rediscovered. It was a real-life treasure story and the opening of a secret hiding place of a famous bandit-hero type from the late 1800's. I felt so lucky.

I shuddered to think that this story had been a legend even then. I remember walking into the King Tut exhibit in San Francisco in 1980 and seeing part of that incredible treasure. The gold and jewels had a shine from a different era. Besides the overflowing beauty of the objects themselves were the photographs of Howard Carter which froze the time around the spectacular discovery of the tomb of Tutankhamen in 1922. He looked tired and scared. Howard Carter had been searching in Egypt since 1890, a period with an interesting parallel to this story.

I felt honored to be invited, being the last member to join the cadre of Blaine's team who were going to assist him at the opening of a large treasure buried on a mountain near Culiacan, Mexico. This was going to be an exciting adventure with historical significance. There was more than enough fantasy and adventure for the group. It was exciting beyond words.

As before, nobody was permitted any form of recording or electronic equipment. My cameras were the exception, since my role was to document the discovery. The behavior appeared to be paranoid and ridiculous, but that may not be a fair assessment in light of my lack of previous involvement in the project. Blaine was convinced that he was being followed, and don't get him started about telephone wire-tapping. He didn't trust the mail either. I thought his silver gray hair and beard were telling me something. My inexperience at that time served as an actual shield to the danger ahead. I disregarded the wisdom of his carefully chosen words.

All expenses paid? And I would get to personally experience and photo-document the story? As I said, I was hooked with the first "T" word. I was not briefed in one sitting. I was surprised when I first heard of the church objects, possessions from earlier civilizations that walked the earth, and items of religious significance. These required a different level of care. We had to be sure that they went to the best recipients for their proper placement in the public domain.

The photo-documentation process would be made with Nikon cameras. We used 35mm film. It was only film then, years ahead of the digital world that now looks like it was around the corner. The photographer in me was itching to take the shots that would memorialize one special and productive bandit into history.

Blaine had specific intentions for the ancient power objects and I was asked to help him identify them in the overwhelming face of the piles and boxes of gold and other valuables. The hypnotic trance induced by the treasure itself would be enchanting. It was expected to be a very transformative experience.

I was too excited for words. My mind drifted and jumped, danced and dreamed. There was more than a remote chance that the story would rock the world. Maybe there were two remote chances! Would Oprah like it? The time was right for something positive, where the little guy could win, and when the memories of a beloved folk hero could be elevated to their appropriate place in regional historical significance.

In the last few years there have been stories in the newspapers and magazines about expeditions to uncover sunken treasure using newer technology. The introduction of unmanned cameras and exploratory submarines have greatly expanded the range of the undersea treasure hunter. The stories were newsworthy and exciting. I would tingle with excitement when I would compare these discoveries with the mystic and remote Treasure of La Chiva. It was hard to maintain perspective. Worse than that, it was impossible!

There is an intangible something in the universal appeal of a treasure. Why the dreams? Stories? Whatever the reason, we had all gathered to play our respective roles in this current uncovering of a hidden treasure. The legend was worthy of a story already, but we were going to be adding a new chapter. The story would be revived.

Nothing would be the same after the old trap door is opened for the first time since before World War I. And the next phase of our trip was about to begin. The excitement had an electric quality. This was the moment I had dreamed about since the revelation at my first meeting with Blaine in Phoenix. It changed our lives forever, but all that matters now is respecting the fact that it led to this very moment.

We were not ready for the forthcoming encounter. It was much more than we ever bargained for. The gathering took place an hour south behind extensive security. Meetings of this nature had an air of seriousness. Nobody felt funny tonight. The subject was too serious. He must have found Epimineo Corrales, the last known living person to find the site.

Blaine was in possession of the directions to the legendary Treasure of La Chiva. We were about to locate the cave, open the trap door, experience the story and share the legend. The goals were altruistic in part, and rewarding in many others. Charity and education were going to be the primary recipients of the treasure, after the government got its part.

Blaine was strongly motivated about the establishment of schools throughout the area in Northwest Mexico. It was through educating the young that the most dramatic change can be effectuated upon the Culiacan society without any ethnic or value issues.

I was the fortunate benefactor of the story itself, with the responsibility to share it in order to keep it alive. There was another, secret role: my sensitivity levels with certain antiquities help me "hear" parts of their history. Blaine wanted to quickly withdraw the true antiquities, the tools and sacred objects from the Incan times that should be returned to the mountain from which they came hundreds of years ago. That was why Blaine and I had been introduced in Arizona. We had to return the ancient power objects.

The problems had yet to appear in my mind. My positive and optimistic vision clouded the potential for an unusually dark ending. Ignorance is bliss.

∽ ∽ ∽

PART I – THE BANDIT

1. LAREANO GARCIA

Northwestern Mexico – 1862

The underlying story starts near one of the oldest cities in the state of Sinaloa, Mexico. The cathedral was built in the 1830's. It was older than any other major building in the City of Culiacan. It was made of local materials and bore the traditional architecture, a blend of influences and construction techniques from Spain and Italy. From its shadows came forth the origins of this legend. It was the unlikely birthplace for such a dark and mysterious story.

Young Lareano Garcia is amazed at the size of the enormous wood doors. They tower above him. The aged planks are weather worn and heavy. They are dark, oversized and imposing. They dwarf the boy and he wonders why. The rough iron hinges are longer than his arms. Although they look like a pair of doors, they actually represent a huge wall to the young boy, an impassable barrier. The place is forbidding. He has never been allowed beyond these grand doors. That would not change for five and a half more years.

The doors were a source of curiosity for the boy. For some peculiar reason, his earliest memories were of these portals. The doors had no handles. They could not be opened from the outside. Once a week the bells atop the building would ring and the doors would open, almost like magic, from the inside. They would part in the center and reach outward, stretching to the waiting believers outside. The doors would extend their robust arms towards the street, transformed into an invitation, a welcome.

Young Lareano wondered what made the doors move. He asked, "How did this happen?"

"Did the sound of the bells have anything to do with the opening?"

He wondered why children were not allowed inside. His friends shared the curiosity but accepted the condition without comment. That was the way it was to them.

One time he questioned, "Was there no fun within the big old building?"

He simply couldn't understand the secrets held within or the impact of that moment, and each and every similar one. The questions would have an answer, and the reaction would trigger a chain reaction throughout the entire area.

Life in his country was difficult for most. It was even harder for women and children. We are talking about the middle of the 19th Century, more than fifty years before the revolution. The Revolution of 1910 was a turning point in the history of this nation, but almost all of the events of this story significantly pre-date that time.

The town is located in Northwestern Mexico, far from the comforts of the sea. It is dusty and hot, but never blazing hot. The air is parched. It has not rained for weeks. The dry sandy soil sticks to everything. Cactus is the predominant native species. Agave. The landscape encompassed miles upon miles of cactus. At that time large trees were rare and, when found, ill shaped.

What does the word "poor" mean to a boy of five? His worldly experience does not extend to economic status or possessions. The caste system is unknown to a child. He can already experience the consequence without understanding the concept. Life is its own cruel teacher.

Lareano is too young, but he wants to learn. His mind is like a sponge as he watches and listens. He wants to know everything in unique detail about the things that surround him. He possesses a subtle comfort in the fact that he will know more when he is older. He is confident that he has the time. Patience is not usually innate at such a young age. He would be a leader in time. Was it the glisten in his bright dark eyes? Was it his air of confidence? What could foretell the future?

Lareano Garcia was different, but more in the way he would connect with strangers. Some say it was a passion developed by the extraordinary love and care from his family, especially his paternal grandmother. He felt special. He radiated strength and understanding.

We could also consider his drive. It was outstanding and unusual. He had tireless energy when any goal was in sight. He was project-oriented, fastidious, and self-motivating.

He did not understand the value of limitations. His belief system was developed with a robust level of conviction. He could do whatever he pleased in the world of his dreams. In time he would be able to manifest them too.

The place where light and dark begin to touch has been said to be the place where miracles arise. The sense of wonder manifests out of these ethers. Perhaps this is the story of a dark dream, the creation of the negative. The story is not always happy, and the opposites here are equally true.

This was more like a recipe for disaster. At the beginning, it reflected a destiny to be the worst, the balance to all of the good. But his motives and methods of sharing may reveal a different value judgment.

The catalytic event was major. His grandmother's life has been robbed from him. Maybe he should return the favor. The imagery is simple, the solution so obvious. To become a thief was the decision, the best thief and nothing less. That would be his destiny.

What would you do if your favorite person in the whole world was taken from you? What if it was by the slow process of starvation? The town was poor, but not behind the huge wooden doors. He hated the world behind the doors. That was another world, the world of the church. Something was wrong in that large cathedral building. The contrast was evident, the paradox puzzling. It did not make sense to him. In fact, not much about life was easy to comprehend. He was young and quickly learning.

To Lareano the church was the enemy. Nobody was sure how this really developed. He detested them with all of his might. His anger was deep and empowering. How could they allow such poverty, hunger and even starvation outside while there exists such opulence and richness behind the doors?

Life was suffering for his family. There was barely enough. His father worked very hard in the fields. The demands could be great with physical pain adding to the combination. He was able to get extra food when the crops were good, but the sun and the rodents often got there before him. Hunger was a normal occurrence. Fortunately, the experience was never lasting.

2. GRANDMOTHER

State of Sinaloa – 1860's

Grandma Eva was the most precious person to Lareano. His whole world revolved around her. She was there for him when he was tired or lonely. She would share her cot with him on cold nights. Her blanket seemed softer than the others, perhaps because it was old and worn. Grandma was getting older and thinner. Food was in short supply and money was scarce.

Grandmother always had time for him. She seemed to radiate joy whenever she was around him. The intense love of his grandmother was evident to everyone. She had a smile painted on her face. She never tired of his endless questions.

It seemed that his initial bonds were much tighter to his grandmother than even his parents. He tried to spend as much of his time with her as possible. She was clearly his favorite person, including even his friends. His happiest time was always at the side of his grandmother.

She clearly understood the value of the old saying, "hay mas tiempo que vida." It means, "There is more time than life," and a lot more. Those were the words he most remembered from his grandmother.

Grandma Eva seemed to enjoy every moment of life itself. Her positive contributions to family and friends had a unifying effect. She was happy, peaceful and content at all times.

The neighbors were close, very close. Most of the families had lived in the same place since the birth of more than one generation. As a result there was a very strong bond that would mean great things to a future bandit in training.

Grandmother would play with the little boy when others were busy. Her tender love and constant smiles would make him feel safe and special. She would share his world of imagination. A stick could become a caballero or cowboy at one moment and a horse at another. Any little item could be a stimulus to his imagination.

She took great delight in stretching his mind and creating fascination in his environment.

Walks with her had a special quality. She had an air about her that seemed to attract birds, or at least she was always the first to point them out to the boy. She trained his sight by looking for hawks and birds of prey. These aerial hunters were searching for the rodents, snakes and small rabbits.

She loved the shapes of the cactus. She was proud of the way the corn stood tall and straight up to the blistering hot afternoon sun. After the rains, she would laugh at the worms and their silly motions.

She made him aware of the beautiful world of flowers. She was fascinated with colors, shapes, textures and sizes. The variety made the message more meaningful.

She saw beauty in everything and did not have an enemy in the world. Her positive radiance was a brilliance to behold. It was noticeable even at a distance. The joy was that strong.

There was no limit to fun when playing with Grandma. Many elements from their immediate circumstances were used to create recognitions for the two. She could make fun out of wherever they were and whatever was available to be used as a prop, either real or imaginary. The play sessions had an additional benefit for the young boy. Time passed quickly and most every action was fulfilling. The two bore radiant smiles when together.

Grandma Eva had the unique ability to see the good in everything. She enjoyed the sunrise and beginning of each new day. She would welcome the afternoon heat with open arms, saying it was beneficial for the crops and provided work for the farmers. She shared with her grandson her love for the sun, the moon, and the stars. She saw the sun as the great bestower of gifts. The sun helped the corn seeds sprout into great plants. It made them strong and gave warmth to the day. The sun was sacred in many symbols of their culture.

The moon was noteworthy to grandmother. It lit the path to the homes of her friends and through the fields. It came with the cool evening air, bringing a refreshing change to the hot days. The moon was a symbol of magic to the old woman. It held great mysteries to the generations who came before her and was part of the local lore.

The stars were a jeweled present from the sky. They were memories of the past and symbols of the future. She understood a few of the constellations, and was able to see patterns in the night sky as the seasons changed. The time spent outside in the evening was always considered as sacred. They were alone, alive, and happy.

The planet Venus was a bright addition at special times. It was so intense and easy to discern since it did not blink. Nobody knew how Grandma obtained this knowledge of the heavens, yet they accepted her words as truth. There was a ring of sense to them. Nobody would doubt the old woman. She clearly knew so much, being reflected by the strength and magic of her inner wisdom.

Simple things meant a great deal to her. Her needs were small but her heart was large. She was content with very little. She worried about the state of her people. Her country was old, yet progress was slow. The people were oppressed and living conditions were poor. Power was held by the very few.

The newer nation to the north, the United States, was growing quickly. Her country was not. The Treaty of Guadalupe Hildago ended La Intervencion Norteamericana or the Mexican-American War in 1848. Her republic came up on the short side.

Crime did not impact the locals in their immediate area. It was far enough from town and away from the roads that bisected the state. She heard stories of roving bands of bandits, but understood little of their means or motives. Politics was also a foreign subject. It did not merit attention or discussion.

Her life was simple and pure. She taught and lived by example. Her model was love, overflowing love, and she was a gift. Grandmother was a living light to all that encountered her. She was special to the community and her grandson was special to her. That was empowering, and helped the boy grow without the development of denial and the normal defense mechanisms. His energies and focus were in other skills.

The reaches of her government did not actively extend to her small farming village outside the city limits of Culiacan. The benefits were few. Survival was the main ticket for each day. She tried to smile and make life a little bit better for her family. There was little else she could do. Grandma Eva was old and tired. She had lived a long time but traveled little. Her world consisted of the valleys and hills of Sinaloa, Mexico. The state has many microclimates and she had been to a few, from which she gathered strange powders, herbs and flower teas.

She had never been to the seashore. She was without experience of a wave, and the cycle of breaking and returning. The movement of large water was never experienced, not even once. The Sea of Cortez was described to her in songs and lore, but how do you explain the ocean to one who has never seen an almost endless body of water?

And what could be the value of salt water when the taste was so foul? For her the water meant the creeks and streams in her little valley. The waters blessed her life with the tasty liquid refreshment, the basis for twig, flower and herb teas, and the nourishment for the corn and other plants trying to grow in the desert sands.

At times a choice had to be made regarding the allocation and use of water. Bathing was a luxury when the corn was in season, because it was thirsty too. The family needed the corn to grow to pay for its survival. The balance was tedious and the family usually won.

Lareano was too young to understand the cycles of life. His eyes were usually focused straight ahead. He had not experienced and observed enough years to comprehend the return of the seasons. He knew at times it rained and at times it was very dry. His father seemed to be gone more when the sun was shining and there was extended activity upon the earth.

Lareano understood more over time. His father, Esteban, was a farmer, as were the fathers of many of his friends. He worked long hours on the land. He would borrow his uncle's mule and walk behind it making straight rows in the earth. Back and forth he would go. The progress was extremely slow. You could hear him singing to the mule. It was quite a show in its own right.

The boy could not understand what was happening to the ground with each pass of the mule and its simple but effective apparatus. He would watch his father reach down at times and throw rocks from behind the mule. His father did not appear to be happy with the rocks. He would just toss them into piles and later remove them.

The boy loved stones. He had his personal collection divided into roughly thirds, with each in a different hiding place. He treated them like they were special treasures. His sense of space and geometrical balance was innate. He could make the stones into different shapes by piling and balancing. He would pretend to create caves and caverns with them. He would hide little sticks and smaller stones under the larger rocks. They developed qualities of their own world.

He would discern the difference of his collection based on color and content. As he would grow older he pretended that the flakes of pyrite were real gold. He did not understand the intrinsic value of gold at that stage of life, but only its inherent beauty. The sparkling gold flakes radiated and intensified the light of the sun. They bore a sparkle of wonder.

Some nights when his family had visitors he would share his favorite rocks and minerals. Lareano quickly learned that the metallic flakes in the pyrite would draw an initial inquisitive eye from his father's friends. The men went for the pyrite pieces first. There would be an instant sparkle in their eyes similar to the light emanating from the stone. Why? And then the men would often engage in stories about gold and lost treasures. What did that mean? For ages man has sought and treasured this precious gift from the earth. And what did it mean when they called his stone "fool's gold?"

There was something to learn here about this subject. He knew it would be safe to ask his grandmother. He could trust her response to be the truth. She would not laugh at him. She would never call him or any of his special treasures a fool. She was too kind and supportive, and that special glisten in her eyes was real.

She understood more than those men who came to visit her son, Esteban. They had been coming for years. At times their words conveyed great anger. She said their harsh talk was actually a release of steam. It was just time to observe and complain for them. Nobody expected actions or results. Any attempt at change would be futile.

She bore the grace and understanding of a family elder. Only certain matters would involve the senior members as counselors, and those were usually of a family nature. Intervention was used to facilitate communication when feelings were hurt and actions or intentions misunderstood, including between neighbors. Grandma Eva radiated peace and understanding. Around her problems would simply dissolve. She considered it to be a matter of perspective and nothing else. Her humility was always evident.

Mother, Carmen, was in and out of the boy's life. This probably had a strong part in developing his independence and free-thinking. She would travel to see her parents who had gone north to the place called Arizona. Mother greatly enjoyed these travels and would always be happy and radiant when she arrived back home. Horses and long rides pleased her. She loved the time in the saddle, and demonstrated a special skill and understanding with these large animals.

Carmen would be gone a couple of times each year, leaving the boy in the care of his grandmother. She would return home with fabrics, dried meats, and lots of sugar. She would make clothing for her husband and son with the new fabrics. Her creations were of a high quality of craftsmanship. This too added to the unique style of the growing boy.

Carmen would also bring home seeds for her husband to plant in the family plot. The new varieties of corn and beans helped increase the yield and better provide for the family. There were bright colored tomatoes and varieties of squashes too.

Seeds were like magic to the boy. He loved to watch his father plant them in freshly tilled soil. His father was always careful with the small seeds and treated them with great respect. He planted them only after diligently working in the earth. He would add water almost every day and watch for signs of life to sprout up out of the ground. It was like a celebration when the tiny seeds burst forth and stuck their tiny heads out. After more attentive watering the small shoots grew into plants and often provided beans and fresh vegetables to compliment their afternoon meal.

The boy occasionally watched over the plantings and tried to keep away the rabbits, rats and birds. These animals and rodents also found a special attraction to the new greens grown from the imported American seeds.

One year his mother took the boy to the local school. He was extremely scared. He did not understand why he had to leave his grandmother and go to school. He asked if his grandmother could come and was surprised when he was told that she could not. Although she had been his primary educator to this point in life, the townspeople did not consider her to be a teacher, whatever that meant. Mrs. Ruis had that role. It was time for school.

The teacher enjoyed the boy and quickly noticed his special qualities whenever he was introduced into a new group of children. Lareano made an incredible first impression. He was neither quiet nor shy. He appeared to be responsible and interested in pleasing his teacher. The boy was happy to learn that other new children were a source of fun. They looked up to him and would follow his lead. They would listen to his stories about the land that his mother visited up north. They would play with his stones and laugh at the various made-up games. His colorful imagination was greatly stimulated by the new friends. He entertained them and everyone grew from the experience.

Mrs. Ruis quickly observed and reported to his parents that he was a natural leader. They were surprised to hear that this quiet, only child had developed such a comfort with the other children. They had harbored a secret fear that he would not blend with the group. Obviously the isolation had not hurt in the socialization of the young farm boy.

What they did not understand was the valuable role played by his special relationship with his grandmother. She taught him so much about people and things. He was wise beyond his years in organizing his beliefs. His perception was tuned. He understood a lot about life from his observation of nature. He motivated and inspired his new friends. He was a potential leader, a born salesman.

Lareano walked a long way to get to school every day. Often his feet hurt, but he did not complain. He had a high tolerance for pain and discomfort. This added to his strength and endurance. He was not a complainer. The extreme heat did not bother him at all. He often walked to school alone. Life was safe for children in the 1860's, when the greater dangers were from small poisonous snakes and Gila monsters rather than from people.

His early childhood years passed with the development of his special qualities. He seemed to possess something called "The Gift." It was akin to a psychic ability to foretell something in the near future. Perhaps that would become useful, but it served no purpose to Lareano at that time.

3. RESOLVED

Culiacan – 1867

Lareano was now ten years old and nothing in life could prepare him for what he was feeling. The pain was like he had been sliced up. He felt like his stomach had been cut out and his heart was likewise removed. He could not eat, or even think of keeping food within. He was a mess. He was angry, tired, and in crisis. He had cried so long that the tears were dry. He had screamed so loud that his throat hurt. He was mad at the world. He was totally out of control.

Ten years on the planet had not prepared him for this. He had come home after a strange day in school to hear that his grandmother was dead. A sickening feeling had overcome him about mid-day, and this was the answer. Grandma was dead. She was gone, never to return to him.

The images before his mind were a mass of confusion. This was the wrong moment to arrive home. She was being taken out of the house in a pine box. Why was Grandma in the box? His mom said she would never return. That was going to be a real problem for the boy. It would ultimately translate into a bigger problem for others as the years progressed.

This was the birth of something new, the spark of empowerment of his dark side. Here was the place that fury blended with pain in an alchemical nightmare. The simple script of his life was to be changed forever. He would become a living cauldron of trouble.

It only took one moment. The change in momentum was almost instantaneous. A far-reaching force occurred that would have an impact for generations. The playful puppy had become a rabid dog, or worse. His current view of the world was not a pretty picture. The shadow of his dark side would create and then cast an ugly spell.

The boy followed his father, relatives, and family friends as they loaded the box onto the wagon. The old brown horse sensed his important role and held his head tall and proud as he pulled the remains of the grandmother into town. The men and women openly wept as waves of sadness overcame all of them. The creaking of the wagon wheels made the only discernable sounds as they rolled along the dusty dirt road. A deep cloud of silence overcame the mourners.

When they reached the town Lareano could hear the bells in the tower ringing. The horse and wagon were brought up next to the large doors and suddenly they opened. Today the grand doors were open to him for the first time. He could not understand. Why today? He had been to the small chapel a number of times but never the large cathedral. Padre Ramone was standing at the door and clearly had something to do with the special venue.

The men carried the casket through the great doors. The boy wondered why they were taking his grandmother inside. He waited his turn and quietly entered where he had never been before. Six years had passed since his first experience outside the wondrous doors, and now he was going inside. A personal mystery was about to be uncovered.

It took a few long seconds for his eyes to adjust to the dim light within. It was a sharp contrast to the bright sunny day outside. His footsteps created an echo once inside the doorway. He realized he had never been in a structure so large. Lareano's senses were on overload and his emotions were out of check. Everything was different than he expected and the largess of the unknown had a compelling quality to him.

He became acutely aware of the incense. The mysterious smell of black copal overcame him. It was a rare and exotic scent, totally unlike any odor he knew. He had never been in a place where ceremonial incense had been burned. The pungent aroma was refreshing and unique. Almost by reflex he found himself taking in an extra deep breath. The scent was strong but beautiful.

When his eyes adjusted the boy was astonished. As he crossed the threshold he first looked upward. He gasped at what he saw.

Inside he found towering ceilings, dark hand-hewn beams and reflections from richly painted glass. Never in his life had he experienced a place so grand. It was beyond all of his imagination. The interior volume of the old cathedral was immense. He felt tiny and insignificant.

There were neatly designed rows of benches made of beautifully carved woods. Their finish was dark and shiny. They had a waxed luster unknown to the boy. Everything was so old and stable, but it was new to the boy.

As he adjusted to the darkness his eyes became fixed upon a huge crucifix. He could not believe the magnificence of the sacred image. It was huge compared with the small cross that adorned his small local church. The sculpture of Jesus appeared to be made of gold, and the cross was adorned with colored stones, speaking of opulence unknown in the town. The colors danced in the light. They cast a mystical eye to the boy.

On the walls he noticed numerous tall statutes. He heard them called "Saints." They appeared to be made of a bright, silver colored metal. The boy never dreamed that they could be real silver, not in this poor town. But they were.

The funeral mass seemed to never end. It was stuffy and uncomfortable. The boy did not understand anything that was going on. The man in front appeared to be speaking in a different language. The boy could not understand the words or the reasons for the actions. Lareano was sitting in the cathedral and was lost, both in his own thoughts and personal pain. He did not know what to do but it didn't seem to matter. He saw smoke coming from the incense burner. He watched the priest twirl silver objects in some type of rhythmic motion. The people stood, kneeled, and sat in unison. The boy did not understand the differences in the movements.

The only thing that was obvious was the fact that Grandma was not coming out of the box in front. She was gone forever. He reflected on her illness and remembered that she was getting thinner in her last few weeks. She could neither eat nor drink. The family was too poor to bring a doctor from the city. Grandma was too sick to travel. It was horrible. Nothing could be done. They said she was old and running out of time. That didn't matter to Lareano.

The boy studied the interior of the church. Somebody here was definitely rich or important enough to have the answers. He could have helped save Grandma from her fate; at least they could have tried. Why was no assistance offered? The subject of human loss and death was novel at this point in his experience. He would become an expert on the topic before his life was over.

Grandmother had spent all of her years within miles of this city. She helped both friends and strangers alike. She would share the food from her kitchen whenever visitors were in the home. At times she ate less just to ensure a larger portion for her friends, or her son and his family. Grandma Eva rarely if ever used the word "no."

The boy did not know his grandfather. His father never spoke about his own father. Somebody in the church said she was going to join him, but that was beyond the scope of the boy's imagination. How would she leave the box? How would she find somebody that he never knew? Some parts of life are too complex for a boy of only ten years to understand.

At the point that Lareano was hurting from sitting on the wooden bench, something different began to happen. The priest left the altar and stepped down towards a door in the rear. One by one people got up and walked to the side of the church, in an area where there were many colored candles. When it was their turn his father and mother took him over to the rack of candles in red, yellow, green and blue containers.

He took a long stick with a flame on the end and a red candle was put before him. According to his mother he lit the candle as a memory for the soul of his grandmother. That was what she thought. In his mind the lighting ceremony was to confirm his new resolve. He had made a decision, one that would last the rest of his life. At times a decision or resolution can be made out of sheer circumstance. Like a seed, if the soil is fertile and it is properly nourished it can grow and grow. Today was one such day, and he would remember it forever. He walked in a young boy and walked out a very young man. He entered in pain and left with a purpose.

The bright afternoon light blinded him as he slowly stepped out of the cathedral. This would not be his last visit to this church. In fact, he intended to come back when he was older and better prepared. Then he would rob it. His goal was to take what he deserved and feed the poor so they would not die like his grand-mother. He would visit many churches, and rob each and every one of them. First he had much to learn.

His name was Lareano Garcia. He was so young but mighty in many ways. He understood only winning. His gang would become known as the Lareanos, and in time grow to a strength of almost two hundred fifty strong. In the terms of their era, they would be nothing less than a small army. They would demonstrate leader-ship, training, and a significant understanding of their own par-ticular skills. They would be specialists, professional bandits, in a country with a tradition of excellent banditos. They would not be ordinary thieves; they would become the very best. Their destiny was established with the lighting of the red candle on November 2, 1867.

Grandma's coffin was taken to the old cemetery outside of town and buried among those that preceded her. It was another hot and dry day, making the whole procedure more difficult. Emotions were running high as the family and friends present completed the task. The new Lareano was tired, thirsty, and angry. He felt iso-lated within the large crowd. He became fixated on his belief that he should honor his grandmother's death with one of the oldest and most primitive motives known to mankind, revenge.

4. CAMACHO LOPEZ

State of Sinaloa – 1868

There was an attempt by everyone in the family to have life return to normal. They all bore their sadness about Grandma Eva silently within. It was a deep pain with an impact that would last for years. Their eyes would be a witness to their feelings.

Esteban went to the fields to tend to his crops. Carmen cooked more than before now that grandmother was not in the kitchen. Lareano returned to school, though he began to skip class. Without his grandmother's company he found diversions on his walks to town. Sometimes he would stop to visit his friend, Camacho Lopez. Camacho did not go to school. He would help tend to the family goats and do other chores around the homestead.

Camacho and Lareano often played together. They loved to entertain each other with mental games and imagine they had their own fine steed horses. They acted like great cowboys, full of control of large exceedingly fast horses. In truth, neither had ever been in a saddle. Their families were too poor to own a horse.

Young imaginations could be free and open. The boys made pretend toy guns out of sticks. They would shoot at each other and make believe enemies hiding around the corner of the house or shed. They discovered tactics and gained an understanding of the advantage of silence and surprise. It was a form of union with the animal world. Grandmother still lived in Lareano and was his guiding light. Her lessons were not lost.

Lareano and Camacho were each showing signs of a young shaman. They were innately stealthy and continued to develop an ability to move silently, to observe unknowing people, places and things. They evidenced an innate kinship or familiarity with the dynamic world around them.

They practiced often and developed a strong sense of selective invisibility. Each could sense the movement of the other, so they could act more at will. They could almost sneak around unnoticed and undetected. Instinct and intuition were being exercised. They knew too much for boys of their age. Their curiosity was grandiose with a strong blend of anger. They bore a unique viewpoint and did not accept criticism well. They were paving new territory and there were no rules. It would be all outside the law, way over the line.

One day Lareano asked his father if he had a gun. The father was initially surprised at the question since the subject of firearms was never mentioned in the house, and the family protection was hidden. While the question was not totally unforeseeable, the timing and stage of life made the query uneasy. He was younger than expected but the inquiry revealed the need for more information. Nothing was served by concealment and it was now time to address the experience.

Esteban remembered his own father teaching him how to use the rifle many years earlier, and decided that Lareano was at a good age to learn how to shoot. It was time. Their dwelling was located far outside of the town limits and one never knew when a poisonous snake, desert predator, wild animal, or other danger would present itself.

Father was proud of the fact that his son was growing up and thinking of personal defense. There were many long days when he would be home alone with his mother. He was growing fast and showing signs of responsibility and independence. Father agreed to teach Lareano all about the use of the gun. He had no idea that the decision would have an impact of any significance. Esteban saw no harm in this endeavor. He was wrong.

The instructions were few and easy to remember: "Always treat the gun as if it was loaded. Hot. Never aim at anything, never, that he would not voluntarily use deadly force upon. Never."

It seemed like days until he would be seeing his friend again. Lareano could not wait until he could tell Camacho that he was going to learn how to shoot a real gun. No more sticks and pretend guns for him. The excitement about this overcame Lareano. He believed this to be the first major step to reach his concealed goal. Not even his best friend was aware of the brewing plot. It was his inner secret until the time was right for sharing. He still had so many questions that interfered with his clear vision of implementing the goal. He had the time to wait.

Father surprised his son with the speed of his response. He awoke Lareano very early one morning and took him out away from the familiar direction to town and toward the hills. It was not a usual morning activity for his father to spend time with him. Lareano felt excited and proud as he rode along with his father on borrowed horses. He wondered where they were going and what they were going to do. Father brought with him the pistol and fifty-one bullets, leaving only twenty-six extra for protecting his home. They remained stored in the back on the top pantry shelf.

Lareano and his father rode until they were at the foot of the distant peak, which they could barely see on a clear day from their home. The locals called it Tacamonte. From the top they could look back down into the valley below and see Culiacan at the far end, many miles away. Looking in the other direction, to the South, they could see the sheer white face of La Chiva. Father said that mountain was aptly named "The Goat" because of its steep approach that looked better fit for climbing by a four-legged. The white rock at the top reminded Lareano of the beard on Camacho's favorite goat, Onofre. He wondered if that was the reason for the name because the summit area sure looked like a goat to his way of thinking.

Once they began the ascent of Tacamonte the dual purpose of the venture was made known to Lareano. There were many wild rabbits roaming the hills and father wanted to use the valuable bullets for food, if possible. It would also be better for Lareano to try and shoot at a moving target. Father did not believe that firearms would ever be needed against a stationary target. Besides, that would be too easy. Now the challenge was evident.

Father began by removing the ammunition from the cylinder and explaining the pistol to Lareano. He called it a revolver, based on the rotating mechanism that held the bullets. Esteban carefully showed Lareano how to load the bullets into the chambers. He also told him again never to aim the pistol at anything that he did not want to shoot and kill. A gun was not a toy. It never would be. In Lareano's mind, it was going to be an important tool.

Father treated it with both fear and respect. It was the easiest way to hurt something or even take its life. Father hoped that it would never be necessary to shoot at another person. Lareano thought otherwise but kept his thoughts to himself. Nothing would be served by upsetting his father.

As in school, Lareano learned his lessons well. He had a secret motivation to be an excellent shot. He learned to calm his mind and shoot by reflex. He held a steady trigger finger and quickly developed the uncanny ability to anticipate the correct movement of the rabbit. His father was surprised at his natural ability with the pistol. It was another manifestation of "The Gift."

Esteban taught his son about the working parts of the pistol and the means of cleaning it. He focused his instructions on mechanics and safety. The knowledge, skills and training acquired at this time would be valuable for the future.

Father and Lareano would go hunting in various places numerous times over the ensuing years. No matter where they went, Tacamonte and La Chiva were always Lareano's favorites.

Lareano acquired a rifle and became equally adept at its operation. The family was too poor to afford a second gun, but suddenly it was there. When questioned, Lareano's response to his father was neither logical nor satisfactory. Somehow the subject was never discussed again and no questions were ever asked about the source of the additional firearm and ammunition for both weapons.

Father was proud of his son's ability to hunt. The beans, corn and vegetables at their meal table were often supplemented with birds, rabbit, and small wild game shot by his son. Lareano quickly learned which of the birds were satisfactory to his taste. The others he would leave alone. They were not within his sights.

5. Buried Assets

Mexico – 19th Century

The financial backdrop and depository conditions of 19th Century Mexico were much different than we are accustomed. At that time the banking system had not been sufficiently developed and did not hold the highest level of trust and confidence of the populous. It would not be until years after the revolution that banks would be trusted again. This simple fact was the precipitating cause of many stories.

People considered themselves personally responsible for the safekeeping of their own money and valuables, however great or limited. Often they would be carefully hidden within a dwelling or buried someplace outside for safekeeping. It was common to bury one's valuables and then perish without sharing the location with anyone else. Sometimes they became disoriented and could not locate their secret spots. Natural events such as weather and storms often changed the relative position of landmarks and other noteworthy objects of reference. There was also the risk of discovery and theft.

At times a death in the family would erase all hopes for the heirs to find the keepsakes and valuables. Many times only the senior male in the family held the secrets and knew the exact hiding spot. The role of women at that time was not greatly evolved. Many families lost hope for recovering all of their hidden wealth when the man of the house, or patron, died. This was not an isolated personal loss. It seemed like every town and every valley beckoned with stories of buried valuables.

Stories remain to this day of lost or hidden treasure. They are part of the core folklore of each region. It has been a long time since one of the regional tales has proven to be true.

6. THE LAREANOS

Culiacan – 1876

To the townspeople Lareano was an exception. There was an indescribable something that sounds so simple yet it is so accurate and true with relationship to Lareano. He emanated a light, an inner sense of purpose, and used his enchanting smile to engender comfort and trust. His strength and convictions had a strong and penetrating impact. They added a convincing quality to his personality.

In some ways Lareano represented the collective ideals of the people, a natural unifier. He behaved like a magnet. People saw him in their future. It would only be a dream, but it was contagious.

The girls thought he was handsome and would giggle with delight when he paid extra notice of them, but such occasions were often rare. He developed strong independent qualities and was respected and not resented by the other males.

There was another side to the soft and compelling demeanor. He was as tough as can be with a periodic short fuse. He was wound tight and the spring could pop when you would least expect it.

He grew stout and strong. He helped his father in the fields and could handle a mule and crude plow as well as a grown man. Farming did not excite Lareano. He did not want to follow in the footsteps of his father and grandfather. His mind was focused and preoccupied but his secret goal was never disclosed at home.

One evening Lareano was drinking tequila with Camacho and a couple of other friends. They were sitting in the garden of a café relaxing and talking. The bottle of fresh alcohol was a rare treat. The youngest of the group obtained the bottle from his oldest brother, who worked at the plant. The discussion became impassioned and inflamed. The subject of the church and the treatment of the Mexican people got out of hand. A stranger put Lareano's motivation and character into question. He was insulting and degrading. Without warning, Lareano flew over the table and grabbed the man by the throat, wrestling him to the ground. His strength was Herculean.

His friends were simultaneously scared and proud of his stance. They had no idea that he would become so visibly strong and demonstrative for his principles. They had never heard about any visits to the church, and did not understand the sudden outbreak of animosity when the subject of the repression of the towns-folk came into focus. Lareano retained a short fuse when it came to the church. It was that single moment that made them realize their need to listen more closely to his words. Their future became instantly aligned with this special friend. They shared common feelings and repressed them all. Each had his own reason and not one was less serious than the other.

Generally speaking, the overall population felt neither comfortable nor secure at that time. Life was a struggle and the safety of the townspeople was always in question. The prevailing attitude in the country was tenuous. People lacked confidence in their leaders and nobody was pleased with the government. The corruption of politicians was commonplace. Everyone had numerous examples. The military appeared to be a sanctioned and independent band of thieves, and the church represented corruption to the core. It would take many years for the big picture to change.

The turning point came much sooner for some in and around Culiacan. It was on one special night that Lareano and Camacho made their personal agreement with the devil. They had witnessed enough and decided it was time to fight back. The enemy was known. It was time to beat them at their own game.

Lareano would be the leader of the band. It was by unspoken consensus. Nobody would dare challenge his authority. His leadership had been developed over time. His distinctive qualities were greatly admired. His radiant nature and confident aura extended through those around him. There was never a question or discussion about his authority, he merely seized it. Such was his way.

The respect of his friends was now rewarded. Nobody would cross his word. To do so would be a certain risk of personal injury. He had been tested many times while growing and nobody ever got the best of him. His physical strength was without equal. His speed and anticipation made him lethal.

Nobody knew if he ever killed a man, but he easily could. While an incredible marksman, he seldom used his gun on living things. It had something to do with his grandmother, he would say. It may have had to do with much more.

Lareano behaved like a man possessed. There was little doubt that anybody could stand in his way. Yet, by contrast, he was intuitive, understanding, and fair. Lareano displayed a gentle nature until challenged, and then an imposing wall of anger would arise out of nowhere. It was scary. He was a gentle giant. Though relatively short in stature, he was wide and muscular. He was as deadly with his fists as with a knife or a gun. He could look through you with his dark brown eyes. Lareano was an irrepressible force to be recognized.

He spoke with clarity and distinction. His words could not be ignored. He made promises, not threats. To say "No" to one of his requests was to invite disaster. It would be easier to just run away and live for another day. Dissent was neither encouraged nor popular. No confrontation was accepted. He was neither a tyrant nor a bully. His whole power thing was a result of the collective acquiescence of others rather than a preponderance of his strength and misdeeds. He cast a larger shadow than realized.

Lareano began closest to home declaring the first project to be the protection of the farmers and townspeople. It was an early version of neighborhood watch. In the past, bandits passing through on the main north-south roadway could occasionally detour and raise havoc. The men, women, and children of the town would be protected from outside interference. Nobody would ever victimize their families and get away with it again, not while the Lareanos were around. This would turn out to be a surprisingly easy goal. The vigilante system of self-defense was convincing.

Enforcement would be simple. Excessive force was the rule rather than the exception. Shoot to kill would be one of the commandments. Enemies would perish. The elimination or destruction of the opposition was encouraged. Families would be safe. The women and children should live in peace. This created an absolute shield of protection for the gang. Nobody would ever snitch or complain about their protectors. They could hide in plain sight.

It was victory for the little guy. The townspeople felt safer. Commerce could grow. Life could improve. The corrupt politicians and leaders could exact their penalties from others. The people in the farms and villages outside Culiacan would be relatively free.

Following the establishment of protective services, Lareano began to implement his personal goal. He could not sleep until revenge was exacted from the church. This would not bring back the lives of those that died of hunger and starvation, but it would make their descendants feel better.

7. A Promise Fulfilled

Culiacan Cathedral – 1876

The main cathedral in the center of the city was the first major target. It was an ideal extracurricular project and served as a confidence builder along with fulfilling major retribution points. The political and social ramifications of this primary target made the objective challenging and fulfilling. It reflected arrogance, defiance, and a new level of nerve.

This combination of structures was the heart of the church in Culiacan. It was strong and massive in comparison with any of the other buildings of the day. It was believed to be constructed of lasting materials and reflected careful consideration and effective execution. The size of the structure for the time was massive, and huge imposing doors had guarded the entrance since the 1830's. Lareano knew them well. Those doors!

He did not care if the doors were locked, barred from the inside with some unseen lever or barrier. Surprise was on his side. Nobody could predict his intentions. He would open them by his own hand under cover of darkness. A church robbery was unknown since the founding of the complex. The original small church was absorbed into the much larger cathedral grounds countless years earlier.

The mere thought of this church evoked a different side of Lareano's complex personality. He had developed a kill-or-be-killed mentality. His focus was one-pointed and his intentions were unbending.

The church in Culiacan had been collecting money from the community since the previous century, yet gave little back to the people. Lareano held them responsible for the death of many, including his beloved grandmother. The church was filled with precious metals and bejeweled artifacts, while the people were starving outside. The extent of the holdings were strongly symbolic yet unknown to him. Their quantity was not important. There was a point to be made and a cause to be served.

It has been said that the point of intercept determines the outcome. When and where one starts something has a major role in the prediction of the ultimate result. Unseen factors can come into focus and importance based on timing and circumstances, with the mystery of life lying hidden in the details.

The choice of the massive cathedral in Culiacan was a daring decision. The impact of the selection would create reverberations throughout the entire area. Lareano believed the appropriate revenge must first be exacted from the closest and largest resource. It was a venture into the unknown, but the church appeared to be confident without reason. History was on its side, but the tides were about to change. To Lareano the rewards greatly exceeded the risk.

Lareano had never heard of the Robin Hood legends or even the land of England, yet his motivation could be compared to the lad from Barnsdale and Sherwood Forest. Lareano wanted to take from the rich and share with the poor. He considered himself to be a prime representative of the lower class as had generations of his family before him. He was angry and wanted to see conditions change. He did not possess even a small bit of doubt or regret.

Lareano still remembered his first entry into the huge cathedral. The glitter of the gold and silver ornaments burned a brilliant image into his mind on that stressful day. Soon they would be his.

The planning stages took just short of a month. It was agreed that Lareano and Camacho would need at least two more accomplices. That was satisfactory to them since they had numerous friends and associates from whom to choose. Each was worthy and every one could be trusted. After more inquiry and surveillance, Elias and Omar were chosen, and the band of four began their plans in earnest. This was going to be a dangerous mission.

Correct timing was an essential part of their task, since armed guards patrolled the plaza around the cathedral. Once they passed, a quick return was not part of their usual pattern. They would be gone for a minimum of one and a half to two hours. This was plenty of time for the contemplated larceny. But Lareano needed to know more.

By this time Lareano had proven himself to be an ample marksman, but the shooting ability of his friends was clearly in question. Shooting at a man or defending oneself from an armed guard was different than target practice at a cactus or the hunting of a small bird, rodent or rabbit. The men would shoot back with some presumed degree of accuracy. More likely than not, their skill level would surpass the novice bandits.

The decision was made to do the heist without firearms. The consequences would be less and at least one of the dangers removed. The church was not internally protected. Nobody had ever robbed the cathedral before, and Lareano doubted whether the priests would have any weapons. Intrusion from the inside was the goal, and avoiding detection from the outside would increase their odds of success.

Lareano decided to create a timetable and determine if there was any regularity to the cycles of the patrols. He went to a small café across the plaza and down two blocks, and saw an old friend serving there. She turned out to be a valuable source of information. The patrol would frequently eat at the restaurant and she knew all of the guards, not only by sight but also by name.

According to local stories, the cathedral had not been violated in the previous four decades. Nobody would dare cross the line with the church, at least not in that time. Respect had been earned out of fear. The guards thought their job was more of a joke. Their presence was all that was believed to keep the townspeople from even considering any foul play. That would not be true tonight. The timing of the patrols was a farce. Lareano and his group would have all of the time they needed as long as they began their efforts after midnight.

From years of observation Lareano knew that he could not enter through the massive front doors. He found an excuse to survey the premises when he assisted the local baker in making a delivery. The old man had almost severed his foot when his wagon began rolling prematurely. His limp was horrible and it took most of his strength just to balance himself in an upright position. He welcomed Lareano's offer to assist. A strong young helper was a welcome addition.

Lareano was all eyes as he offloaded the cart and began carrying the tortillas and flat breads into the commissary of the church. He was absorbing everything he could to the finest detail. First he noticed how small the bolt was on the small door that entered the kitchen. He was surprised and disappointed. It looked to him like it could be forced open with a simple straight wedge. He also noticed no living quarters on the main floor. That meant all that stayed on the grounds were living away from the main structure or over the kitchen area. He doubted whether sounds could travel through the cathedral's thick adobe walls to the rear of the building. The construction materials served as a natural sound barrier.

The size of the structure would be his ally. The first trick would be a silent entry, and the second was a safe escape. In between required careful maneuvering and quiet mobility. The easiest point of entry was determined to be from the rear near the kitchen. He wondered if they bore a false sense of security as if protected by a higher power. Fear could be an important deterrent. Whatever the reason, Lareano found the task to be much easier than expected.

The entry was made on a dark and cloudy night. The moon phase was an ally to the bandits. It was waxing crescent, only five percent of full. The moon did not cast much light, being only in a small sliver shape. The canopy of tall trees blocked most of the illumination. The wind was blowing mildly, almost as if to mask the sounds of the approaching trespassers. The rustling of the trees was an excellent cover.

The would-be bandits believed it was their destiny to rob from the church. They saw it as a blessing, to share with their families and friends. The obvious ethical considerations were totally absent. If anything, it was the completion of a commitment Lareano made to the memory of Grandma Eva. The others had their own personal motives. The unity of purpose overshadowed any reflection on the appropriateness of the action. There had not been any doubt.

Lareano found no obstacles to his goal. The entry was easily made, and the coast was clear wherever they went. There was nobody awake in any of the passage areas. There was no form of barrier from the private area into the chapel. The massive front doors remained locked from the inside, with a large horizontal timber bracing both doors in a secured position. No wonder they wouldn't budge. They were as impenetrable as the gate at a fort. Entry through those doors was impossible. They would now serve to protect the bandits as they began their larceny.

A decision had been made to remove everything through the kitchen and take the items for temporary storage to the bakery across the plaza. From there the items would be removed in the delivery wagon during the normal early morning delivery run. This decision would be quickly changed when the bounty was collected. By sheer volume there was too much loot.

Lareano became disoriented in the darkness, and lost sight of his cohorts for a couple of minutes. The cathedral in Culiacan contained multiple chapels or niches along the perimeter walls. Some were filled with flowers, others with statutes, and even one with drawings. It was absolutely huge inside. Looking up he saw incensor cables or lines to swing very old frankincense containers above the worshipping congregation. The sense of smell was powerful and truthful. One rarely forgot that unique experience after the fragrant frankincense, copal, and whatever else the priest burned. It evoked a sense of timelessness and calmness.

Camacho first removed the large cross. Lareano was surprised how easily this was going. His boiling contempt was mitigated with the removal of each object. At one point, Lareano grabbed a small silver statute and placed it at the pew from where he witnessed his grandmother's ceremony. Again he thought about how things looked so different now. Had he changed that much?

He approached the very same area where he lit the special candle for the spirit and safe journey of Grandma Eva. He found a match and repeated the act. He selected a red candle as he had before. Tonight was his glory. It was happening this very instant. He was inside and overcome with power and excitement. His senses were heightened and his ears were on super alert.

The selection and removal of the items also evoked a contrasting horror in the mind of Lareano. It was obvious that his grandmother would not approve of his decision and actions. The problem was, he felt energized and alive from the thrill of the experience. He could enjoy a rush of pure energy. It made him

feel better than he ever could remember. It was a mixture of satisfaction of a dream and the realization of a new power. He had
made the choice and now it was too late to change. The path would
make many twists and turns, but the starting place would always be
this church.

The beauty of the moment even overcame his fear. He was fulfilling a dream and discovering a new power. The psychological
value to the event may have had even more significance in the
development of Lareano than the intrinsic value of the converted
items. He did not have significant economic needs, and his life
was simple. That would change following this evening, for nothing
could ever be the same for him again.

Lareano was unclear about his feelings. He was overcome with
excitement and could sense the rush of blood pumping through
his body as he walked about the chapel. At the same time, he was
saddened by the realization that nothing he was doing would bring
his grandmother back, nothing at all. For a moment he thought
revenge was not a sweet feeling. It did not replace or nourish anything. It was an incomplete empowerment. Nevertheless, the die
was cast and the path was set. Lareano would steal until he felt better. It would take a very long time.

Failure was not an alternative in Lareano's personal psychology. His temperament and practical makeup did not entertain
even a moment of doubt. His confidence was always at the highest
level. He was an optimist to the core. No task seemed impossible,
and no obstacle or danger was perceived as insurmountable. The
goal was always maintained as a clear and present focus, the success of which would be the normal and expected outcome. Think
and prepare; act without warning. Deviation from that level of
achievement could easily result in capture and death. The stakes
were high but the rewards were great. With that in mind, Lareano
continued with his plan.

Lareano was a true leader and a compassionate young man. He
clearly understood the value of charity and gathered an intense
sense of loyalty from those he encountered. He shared so much,
and he was a symbol for even more. He was the outer manifestation of their repressed inner feelings. His arrogance and defiant
conduct would later ascend to a level of enduring folk hero and

ultimately a local legend. Tonight he was merely an emotionally confused and troubled being who crossed the line and decided in favor of crime.

The aspirations of the Lareanos could create hope. Besides the symbolic issues, they also threatened and angered the authorities. What could be better than a local level rebellion? It was a protective state within a geographical area. An "out of bounds" zone for local autonomy.

He saw cruelties inflicted by the government and the military. Politicians were the greatest disgrace. The rights of the townspeople were never considered to be paramount. There were no rights. Almost everyone survived at the grace of the volatile Military Governor. Even that title angered the people.

This was a horrible time for human rights. The subject was non-existent, as was the lack of a jury system. Those entrusted with enforcing the law were often the most lawless. It was a horrible situation that did nothing to police itself. The positions of greater power were coveted, and often passed between relatives or friends. Fairness had no standards. Justice was blind. The people suffered and nothing changed at all. The Lareanos became a balance to this condition.

8. DESERT YOUR POST OR DIE

State of Sinaloa – 1880's

As time passed the gang continued to increase in number. Only Lareano, Camacho, Elias and Omar were on the first job. The Lareanos grew to an unbelievable two hundred fifty loyal participants at the apex of their activities. The expansion was a natural progression in light of their immense success and overflow into other territories and opportunities. At least one of the four originals personally approved every additional member of the gang. They did not permit strangers to join the Lareanos. They knew that one bad referral could be deadly for them all.

There was a feeling of unity, strength, and solidarity within the gang. As their fame became more widespread, internal security became more of a concern. The code of silence was strictly maintained and their membership was never permitted to be acknowledged or disclosed with anyone else.

The newest initiates were always given the most dangerous assignments. Their behavior and reaction times were carefully monitored and regularly reported back to the leaders. There were never lingering doubts or issues. All questions were quickly dealt with and all decisions were final. Their concept of justice was not fair, and regret was never a factor.

The Lareanos brought the definition of stealth to a new level, the invisible hiding within the visible. It was a secret underground society existing silently throughout the northwestern portion of Mexico.

The gang operated by a unique sense of frontier justice, and the implementation of their rule was swift and decisive, often with extreme harsh results. Lareano's word was their law. The dual aspect of Lareano's personality would become immediately apparent if trouble was suspected. There was rarely time for whining or complaint. The benefit of doubt was never given. The sword of justice was faster than the word. Room was never consciously left for a mistake.

They were a family of a different order, with the survival of each member irrevocably connected to the others. The gang was a one-way road. There was no quitting and no opportunity to turn back. The hierarchy was complex and yet simple. You always knew where your neighbor stood, at your side. The Lareanos existed seamlessly in their former neighborhoods, farm areas, towns, villages or cities.

This gang was hidden in plain sight, and security was paramount. No talking was permitted. Walls had ears. Silence was richly rewarded. Suspicion never grew beyond a warning. It could be ugly and cruel at times.

Camacho had a memory for names and faces. His role was similar to a one-man human resources department. He appeared subordinate to Lareano but was not thought to be so by the leader. They were true partners.

Suffering was often a normal part of their days. They traveled numerous miles on horseback and often slept in camps away from their families. A majority of the band consisted of friends and relatives, with a strong common history and belief that their means were the best of all available alternatives for survival. All had experienced suffering firsthand.

None of the Lareanos were overly scholarly, and religious zeal was not a component to their lives. Due to the prevailing conditions and family pressures during their youth, all had been exposed to the church on at least an infrequent basis. The church was not a popular institution with this group of men. Their belief was in survival and personal gain.

They were bandits and operated within a primitive hierarchal system. Lareano's law was their rule and guideline. He treated all of them fairly well. Considering where they were from it could be said that their roots were not good. Each made more money than they possibly could ever dream. They helped others too. Their self-esteem was boosted and happiness was experienced by their increase in life qualities. Most important, they felt safe in this endeavor. That was a key to their strength and success.

A bandit's loot was greater than the earnings of a farmer, merchant, laborer, or almost any other job or profession. They clearly exceeded their wants and needs, and felt rich and powerful in the process. There was an unexplainable influence from the connection, and everyone's desires were met by the enterprise. They were all winners in the process.

The camaraderie within the Lareanos was something to behold. They functioned calmly with a sense of righteousness and fairness. Everyone was proud to be with the others. There was safety in numbers, a unity of purpose, and pure potency in the conviction.

For years they talked among themselves of that day when a boisterous and aggressive man was trying the wrong way to make a name for himself. He was substantial in size and build. He radiated strength and confidence. He approached Lareano's table at a café making insults in rapid succession. The rest allegedly happened within seconds. Six men were standing with weapons drawn. Only Camacho's gun went off, a perfect hit in the foot, causing more pain than permanent injury. All of the time Lareano just sat and smiled. Nobody would ever get near Lareano.

The group consciousness took on a life of independent significance. The gang expanded their abilities and remained competent to protect themselves as the level of danger increased geometrically. In this case, it helped to have skill and experience in the use of pistols, rifles, knives, machetes and other forms of self-defense. They helped train each other and they became highly proficient in their craft. Might often made right.

Practice and training was an important part of their routine, but on-the-job experience had no substitute. It was easy to shoot at a fixed target or a defenseless animal. It was different dealing with an armed guard whose job was the protection of somebody's property, though never or rarely their own.

It was often the circumstance that a lone sentry or small group of guards would abandon their post at the sight of the Lareanos. It was too easy to calculate the outcome when outnumbered and outgunned. Life was an easy choice over job and certain death. At that moment of decision, it was usually clear that the secured objects belonged to their employer. To lose one's life for a job or protecting somebody else's property was not a common mind-set for those that were not dedicated law enforcement officers. It was different for the police, military or government. So, as time passed, it became easier for the Lareanos to accomplish their desired objectives.

The command, "Desert your post or die," was often shouted and rarely resisted. It was a familiar greeting from the Lareanos. It would not make sense to resist against great odds and with such an obvious outcome. Suicide for things was not highly rewarding behavior. It had no future.

Word traveled fast even before the modern forms of advanced mass communication. The Lareanos were known because of their daring efforts, strength, and size. The good deeds spread among the people in many communities did not go unnoticed. The concept of sharing was a proven form of prepaid insurance.

The Lareanos became enduring folk heroes in a time when daily life was a difficult struggle for meager subsistence, when government was corrupt, the church was insensitive, and the power and material wealth were vested in a select few. This control was often passed down through the same family lines. Of course, the Revolution of 1910 would change this situation temporarily, but that would be half a century in the future. Until that time the conduct of the bandits was diametrically opposed to the rules of law of the land.

Legends develop with qualities greater than life. A person's reputation can cast a shadow much larger than the actual physical being. The story of the Lareanos had those characteristics. They were repeated so often that what started as mild exaggeration ultimately increased the stories and exploits threefold. While it is true that the gang was open and notorious about their activities, there was nobody or nothing to make them cease and desist. They set the rules. Safe travel through their domain was in doubt without their patronage or protection. People were likewise afraid to cross them because they could not be sure that whomever they were talking to was directly or indirectly involved or associated with the gang. To create suspicion would be an act of sheer stupidity bordering on suicidal behavior.

The absence of noticeable or effective resistance allowed their area of influence to naturally expand. There were no constraints. Lareano's conquests began in the surroundings of Culiacan in the state of Sinaloa, and ultimately spread to the neighboring states of

Sonora, Chihuahua, and Durango. There were too many churches and other vulnerable targets with too much bounty to contain their efforts. They expanded their sights.

The Lareanos were treated well whenever they entered a strange community. It was as if they were a friendly liberating force. The locals would feed the men and care for their horses and pack animals. It was not unusual for a feast to be prepared in their honor. At times the offerings were staggering. Other delights and treasures were also shared, including those of a personal and physical nature. They were treated like conquering heroes.

A perverse joy and happiness spread throughout an area whenever they were around. It was a festival of liberation. These were the men that resisted authority. They were symbols of the current Mexican dream, where conditions would not enslave a family, where the poor could rise to a level of power and possess an actual voice to be heard. The bandits were powerful and handsome. They were all the declared enemy of the despised Military Governor.

The villagers could easily relate to the Lareanos. The men were proud and rode upright. While their lives were far from easy and comfortable, they did not endure the daily suffering of tough physical work tending the land and bending over the stubborn soil. Their pain was more of an emotional one, a loneliness living the life of an outlaw away from their families and loved ones for significant periods of time. Nevertheless, the rewards were great and the benefits were more than subtle. Lareano was generous to a fault, and they all shared in the cash portion of the bounty. Lareano and Camacho would keep most of the church pieces, jewels, and ancient power objects of the priests. The cash equivalents, coins and currency were liberally shared. Nobody complained and life was very good. There was more than enough for all of them. Everyone entertained the belief that they were overpaid. The job was that much fun.

The first message that their symbolic voice proclaimed was a loud and vigorous protest to the practices of the church. They clearly adopted Lareano's view that the church lent a deaf ear to the problems of the people. Topics such as hunger, poverty, medical needs, crop failures, water issues, and the impact of the heat and the cold were not unique to any one specific area. They were the standard conditions of life for a majority of the population. Yet the church was either blind or callous to these issues. It took a percentage of their money but did not return any physical dividends. It did not lend a hand, in any manner, to those that resided outside its walls. Even the workers or employees on the church grounds were among the lowest paid and least rewarded. Unfair treatment was a common complaint.

It was the same old story. The spoils belonged to just a few, and the status quo was to be maintained at all costs. An informal caste system was in place and change was not welcome. Many believed that the church was responsible for perpetuating this problem. It had wealth beyond all reasonable needs, including land, tools, livestock, money, jewels, collectibles, and other valuables. They also had the politicians, lawmakers, military and others strongly under their thumb. The church was the storehouse for their power, the steady base that assisted in the maintenance of the current order. It was a complementary relationship.

The history of the church was one of expansion. Its stronghold on control included thriving on oppression. Sharing was taught, but never practiced. In short, it served internally as the exact opposite of its intended and stated purposes. The church thrived on pain, and had its own special role in perpetuating the same. Unfortunately, the fine history of Mexico was no different than in Europe or on the other continents. The conversion of the masses was the mantra and reflected the ever-expansive objectives. The means were somehow excused to serve the desired ends.

Whatever the reasons, the majority loved their church and rarely placed blame. They exhibited a form of blind faith. That may have been different if they had even the slightest glimpse of the disparity between the holdings of the church and those of the people. The scales of need were deeply out of balance. There was no semblance of reason or parity.

9. The Cave

La Chiva – 1880

After a few years passed a unique problem evolved regarding the storage of the bounty. The loot had grown to unmanageable proportions. After a generous division among his men and the people in need, Lareano still possessed unbelievably large quantities of gold, silver, coins, artifacts and jewels. There were also unopened crates that were never discussed. Since his family unit was small, a number of friends had been entrusted with a portion of the captured items. But it was growing too rapidly. Out of this problem came the oldest solution, to bury it.

Lareano considered many alternatives. Privacy and safety were two important considerations. But so were location, access, and long-term issues relating to the powers and changes of nature herself. It needed to be safe from the elements, away from human sight, suspicion, and capable of an advantage in defensive protection. It also had to be suitable in size with some relative ease of access.

For a passing moment, Lareano remembered the childhood day when he saw the cave on La Chiva for the first time. He was climbing behind his father on one of their shooting sessions. It was horribly hot, and thunderclouds were building above. His father predicted a storm within the hour, and lightning was already visible over the eastern hills. As they ascended the rain suddenly began to fall. It was as if the heavens rumbled and the clouds opened simultaneously. The chorus was deafening on that steep slope, with the sounds reverberating in the canyons below. Lareano remembered his sensations. His father represented strength and courage, and he did not want to show any sign of weakness or fear. He was shaking inside, but he kept that a secret from his father. The moment was important.

When he thought about it the decision was so obvious. The regional folklore was on his side. There was at least fifty years of

terrifying legend to help keep the traffic away. The locals were traumatized with the bloody details about a large resident cat. Others
heard stories of people who lost their lives almost spontaneously
from attack by poisonous snakes. Even the nearby Tacamonte
was considered off limits. The canyon between the two was rarely
explored. The areas formerly best suited for camping or transient
living were almost always vacant. The ideal spot he had in mind
was also protected by steep terrain. It discouraged casual inquiry.

The site was an arduous climb from the valley floor. The footing was unstable and the bugs were annoying. The vegetation
consisted of numerous varieties of thorny brush. It was a perfect
natural barrier to the hidden treasure above. Lareano knew that
his precious share was perfectly hidden. The chances of accidental
detection were slight. Nobody would be walking around up on that
lower face, and the opening is perfectly concealed unless directly
upon it. That would be unusual since the entrance was partially
under a stone overhang that sealed the deal when the bandit created a rockslide and covered in the purloined materials.

Lareano had a solution for the access to the site. He used to
camp much higher above and knew of a deer trail on the ridge hidden from view. Approaching from the top appeared to be treacherous, but it was actually easy if you followed a route well-known
to Lareano. He would access the location by mule from an almost
hidden passageway two-thirds of the way to the top, and store his
bounty in the safety of the isolated mountain shelf. His chosen
spot was a natural.

There was a large overhanging rock, so initially the loot could
be stored there and loaded though the open front. There were
years of fallen materials to create a temporary barrier to the opening. It would be invisible except from one spot on the next ridge,
which was significantly lower and a decent distance away. From
that ridge one would be looking into the sun during the mornings
to mid-day when Lareano would usually visit the site. The bright
light over La Chiva and the dense shadows around the cave area
combined to make a perfect camouflage.

Most of the trips to the site were made alone or with Camacho,
often ending in the cover of darkness. The site was always a mystery to everyone else, including his wife. The world was too hard

and the risk grew with every indiscrete activity. The bandits modified the original site after a large landslide hid the trail. It gave them the idea to dynamite a slide and totally cover the overhang at the proper time after the treasure was unloaded and strategically organized.

It was indeed a great day when he had stumbled upon the cave with his father. It was high up the mountain far away from town. The terrain was difficult and not the hiking grounds for the normal hunters. Everyone left the place alone. It was too steep for cultivation and extremely hot in the summer months. The only water was far below.

The actual cave site was perfect. It was forbidding, protected, and yet familiar to Lareano. The mountain was known by its traditional name, "La Chiva."

10. Good Time For Bandits

Northwest Mexico – 1880's

After a time the targets expanded beyond churches and hostile businesses to shipments from the mint. Coinage had been developed and was in plentiful supply. The bandits overtook transports of various sorts and relieved them of the monies.

Events could easily be viewed as opportunities. That perspective helped release fears that would otherwise be based upon the timing. One of the facts of life is the known realization that opportunities do not come in the order that you want. We are not given dominion over those choices. They are part of a higher order.

The weather was highly cooperative. The area is generally temperate with significant rainfall only in the extreme winter months. It rarely gets as low as freezing. The gang could move about almost at will without the weather being a factor to influence their objectives or decisions.

The success of the Lareanos created numerous logistical issues. The quantity of the stolen goods required sufficient coordination to safely distribute, transport, and hide. They were secretive individually and collectively. They needed no coaching and said little to nothing. Concern and concealment were not frequent discussion topics. They were bandits and they knew what to do.

The band made its own law, and Lareano Garcia was the one member Supreme Court. There was no true opposition. Resistance by the guards was generally light. The band was cautious and alert, but never afraid. Self-help was rarely encountered. It was easier and much safer to submit than to fight the Lareanos.

Occasional attempts would be made to capture some of the men. Rather than weakening the morale it had the opposite result. These men were indomitable. The code required confidence and arrogance. No captive would talk, not even a hint or a whisper.

The leader, Lareano Garcia, led a surprisingly more normal life than one would expect. He grew out of the people and was universally acknowledged for all that he was, the leader of a huge gang that was more successful than any other before its time. He was operating on a pack level with a tradition of order. He was a hero. He was bad and good simultaneously, a constant study in contrasts. He lived a powerful but normal life. He fell in love with his majestic wife, Arlena, and had two happy children.

Like his mother, riding on a horse was an elixir for his wife, and her time in the saddle brought great contemplation and personal reflection. She would have stories of the journey north through Mexico and across the border. She talked about the wonders available to people living in Arizona and dreamed of a time when her husband and children could travel with her and experience the life-altering opportunities to the north. She had dreams, but told nobody. She did not share her private mind and inner thoughts. From the outside she was reserved and somewhat traditional.

Arlena was a bold and beautiful woman. She was stout, strong, and decisive. Her hair was the first thing you would notice. It was a copper red color of sufficient length to cover her neck when wearing a riding hat. She had been married to Lareano for some years, and was precluded from leaving the absolute protection afforded within their specific area except with a guard or on extended trips far away. The Garcias had been hidden, guarded and protected for years.

There was a time when Lareano started developing mixed feelings about the gang's pursuits. He wondered if they should take a break. Their success had been a blessing. It could be a good time to stop, rest and enjoy. He even met with Camacho about shutting down the operation. Camacho had been a catalytic member from the beginning, and the concept of quitting was unquestionable to him. No way. Not now. Not ever.

However, it was getting more dangerous for the Lareanos. The Military Governor was taking matters personally and beginning to put up a front with the train shipments and cargo convoys with the coins. There were armed guards in the territory asking questions and getting wrong answers.

Lareano wanted to slow down. They could all integrate back into their places and enjoy their personal lives until things cooled down a bit. Each clearly had enough. Land and lifestyle became more important than attacking government protected installations. Growing food and raising children had more appeal than being on the road. Shelter was feeling comfortable and alluring. Conquest and challenge had lost their appeal and shine.

There is no proof that the gang ceased or even reduced its efforts. They had a momentum and the conflict factor was light. The die had been cast and there was no way to turn back. Shooters from the government reportedly gained a surprise advantage over a splinter group of the Lareanos and inflicted numerous casualties. According to the local stories, there was not one survivor. Again notice was duly served.

Their loyalty came from a code of conduct that died many years ago. They had honor and respect in a very dark time. Many new children were born after the gang reached its apex of fame and influence. The name of Lareano's daughter, Esperanza, was the most common name for the new girls. It means "Hope."

ભ ભ ભ

PART II – THE MILITARY GOVERNOR

11. JESUS BORELLA

Culiacan – 1886

Jesus Borella was born in Culiacan in 1836. He lived seventy-four long years, and died in 1910 as one of the early casualties of the revolution. Jesus Borella was commonly known for two major things. First, he became the Military Governor of Sinaloa. With that position he had an unusual amount of power and influence, but nothing that rivaled the changes that occurred in his life following his personal encounter with Lareano Garcia. Second, he would ultimately be recognized as the richest man in the area. He may have also been one of the oldest.

The story of his wealth and power did not relate to family circumstances or their rumored inheritance from Spain, but rather to his private deal with the bandit, Lareano Garcia. No, Jesus Borella was not a member or supporter of the Lareanos. That would have been too simple. His story is much more devious and complex.

As Military Governor of the state of Sinaloa, Jesus was technically the chief legal officer of the region. In his official capacity, the order from Jesus Borella was the word of the law. He had at his disposal all available forms of enforcement. A few corrupt judges enhanced the package. He would say it was a prosecution-oriented legal climate, but the general population had the opposing view. The conduct of the Lareanos was a true challenge to his rule. The major irritant to his power was the continued irreverent and unlawful conduct of the defiant bandits. The churches had all been disrespected and looted. Some of their precious jewels, artifacts, and history were callously removed. Many of the historical

objects tracing back to the Mayans and Incas were now part of the
Lareanos' treasury, or sold or used as barter to places unknown.

Nobody ever seemed to question how the churches became
the original depositories for such historical treasures, but the raids
by the Lareanos had clearly redistributed some of the goods. Like
the church, the Lareanos were not the appropriate benefactors of
these sacred and powerful relics.

Lareano did not feel sorry for any form of organized religion.
While he took a significant amount of items, the church was never
completely cleaned out. The gang always left the practical ceremonial objects and other items of regular use. Their childhood
upbringing left a small stamp of tradition and respect. All had at
least some exposure and training by the church.

It has often been said that might makes right. As the Military
Governor, Jesus Borella was clearly seduced by this framework of
thinking. After all, he was selected by the president of his country
to be responsible for upholding the law in that entire multi-state
area.

He was also the chief political officer in the state. The implementation of a very tight rule was symbolic of his regime. With the
color of authority, seemingly unlimited supplies and sufficient government troops, nothing should inhibit the power of the Military
Governor, at least in his thinking. Factually that was quite inaccurate. While the people were afraid of their leadership, and passive
submissive behavior was the normal outward appearance, the true
spirit was one of quiet rebellion.

The people held their government, both the local and national
layers, in ultimate contempt. The masses lived in horrible conditions while the so-called elite prospered greatly at their expense. It
looked like there was a two-class society, consisting of the very rich
and the poor. There was nothing in between. The barrier between
the two was absolute and inviolate. It was an unofficial caste system
based on economics, history, and a tradition of oppression. The
enforcement mechanisms were securely in place and dissent was
not acceptable conduct. All resistance was dealt with quickly and
decisively.

There was little, if any, vertical mobility. One's birth and family
status almost always predicted the story of their entire life, from

education through employment, from living conditions to comforts. Life was hard, and the political leadership profited by suppressing the majority. It was the universal story. This was the history for many decades and nothing changed.

In direct contrast to the bandit, Jesus Borella was born to a family of privilege. Both of his parents were from Spain, and came to Mexico only a couple of years before his birth. They immigrated as cultural ambassadors personally chosen by the King of Spain. Their primary role was to expand commerce and seek natural resources of benefit to the mother country. It was understood that the required vehicles for personal gain were likewise afforded to them. Opportunity was at their doorstep and nothing stood in their way. They were the chosen conduit for riches. They were watchdogs of a sort, always maintaining their allegiance to their homeland and place of birth. This birthright had a significant impact on their son.

There was an arrogance surrounding his family situation and history. Being of Spanish ancestry helped Jesus feel different and slightly superior to his friends as they grew up. His family lived well beyond the norm in the area, residing in a hacienda more similar to a European compound. Their large house and gated grounds afforded them privacy, and the staff quarters were filled with servants and others to help with all of the maintenance and chores. Daily life was actually simple for these selected few. They prospered and grew upon the backs of their neighbors.

In spite of this ancestry, Jesus was born of and belonged to Mexico. As he grew he found himself in love with the land and its people. This was his birthplace and he knew he would never leave its soil. His goals were mighty, but he had a large head start over all of his friends and contemporaries.

Jesus was born to a Catholic family. They worshiped regularly and maintained a strong relationship with the bishop, priests, and staff at the cathedral. There was an informal seating arrangement that favored the entire Borella family. They enjoyed the benefits of a second row pew, a product of their steady support, generous gifts, and regular patronage of the staff. Nothing was forgotten.

From early childhood Jesus loved the ceremonial nature of the events, along with the size and majesty of the surroundings. The brightly colored trappings of the priests enhanced the connection with his senses. The light bouncing off of the gold, silver, and colored gems dazzled him. The entire religious experience was highly influential in giving him a larger working philosophy of life. The church provided a comfortable structure for him. He liked all of the rules and conditions. He was a true believer.

The privileges for Jesus began at birth and continued throughout his schooling and into his adult years. The family connections enabled him to move to the top of his class and stay there. Nothing was lost on this young man. He was strong, smart, and extremely aggressive. His competitive spirit would manifest itself at everything he attempted. Even as a child he had brash confidence. The concept of fair dealing was not part of his script. He was more of the win-at-any-cost mentality. He wanted things his way. He was fearless and mean to the core.

Jesus personalized many of his encounters. The school was his school, the town was his town, and even the church was passively thought of as his church. His opponents were treated like enemies, and conquest was his primary goal. He was a control freak in every sense of the word.

This personality trait ultimately turned into an absolute obsession when it came to the Lareanos many years later. Jesus would even experience trouble sleeping at night when he thought about the exploits of the gang. He was deeply disturbed with the fact that they took items from the church, his church, and treated themselves to favors from every available establishment of their choosing. They were indiscreet, disrespectful of the law, and disparaging of the church. The gang members thumbed their collective noses at the established order. They were true outlaws and had to be dealt with.

Jesus could not understand why the townspeople in every area would actually cover the tracks for the Lareanos, hide them, assist their efforts, feed and even share their homes with them. It made no sense. These were bandits and deserved to be caught and punished, even killed. Their individual and collective success was a major irritant to his job as Military Governor. He became obsessed with the capture and elimination of the Lareanos.

The attempts to catch the bandits became a cat and mouse game. When the patrols and protection of the churches increased the bandits expanded into different arenas. They robbed the banks, such as they were. Then the ultimate disgrace of authority, they attacked the pack trains from the mint at Durango. The federal guards were no match for the local knowledge and the skill of the Lareanos. They knew the terrain like the backs of their hands, making each ambush a unique work of art. The protective troops were no match for the coordinated skill of the Lareanos, and the amount of bandit wealth continued to grow.

The obsessive nature of the Military Governor was overcome with these attacks. It was a personal affront to his power, position and authority. He wanted the gang and he demanded restitution and revenge from the Lareanos. He had to get them at any cost.

12. Trapped

Northwestern Mexico – 1890

The Lareanos ran wild for another couple of years, until a potentially successful plan was ultimately devised. Jesus Borella and his forces would set a trap unlike any in recent history. It was a full military maneuver, including the latest of weapons and long guns, a surplus of specially trained soldiers, and the benefits of planning, timing, the specific season, and unlimited resources.

A comprehensive plan of misinformation initiated the maneuver. Jesus came to believe Lareano was getting facts from within his ranks, so some intentional bait and totally incorrect information was given out to all but a select and trusted few of his men. The misinformation plan was a secret. Most of his leaders were not privy to the real goal.

The entire mission was aimed at the elimination of as many of the Lareanos as possible, the capture of the gang leaders, and the restoration of law and order in the territory. A prolonged amount of time and planning went into the operation. It involved moving the largest run of coinage to date, including boxes of the 8 Reale silver coins with the face of King Ferdinand VII, and the use of a train to transport them further north.

The train contained passenger cars as well as sealed freight or boxcars, which were alleged to contain the largest historical shipment of gold bars and freshly minted silver coins for delivery. In fact there were nothing but soldiers, weapons, and more skilled guards comprising the entire group of passengers and working crew. The train was an armed fortress, a Trojan horse.

In the past, the Lareanos would merely confiscate the pack animals with their valued cargo. This time they would have to unload the train in order to escape with the bounty, requiring additional time and necessitating a surplus of pack stock. This element of time was a secondary benefit in the plan skillfully executed by the Military Governor's trusted few, because a counterattack would also be launched by a following train filled with soldiers, horses, and more weapons. A huge number of soldiers were assigned to this mission, and the trap turned out to be successful.

The Lareanos had become somewhat complacent due to the lack of effective resistance. Their reputation for swift and decisive action had demoralized the guards and other guardians of the earlier shipments. For years they had been the beneficiaries of detailed and accurate information from compliant guards. The gang was richly rewarded with frequent inside information. The history of accuracy bred contentment. The edge had been lost. The sympathetic guards posed no opposition and provided clear and highly accurate details for years. Nobody had any reason to believe this dual loyalty had been compromised. The poisoned information was effective because everyone believed it to be true.

A number of additional factors all contributed to a decreasing lack of sharpness. The gang enjoyed their liberties as folk heroes and local favorites. They were eating well and drinking more. They did not practice their shooting and other skills with the same degree of conviction. They failed to maintain peak physical conditioning. At times they were getting lax.

It had all been too easy. The political climate also was a factor. The locals were becoming increasing outraged at the perceived corruption of their leaders. The class struggle was lost, and living conditions were deplorable for the majority who were poor. It was a perfect climate for a gang of bandits to prosper.

The protection of the bandits was a mandate to effectuate change. The people vicariously enjoyed great pleasure through the antics of the Lareanos. Sometimes it is that way with real folk heroes who carry the dreams of the others on their backs. Rebellion takes many forms.

The capture scene was an ugly sight. It was bound to happen sometime, but this was an unusually brutal day. The objective was to kill as many bandits as possible, using a combination of tricks.

First of all, the train contained nothing but armed guards and hired professionals. In addition, armored shooting platforms had been installed in many of the boxcars. It was a moving death train, with a mission to exact final and complete revenge against the outlaws. The onslaught was memorable.

Next, there was a following train loaded with federal troops. The Lareanos were not ready for the second train trick. The sympathetic guards were equally surprised. They found themselves to be in a strategically difficult position.

The Lareanos could quickly see that the odds were overwhelmingly against them. Nevertheless, they kept shooting, moving, and defending. The government troops were the obvious aggressor. They had every advantage. The bandits appeared to strengthen their personal resolve when one of their neighbors went down. This was a fight to the finish.

Every one of the bandits fought together until the massacre was too great. They were surrounded with no option for retreat. The bandits were outgunned and outmanned. The government weapons and ammunition were more powerful and part of an apparently endless supply. There was no easy way out. After hours of fighting they were forced to surrender. They had no other choice.

The caboose held the Military Governor, who wanted a ringside seat for the carnage. He walked about after the deadly battle gloating with his success. He felt vindicated and overly confident. It was a special moment for Jesus when the bandits surrendered before him.

Lareano, Camacho, and the other leaders were separated from their men and from each other. They proclaimed no knowledge or responsibility for any of the previous holdups. They protested their arrests and claimed this to be the first robbery for the group. On that story they would not bend. They would not admit to holding any of the previous loot, and denied any knowledge of where such items may be stored. No one violated his oath of silence, even in the face of numerous executions. Their lips remained closed.

The shooting of gang members in front of the others did not weaken the exceptionally strong will of the survivors. They were tough to the core. The brutality of the guards only strengthened their commitment to silence. The condemned had a look in their eyes that was different than most. Not one member of the Lareanos exhibited any fear. They had lived a life of meaning and adventure since joining with Lareano and Camacho. Their faith in the afterlife gave them strength as they witnessed their fellow riders needlessly shot at close range by the troops. There was victory in death too. They loved their leader and would easily die for him. It was a small price to pay for the years of joy and glory. Lareano had given them their zest for life and the reward was their dignity. This was true for every single one of them.

Sixteen of the men, including the four original members of the Lareanos, were chosen by the Military Governor to survive. They were bound by hand and foot and taken on a long wagon ride to the fortress and jail a number of miles from Culiacan. Their conditions were deplorable and they were treated worse than enemy soldiers. They were given very little food and water.

The Military Governor wanted to establish who was boss and also weaken both the physical strength and the will of the captured men. He demanded what they had. He needed information. Nothing was effective. He gathered no clues to the location of the missing valuables. Not one coin was being recovered as a result of his efforts. Something else was required and violence was his favorite communication tool.

"Where is the gold?" he screamed.

There was no response.

"I will kill you slowly and then you will tell me," he promised.

Not one of the captured men spoke.

"You will want to talk to me in time," he snapped as he walked away.

The few surviving gang members were separated from their leaders when they reached the jail facilities. There would be no trial. It was a frontier justice system, quite unlike those that we currently enjoy. There was no such thing as due process. The detainees were determined by the Military Governor to be guilty as charged, and publicly sentenced to hard labor while secretly condemned to a very short life.

In the animal world there exists an instantaneous scaling and determination of the immediate environment, with an emphasis on everything in close proximity. Almost by reflex an effort is made to locate any possible opponent and evaluate the strengths and then the weaknesses of the potential enemy. It is a primitive reflex which helps prolong the lives of the species. The very survival requires an ability to monitor the environment, determine friend from foe, and secure a safe position relative to the perceived danger and available choices. Nothing is different with mankind, other than the filter of the cognitive process. Men almost instantly size up their situation, evaluate the competition, and determine their relative strengths and weaknesses. It is an automatic process and happens within seconds. We are hard-wired that way.

The skills of a bandit were further honed by the knowledge that they lived on the edge of society, or at least far beyond the promulgated rules of law and recognized standards of social order. To survive at his level, Lareano had developed these skills to a fine art. On more than one occasion his instinctive reaction prevented bodily harm or loss of life. He could look at a gathering and almost climb within their minds. To the outside it looked to be by reflex that Lareano could determine who would react first and take precautionary steps to eliminate that threat. He would know who would draw their gun and shoot and who would merely stand and watch.

The old story of killing a snake by cutting off its head was true. The injury or death of the most reactive guard would often cause the rest of the men to surrender. This uncanny ability of selective culling actually prevented a great amount of bloodshed and loss of life during the raids. The Lareanos had been excessively violent only in unique situations. They were dominant and cast a tall shadow at all times. For the most part they used their reputation to effectuate their will upon others.

It was different now. Lareano was not only confined, but he was also seriously restrained. The shackles were more fitting to hold a bear or huge beast. He knew he was going nowhere. The only key was rumored to be in the safe behind locked doors in the Military Governor's private quarters. The bandit's sympathizers inside the prison could never get close enough to the key to be useful. The inner circle of guards was too small to pierce. In spite of his predicament, his spirit was strong and he felt himself to be in a decent bargaining position. That confidence was carefully hidden.

What did he gather from the power objects and other items of religious and historical significance that he had secreted away? Where did he gain this strength of an elephant? He felt like he had the energies of his grandmother on his side. He also had the special training from the shaman priests that lived on or near the dual mountains of Tacamonte and La Chiva. All was not lost. He was alive.

Loneliness set in after a number of months. It was obvious to Lareano that the current stalemate would not change. There was nothing that could be done to challenge his incarceration. He had underestimated his adversary. Many of his men had been brutalized. Those that remained were caged like animals with no way out.

He often thought of his beautiful wife, Arlena, and two happy children, Esperanza and Hector, and wondered if there was any chance that he would ever see them again. These thoughts would weaken him to a point of utter despair. Putting being tough aside, he missed his family and the time to be together.

It was then that he hatched his plan. He would use the treasure as bait. It would be irresistible.

13. MINDS OF STEEL

Detention Center – Early 1891

Lareano sent a message through one of the guards to meet with the Military Governor. He knew he could make a deal that could not be refused. Lareano would communicate nothing further on this subject other than directly with Jesus Borella. He would say no more other than request an important meeting with the Military Governor. The contents, timing, and conditions were unknown.

Wanting to establish his dominance, Jesus declined to meet with the bandit leader. Instead, he had the guards shoot and kill Camacho and three key men, Elias, Omar and Emory. Lareano was the sole survivor. There was no doubt in the Military Governor's mind about who was the boss. He was brutal and had no boundaries.

This began a time of severe isolation for Lareano, locked in a wooden cell, and chained to an iron ring that was anchored deep into the ground.

After a couple of months Jesus Borella decided to go and visit his prisoner and vent his superiority in a shallow and demonstrative manner. Before Jesus did or said anything the bandit broke his silence and made a shocking proposal.

"How would you like to be the richest man in this territory?" he asked.

The silence was thick after his first words. It was as if he had not said anything.

Then he smiled and continued, "You know I can make that come true."

The words coming from the bandit were overwhelming to the Military Governor. He had often though about the purported wealth and status of the bandit. The bandit was correct. He, Jesus Borella, could be the richest man in the state of Sinaloa, and maybe in all of Mexico. In addition to the power of his office and unyielding administration of justice, he would have the wealth to back it up.

He quickly scanned his mental pictures about the social status and respect he would have as he walked down the streets. Everyone would look at him with envy. He could own businesses, many of them, and have employees, and make money off all of them. And the church, yes he would be held in even higher regard than even his father had before him.

His thoughts were not all positive. Was he worse than the criminal himself? Only if he got caught! He quickly evaluated his ability to maintain and protect his secret. Then he realized the consequences, for he would have to make a deal with the devil, the despicable character that was in chains before him.

At least three long minutes passed before he spoke. To his perception it seemed like an hour. It was becoming a match of wills. This could take awhile. Both sides saw patience as a psychological weapon. Beads of sweat were forming all over his face, his eyes became out of focus, and his mind ran wild as he thought about the impact of those simple utterances from the bandit.

Jesus felt the sweat drip from his forehead. His lips became dry, his voice cracked. "Tell me more," was his only reply.

Lareano started to stand, but the chains about his legs made any graceful effort impossible. In order to avoid showing anything more to Jesus, he elected to remain in place on the ground. Although he was sitting on the dirty floor of his cage, imprisoned for an unknown amount of time, the bandit was still able to clearly visualize life outside of the prison, happy times with his wife and children, and a new beginning in a land far away. It was as if his entire future lay before him, an alternate reality far different than life in the filth of this cell.

He contemplated his options, as he had numerous times before, and then he spoke. This was his moment, the best opportunity he could see. The time had come to play his cards and win his freedom. His hand was that good. Of that fact he was confident. His actions were calm and calculated.

"Suppose we make a deal," Lareano uttered quietly, with his eyes downcast at his dirty bare feet.

His boots had been removed and taken weeks before. The iron shackles had made rust-colored stains around his ankles. His feet

were swollen and his body ached from inactivity. He felt so sick
with the sound of those words that he fell silent again.

Dealing with this man was worse than he thought. At times the
relief of a quick death would be easier. It was becoming harder to
care. He needed this to work.

"Si," said Jesus, with his only motion being a slight affirmative
nod.

"I am of no value to you here, on the floor of this filthy cage,"
proclaimed the bandit. "But I am worth more to you than you can
ever imagine if I was set free."

These words were uttered with his defiant gaze fixed on the
only object in the cell, an old three-legged stool that he could not
even reach. It was beyond the length of his chain. The carvings on
each leg represented something to the various men who had occupied that cell before him. Their history would not be filled with
favorable outcomes. This was a horrible place and a brutal time.

Jesus followed the bandit's eyes back to the stool. He unlocked
the door, entered the cell, and pushed it with his boot over towards
Lareano, who promptly pulled it under him and propped himself
up as if on a throne. This had been the first sign of respect shown
to him since the capture.

Jesus then reached into his pocket and pulled out a cigarette,
which he lit and gave to the bandit. This procedure was going to
be slow and deliberate. The posture had changed and a major
acknowledgement had been made. Serious negotiations had been
commenced.

Jesus addressed the bandit sternly when he asked, "What have
we before us?"

"How can we help each other?"

"What do you have for me?"

The questions came faster than the bandit wanted to respond.
He patiently waited until his visitor stopped.

"I can make you the richest man in Sinaloa, and you won't
have to worry about it. That means gold, silver, jewels, and precious objects that date back to the ancients. You would have currency, coins, and ingots that can be spent here or in the United
States. There are old coins from Spain, and newly made ones from
your government mint.

Lareano took a deep breath and continued, "I even have ceremonial pieces and power objects stolen by your church from the Mayans and other travelers upon our soil."

Jesus was silent. His heart was pounding and he was unable to say anything.

The bandit waited and then continued by lowering his voice as he whispered these words: "You have the chance to be very rich. The choice is yours."

Jesus felt his chest tighten and he almost choked on his own selfish desire. While he had secretly hoped for this type of outcome, he rarely believed it could ever come true. Up to that point the bandit had not shown any signs of remorse. He never admitted to having possession or control over anything at all. He never weakened in his resolve. It looked like his secrets would remain until his death. But now, there was hope. He, Jesus Borella, could be the richest man in the area, and nobody would know why or how. That was to be his secret. He already had an alternate plan.

Although Lareano had never been a fisherman, he understood the concept of baiting the hook and waiting. He delivered his message and then said nothing more. The room was filled with excitement and amazing potential, yet he remained silent and calm. He was in the center of the action and he was comfortable with the strength of his game.

Time passed. It felt like the temperature rose and the air became thin and stale. Jesus waited and hoped the bandit could not hear his rapidly beating heart. Concealing excitement was not one of his personal strengths. He was never one to mask his feelings. He broke out in a strong sweat and was noticeably affected.

This was Lareano's time, perhaps one of the few intersections of chance with destiny. There was an opportunity to see his children and be in the arms of his lovely Arlena again if he could sell this proposal to the Military Governor. He saw the potential in his adversary's dark eyes. Greed and lust were alive and healthy in his opponent. Jesus was the law but his corrupt values were known. The treasure was too much to resist.

Lareano sat quietly and did not move a muscle. Time was his ally. To him the air changed in the cell. He could see the dust particles floating through the rays of light, the stripes of the bars forming a complex of parallel lines in the opaque light. It was late afternoon, and the temperature was beginning to cool outside.

The anticipation of unlimited wealth teased every sweat gland in the Military Governor's body. His mind was whirling, and his thoughts were unclear. He was intoxicated with the moment. He wanted to hear more, but was concerned with how he would extract the information from the bandit. He did not want to make a mistake. Perhaps it was easiest to simply cooperate, and see what his adversary demanded. After all, he knew who was in the superior bargaining position.

Lareano sat and waited. It was similar to a state of suspended animation. His breathing was slow and shallow. His gaze was fixed on some imaginary point through the walls and into the distance.

Tension and anticipation filled the air with electricity and a strange odor. The pause was so long that it felt like the temperature rose another few degrees, or was that hot breath on his neck as if from some imaginary person?

When he broke the silence, his words were soft and calculated: "We have been bad enemies, and now we can become good friends. Both of us can succeed in a lasting way."

Jesus sat at full attention as the bandit continued. "I can give you countless riches, beyond the reach of any man in his lifetime, and you can give me my freedom. Just that. We can make a fair trade. No?"

Lareano maintained his steady eye contact. This was serious business and he was giving away something larger than anyone could possibly imagine. The treasure was beyond comprehension.

The bandit practically stared down his adversary. He had learned long ago to trust the face as a predictive indicator of behavior. The Governor's eyes filled with delight. His heart was beating so noticeably fast that it was difficult for him to pronounce any words. His inner joy was overflowing. This was going to be easier than he thought. The best outcome was now possible.

Jesus took a deep breath. As he exhaled he said, "Yes, I will consider your offer."

The pause seemed to annoy the bandit. Then Jesus made his inquiring move. "There are rumors of your generosity. I know that is why it was so hard to stop you and catch your gang. It is good to know that you retained some share. That is very good news. It may even save your miserable life. That is, if we are both lucky."

Jesus began to smile and he continued, "So the treasure is not a rumor. It is real. Now, tell me where you hid my treasure. What is in it? Is it far from here? Tell me now."

Jesus stopped and laughed. "I sound as excited as a young boy. This is good. You amuse me, my new friend."

Even as the last words were spoken Jesus knew that part of what he just said was not true. The bandit was never going to be his friend. In his concept of a strict system of law and order, a bandit is a criminal, forever. And justice was what he decreed it to be. He was the Military Governor and, as such, he was personally the embodiment of the law. It was his will which the judges, jailers, guards and executioners would implement. Unfortunately, his concept of justice was personal and primitive. He believed in solid retribution and always taking the upper hand. Violence and over-reaction were the normal means of distributing punishment. Cold and brutal behavior was the norm rather than the exception.

Lareano folded his arms and sat back with a snicker. His head became more erect and his gaze became fixed on his captor's eyes. He waited.

"There is no way I will tell you anything. The distance is great and the location is close to impossible to detect. You can be within feet of the hiding spot and still seem miles away. You need my help."

The bandit then revealed the essence of his deal when he said, "I will personally take you to the treasure after you have ensured and delivered the permanent safety of my wife and children, and agreed to set me free."

"This cannot be done," growled the captor.

"It has to be. There can be no other way."

"Everyone will know I made a deal with you. I cannot simply set you free. No, never. Your demands are unreasonable and impossible. Do not take me for a fool. Look at you. Look at the leg irons. You are an animal. I am in control of you and not the reverse. Do not insult me."

The tone changed. Lareano sensed this to be his moment. He would risk his life now, and the outcome would become clear soon.

"Not true," said the bandit, "just listen."

More than a minute passed, and then Lareano continued, "I have learned a lot about you, first as your adversary and second while captured in this hellhole you call a prison. Your family came to Mexico from Spain. You were born here, and not in Spain as you so often pretend. You and I are brothers of this soil. Your father was in government service. There is little or nothing known of his fortune, other than he had the blessings and support of the King. Odds are he came with sufficient wealth to start a complete life on his new soil."

Lareano chose his words carefully. "Your father died two years ago and you inherited his business and funds. I would suspect that they are not as great as desired, or you would have retired from this job and ceased chasing me. Or, should I say, his position and his debts! There is a lot of responsibility and problems, but little reward. I can give you the reward. It can seem like it was part of your family legacy, even the coins from Spain. You could disguise the use."

Lareano waited for the impact of his words to be understood. Then he continued, "It is a simple trade; freedom is worth that to me. My freedom is worth more to you."

Minutes of silence followed. The conversation was not being advanced. Neither of the men appeared interested in speaking any further. Each held his ground firmly. No clarification would help. They were at a procedural impasse, nothing more.

The rivals sat isolated at this crossroads of silence. Not a word was spoken. Neither wanted to breach the silence. They both considered it to be a sign of weakness to be the first to talk in this situation.

For any deal to work, the transaction must be bilateral. Jesus wanted the treasure, and Lareano wanted a new life in Tucson. The successful implementation of a fair trade was a far stretch for the minds of these competitors. Neither was an inherently fair person.

Lareano's heart burned to be with his wife and children again. He could easily gather more riches. There must be opportunity for plenty of crime across the border.

They were deadly rivals, and the competitive spirit was enhanced in both of them. Neither trust nor respect were present, nor were they a requirement. Their collective history prohibited that much faith in the other.

The two excited men had the outline of a deal, or at least the potential. Both men sat and thought. Neither would break the silence. Each saw it as impotence, and this was not the time to signal any concession to the other. This was intended to be simply a business deal, a trade. The difficulty would be in the details.

How in the world could it be accomplished without detection? What can be done to maintain safety? Security? How many men do you take into your confidence?

As the opponents sat their relationship needed to morph from hostile to complimentary. The transition necessitated an almost simultaneous reversal of anxiety to trust, sarcasm into respect, and loss into profit. The element of trust would be required to coax the cherished secrets from the bandit. By taking this step he would become a brother in crime. The Military Governor would be involved up to his neck; his conduct would ratify the theft. He had no intention of returning anything to anyone else. He was comfortable with his own secret.

They sat and they waited. Jesus finally spoke first, his lips started to move and only one word came out, "How?"

Lareano took that word to mean more than it sounded. Lareano knew that he had obtained the necessary consent. Jesus wanted to do the deal. Of course he did.

Now came the rules. Could they reach agreement? This would prove to be a critical point in setting the tone of the new relationship between the two men.

Lareano replied, "You will need to show a sign of good faith. This is absolute and essential. I will do nothing more until you take the first step. It is the only way this can work. It is not negotiable. Never."

Jesus was surprised at the bold response. He decided to ignore the arrogance of his captive and new partner, and he quickly repeated, "I said how?"

The bandit then shared his deal points for their undertaking. He spoke more slowly and very clear, "It is very simple. First, you will provide the safe travel of my family to Tucson, in the Arizona Territory. This must happen quickly. They should be able to bring whatever they want and start a new life in America. That is the only way you can accept this deal. It requires safe transport of my family to start a new life outside of Mexico. Tucson, Arizona to be specific."

The reference to his family surprised the Military Governor. It was a total shock to hear that the bandit had a wife and children. That was a perfectly kept secret for so long. Jesus was floored with the realization that the bandit had roots somewhere in the greater area. It was taken as a personal slap in the face.

At once Jesus was overcome with a feeling of being small, of realizing that acrimony was brewing between his office and the people. He knew his public image and community respect were at a longtime low, if it happened to matter. There were no polls then, just an accepted understanding. The thought of the bandit's family domiciled somewhere in the state of Sinaloa was irritating. This was his jurisdiction, and his knowledge of his number one adversary was obviously missing key facts.

The Military Governor hated secrets, unless they were his own. It bothered him that his information was deficient. He was upset over the manifest lack of communication and ultimate disrespect.

Questions from Jesus, uttered quietly and slowly, filled the air. It was different than the earlier part of the conversation, when Jesus began repeating questions in a rapid-fire manner. He was still speaking too fast for reply. The bandit waited. His patience went unnoticed.

"How will you know that I complied with your request?" asked the Military Governor.

"What if I have them killed instead? What if I do nothing? How can you trust me? How can I trust you? Can this realistically be accomplished?"

After a pause he continued, "Are we both crazy? How can you possibly know if your wife is delivered to Tucson if you are locked in this cell?"

He thought for a moment, eyes downcast, and mumbled, "How is that possible? Why do I wonder?"

Lareano stared at his captor. His eyes remained clear and bright. He spoke slowly and clearly. His response was short and simple, "You are a smart man."

Jesus challenged the inquiry, and asked more with an inquisitive twisting of his head and a warm and open look in his eyes. It was a visible softening.

Lareano then replied, "I will know when they arrive safely."

He paused for impact, and added: "At that point we will be able to proceed to the next phase of our exchange."

After a couple of moments of further reflection, the bandit said, "My wife and children are of no consequence to you. Your life would not be enhanced by taking theirs. You have me as collateral."

Jesus asked about further details. "What more will be required of me than the safe passage of your family? Will you blackmail me, my new friend? Even worse, will you betray my trust?"

Lareano replied, "My life. I want my freedom with my family. I can get safe transportation across the northern border and I will leave you alone forever. I will stay away. You will never see me again. I will be too far away."

"A treasure to the Borella family in exchange for transporting my family to another county and sending me after them is such a good trade for you. You have my word."

The Military Governor spoke, "And if I just kill you now and then hunt them down?"

"You would not live to see another year. And even if you were lucky enough to survive, you could never find my treasure trove. Never."

His smile had a peculiar twist to it. He reflected a confidence beyond words. Of course his treasure was well hidden. But somebody may know where it is. One may question.

Jesus asked if the wife or children would be taking any part of the treasure with them. The question was a trick, a deception, because the removal of a portion of the treasure was not considered as a threat to Jesus. No, he wanted to know if they were aware of the hiding spot. He was trying to determine if his efforts would be better spent searching for the family and torturing the location out of the wife. His level of cruelty actually favored that approach, but the risk was obvious.

Lareano was gratuitous when he replied that they did not even know where it was. His children were very small. They did not know he was a leader. They lived a simple protected life with their mother. He also disclosed the fact that his wife had never been to the area at all, let alone the treasure itself. Only Camacho shared the secret, and strong rumor had it that he was murdered here.

Lareano believed it was a security risk to have his wife know anything about his business. She did not have the slightest idea of the existence or location of her husband's cache. It was a form of life insurance for her. That was his thinking, whether right or wrong. Life was planned that way. Arlena knew noting at all about the treasure. She knew he was the bandit leader and loved by the people far and wide.

He was a folk hero and she was his protected spouse. She could ride her horse, which was her favorite diversion, feeling safe wherever she went. The reaches of her husband's influence covered her with a mantle of protection.

She was not aware of any depository for the illicit fruits of his labor. It was unnecessary knowledge. She knew there was always enough, maybe too much at times. She could not remember a time of scarcity since she married him. He was very good at what he did.

"I will know if you do not proceed," snarled Lareano. "Don't make that mistake, for it will cost you."

"I could have you killed right now," growled Jesus, flexing his superior bargaining position over his captive rival. His breath became hot like fire, and he had clenched his fists. Patience was never his best personal attribute. Fairness in negotiation was never one of his noteworthy achievements. Kindness and subtlety were always absent. He was decisive, rough, and selfishly brutal.

The bandit was quick to reply this time. "But you know I will never talk. The Arizona Territory is out of your jurisdiction. Worse still, you will lose a fortune. You are too smart for that," whispered the bandit, his head down and his eyes focused on the leg shackles. He clearly disliked the disparity in freedom, the chains were not humane. He had too much pride and inner dignity. He could wait.

Jesus admired the inner as well as outer strength of his adversary. In the face of sheer defeat, shackled like an animal, and locked within a cell, undernourished, the bandit was able to project conviction, strength, and a powerful air of knowing. His confidence was convincing. The bandit earned the Military Governor's respect.

He looked about the cell. This would be a horrible contrast for the man who was rumored to amass one of the largest treasures in the history of his young and proud nation. The defeat associated with being captured should have a bigger impact on the psyche of the bandit, but it did not. The boredom and minor abuse since capture could impact the drive of lesser men, but not Lareano. He was something special. He was not prone to talk and nothing could change the strength of his resolve. He functioned with an inner vision and knowing. Much of the shamanic training paid dividends at this time.

What the Military Governor did not understand was the loyalty of some of his guards to the captive bandit. Food wrapped in a checkered cloth was found at the door to his cell at unusual hours. His ragged appearance was more from the lack of shaving and dirty conditions than a malaise from inadequate diet and nutrition. He needed to be free of the bondage, the unbelievable frustration from forced captivity. He knew what he would do.

Jesus reflected momentarily on the old game of chess, taught to him by his father when he was a child. He remembered countless candlelight evenings spent at the old wooden board with his family. He could visualize the checkered layout, with carving and beautiful contoured inlays around all four sides. The wood was smooth and dark. He wondered how the finish could be so smooth. The mind polishes it to a perfect gloss. The memory included visual images of the chess pieces themselves, carved out of wood and hand-painted by a craftsman who lived in a Spanish fishing village long before the family moved to Mexico. One team was cut from light birds-eye maple, and the opposing team was made of a dark hardwood resembling walnut. The pieces were heavy and represented a mythical time of a few centuries before. The antique chess set was one of his father's prized collection pieces from their life in central Spain.

It was always a special time when chess was the activity of the evening. He loved the discipline of the history-rich game. He thought about the variance between the lowly pawn and the mighty king. The similarity was not lost upon him.

If he played this move correctly he could become instantly one of the richest and most powerful men in his country. His desired outcome required little else. His destiny was before him and he could easily disguise the repatriation of specific items. It would not be difficult to assimilate and conceal his mighty asset acquisition. But, he still had no idea of the extent of the bounty. He dreamed big, and he would soon find the proportion to be beyond his capacity of imagination.

The deal would have to remain a secret, forever. This would take more thought and very careful planning. He wondered if he could trust the bandit, and his mind instantly went to work on possible alternatives that would ensure his objectives. He was consistently ill willed in his approach.

The primary concern was the treasure. Capture the treasure and control the man. To obtain the treasure would elevate his life beyond his means. Although he clearly had power and authority, he did not radiate culture or respect. He did not maintain the dignity of Spain as reflected by his parents. He lacked the style.

This wild and rugged land influenced him. While it was home for his whole life, the family stories from the old country were filled with images from a different life, from a century when lavish elegance was the lifestyle and birthright of the more privileged.

He remembered his father's stories about Madrid, the capital and largest city of Spain, with the squares, fountains, monuments and statutes to celebrate soldiers and events of long before. Apparently there were many such leaders and milestone events. Spain was where he believed kings and queens, as well as their consorts and friends, enjoyed rich food, luxurious surroundings, tender song, and fine craft. These were not descriptive of his experiences in Mexico. The rich quality of life was in sharp contrast to Culiacan. The history and traditions differed greatly. Mexico was totally unlike Spain. It had no royal family. The architecture was a planned defense against the climate rather than a statement to the higher life. The standard of living was much less. No fair comparison could be made.

To Jesus, there was no history in Mexico other than change. To him, the land was not rich with the tapestries of tradition. It bore witness of an unleashed future ahead, rather than a monument to lives of the past. The power, potency and potential were there, but the tradition and motivation were lacking. Europe was more than an ocean away. It represented a time that never reached the North American continent.

The contrasts and comparisons were endless. The secret truth for Jesus was his longing to enact the life of his childhood fantasy, his imaginative re-creation of Madrid and its environs during the glory days of Spain. That was neither his experience nor his future. He was born two years after his parents moved to the new land. His heritage and memories were of Mexico. He will die in this country having enjoyed a good life resulting from the inheritance of his father's status and appointment, but not by his own merit and achievement.

Lareano reflected upon the circumstances of his capture. There were scenes from that day that regularly haunted his consciousness. Preparation and planning were his mandates. He often dissected all moves and decisions in his memory. He ran a ballet of crime.

The bloody ambush and capture of many of his men was disturbing and destructive to Lareano. He missed his loyal followers, each and every one of them. They were more than associates in crime; they were part of a large family. He was troubled with the obvious fate of his amigos. It looked bleak under the iron and brutal control of the Military Governor.

Camacho Lopez was now dead, and the treasure in the cave on La Chiva was Lareano's ticket to freedom. The treasure was the best reward from a life of crime. It was also the best place for revenge, for getting even, if Jesus Borella did not play all of his cards correctly.

The Military Governor shuffled his feet, cleared his throat, and Lareano's mind returned to the present. The contrast with his current situation was sickening to him. He had the riches of a king yet he was trying to survive in conditions fit for a rat. He had to get out. His assets should be converted into his freedom. His plan to retain them would remain a secret. The bandit never lost hope. He reflected the positive spirit that drove him on. He would have to act alone.

Lareano could easily envision the wooden boxes with rope handles stacked high in the back of the cave. He lost count of the number many raids ago. He had surplus for his entire life, which he had always believed would be a long one. Now that was in question. The surrounding ground was covered with large piles of sparkling gold coins. There was also so much money of that time, Pieces of Eight, Reales, Escudos, Spanish Doubloons, and assorted other gold and silver coins. There was even a bag of tokens for goods or services, including 1887 corn tokens from Cortez. The orderly stacks of gold bullion and silver ingots were impressive. The quantities were excessive.

This treasure belonged to Lareano as his personal stash. The location on La Chiva was always Lareano's secret and Camacho was the only person to help him there. The exact location was a mystery to everyone else. His men would always wait miles away at the base of the canyon. They respected their leader and were also afraid of the shaman reputation. Every Achilles has a heal.

The gold and bejeweled artifacts stolen from the churches represented the most visually exciting part of the bounty. Some of the Spanish coins had an unknown currency value yet an obvious beauty, and the gold and silver statues and icons added a reverence. The value of the Incan and Mayan power objects were not fully understood. To Lareano they meant special magic. He treated them with respect but without understanding. They sat on the flat surfaces above the boxes of coins. The bags of small stones and rubies sitting at the base of the cave shimmered in his mind.

Other artifacts and empowered objects represented a minor portion of the treasure. Metal plates from Incan lands to the south were from the initial raid of the cathedral. Carvings, sculpture, statues, and relief plaques all added to the magnificent bounty of stolen objects hidden by Lareano in the sacred and protected mountain cave.

Lareano sat in a much different reality. The present situation was ugly and memories were a wonderful means of escape. The dreams of the past were replaced by the reminder that he was restrained and in captivity. The bandit was strong and brave even when chained. Nothing could be done so he tried to relax and wait. For that day he had no options. It was a hybrid of entertainment and gambling. It was his job for the day. The stakes were very high and he had to be ready to win.

On the other side of the room the Military Governor sat quietly. He had nothing better to do either. Jesus Borella thought about the pending offer. He went from random thoughts and old memories to the place of confinement in an instant. The silence was deafening, and he vowed not to be the first to speak. He would outlast his opponent, and saw it as a demonstration of his strong will and carefully developed mind. This was competition at its core, and defeat was not within his mindset either. He would demonstrate his superior bargaining position by appearing not to care.

As an ultimate act of defiance Jesus slowly rose, kicked the dust off of his boots, and walked out of the cell. He did not want the bandit to know he was interested. But interested he was.

Lareano did not acknowledge the silent departure of the Military Governor. This was just a game. He knew a return was forthcoming. There was no conceivable way that any rational man would walk away from the opportunity for unlimited wealth and a full inventory of treasure. It was too tempting. Nobody was that strong.

Furthermore, Jesus was not asked to give up much. Safe passage to America for the family as his deposit, and then permitting the bandit to escape would both be easy efforts to conceal. It would never look like the Military Governor compromised anything. Suspicion would not be aroused and nobody would ever hear or see a thing that implicates Jesus. He would just have to be patient and remain silent.

The commitment required by Jesus was minor compared to the benefits he would receive. The insurance factor was high and nobody should ever know of the conspiracy. He was in the perfect position to implement a total cover-up, and not many would believe the bandit should he abuse the deal and publicly implicate the Military Governor. There would be no credibility to any such claim. The bandit had no standing. Jesus knew that would never be a real issue, not because he absolutely trusted the bandit leader, but rather because he was developing an alternate plan of his own.

Jesus was having a recurring vision that scared him greatly. He would get cold chills when he realized what was on his mind. The Military Governor was afraid he would exit the treasure one day only to be looking out at the barrel of Lareano's gun. Lareano would know that the location of the secret would not be shared by his adversary with many. Jesus would go to the treasure alone and possibly be followed and killed. Or, even worse, the bandit could ambush him by rifle at many opportunities without ever coming into his immediate sight. No, the bandit would have to die at the proper moment. Then, and only then, would the secret be safe. Jesus must secure the location of the treasure before that event. He too had to be patient. Dead men tell no tales.

14. ACCEPTANCE

Arizona – April, 1891

The offer was accepted by conduct six days later. Action always speaks louder than words. Jesus communicated his agreement to the exchange without any further event or interaction with Lareano. His clear and convincing signal of consent was unannounced. Without meeting, negotiation, or even further discussion, the Military Governor effectuated the safe transport of Arlena and the children to Arizona. He used three of his most loyal personal guards to find the family, communicate as required, assist with the packing, and act as escorts to make the safe transfer to the border. The small group did not appear to draw any attention at any point along the way. It went better than planned.

Although skeptical at first, the family found themselves without alternatives when the guard spokesman arrived at their house and explained the safe transportation offer. They packed their key items quickly and were ready to leave the next morning when the trio of guards arrived with horses, a wagon, and pack animals for their journey north to safety.

Nobody remembered how the family was found, only how they were transported. This was done using a government wagon and three special guards, all of whom believed Mrs. Garcia and family were being removed from her home and deposited somewhere else as a punishment in furtherance of a decree from the chief lawmaker and enforcer. The guards would have been shocked if they ever knew themselves to be involuntary accomplices in a criminal conspiracy between their superior and the legendary bandit. That fact would remain a secret forever.

It is surprising they did not suspect foul play based on the time given Mrs. Garcia to gather her key belongings and the assistance given her by loading her selections into the storage area of the wagon. Her treatment was not like any previously given to somebody on the receiving end of the Military Governor's punishment.

Perhaps the respect held in the community for the bandit had a carryover effect for the family. Their boss may have even considered it life insurance.

Secret lines of disseminating information and underground railroads of various forms have existed throughout the centuries in Europe. This area likewise had a communication network facilitated in the immediate area by a couple of the local guards. It was speedy and more reliable than the tentative mail system being attempted by the national government. The means of using this underground system was known by the contact when the bandit's family arrived in Tucson. News of their safe and surprising arrival was possibly the most positive information to ever flow across the border and south through the pipeline.

Less than a week later Lareano got word that his wife and family were safe in Tucson. This came from a credible source that also possessed the secret coded identity or password phrase that would not be known or used by anyone other than his wife. They each had "proof of life" words or phrases should the need arise to have a code.

Lareano rejoiced with the news. His heart overflowed with hope and renewal. His dream of being reunited with his family was going to be fulfilled. Things looked instantly brighter from his dirty and dingy cell. It would only be a matter of time before the Military Governor would be visiting. He suspected a few days at the most.

Jesus was at the cell door late in the evening a couple of nights later. He did not want anyone to see him meeting with the former bandit leader. There should be no further connection between the two men. This communication would be private and privileged. It meant too much to both of them.

Jesus spoke to Lareano through the bars in the back section of the cell. His captive was not chained since the day after their last meeting, and Jesus had no intention of testing the new friendship with a silent meeting inside the cell. His trust did not extend that far.

Jesus began, "They are safe."

Lareano replied confidently, "Thank you. I know."

Jesus withheld further conversation and expressed his natural curiosity. It defied logic that messages could travel from Arizona to this area of Mexico and then penetrate through the walls of detention so quickly and efficiently. He had heard about it for years, and now he had personal proof. There had to be a simple answer. There were more important items on his mind.

Jesus was ready to implement the next phase of the procedure and thought it was appropriate to ask for directions. He wanted to know how to find his reward. He couldn't wait to learn about the hiding place for the treasure. Lareano requested writing materials so he could prepare a map. When the Military Governor returned the bandit gazed at the size of his rival's midsection and smiled.

"You are going to have a tough time climbing the trail to the treasure. The mountain is steep and you will have to be careful not to roll back down," he chuckled.

Jesus did not appreciate the humor. The personal attack on his large midsection was not understood, for that was a symbol of his masculinity, success and power. There was no doubt he lived and ate well. By contrast in belief, Lareano thought it would impact his ability to climb. The mountain was tough and there were no shortcuts to the treasure site. He had no intention of disclosing the alternate routes. He may need them for ambush or escape.

The first phase of their deal was concluded. It was now Lareano's turn to show good faith and produce the location of the main treasure stash. One of the best-kept secrets of his life was now being disclosed to his greatest adversary. This decision was inescapable; there was no other viable alternative.

Lareano gave Jesus directions through the town of Culiacan, south through the valley, over to the Tacamonte Canyon entrance, and all of the way over to the picnic area at the base of Tacamonte. Lareano's thoughts seemed to regress to his childhood years when he would first play and later learn to shoot at that remote area. It was a beautiful and lengthy ride from home and clearly out of the sight of anyone.

Lareano then got to the first important marker. He described a fence line at the edge of the wash and told Jesus about three consecutive fence poles that were different from the others. Each pole was just a small bit shorter and bore a cross carved into the back face about two to three feet above the base.

Jesus was not happy with the bandit's choice of a marker symbol. The cross was the primary icon of the church, and the treasure was obtained because of and at the expense of the church. His attention floated back to his earliest memories of the church, and the impact those experiences had upon his life. He was drifting and losing focus.

There were various markers along the path, each of which bore a special symbolism. Jesus was instructed to stand at the center of the three poles, align his body perpendicular to the white peak of La Chiva, and begin in that direction.

Landmarks included three birches, an old rockslide, a large boulder resembling the front of a boat, dry falls, a rock pile that looked like the front of a building corner, an upper elevation creek, a switchback near two dangerous ledges, an area on the lower face of the mountain apparently beyond the tree line, and a most unique entry into the treasure itself. That he would have to see to believe. A dismantled door cover from a bank safe!

Lareano sketched a map with the landmarks and distances adequately spaced. The map itself would be a problem. The mountain was too steep to accurately represent on a two-dimensional piece of paper. The distances seemed compressed or shortened as compared with the actual locations on land. It would be confusing without him, but there was no chance that he would be invited along. It would be the Military Governor's last day to live if he invited the angry bandit to join him.

Jesus searched on the mountain for two days with the detailed directions and map. The scale was horrible. Lareano never had to draw it before and his use of distance was off too. To make matters more complicated, Jesus was absolutely unfamiliar with that type of terrain, and a few errors in his calculations did not help.

He found the warnings from the bandit to be understated. The hillside was far more difficult than any place he had ever traveled. There was little protection from the hot sun. The plant life was sparse. There were scattered trees and very thick bushes. The vegetation was sticky, dry, thorny, and unrelenting. The biggest problem was the scarcity of water.

He quickly became disoriented and had to retrace his steps numerous times. There was something about the whole area that created an eerie feeling. His body hurt badly and his mind was playing tricks. As the temperature rose the Military Governor began to hallucinate.

Overcome with heat and thirst, the realization that he was not prepared for this adventure became obvious. Thoughts and images laden with doubt began to depress him. Although his experience told him this was the worst day of his life, his unusually strong spirit drove him on. His feet moved without a second thought, one after the other. At times he cursed out loud. A large frame and developed belly were not assets on La Chiva.

He climbed upward with the steadfast faith that reaching the goal would change his life. He visualized himself in a new status, with money and riches beyond anyone else in this developing land. Thoughts of the treasure were converted into a form of mental energy, driving Jesus higher and higher in spite of the physical pain.

Memories of his father troubled him in this agitated state. He rarely permitted any comparison with his father, making him realize how competitive and inferior he felt to the senior Borella. How did this happen? Why? He listened with envy as his parents and their friends discussed life in Europe. It sounded much better to him. For one, he imagined a climate more temperate and conducive to life. The water, fountains, and the giant Mediterranean Sea were part of his image of an ideal geography. He found Mexico more supportive for reptiles than humans. His spirit spiraled downward as this forbidden topic filled his mind. Jesus wished he had been born in Spain, like his father and six elder brothers. Although he had never traveled there, he had vivid mental pictures of that land.

The death of his own father had made him incomplete, losing his key link to the stories of his ancestry and memories of the past. Jesus also felt condemned to his country of birth, and had realized many years earlier that there would be no way out. For a majority of the time his efforts in repressing this confinement were successful. Today was not one such day. This was a day to suffer and curse the heat.

He was determined to exploit the situation and make a difference, and the opportunities created by the treasure were to be the
focal point of his renewed life. He still had no idea of the scope.
The trip up the mountain continued to be his worse nightmare.
He would make it. Quitting was not an acceptable option. He was
close and he knew it. A major change was about to come.

After a few more hours the Military Governor felt betrayed.
What a fool he had been. He was running around the mountain while the bandit was probably laughing in his cell. Despite
moments of despair, at times he still felt contrasting waves of hope.
After all, the bandit was still in his custody, and could easily be
eliminated if he deceived or tricked Jesus.

He must continue on. The lure of the treasure was too strong.
He needed more patience. He had to keep searching. The bandit
had warned him of the potential difficulty in locating the markers and then the trap door. Jesus remembered the look and the
snicker. He will prove him wrong, or kill him. There were no other
reasonable alternatives to be considered. Drastic choices for a dangerous man. Once again the captive had been correct. Jesus simultaneously respected and detested his rival.

Jesus developed a quick distaste for La Chiva. He was over-
heated, tired, and confused. Every rock outcropping began to
look the same. Didn't he pass this way before? The pathways, what
there were of them, were narrow, worn, and slippery. Little has
been said of the sheer steepness of the area, and the footing was
horrible too.

Jesus sat and pondered. There was something very confusing
about and around the whole place. He was horribly out of his
element, and he knew it. It was as if there was a flow of energy
unlike any he experienced before. It did not feel like he was near
Culiacan. He was teetering on the brink of another dimension.

All at once he felt weak, his knees would not move, and his
mind was becoming foggy and unclear. Was it the altitude? The
heat? He finished his water supply twenty minutes earlier. His
heart raced and he pondered his alternatives. A difficult series of
decisions would have to be made.

By late afternoon Jesus had made the decision that would
change his life forever. He decided to climb back down the

mountain, regroup, and return early the following morning to follow the bandit's map and directions and reach the bounty. It would fulfill his destiny on that day. He had planned and plotted the capture, not killing, of Lareano. This moment was three long years in the making. He could rest, restock, and wait until another morning.

Jesus camped at the base of the mountain near the small hill of Lareano's childhood. He needed to regroup and try again with a fresh set of eyes and a better attitude. When he looked across the canyon and up at the face of La Chiva he instantly understood his error. He had traversed the approach hill too far to the left. He now knew it was true because of his overlook of Culiacan out in the distance. There was no possible way to have that sighting and be simultaneously on the correct ridge. He was over to the left by at least two minor ridges. Wrong canyon, wrong result. Jesus smiled with that understanding. The mountain looked much larger to him now. He would be the richest man tomorrow. With those thoughts he fell asleep in his secret tent encampment in the canyon between La Chiva and Tacamonte.

Jesus awoke early with the sounds of the first morning birds. The shrill call seemed to awaken the whole area, and sounds of life began crying forth. Jesus loaded his bag with more provisions. He also took a narrow strip of cloth to use as a headband. His intention was to moisten the fabric and use it under the brim of his hat as a cooling tool for his steep ascent to glory.

Jesus walked to the fence markers and marveled at the irreverence of the bandit. He used the very emblem of the church, the cross, as his identifier. The reason was obvious. Upon detection someone would think the posts were also being used as a burial marker for the remains of someone who could not afford the expensive cemetery in town. A significant number of families could do nothing more in these troubled times. The government was still not responsive to the people and the people were sowing the seeds of unrest. These seeds would ultimately grow into a full revolution, and later the history would revert again to a government of corrupt motivation and individual self-promotion.

The first welcome break was taken at Boat Rock, aptly named because its face resembled the prow of a large boat, which is the part of the bow sticking above the surface. It sat at a forty-five degree angle from the main face of La Chiva. The unique striated red bands were also marked on Lareano's map. Jesus was confident that he was standing at one of the identification points or markers. He was already exhausted, sweat was pouring off of his body, and he needed immediate rest.

After the break he hiked up the hot and dry hillside, past more of the landmarks on the map carefully prepared in the detention cell under poor lighting conditions. His respect for the toughness of the bandit magnified. The strength of the bandit was amazing if he could traverse this hillside bearing weighted objects. The Military Governor did not understand the history of the cave nor was he aware of the alternate entrances to the area from a ridge out of sight to the right and above the treasure.

Despite his initial positive thinking and inner drive, he could not find the cave. He hiked around and around without success. His confidence level crashed and his attitude became stubborn, bitter, and ugly. Beyond the expected difficulties of map navigation in strange territory, and pure physical strength and balance requirements as he climbed the base of the mountain, a new test was to present itself. This was the next test of this day.

15. EL TIGRE

Tacamonte Canyon – April 27, 1891

In the legends of the region, perpetrated by oral tradition, there exists a spirit guide or animal spirit for most of the mountains. This was the way it was, when man was more connected to the earth and his surroundings. The locals often established a small altar at the start of a trail, with meager offerings left for protection and a safe return. It was as much a superstitious ritual as one sanctioned by the church. What mattered to the people was the knowledge that it worked.

For generations it has been known by the medicine men and wise ones that the spirit totem of La Chiva was a panther. They called it "El Tigre." In fact, hunters have spotted the animal we would call a mountain lion in the area on many occasions. The range would provide a natural hunting ground for a large, territorial cat. Small rabbits, rodents, and the occasional domestic cat from the neighbor miles from the base of the hill near the entry to the canyon would supplement the diet of El Tigre.

Occasional paw prints in the mud left no doubt that a large animal of some sort had been prowling in the area. This realization heightened the senses of Jesus. He listened with all of his being. He ascended the mountain with a minimum of noise. In his enhanced state of alertness the calls of the birds overcame him. Everything seemed loud. He felt touched by the contrast between the soft beauty of the birds and the wicked brush along the climb of La Chiva.

He appreciated and acknowledged his elevated sensitivity and felt more alive than before. The adventure was nourishing for him.

He stopped and caught his breath. Then he removed the map from his bag and studied the landmarks. The bandit was so precise with his drawing, and all he had to do next was line up and proceed in the direction of one thing or another. He tried to figure out his next goal and smiled with anticipation when the marker was in sight. Once again, the bandit had selected an excellent landmark. It was similar to connecting the dots. Waves of confidence overcame Jesus and he proceeded forward.

The benefits of his good night of rest and early morning start were becoming apparent to him. It was still relatively cool, and La Chiva actually blocked the sunlight as it rose in the early morning. He felt like the spirit of La Chiva as he drove upward, constantly upward, toward the point of the beard. It was easy to keep that promontory in sight. It towered over the next ridge. Now he knew what he had done wrong before.

Jesus slowly took a long drink of water from his canteen. He looked out at the territory beyond and felt a strange pride in this part of his jurisdiction. He was the Military Governor, the strongest man in the territory. Soon, maybe today, he would be the richest man in the land. That fact he has determined to prove. He felt bold and confident. There was no doubt evidenced anywhere in his thoughts. He was steadfast on his goal and ready to proceed.

He reviewed the map and notes. Proceed southeast to the tall Mapa Tree with nine large roots. It would be directly on line between Tacamonte, below in the West, and the center of La Chiva, rising in the East. Beware of the cactus field at the south of this marker.

The translucent cactus needles were no friends of Jesus. Everyone growing up in the area had at least a few encounters with this defensive succulent. Jesus once fell onto an isolated piece of cactus and it took thirty painful minutes to pull all of the sharp needles out of his left hand. That was tough on him when his hand began to swell, and even more difficult because he was strongly left-handed.

Jesus fought back his memories and returned to the present. This mountain was playing strange tricks on him again. Was there really El Tigre? Was the area protected? How would he get into the treasure?

He realized he was unprepared to dig significantly. He did not have the shovel recommended by the bandit. Why would he have a small shovel? He was a leader, not a worker. He had workers and servants doing the digging at his home. Now there would be more work to be done.

He proceeded until he found the Mapa Tree and knelt in prayer as instructed. The bandit told him to look for a sign. Although this seemed a bit silly considering the location, the Military Governor complied. His faith was promptly rewarded. Carved below the first main branch was a small cross. He thought about that symbol again and what it must have meant to the bandit. His heart began to pound rapidly as he considered the significance of the marking, for it was the ratification that he was almost there.

The stress and strain of the hike were quickly forgotten. Jesus was shaking with excitement as he proceeded down and around the rock jutting out from the side of the steep bank. The rock cap was sitting like a shell above him. You could be at this site and never see it. The bandit had loaded the natural cave and then blasted it closed by forcing a rockslide above the site. Genius.

He climbed around the rock to the spot described by Lareano. He moved away some brush and a number of loose stones and saw the shelf above him. He climbed beneath it, as instructed, and looked directly above his head. Again, he found the same symbol. This cross was carved in relief, with the background cut back and the cross standing forth. The bandit must have taken extra time to carve this marker. It was different than all the rest. Jesus was at the goal.

The site was nothing like he envisioned. It was much better hidden than Jesus believed was possible. He did not know he was there until he was standing upon the trap door, or rather stooping. It took great courage just to go around the large flat rock apparently hanging over the edge of the steep ledge. That was the illusion. As soon as one peered around the rock you could see a perfect trail leading underneath. It was brilliant.

Jesus took a large stick and began loosening the dirt and gravel below the cross. They came away differently, at the exact place measured and disclosed from the bandit in the map. It worked. The trap door was comical in its simplicity. It was the front of a bank vault door from one of the robberies by the gang. He pulled on the door and it slid away. A blast of moist and cool air was coming out from the portal. It had a smell from time long past, but it carried the sweet aroma of the future.

Jesus could stand it no longer. He grabbed his candle and proceeded very slowly down into the secret vault. During the afternoon
of his second day on La Chiva he found the fabled treasure. There
was nothing that Jesus Borella could have done to prepare for this
moment. He would never forget the date, April 27, 1891. It was
different than expected. This moment would be transformational.

An observer would have seen the flash of change pass over his
eyes. He had been initiated into a secret order, and his life would
never be the same. His whole body began to shake with excitement as the glisten of candlelight on gold marked his way. In time
he could wonder if it was actually worth it, but at this moment it
was sheer ecstasy. It was a time for private self-fulfillment.

The first thing he saw was a pile of gold ingots, neatly stacked
in the rear corner from the floor to the ceiling. It was impressive.
He had no idea what that much gold would look like. He found it
to be awkward to adjust to. It was beautiful and it was his. He began
to shake uncontrollably.

16. Waiting

Cell 6 – April, 1891

Lareano sat in his cell that night and wondered if the comman-
dant had made it to his secret hiding place. The price was high,
but it did not cost all that he had. This was not the only stash of
treasure, just the largest and most special. His freedom was costly,
but you can't spend any of it if you are in prison or buried in the
ground. He was at peace with the price.

From a jail cell you learn the value of life. With incarceration
comes the strong appreciation for mobility and freedom. The set-
tlement was fair. Arlena, Esperanza and Hector were already safely
across the border. He was comforted with the belief that he would
be joining them soon.

Lareano thought about the next stage of his drama. The
Military Governor did not want Lareano's release to be attributable
to him, much less happening on his watch. It had to occur from
a neutral location where nobody would ever harbor any doubt
about mutual involvement or presume a conspiracy. His adversary
had come up with a sensible plan. He would ask the local judge
to implement Lareano's sentence at the larger jail facility at Vera
Cruz. This permanent prison was more secure and distant from
the land where the gang formerly operated. This increased security and decreased the chance of retribution by remaining gang
members to free their leader.

The plan was to release Lareano in Mazatlan, on the way to the
Isthmus of Panama, before he would be taking his final boat ride
to Vera Cruz. The timing of the release was to occur while they
were marching overland to the boat. A loyal guard would unlock
the handcuffs on the prisoner as evening approached. The bandit
would be responsible for the timing and means of his departure.
There would be no additional assistance and no guarantees. It
was anticipated that a horse could easily be confiscated to implement the getaway. A guard was not usually placed with the horses

when they camped for the night since the prisoners were always restrained.

No representations were made to the bandit leader. He would be released without fanfare. There would be no witnesses to this conspiracy and Lareano would be responsible for his own safe conduct through the badlands of Mexico and north to his new home. It was anticipated and discussed thoroughly. Getting to America would be his own difficult responsibility. That was not a concern for the bandit because his network was still in place. The initial obstacle was getting free.

Lareano was looking forward to the opportunity to be on horseback again. As far away as possible from the jail cell would be his immediate goal. He knew the territory well and had numerous friends along the way.

Dreams of reuniting with his wife in a new land filled his mind. The memories of his children's voices rang in his inner ear. First he had to escape. He knew there would be few chances to gain freedom, and he constantly watched for such an opportunity even in advance of the proposed release by the Military Governor. He would take the first chance out, whenever and however it appeared. The bandit never completely trusted Jesus and an advanced departure time would suit him just fine.

Lareano had serious doubts about Jesus and the quality of his word. Although he was forced to trust this man, sensations throughout his body told him to beware. He knew the eyes and watched the behavior of his adversary, giving him a visceral reaction that the Military Governor should not be trusted. Meanwhile Lareano had nothing he could do but wait.

17. THE SECRET

La Chiva – April, 1891

The picture was entirely different back on the mountain. The despair of the bandit was in direct contrast with the elation of his captor. At this very moment Jesus Borella was back outside of the cave gathering his nerve. His exit had been rapid and unexpected. Nothing can reverse a man's direction more quickly than the sight of a rattlesnake. The flat head, diamondback pattern, and forked tongue automatically engage the human reverse gear. The survival instinct is fail-safe. In this case the snake was not coiled and thus not in a position to strike. The snake was as surprised as the man.

Jesus reflected on his alternatives as his rapidly beating heart returned towards normal. He sat outside and hoped to see the snake make an escape. He wanted to go back inside. The golden glow from the candlelight on the ingots permeated his awareness. They had their own magnetic attraction. It was overpowering and indescribable. He needed to climb back in, and quickly. His alternatives were few and he pondered them. He thought about finding a long stick and prodding the snake. Knowing that snakes are territorial, this could cause the rattler to retreat further into the cave if that was his home.

He thought about using fire. While he possessed a candle, he had nothing combustible to burn. There was dry brush outside, but that could start something in the cave on fire. He wished he had a pistol, but he was never known as an accurate shooter. Besides, he did not have a firearm with him.

Throwing a large rock on the snake was perhaps his best choice, but he was worried about the outcome if he missed. Jesus was sweating profusely. His breathing was shallow and labored. His alternatives were not promising. He did not know what to do. He was confused and having moments of real fear. He had not prepared for any adversity other than hunger and thirst. He was scared and frustrated. He hated snakes.

The situation was resolved within minutes when the diamond-back slithered out into the sunlight. It was as if this guardian of the treasure was pleased with his release. Jesus did not try to figure out how the snake had negotiated its way into the cave. Instead he wondered if any other form or level of unknown adversity awaited him. He tried to decide if he believed snakes traveled alone.

His mental state deteriorated rapidly. Had the bandit booby-trapped the entrance to harm or even kill unwanted intruders? Was there any type of trap past the entrance? What other precautions had the bandit taken to protect his loot? He began to think of the legend of El Tigre. La Chiva was allegedly the heart of the cat's domain. Was the cat nearby? Paranoia was getting the best of him.

The magnitude of the event overcame him. His mind drifted into an altered delirious state as he tried to compose himself. He was hot, thirsty, and out of breath. He was moving in slow motion yet felt like he was in a hurry.

The Military Governor looked out at his surroundings and took a couple of deep breaths. This seemed to clear his consciousness and reveal a renewed perspective. Clearly the bandit did not expect anyone to find this treasure site. Things should be just fine. It was time for his personal celebration. He was now unquestionably the richest man in the land. Unfortunately, nobody could know. He had the most amazing of all secrets.

Jesus felt great relief as he re-entered through the narrow passageway. Again he was overpowered by the reflection of light from the pile of candlelit gold ingots. They were stacked all the way from the dirt floor to the stone ceiling above. His knees felt weak as he stepped closer. There were bags of stones piled up against the lower gold bars. He had to sit and just stare. Still along the back wall he found wooden boxes with rope handles. They bore the brand from the Durango mint. He remembered when the brave gang had stolen an entire wagon train from the mint, including the pack mules that carried these boxes. The threat of the federal guard proved to be no deterrent to the bandits. He hated the bandit gang and felt good about his exacted revenge.

The cave was a gift beyond the Military Governor's comprehension. The scope and depth exceeded his understanding at that time. Lareano's loss was a newfound gain for Jesus. He had the most wonderful secret and he was joyous as he rose, and then danced about the cave. There was wonder in every direction.

Jesus reached back for his bag and lit another few candles. The cave was larger than expected and the tunnel opening was at such an angle that only a small amount of direct sunlight entered. When he reached to place the second candle on top of the boxes of coinage he discovered cloth bags, neatly tied. He opened the first one and found rubies, more than two hundred of the red cut stones. His heart went up to his throat when he opened the second small bag and found various small stones of different shapes and colors. The third contained only pearls.

Jesus smiled and chuckled to himself as he reflected upon the organizational skills of the bandit leader. It was a sight to behold. He maintained his treasure as he had directed his gang. The man was detailed, efficient, and orderly. Jesus Borella was beside himself as he moved the first candle to the other side of the cave. There were large piles of objects stolen from the churches. The shimmering colors from the bejeweled artifacts helped evoke a heightened state of awareness. This was entirely too good to be true.

The perception of time began to change. Things moved more slowly and his vision became more tunneled in the dim light. Chills went up and down his spine and he was overcome with waves of joy. He was over the top with excitement and was actually challenging his tired heart. He was beginning to overload.

He had made it. It did not occur to him to return the bounty to the rightful owners, for that he could never explain. Much worse, his level of personal need and sense of accomplishment overshadowed his responsibility as the chief governmental figure in that area. He was no different than the bandit in many ways, and he did not even care. This would be his secret for as long as he lived. No conspirators, no partners, and no leaks.

18. PROOF

Treasure Cave – April 28, 1891

Jesus grabbed a large handful of the newly minted local coins and filled his left coat pocket. In his right pocket he placed sixteen large gold coins, a small gold rosary, and an assortment of gems and stones. Before he left he grabbed two gold ingots for his pack. At the last minute he added a few old coins. It was a wonderful assortment and a just reward for such a difficult day.

The candles were placed closer to the opening before he blew them out. He knew they would be helpful when he returned. He then noticed some flammable torches left on top of one of the boxes by the bandit. More light would be necessary to help him see the rest of the treasure. In the shadows were bags, boxes, and piles to be further explored. He was delighted with the awareness that there was much more to discover. The unknown had great appeal.

Jesus reflected on his bandit adversary and the possible uses for the treasure. The price had been high but there was value to every part of the agreement. Jesus was pleased with his cunning ability to position himself to this point. He now had a renewed sense of heightened self-importance. He would never again have to stand in the shadow of his father and be subject to comparison. Although his father would not be proud of the means of his acquisition, the value was apparent and the deed had been done. It was quick and clean.

He justified this exercise on some distorted belief that the treasure had been stolen by the gang, not himself, and the sudden possession of the gold, coins, and artifacts did not implicate him in the original crimes against the church and the state. He had a childlike "finders keepers" way of thinking. It is ironic that he applied that to himself, but never anyone else. Rationalization can be a powerful coping mechanism, and justification has its own cleansing effects, however imperfect or incorrect.

He was staking a personal claim for his own benefit. The money would be spent wisely and used to improve the quality of life for his family and descendants. Forever more his heirs would be respected. He already had position and he could now easily buy respect. There was more than enough to help himself and plenty of others.

Jesus incorrectly associated assets with esteem, which was not the norm in this financially struggling country. He rejoiced with the comfort that he would no longer live shackled to the shadows of his father's legacy. He was now his own man, and a surge of independence strengthened his stand. His wife would enjoy more servants, his grounds more gardeners, and his family even better food. He would now hire a cook.

Jesus Borella would become the envy of his multi-state territory. For reasons dating back to his childhood he needed that recognition. His yardstick was warped and he was incapable of accurate self-monitoring. He would have his distorted needs filled now. His self-perceived stature would soon be based upon his wealth and acquisitions, rather than his political status. After all, it was his father's position that enabled his seventh of eight sons to achieve the designation and responsibilities of Military Governor. The friends of his father had seen to the elevation of this young man to a position beyond the reach of the locals.

His father had been sent to Mexico with the authority of the King of Spain, changing the destiny of his family. Now the first of his two sons born in this new land could rise to a level of wealth and standard of living heretofore unknown in this young and developing republic. Jesus could become an empire builder if he used this treasure properly. He knew he would have to be patient for many years and remain silent forever.

As he left the cave another decision had been spontaneously realized. It bore the quality of an instant revelation and required neither deliberation nor reflection. It was a clear visual insight. As Jesus climbed out of the cave opening his vision was diminished. It took a few moments for his eyes to adjust to the daylight after the time spent in the relatively dark confines of the cave. Jesus felt almost blind and defenseless. These feelings instantly reinforced his resolve. If Lareano was freed, Jesus could easily envision a scenario in which he was climbing out of the cave into the barrel of the bandit's gun. There was too much value here to protect, and no need to risk any part of it.

At this point there were probably only two living people who knew the location of the treasure, and one was in the custody of the other. The solution was simple. Jesus was presently in the superior position, and he did not have to relinquish it. He did not evaluate this as a moral dilemma. He did not care. Who would enforce the deal with the bandit? What agreement? Nobody would ever know.

This was the birth of the breach. He would never permit the bandit to leave for the Tucson area. Jesus had the power to reduce the chances of any further problems to zero. Dead men can't talk.

The descent from the treasure site was as difficult as the climb. It made no sense to Jesus, who was fatigued from too much excitement. In later years we would learn that the area is an "upslope vortex" of energy, making it appear to be harder going downhill than uphill. It was like climbing downhill into an energetic headwind. It added an intense fatigue factor to an already hostile environment.

The sun was at its zenith and the temperature was hot and rising. The light-colored ground seemed to radiate more heat than the air. The plant materials were equally hostile. Stickers, thorns, and nasty flying bugs made the entire descent uncomfortable. The physical discomfort was a mere inconvenience when compared to the articles in his pockets and bag. Nothing could put a damper on his excitement.

Jesus was sweating profusely as he navigated the rough decent. He was thirsty, nervous, and uncomfortable. The sounds of the rodents and birds in the brush made him keenly aware of potential danger.

Questions continuously filled his head as he made his way down the mountain. Was anyone watching him? Were there any free members of the gang who knew of this site? Had the bandits divided the take after each heist, as was their reputation? Was it the stash for only Lareano and Camacho? Did Lareano know that Camacho and most of the other gang members had been executed at the orders of Jesus? Had the guards kept their secrets?

Further questions worried him. Did Lareano have guards loyal to him who would defect and release him? Did he promise them any portion of this same treasure?

19. REWARD

Culiacan — April, 1891

Another day was passing without word from the Military Governor. The isolation was almost unbearable to Lareano. The lack of information was troubling. The conditions had improved slightly since the deal was made with his captor. First he was unchained. Then he was now given regular meals and sufficient water, a poor trade for the vast riches at the other end of the treasure map. Lareano had used his major bargaining chip to secure freedom. The wait was getting long. His reservoir of patience was depleted.

Lareano could not rest this hot afternoon. His mind wandered as he thought about the trail to Tucson and the joy of being free and mobile again. He was finding it difficult to remain patient and hopeful.

It was a different mood on La Chiva. As he neared Boat Rock, Jesus stumbled and fell a second time. The footing was loose and he had difficulty concentrating on the path. His shirt was torn and his left arm was scratched and bleeding. He cursed himself for not paying attention to the slippery footing. He wondered if he was carrying too much. There was something about this mountain that made him act strangely, as if his mind was continually drifting without the ability to focus.

He assessed his injuries as minor while he sat and finished drinking the last of his water. He felt refreshed as he gathered his belongings and prepared to complete the descent to the canyon below. He convinced himself that the next trip to the cave would be much easier. The weight of the precious objects in his pockets and bag served as a reminder of the joyous times ahead. Things would never be the same for Jesus Borella.

20. Drink With Me

Cell 6 – May 1, 1891

The bandit awoke with a chill to his body. The coolness of night-fall indicated that hours had passed. He had a strange feeling that he was being watched. He could sense somebody was staring at him. As his eyes adjusted he saw the robust figure of the Military Governor outside the cell door. He sat up erect and stared at the door without speaking.

The Military Governor broke the silence with a gravelly whisper. "You did well, amigo. Your hiding place was perfectly located to avoid detection forever. Nobody will ever stumble upon the exact spot. Your secret is protected."

"Obviously my map and directions were good, so what took you so long?"

Jesus paused, and then explained, "Perhaps you were right about the difficulty of the climb. It must be easier for a man with less ballast, such as you. The directions and markers were good, but there was no discernible path. A couple of the site lines were difficult to follow. The footing was terrible and the heat unbearable."

The Military Governor continued almost as an explanation, "To make it worse, I became confused by the markers and became light-headed on that mountain."

Lareano felt frustrated with that response. He had an easier way to approach the site, from a spot towards the top of the ridge, but did not want to make it less difficult for Jesus. He wondered if the treasure had been reached, but would not ask the magic question. He grunted and waited.

"My friend, you did an excellent job in hiding the stolen goods. Your sense of humor shows with your choice of entrance cover. Also, the use of the sacred symbol of the church is insulting yet fitting."

"So you got in, that is good news. It took great strength," replied the bandit.

Lareano paused only momentarily and then continued, "I have fulfilled my part of our agreement."

"Yes you did, and so will I," responded the Military Governor. "But, first there are details to be arranged."

Lareano had to control the tidal wave of anger welling up within. The caged man had enough sense to withhold saying the wrong thing. His inferior bargaining position mandated patience and silence. He was forced to trust the process, for there was absolutely nothing else he could do. He sat on his words, contained his frustration, and hated the need for submission.

During the following silence Lareano reflected on the folly of his life. In a short period of time he fell to this abysmal low point, existing no better than a caged animal. The humiliation of the present situation was difficult for this respected gang leader to accept. Being confined behind bars was never a part of his life plan. He was accustomed to much more power and control.

If he wasn't going to be released right now, at least he should be able to obtain some satisfaction. He pondered the moment and asked the question that had been bothering him for so long, "How did you catch us? How did it happen?"

Jesus smiled with a broad grin, looking like the personification of the cat that ate the bird as he spoke, "I had my men chasing after you for years, always behind and never in the right place."

After a pregnant moment he continued, "It took six months to put a spy in your gang. He let us know when you were planning the train robbery."

"Impossible," protested Lareano, "That cannot be true. Our intentions were not shared with the gang in advance. You are not telling me the truth."

"Actually, my friend, I am. But it took more than you know."

Once again there was an eerie silence. It felt like a large shadow had overcome the already dark quarters.

"Tell me more, my partner." Lareano wondered if the added familiarity and subtle reminder of their deal would help expedite his release.

At that very moment a guard approached. His boots announced his presence before his words. Both of the men were startled by his sudden appearance.

The guard broke the nervous silence by asking, "My governor, is there a problem?"

Receiving no response, he added, "We thought you were gone. What are you doing outside this bandit's cell? Is anything wrong? Can I be of assistance?"

Jesus realized that his conversation with the bandit had not been overheard. He slowly stepped away and spoke to the guard, "I just returned to town and wanted to make sure the prisoner was still alive and well. He is a popular and dangerous man. I am checking on your job. I needed to know that my men had followed their orders and continued to secure the safety of this treacherous prisoner."

The governor raised his voice a touch and added, "We do not know how many of his men are still free out there and whether or not they will try to liberate their commander. It is widespread knowledge that he has earned the respect, even love, of his men. They may stop at nothing to rescue him. I was worried, but that will be over soon. On Tuesday he will be transported to a safer location. The details will be explained at the appropriate time."

With that Jesus turned and walked back to his office as the guard checked on the prisoner and left. Lareano's heart jumped with the news. He rejoiced with the knowledge that soon the window of opportunity to escape would be opened for him. On Tuesday he would be given his freedom again.

He thought about the perfect plan and his resulting chance to flee. It was the brainchild of Jesus to make it look like an escape rather than a release, and fewer questions would be asked if it did not look like there were any accomplices within the prison encampment.

He was lost in time. The question that troubled his mind centered on what night it currently was. There was no sense to differentiate one day from another when you exist in quasi-isolation within a cramped adobe and wood cell. He tried to figure out what day it was, and fell asleep wondering how many more days until Tuesday.

Lareano awoke to some different treatment including the smell of coffee. The guard brought him a breakfast much improved over any other meal he had been served since the capture. This was far from consideration as a great meal, but rather relatively better taking into account the low standard and small quantity of normal prison food. The most noticeable improvements were the food was warm, the portions were large, and there was plenty of hot coffee too. This was his first cup of coffee since he was thrown into the cell. It smelled wonderful and tasted even better.

Lareano tried to find a routine. Was there a pattern to the guards or other behavior at the encampment? He realized that each and every day merged into the next without any discernable pattern. Was this Tuesday? There was nobody to ask. The deaf guard with whom communication was impossible brought the improved version of the afternoon meal.

When nightfall came he knew only one thing, this was not his day of release. His optimistic spirit wanted it to be Monday, and hopefully tomorrow he would ride again. He wondered which of the guards would be the one to release him. He could not tell if any of them showed any recognition or preference when the Military Governor was in the vicinity. He simply did not know.

He awoke early at the sound of footsteps coming toward his cell. Again it was the deaf guard bringing a large warm breakfast and coffee. There were more varieties of food today and the strong aroma of the hot coffee permeated the air. The larger meals would enable him to gain strength before his long ride to freedom. His belly appreciated the change in circumstances since the Military Governor had found the cave.

Periodic images drifted through his consciousness as the hours of this day passed. He wished he had the opportunity to discuss more than his markers with Jesus. What was his reaction to the treasure? Had he actually ventured deep into the cave? Did he understand what he had there? Were the sacred objects from the cathedral and churches to be returned now?

The strong coffee had a stimulating effect on his thought process. It was difficult to remain focused. Questions filled his mind in rapid succession, at a pace that prohibited contemplation and reflection. Confinement was getting to him and his mind was jumping with renewed life. He could feel excitement at the base of his being, the contrast being noticeable as he continued to sit and wait. His training and experience never fostered the development of patience. He hated the process, and his disposition noticeably changed when he was bored. He was usually impatient and detested waiting. At least the chains had been removed.

The sharp contrast between incarceration and life outside brought about long periods of depression. They had been replaced with hope as he had negotiated his way to freedom. The price was high and the risk was present, but Lareano valued his freedom, life, wife and family much more than his loot.

As he drifted into a nap, Lareano thought about the placement of the power objects in the cave. They elicited great care, as if the man was respectful for or afraid of their qualities. From the beginning, the bandits understood the Mayan crystals and artifacts to have secret magical properties living inside them. Each of the churches kept them hidden and rarely discussed, under a false sense of security that they were safe.

From the main cathedral in Culiacan the gang took the most impressive of them all, a silver Incan plate, encircled with colored stones in a synchronized pattern, with a sacred shape from occult geometry on the outer rim. It had a strong luminescence that was a reflection of the radiating source of power contained within.

He did not tell Jesus about these special objects, and they would be protected from his scrutiny and use until he moved past the large boxes of gold coins and newly minted Mexican coins. The old coins from Spain were on a different wall. That could take years to uncover, or they could also be reached quickly if the Military Governor was curious and thorough.

The day passed and Lareano hoped that tomorrow would be Tuesday. He napped frequently and dreamed of the past. His thoughts were dominated by the troubles he encountered and the obstacles to his freedom, his inner urge to rebel and defy what he experienced to be a corrupt situation. He missed his family and couldn't wait to be out of there. Progress would be slow in his Mexico, and the people would suffer until a drastic change would be made. He was a former soldier of fortune, but he will be living in Arizona, far from the concerns of the state of Sinaloa.

Lareano had no remorse. He had stood up proudly in defiance. Apology and confession were not behaviors he could embrace. He didn't have to. He felt comfort in his role and accomplishments. He operated from a frontier sense of equity and justice that made perfect sense to him. He reflected upon his achievements as noble and noteworthy. His recognition, reputation and standing proved his point. He was not sorry.

His awareness drifted back to his schoolboy years, and the impact of his teachers was burned deep into his being. It would be wonderful, he thought, if he could have continued to gift some of the treasure to help the schools, to make education more accessible to the children, and to help their minds. His people felt passion, but often lacked the ability to read. It was from his mother's few books that his imagination and inner vision developed. That was so many years ago. He realized that he was a teacher in a different forum. The love of his constituents helped him reflect positively on the years of eccentric criminal behavior. It was all without regret.

The evening meal came a little early. The guard had a crooked smile, holding back his secret in a taunting way. Lareano took the mental jump, questioned about his secret pleasure, deduced that it was now Monday night, and tomorrow he was reportedly being transported to his permanent prison site. He asked the guard about his joy on this Monday night, and he replied he would not have to see his face again. The scrutiny and pressure of being under the watchful eye of the Military Governor would abate. It would be a relief to all of the staff.

This was it. It was the eve of his opportunity. He wondered if he could fall sleep before he leaves tomorrow. He visualized his release, especially the part where he is secretly permitted to slip through his restraints and disappear at his appropriate time. His heart beat more strongly as he thought about Arlena and the big step to getting closer to her. He would be on his way to their new home soon. How much had the children grown? How long had he even been in this encampment?

The visualization was positive but this image was not to be. Reality can be rude and cold-hearted. This was not a Walt Disney story. He must have drifted off and slept for at least a few minutes. It was now dark and a bit chilly. He pulled his blanket up over himself, and saw the reflection of the candlelight illuminating the erect figure of Jesus Borella in the shadows outside of the cell.

"Good evening," whispered his captor.

Lareano had a small smile on his inquisitive face when he questioned, "Tomorrow?"

The Military Governor smiled back and answered, "Tomorrow is your day." His breath reeked with the smell of alcohol, apparently having consumed a serious amount before coming to give notice to his prisoner.

"Let's celebrate," slurred the Military Governor.

Jesus slowly smiled and continued, "This is the last time we see each other."

He lifted his coat and withdrew a half-filled bottle of locally made tequila. Lareano wondered how Jesus knew it was his personal favorite. Perhaps they shared that in common. From the looks of the bottle Jesus had been at it strongly for some time.

Jesus reached into the cell and repeated his offer to celebrate, "Drink with me."

Lareano loved the hot taste of the enhanced local agave. It had been so long since he had his last drink. With the warmth came a feeling of general goodwill, his body was a bit toasty and his mind was hit with a slam.

"Why the change in behavior? You treat me well only since I told you of the treasure. But this is our first time with tequila, and a local special too. It is my very favorite."

The governor smiled and looked down. "Mine too."

He handed the bottle back to Lareano without taking a drink. That went unnoticed by the bandit. Nothing was said.

Lareano took another gulp and then he began to feel it. Rather that the heat from the throat and the lightening of the brain, he felt something change from the level of his legs. The drink was overtaking his body. His feet became cold, then stiff. He noticed a lack of contact with his hands too. Something was happening to his extremities; a loss of control was becoming noticeable.

Things were going wrong quickly. A horrible numbness instantly spread through his body and he looked back at the governor and shouted, "You have broken our agreement and will subject yourself to dishonor. In the name of my grandmother I curse you forever."

He stumbled to the ground; the effects of the poison were accelerating. "May evil come to you and your relatives. May the power of La Chiva bring ill unto you. I curse you to hell for an eternity."

The last sounds were slowly and quietly uttered by the bandit, "You have made a mistake bigger than words, and you shall suffer greatly. You are cursed in the name of La Chiva. Be prepared to suffer."

His lips continued to move for another minute, but his words were inaudible. There is no reason to believe that anything complimentary was being said to the Military Governor, who stared through the cell door at his dying adversary, the bottle of severely tainted beverage in his left hand.

When he was convinced that the dosage was terminal Jesus poured the remaining contents of the bottle onto the ground. It would not be needed any more. It had performed his evil assignment. He then tossed the tequila bottle against the corner of the building, shattering it into innumerable pieces like the dreams of the bandit.

He walked back to the cell and stared at the body of the bandit lying twisted on the ground. He was immobile and had an expression of pain on his face. His eyes were open but staring elsewhere.

When it was over the governor knew his way was the safest. There would be no handoff, no escape. Nothing can go wrong at the release. Jesus knew the immense value of the treasure necessitated more violent protection. The clear vision he had at the treasure site was enough to convince him that the only safe way of freeing Lareano was to the Lord. Now he, Jesus, was sure that the treasure would always be his, and only his. Nothing can go wrong, no secrets can be told, and never will he have to worry about ambush or theft.

The bandit was gone. He believed him to be with his gang again in a far more different place. The final words of the bandit haunted Jesus as he sauntered back to his office. With the last shudder of his body a few words had come forth. Jesus was a believer, and the impact upon him had their desired impact.

The bandit said, "You are cursed in the name of La Chiva. Be prepared to suffer."

Jesus rose from his desk, took another shot of tequila from an identically marked bottle, and proceeded to his private quarters. He would not go home tonight. He knew he had been through enough, and he was safe within this domain.

21. Signs of Freedom

Culiacan – May 2, 1891

The morning guard found Lareano's body when the large breakfast meal was being delivered. He ran to his superior, who came running to inspect the prized captive.

Oh no, he was obviously dead. There was no blood flowing from the body, and no evidence of any wound inflicted by either knife or gun. From the looks of his corpse, curled on the floor, he died of natural causes. There was no evidence of foul play and the cell was still locked.

The guards were not of one mind. There were many guards who would have loved to shoot or stab the bandit leader, but all were under the strictest orders to preserve the jail's most famous resident. In direct contrast, there were also guards who admired the bandit and felt a great affinity for him. Many wanted to help effectuate his release. They would now remain silent and protect their jobs. There might be some revenge to exact when the time was right. More information would be needed. Direction would be received in due time. They knew who was now in charge.

The guards were afraid. They believed their job security hinged upon the safety of the bandit. They knew the Military Governor would not be happy with this outcome. They had been advised late on the day before that Lareano was to be moved at mid-day today. They wondered if they would still be escorting the wagon south. Lareano Garcia would require no guards any longer. His sentence had been served with his life, and he was now the loser.

The leader of the guards found the governor asleep in his quarters. There appeared to be no immediate reason to awake the raging bull so the decision was made to let him sleep. Perhaps he would awaken in a better mood. Time was not perceived to be an issue. Lareano was going nowhere.

The pretext of calmness was an act, for the guard leader was terrified to his core. All had witnessed the temper of the Military

Governor, and fairness was never a word used to describe the boss. It was even worse when he had been drinking. There was an empty tequila bottle thrown outside his quarters and one apparently smashed to bits around the corner from the bandit's cell, so nobody expected full sobriety upon his awakening. The men saw the signs of a potentially bad day ahead. It would not be hard to forecast the extent or degree under the circumstances.

After another hour the guard leader heard the Military Governor stirring. His heart skipped a beat as the door opened and he had to face his superior with the bad news.

Expecting the worse, he spoke slowly and carefully. "The prisoner is dead. I don't know why. We watched him and made sure nobody entered his cell. We…"

Interrupting him with a harsh cough, Jesus motioned for him to stop. Then he surprised the guard with his words, "It does not matter, my corporal. If he is dead then that is it. Now we will not have to worry about safety, his or ours, as we were to transport him to Vera Cruz today."

The boss looked to the ground and resumed speaking, "The timing is odd but it is beneficial."

After pausing, he questioned, "What has been done with the body?"

"Nothing, sir. We were waiting for your direction."

"Then take him to the town cemetery and bury him. Quickly, continue with your day. Good day."

"Yes, sir," replied the guard as he shut the door behind him.

The guard's feeling of relief was overpowering as he descended the stairs, returned to his staff and announced, "We are fine. There will be no trip to Vera Cruz today. The saddle time will be much shorter but it will also have a high degree of risk. We are supposed to transport and bury the bandit's body in Culiacan instead."

There was a mixed feeling of remorse and elation among the guards. The focus of their attention would soon be released from the special prisoner to business as it was before his capture. It was a major relief, and the immediate reduction of tension was welcoming. The contrasting emotional component was beginning to take hold. It had been a difficult time for all.

The reach of the gang had been far, and success belonged to everyone until the day of the dreaded deception and capture. The massacre at the train left little of the Lareanos. The murder of Camacho and the bandits, along with the isolated incarceration of Lareano were dual blows to the morale of the people.

The word went through the cellblock like a firestorm. The guards and the detainees felt the same on this subject. They were silently unanimous. Lareano was their secret hero, almost all of them. He represented the essence of the spirit of the people. He was the embodiment of disrespect and yet virtue simultaneously. He was larger than life, a regional legend. He was mightier than the Catholic Church and the equal to the military for a number of years.

The guards under orders to protect the bandit were feeling horrible. They knew what must have happened. They did not walk away when the Military Governor appeared with his bottle of peace offering. That rodent never changes his behavior. They knew he was up to no good, so they hid and watched. The scene was so vile that they became sick for their own ineptitude. They were too weak to attack Jesus, even though they should. It all happened too fast. It was the big boss himself who sent Lareano to his death. No gun, no worry.

They knew the Military Governor would never make himself vulnerable to the physical superiority of the bandit. The comparison was too easy to make. The tequila bottle was the perfect weapon. It was strange seeing El Commandante with his bottle of favorite mescal roaming the grounds that late evening. He usually drank behind closed doors. They knew what happened and were overcome with guilt and regret.

The sad news shot out quickly throughout the compound and, ultimately, exploded out to the city and beyond. The report that Lareano died of natural causes in his cell was met with distrust and then disgust. Nobody believed that this strong vibrant persona could die in such a simple and innocent manner. It did not make sense.

Foul play was not evident, but it was clearly presumed. The consensus strongly supported the developing rumor that he had been murdered. The long history of poor prisoner treatment in that compound only supported the overriding conclusion. Few, if any, left alive. The stories that followed, including the details of the tainted drink, made much more sense. They changed nothing and only furthered the lines of division.

Confirmation was quick. Lareano was gone, with memories galore. He would not have to run anymore. He would not have to hide. The people had all been the benefactors of the bandit's influence. Few, if any, objected to his treatment of the church and its possessions. There was an overwhelming feeling of helplessness. It was frustrating because there was nothing anyone could do.

Word carried fast that Lareano was going to be buried in the afternoon. His people loved him. They knew they had to intervene and afford him a fit and proper burial before the jail team directed a pauper ceremony, or less. Mobilization was almost spontaneous. It was as if a groundswell of energy shook Culiacan and local farming regions, and people began doing whatever they could for a service.

They asked Padre Ramone to conduct the memorial. He had ceased working through the church many years earlier. To many in the gang he was simply known as "Father."

At this time only a selected few were aware of Lareano's direct connection into the church. Now it made sense how convinced Lareano was on the timing of his heists. The contended prescience was really inside knowledge from the top. Father had been the procurements officer for the church, and knew the critical timing of shipments and deliveries. The highly secret contents were never a secret from Lareano. It was one big beautiful symbiotic relationship.

Father's seniority within the church was a callous joy, since he could not be removed for any rumored sympathy for the bandit, but it was also about family. It was through a complex code that Father communicated with his nephew. The connection could not be confirmed until this day.

Padre Ramone proudly led the procession in full black collar and ornate bejeweled cross. He flaunted this artifact, which had been taken by the bandit during the first entry into the cathedral. A previously unknown fact was now becoming clear. He could be the secret successor to what was left of the gang. Viva Lareano.

The caravan with the simple pine box containing the poisoned remains reached the summit before 2:00 pm. The guards were more than a mile from the graveyard, and the rest of the path was lined with people, children, and some of their favorite animals. The children held whatever flowers they could gather.

A deep bell began to ring as the procession cleared the ridge and advanced. The resonating sound seemed to come from everywhere. A man was overheard whispering to his son, "Our Lareano is coming home. Bless his soul." Similar words of praise and blessings passed through the crowd.

The guards were shocked to see the throng and immediately realized they were heavily outnumbered and probably outgunned. They clearly wanted to conclude the details and peacefully transfer the body. A quick understanding was reached without a word being spoken.

The leader stopped, removed his cap, and directed his soldiers to tender the horse-drawn wagon containing the casket to Padre Ramone. The transfer was done slowly and respectfully. It was time to let the rebels and townspeople handle the balance of the bandit's journey. The guards tipped their hats in recognition. The act of submission by the soldiers was sufficient communication to the onlookers. The complete transfer was effectuated by conduct without one word being spoken.

The government uniform was of no importance and did not serve as a differentiating factor. They too had respect for the bandit. They knew the wagon contained the remains of a very popular folk leader. Everyone grieved. The pain was great and felt by all in attendance. The guards backed away quietly.

The sound of the procession was unbelievably silent. Not a word was spoken as the casket passed by. The men removed their hats and sombreros, and the ladies grabbed their children to closely share the importance of the moment. It showed a high quality of respect for their patron. Things would be different for them all now. They were deeply afraid of a return to the past, but their collective grief was too great to worry about personal issues at this moment. There would be plenty of time for that.

The silent reverence for the passing of Lareano Garcia became a spiritual event. There was no doubt in the minds of any of the guards that he returned to his people as if larger than life. He was encased as a martyr in an undeclared war that would bring fruits many years in the future. Although unrecognized on that level at his death, Lareano would be considered to be one of the fathers of the revolution when it actually broke out almost two decades later. If nothing else, he represented the spirit of the oppressed people and a symbol of victory in a time of corruption and tyranny. He had the amazing ability to manufacture attitude. Lareano had a contagious air of invincibility, even in death. He was never afraid.

The procession slowly inched along as it made its way to the gates of the town cemetery. Nobody was in a hurry. The group moved on, gaining mass. The grief and sadness were notable and overwhelming, people were despondent, and their emotions were overflowing.

A silent undercurrent among a majority of those present was the unwavering belief that Lareano had been a victim of foul play. The distrust for the government was strong, and the Military Governor was a hated man in all regards. People were forced to maintain their animosity in private. His powers were vast and rumors of his evil deeds were widespread. The small number of survivors from the jail emphasized this point. Too many prisoners perished while in custody, and survivors of his form of justice were rare.

Lareano was strong and healthy before his capture. He was skilled in survival. His mental state was always one of focused clarity. Nobody in the crowd believed the official story that he died of natural causes in his sleep the evening before. Not a soul believed him to be anything less than mighty.

The crowd mourned with the grief reserved for a personal loved one. It was a major loss. They cried for their fallen hero and they cried for themselves too. Would conditions return to how they were before? Who could possibly speak for them?

The sounds of the bells served as a reminder of their distant relatives. Their relatedness as a people gave them profound inner strength. But nobody was ready for the deep void, the feeling of inner nothingness, as the body of Lareano made its last return home.

It has been said that the angels almost dance upon the earth when the call of the people is that great. The deep grief emanating from this area in northwestern Mexico must have served as a cosmic microphone or homing beacon. The angels and protective spirits came by the multitudes.

The empowerment of giving away much of the bounty actually made Lareano a much richer man. Everyone had benefited from his generosity, either directly or indirectly. Every person, without fail, considered himself or herself to be a partner in one manner or another. All had their justifications, yet none needed to explain to anyone. It ultimately was reduced to an individual decision, and the needs of each were part of the private purview of small town life. Viva Lareano.

It had been a win-win situation and all views were supported. The schools were improved with the proceeds of some of the treasure. The teachers were paid with coins and currency taken from the wagon trains. The elders were all fed and clothed, whether or not they had personal valuables. People lived in relative harmony. They felt safe to pursue the smaller things that required their attention. Their plots were expanded and their gardens improved.

The gains had been noticeable in a time of little. The success of the crops gave a sense of stability to the area. The moisture from the improved irrigation canals mitigated the baking heat of the valley. The enhancements to the water storage and distribution systems were gifts from Lareano. His father's corn seeds grew straight skyward as the land showed its appreciation for the extra care and love. They had been shared with all that asked.

Sainthood has been a status reserved for the extreme few believers who sacrificed for the good of the masses. Special unspoken attributes were always understood to be associated with the worldly persona of such a revered person. Lareano Garcia did not fit the mold. He was loved like a saint, for all of the good that he represented. Yet he was a career bandit, and a thief. The magnificent deeds with the ill-obtained loot did not mitigate the means by which he obtained such riches. It would be a moral dilemma now, but not at that time.

In any gathering the argument would be made that Lareano was the true spiritual leader of their time because he was not afraid of the power structure. He fought the Military Governor for many years. He stole from the churches, cathedrals, monasteries, banks, government institutions, the mint, the railroad, and the estates of many self-declared nobles transplanted from Europe.

His trademark horse was brown with a black mane. How many had he ridden over the years? He rode to danger and survived seemingly impossible situations. His level of risk tolerance was very high, but his successful efforts at survival, acquisition and redistribution were living proof that each and every one of their lives was better since his gang had watched over them. The way of life they experienced was a new joy. They had felt safe. That was a rare experience in their country. They were all Lareanos in one way or another.

The political corruption and taxing power had terribly abused the people. What would happen now? What happened to him? How did he die? Would they ever know the truth? Why should they doubt what they intuitively understood? Everyone knew.

Nobody was expecting what next occurred. It was out of the realm of personal experience. It was clearly a thing that legends are made of. It started with an eerie sound. At first it seemed far away, but eventually they realized that they were surrounded by it. It was everywhere. It was a faint hum. People later said they could feel it in the back of their neck more than "hear" it in their ears. Hum. It was a most different frequency, which gained in a bizarre way. Hum. The wind began to blow. It was so strong that it carried a sound similar to bees. Was it a loud buzz?

Some thought they heard a voice in all the confusion, the voice of Lareano. Many instantly fell to their knees. It was the bandit speaking to them.

The prevailing thought centered upon the fact that a miracle was happening about them. They were all simultaneously overcome with a wave of knowing and an inner vision of the consequence. Nobody registered too great a level of surprise as the volume of the unknown sound began escalating. It was all too bizarre for words. The bass notes or rumbling took on powerful proportions of the earth, or was it the wind? Some said the sound was a projection of the voice of Lareano. Others heard nothing, absolutely nothing but silence the whole time. The composition of this group negated any quick generalizations. It was a diverse mixture of the town.

22. GERARDO

Culiacan – 1891

Back at the government facility Jesus could not keep his mind off of the treasure. It was his treasure now, and he was loaded. He believed he had more gold than the national bank. He controlled a monumental pile of rubies and other precious stones. He took a mental journey through the cave. There were at least fourteen crates of silver and gold coins, most of which were still in their original shipping boxes from the mint in Durango. He said it aloud a few times: "My gold. My treasure. My very own cave of treasure."

Jesus was mistaken about his alleged special secret. It was not his alone. Another knew the truth, one that was close but not dangerous. His brother Gerardo was at least six years his junior. He was the eighth and last of the brothers, but only two of which were in Mexico. He had no connection with the family's history in Spain and loved the raw native land of his birth. His home was the Republic of Mexico and he was proud of it.

Gerardo had firsthand experience of the cruelty imposed by his elder brother and was totally sympathetic with the views of the people. He agreed that the quality of life was becoming more and more difficult under the strict control of his brother.

Although never a member of the Lareanos, he identified with them and passively supported their beliefs. Gerardo felt an emotional bond to their cause and was totally depressed when he heard of the capture and later violent deaths of the members of the gang. There was never a moment that he doubted the potential for torment inflicted by his brother. He had been the recipient of undue agony at the hand of his older brother. Gerardo walked the tightrope between his family name and honor on one hand, and his sympathy and love for life on the other. He knew that his familial relationship would serve as no shield from the wrath of his brother.

Have you ever had a moment when you suddenly felt like you saw in your mind's eye a fact, event, or thing that you did not have previous conscious knowledge about? Gerardo had such a dawn of inner understanding when he visited his brother following the first opening of the treasure. It came as a discreet visual picture as Gerardo had dinner at a family gathering less than two weeks after the burial of the bandit leader. He was sitting with his brother after an uncharacteristically lively dinner discussion when he realized that something was unusual. In fact, everything was distinctly different.

It is illusory to believe you can maintain an absolute secret of something as magical as the discovery and possession of an enormous treasure. While an outsider may not notice subtle changes in personality or attitude, a family member is beyond such illusion. It was simply impossible for Jesus to appear unaffected after his first venture into the bandit's cave. There was a huge change in his confidence. His eyes gleamed when he thought of the jewels. An almost perpetual smile appeared on his face whenever he thought of the boxes of shiny coins and piles of gold bullion. At this point he was unaware of the pieces of religious significance, church artifacts, and power objects from ancient cultures adorning the back walls of the cave.

He was over the top with excitement and it showed, at least to his brother. His brother saw it as a golden hue. That would soon become a problem. Gerardo was able to perceive a difference. Gerardo felt there was something being concealed, and his natural curiosity caused him to dig deeper. He had a history with his brother and the challenge ahead was predictable. They knew each other too well.

One day Gerardo stopped by his brother's home when he was confident Jesus would be absent. He had a plan. He hoped to exploit the opportunity and to satisfy his burning curiosity. He sat and talked over tea with his sister-in-law, Rosa, and learned that she was also suspicious about her husband. His attitude about their home had changed. He hired additional household help, and his new acquisitions were out of character.

In the course of the conversation she revealed her husband's recent interest in the outdoors. They had plans that coming weekend to picnic at Tacamonte Canyon. She found this activity to be extremely unusual. Jesus was not a hunter, and a picnic trip to a local mountain was not in his usual repertoire of favorite activities. They had been aware of the rumors surrounding the area and previously did not want to tempt fate and challenge its lore or become part of its history. They were both afraid of the cat.

In spite of her former trepidation, Rosa was preparing for the most complete outing in family history. All of her husband's favorites were carefully packed away for his joy at the mealtimes. Perhaps Jesus wanted a new way to relax and celebrate with his family.

Her brother-in-law had the same idea. He had nothing special planned for the weekend, and the thought of eavesdropping on his brother had some intrigue. Gerardo had a confident understanding that his brother was up to no good. By following him at a distance, Gerardo could learn the truth about his brother's intentions. What was he doing on Tacamonte? Jesus Borella was not a camper, never was, and the call to Tacamonte Canyon had to be something else.

Did this have anything to do with the bandit king? Without a doubt, thought the brother. Jesus Borella, the Military Governor, was going to Tacamonte for surreptitious purposes. His brother, Gerardo, was going to follow and observe.

The weekend came quickly and Gerardo decided to leave for the area very early. This way there would not be any sounds from a horse and rider echoing down the canyon. He was so happy that he kept the spyglass purchased from a seaman more than five years previous. He had no specific reason to buy or retain the item, but it had some unique appeal to him. Now he had a special need for it. The brass spyglass was like another eye. It allowed him to watch and see clearly in the distance. He intended to use it from a hidden vantage point to spy on his older brother's activities.

When the weekend came he climbed to a protected spot well above the best camping area. It was easy to predict where his brother would choose to set up tents and have the picnic. The camping area was level and the brush had been cleared away after repeated use. The stream flowed slowly past the site and the fresh water made the meal and rest areas more enjoyable.

Because of the water at the base of the canyon there were trees, plants, flowers, and the associated birds and small wildlife. The site was almost an oasis, at least at this time of year. The summer heat would soon dry out most of the greenery, making the area much less hospitable. The metamorphosis between the two patterns was quick and direct.

Very few of the locals would make the two-hour plus ride to the Tacamonte Canyon. That is a rough amount of time to spend on horseback, mule, or wagon. The hunting was rumored to be good at the base of Tacamonte, or even better if you could climb part of the way up. The same was not said about the very steep face of its larger neighbor, La Chiva. It was so tall it dwarfed the morning sun. Everyone always quit. The persistent rumors of the large hungry cat cast an unwelcome shadow too. The word was even the shaman and crazy ones would not venture too far up La Chiva. Too many had attempted the climb and never returned. It could be called the mountain of the dead.

Gerardo Borella watched his brother and family arrive at the predicted spot. Jesus used a series of ropes and large pieces of cloth to create protection from the sun. It looked like they planned to spend some time. Gerardo's analysis was correct so far. He watched his brother's family cook and enjoy a large meal, and it looked like they were all settling down to rest. It was not yet siesta time, but the activity level became very low. Gerardo became lazy and almost fell asleep. Thankfully, he retained some degree of wakefulness and was alerted when there was activity in the camp below. He smiled broadly when he saw his brother leaving the tented area alone with a small leather pack on his back. It looked like he was trying to be silent too.

Gerardo got out his spotting scope to follow his brother's path. He was quickly surprised with what he saw. It was instantly obvious that he planned incorrectly. His brother did not attempt to ascend any of the trails or paths that traverse Tacamonte. He wasn't going to climb that area at all. Instead Jesus crossed the stream and was walking in the opposite direction across the small canyon floor. This surprised Gerardo because he was sure that Jesus was going to climb Tacamonte. Jesus was scampering away from Tacamonte, across the canyon, and towards the base of La Chiva.

Gerardo quickly realized that he was in the wrong place to observe his brother. Instead of looking across the small canyon to all of the exposed trailheads, he was towering above the thick brush. His chances of following his brother were lost for this day. He would not risk being discovered. There should be plenty of opportunities to learn more. He had the advantage of time and surprise.

His mind reeled with possibilities. Dreaming up potential scenarios was always a pastime for Gerardo. He spent many long hours alone, and found comfort and a strange companionship with his vivid imagination.

He did not respect his older brother, and the appointment as Military Governor cemented his disgust and dissatisfaction with his brother's aberrant behavior. Jesus had always been a bully. Gerardo thought he was rough, intolerant, and a difficult person to acknowledge as family.

Gerardo had innumerable unanswered questions, and only time would help in solving his little scenarios. At the bottom of them all was his belief that his brother had something to do with the bandit king, a man that Gerardo greatly respected, not from direct personal contact but only by reputation. That added to the conflict that he had with his older brother. It was never nice, and now it was getting worse. It was even difficult for a brother to forgive and forget.

He found no way to explain the sudden expansion of his brother's house, the new jewel necklace that dangled from the neck of his sister-in-law, the additional staffing, and even the grounds and landscaping improvements on the property. His brother was just too cheap to suddenly authorize these expenditures. Jesus must have come into an unexplained windfall.

When ultimately asked, Jesus advised that he had begun each of these projects some time previous and their concurrent efforts and status were just a matter of chance. He claimed they have been part of his plans for years. That was true. But dreams are one thing, and it takes money to pay for work and improvements. There was a lot going on.

Meanwhile Gerardo had to sit and wait. Opportunity was not there in the near term. He had many questions to ponder. Was there some special secret at La Chiva? Could it be related to the bandit's gold? It was yet another challenge to unravel these secrets. Gerardo felt well suited for the task. He laughed at his own overactive imagination and considered many of the possible stories for what he had witnessed. He concluded that there must be a more logical explanation and put the subject temporarily to rest. He decided to quietly descend and quickly leave the area before his brother returned to camp.

The weekend at Tacamonte Canyon was different for the Borella family. It was a relaxed and happy time. Jesus went on an afternoon hike one day and was gone more than five hours. When he returned he was happier than anyone ever remembered. He was smiling from ear to ear, almost glowing. Everything seemed just perfect with him, and he did not smell like alcohol.

Particularly strange was the extra patience and kindness he directed towards his wife and children. Was he overtired? Was the additional relaxation from the extended time in nature that refreshing to his soul? Was he finding some rejuvenating quality from the hot springs at the base of Tacamonte? Where was he going?

The results from his time near Tacamonte were noticeable and everyone appreciated his more jovial state and the extra attention from their family leader. When grandfather was happy the others reflected it too. The increase in harmony was welcome within the family unit. They were great celebrations, with everyone enjoying the camping experience too. Nobody suspected the truth behind grandfather's new elixir. Certainly it was not from his recent communion with nature. There was much more to this change in his attitude and behavior.

The Borella family did not have another picnic session again until the late fall. Jesus was extending an invitation to a grand gathering for a special family picnic. Gerardo wondered why it was to be out in the Tacamonte Canyon, and learned that there was too much work being done at the house to properly entertain. Besides, Jesus found a wonderful site that was perfect for a large gathering. He wanted to share his growing love for the outdoors with his family. Despite the inconveniences of travel, the beauty and the strength of the area were overwhelming, and the tents would be oriented near a calming stream. It was going to be a spe-cial time in a unique spot. It didn't make sense, but it made things easy to observe. Gerardo leaped at the chance to attend.

Gerardo never saw him leave. It must have been carefully planned. By pretending to rest, Gerardo was able to maintain an afternoon vigil further downstream and await the return of his brother. Perhaps something noticeable would give him a clue to this behavior. There was nothing. Jesus returned from a differ-ent direction more than five and a half hours later. Gerardo was puzzled.

The highlight of the gathering on the last evening was Jesus' gift of one small gold coin to everyone present except the young-est grandchildren. Jesus had no big explanation for the surprise, other than to share his success with his family. He had done well. Gerardo was suspicious about the source of those gold coins. He was sure that his brother did not carry that bag of coins from town.

Jesus loved the gold and silver. He would entertain moments of feeling like a joyful child with all of his worldly desires fully satis-fied. He felt powerful and free. He had a wall of boxes filled with coins, piles of gold and jewels, and money of various forms. It was too much for one man to hold.

Jesus Borella had no fear of detection. He knew the treasure was secure and he believed his secret was safe. Gerardo Borella thought otherwise.

23. SUSPICIOUS MINDS

Tacamonte Canyon – 1893

At his death Lareano made a curse, and one that would have an impact on Jesus and others that followed. Lareano Garcia cursed the man who poisoned him, and the little messengers of nature responded. Their relationship was close and the repayment was quick. Karma can work that way. Nobody remembered for sure when the cat was first seen on the mountain. There was no consensus. Everyone placed it at a different point in time.

This cat, El Tigre, was larger and more aggressive than anyone could believe. Its cry was loud and shrill. When asked, nobody could actually say they saw the cat, but they knew it was close enough to create alarm. Hunters quit climbing on Tacamonte and La Chiva. In time the cat joined into the protective totem of the mountain.

Jesus loved the rumors and warnings about the cat in the area. He laughed at the gullibility of people. Superstition can be used to effectively control others, or at least reduce their motivation. As far as he was concerned, it was a creation of the bandit to keep his special area out of bounds. Obviously, the less people hiking around the better. Everyone who visited the vicinity helped spread the rumors about the cat prowling on the mountains or in the long, deep canyons. The blood curdling stories of close encounters and narrow escapes from El Tigre added to the lore.

Opportunity knocked for Gerardo more than a year later, and this time he was in a better position to spy on his brother. He positioned himself in advance along the lower ridge on a companion canyon face with a panoramic view of La Chiva before him. He had ample provisions, including food, water, and extra clothing. The sailor's spyglass was sitting at his side. If he had to guess, it would be a number of hours until he saw his brother.

This time Gerardo believed his patience would be rewarded. He had a good idea that his brother would be climbing, as unusual as it seemed, to a hidden location on La Chiva protected by the thick vegetation. He was ascending from the valley floor and probably following some hunting path to a small fissure or remote canyon not visible from the Tacamonte side.

Nobody in his or her right mind would voluntarily climb upon or around La Chiva. It was common knowledge to stay away. The whole area was taboo. Jesus had to be heading towards the bandit's gold. If he was, the genius of the bandit was to be commended.

Although not religious in any sense, the bandit was a true believer of many things. Lareano further protected his secret area each time by a prayer or incantation that would be performed slowly before he walked away from the site. It would not be heard again. He would not be returning.

Jesus Borella sat beneath the Mapa Tree and looked down at the canyon below. He tried to relax and catch his breath from the arduous climb. Out of his pocket he pulled a small flask, and took a swig of his favorite potent drink. The local product was always a useful vehicle for relaxation. Ironically it was also the favorite brand of the bandit, or at least it used to be. The burning sensation in his throat brought with it waves of clarity to his mind. He chased the tequila with water from an aging canteen. He was here, and again he was happy.

Jesus had never seen and taken note of the full extent of his treasure. It was too dark in the rear. This time he was prepared to explore more, or so he thought. He opened his pack bag and withdrew a handmade torch.

It was his fourth trip to the site, and his precautions were not yet a habit. Each time he became more relaxed and less paranoid. On earlier trips he would stop at odd intervals and listen for the sounds of footsteps. He was always afraid of being followed. This time it was different. He was cautious but confident. He ascended past the landmarks without doubt or hesitation.

This was perfect for Gerardo, who was watching the movements as his brother came out in the clearings and then vanished in the brush again. Gerardo moved to get a better look. His brother was sitting on the side of an outcropping, in the shade of a small tree. Was he singing? His brother didn't sing! Perhaps his brother was talking to himself.

Jesus took another swig from the flask in his jacket pocket and the reason for the rest break was understood. It seemed like a long hike just to find a quiet spot for a drink. Then Jesus arose, something strange happened, and Gerardo could not contain his excitement.

Jesus walked about ten yards to a smaller outcropping and withdrew a small shovel. He then returned to a rock overhang and began pulling on a pile of branches and carefully piling the brush and debris to one side. When it appeared to be cleared he then stooped under the rock overhang and began shallow scraping movements with his shovel. From his angle Gerardo was unable to determine the impact of the digging. He could hear the sounds of his brother's actions, but he had no clear picture of what was going on. He was unsure about coming closer and risking possible detection, so he decided to sit and wait. This proved to be the correct choice.

After another brief rest Jesus carefully scanned the adjacent hills. He had the biggest smile on his face. He was slow and methodical as he either reacted to some noise he heard or just took extra precautions before his next task. Gerardo put down the spotting scope and remained motionless behind a mound of rocks and plants. He had come too far to risk detection at this point. He had observed the rifle leaning upright at his brother's dig, and did not want to be the recipient of any unlucky shot.

Jesus lifted what looked like a metal lid from under the protective rock and then he was gone from sight. Gerardo, watching every move through his scope, stared in amazement at the metal lid. It looked like a door to a bank safe. How did it get there? How did his brother know it was there? Did this door conceal the bandit's cache?

Jesus had lost his fear at the site. He did not have to worry about the bandit or his gang. He was at ease. Earlier fears of a booby trap, spring gun, or other protective device were unfounded. It was his fortune and his alone. He had all of the time he needed to survey the interior and remove what he wanted. He could take or leave any piece at any time. Nobody could stop him and the treasure on La Chiva was his secret.

On previous trips he was forced to rely solely on the daylight filtering through the opening supplemented by some small candles. They could not illuminate the entire cave, so Jesus had a mosaic of mental pictures, but never the experience of seeing it all at one time. He was in store for a major surprise.

The light did not enter or reflect well inside, and only at certain times of year. His goal this visit was to explore more of the contents of this hidden cave. The sun was still high in the sky and he believed he had plenty of uninterrupted time for that glorious project. The torches would enable him to investigate the extent of his prize. He was excited like a little boy and protective like a mother cat. This was his secret and he gloated on his personal success. He became lost in thought trying to grasp the size and scope of the treasure. It was time for an informal inventory.

He sat mesmerized for almost an hour, finally reaching for one of the bags filled with precious stones. He stuck a few fingers into the bag and felt around the various sized jewels, being careful not to spill any. He let them slowly run through his fingers and back into the bag again and again. To him the exercise represented the endless riches hidden in this spot. The cave was filled with large wooden boxes, piled from the dirt floor to the uneven stone ceiling. Jesus had no concept of the depth of the cave. He saw that almost all of the available space was used, but he did not know what was behind the large boxes or around the side. Was it more of the same? The only way to know was to move some of the boxes. He could begin the task by removing the upper boxes to see behind them.

After moving and restacking a number of the heavy boxes, with a few breaks in between, Jesus heard a strange sound that broke him out of his focus. He turned around and was startled to see his brother, Gerardo, coming through the entrance of the cave. Alarmed and caught off guard, Jesus began shouting questions at his brother. "What are you doing here? How did you find this place? Why are you here?"

Without waiting for an answer, Jesus continued, "What are you doing? Why did you follow me?"

Gerardo responded slowly, as he crawled through the opening and began to stand. "Relax, my brother."

Jesus was in his nasty bully mood. His words were accusatory and ugly.

Gerardo fired back, "I'm your brother, please treat me with respect."

Then he continued, "Why are you here? What is going on? How did this get here? How did you find this?"

Nothing positive came out of their words. Each was upset and defensive. Their voices and tempers escalated, and a shoving match ensued. Jesus made the first move and his small brother responded in kind. Jesus became further agitated and forcefully attacked his brother. Gerardo was not properly braced for his large brother's advance, and he fell backward into the recently stacked coin boxes.

Jesus watched in slow motion and could do nothing to stop the process. The cracking sound of his younger brother's skull against the boxes was eerie. Jesus would never forget the sound of the snap, as the fall instantly took his brother's life. There was no doubt from the look in his eyes either. Gerardo was dead on the spot.

Jesus did not know what to do. He panicked. He began to hyperventilate and almost became sick in the cave. He turned towards the doorway, climbed through the opening, and staggered out into the sunlight. He was gasping for breath, weak in the knees. His younger brother was dead, at his hands.

Gerardo was staring out from the far corner of the cave, sitting peacefully forever, propped up by a large bag of silver coins, with a number of boxes behind.

Jesus began to return to his full sensory level as he took in the view of his immediate surroundings. At least nobody knew he was here. Since his brother found the spot could there be others? It was a waffling of ideas and emotions. He concluded that he was sloppy, his brother had been lucky and somehow was able to follow him, and nobody else was involved.

He descended back into the cave, filled his pack and pockets with new coins, and then looked back at his brother's body as he backed towards the door. Jesus took another glance to focus on his brother's face. He could do nothing with the body. He couldn't take his brother back to town and risk his position. Any inquiry would present a problem. Burying him in the stony terrain near the cave was out of the question. Transporting the corpse would be close to impossible.

He put out the torches, stacked them close to the entrance, closed the trap door, and began shoveling sufficient dirt to cover the metal door. He then tossed the branches, leaves and dried brush to the site in a random manner, hid his shovel nearby, put on the pack, grabbed the rifle and departed in a hurry.

The whole event was troubling. Although the death was an accident, Jesus was responsible for his brother's violent end. His speedy exit was a reaction and not a solution.

His mind was filled with questions as he descended the mountain and his worries overtook him. How would he explain the sudden disappearance of his brother? What was his risk of detection? Did anyone know where Gerardo was going? Did anyone know his plans? Was this secret secure? How could he have avoided this crisis? Could any action help now?

There were no answers. He was trapped within a prison of his own thinking.

24. MISSING

Culiacan – 1893

Gerardo's absence was confusing. Gerardo was there, and then he was gone. Nobody was sure when they last saw him. They could not pinpoint the time. To his neighbors, he quietly vanished. Those that knew him were confident that he would return suddenly with a huge smile on his jovial face and stories about a colorful and exciting adventure. There had to be a reasonable explanation.

Speculation was rampant. There was first one theory and then another. They ended with no logical explanation for Gerardo's disappearance. While he did not have public problems or known enemies, it was ultimately concluded that he had met foul play somewhere in another town and was probably buried or left to die in the desert sand.

Neither La Chiva nor the Tacamonte areas were ever mentioned. Had Gerardo been placed in that locale, Jesus was prepared to remind everyone about the tiger rumors and speculate accordingly.

The sudden disappearance of the Military Governor's brother remained a topic of discussion and inquiry for over a year, and then the matter rested. Jesus had demonstrated a fatalistic attitude from the moment it was realized that his brother was missing without a trace. Rosa could not understand why her husband was not more involved in the investigation of his brother's absence.

Jesus successfully rationalized his way out of any personal responsibility for Gerardo's death. In his mind it was his brother's fault for sneaking after him to the secret cave. If only Gerardo had not startled and then argued with him. It became violent without warning. He slipped. Maybe he was pushed. It was nobody's fault. It was an accident. He did not intend to harm his brother. All in all, his excuses were pathetic and void of reality. He always worked things out in his mind in his own favor. His protection mechanisms were acutely developed, and they helped him maintain a self-righteous stance whenever in conflict. That was nothing new for the thinking process of the Military Governor. He was who he was.

One of the most troubling byproducts was his increase in self-confidence and corresponding decrease in kindness and compassion. The additional financial clout also added to his arrogance. It did nothing to make him a kinder person initially. Ultimately that changed. He became generous with his family, workers, and friends in his later years. He loved to surprise them with coins allegedly left to him by his father. They always smiled to acknowledge the source but knew better.

Jesus chuckled when he created a mental picture of what it would be like for somebody to stumble upon the entrance, uncover the door, climb through the entry, be overtaken with the gold and piles of jewels, and then notice his brother, or what was left of him, in the corner staring towards the entrance. That would scare anyone. It became another protector of the treasure.

When he would least expect it, he would feel haunted by the responsibility he bore for Gerardo's violent death. He deeply believed he was right. His brother was wrongfully at his secret place. His brother was trespassing. He didn't belong there. They each pushed the other. Jesus was defending his property. The justifications went on and on.

Horrible nightmares began within a month after his sudden departure from the cave and the intensity and content were troubling. The situation and placement were different most every evening, but the tone was equally terrorizing. It was his personal nightly visit to hell. He became continually troubled, tired and mentally exhausted.

Close to three years would pass before Jesus returned to the mountain. His interest in picnics and camping at the base of Tacamonte ceased as quickly as it began. In the interim, life returned to the new normal in his household. Things were good. Everyone noticed an improvement in his attitude. Change was evident.

Jesus gathered the courage needed to finally visit the treasure again. Necessity has a way of clearing behavioral blocks. He had long since exhausted his gold from the previous visits. He returned to La Chiva with a need to refill his satchel and a burning curiosity about his brother's remains. The death happened so quickly and he had been drinking a little, maybe even too much. His level of denial had penetrated his own memories. Perhaps it was a hallucination. Maybe he wouldn't be there.

The solution to his fears about his brother's remains could come to a head soon. Three years was a long time to stay away. Maybe a treasure fix could solve his problems or complete the mental signal that haunted his dreams almost every night.

Jesus was also aware of the rumors about increased sightings of some large predatory cat in and around the La Chiva and Tacamonte area. These rumors added to his concerns but were not a true deterrent. Years before he didn't even believe them. In fact, he was indebted to the hoax.

When his excess funds were depleted, the ascent of his mountain of fears was imminent. He had no choice. His lifestyle greatly exceeded his income, a temporary problem capable of full resolution with a visit to La Chiva and the ensuing ascent to his glorious cave. The solution was within his grasp, subject only to the possible watchful eye of the protective cat.

Jesus was not sure if he believed the rumors, but he likewise could not afford to discount them too greatly. The stories added to his concerns, but the comfort of his new shotgun would ease the burden of its weight.

25. Alone Again Or

La Chiva – 1896

The climb was more difficult than Jesus remembered. It was steep and unforgiving. The path itself was more slippery and the surface caused him to lose his footing often and stumble repeatedly. The terrible traction forced him to move slowly and with great caution. Nevertheless, he had no problem locating most of the landmarks or markers, and reached the site only half an hour later than anticipated.

His expectancy was so great that he actually felt energized and refreshed rather than fatigued when he reached the goal. He was back to the entry to his beloved treasure and to the renewal of his expendable holdings. He was sweating profusely as his dig had begun. The rains of the last three winter seasons had sufficiently eroded part of a face high above and deposited an additional four to six inches of decomposed granite and silt. It took almost an hour of digging and scraping with his back bent low for Jesus to reach the protective cover. Again, the bandit's precautions proved to be effective against the elements and natural adversity.

By the time he opened the old bank door, Jesus was breathing with great difficulty and dripping with sweat. His heart was beating strongly and his emotional state was on edge. The normally dank air in the cave had an unusually sour smell. It was hard to get past the impact of the noxious smell. Of course, it was not bad enough to stop Jesus, merely an irritant. It forced him to acknowledge and think about the consequences of what happened the last time he was in this cave.

He also reflected on his previous four visits, and the highlights of each. The last one ended in a crippling event that would scar his psyche forever. It haunted him. The undetected and unpunished accidental death of his brother was a heavy burden to carry. Jesus had a conscience, even if he chose to ignore it.

A cloud must have moved in to block the sun, and the air suddenly felt cooler. Jesus felt a heavy weight lift from his shoulders. Things started to get easier.

An ear-to-ear smile filled his face as he again knelt before the entry. The torches from an earlier visit were still piled where he left them just inside the doorway. He lit one and proceeded inside. It felt confining as he stooped through the protected entry and betook the dazzling picture before him.

He was prepared to see something bizarre, for the passage of time had let his imagination haunt him. Seeing his brother's erect skeleton was shocking. The rodents must have eaten his remains. Rats and mice were plentiful. It was such a sickening sight that Jesus went weak in the knees and quickly sat down. He could not move forward or backward, and he needed to gather his strength.

A wave of dark energy overcame him and his situation worsened. He felt threatened and his mind was spinning. His legs and hands were out of his control. He was overtaken by guilt and remorse. He felt sick for what he had done.

He had spent sufficient time in church to believe he could feel spirit. As his head spun he had visions of his brother and then the bandit. He had betrayed both and he felt connected to their presence. He was almost sure they were there with him right then. He looked harder as if he could focus on something from the otherworld.

Jesus was instantly sick to his stomach. He realized he was numb and immobile. Jesus was terrified. He was weak, vulnerable and unsure whether this was contact with spirit or an emotional catharsis. What was he hearing? His fears and beliefs combined to play a symphony of tricks on his mind, continuously gaining volume and momentum.

For a moment he could almost taste the bandit's last drink, and fought to not let the sensations go beyond his own mouth. Could he die if the feelings went down his throat and beyond, an imaginary poisoning in retribution?

The silence was broken with a sound not unlike the snap when his brother fell. He heard it over and over, like an echo. He knew what it was and yet he could not understand. He reflected upon the quality of his life and whether or not it mattered if he could not regain mobility and leave the cave. Could he be at peace if he died on this very spot of a failed heart? Or because his legs wouldn't work?

Ultimately, his inner strength was sufficient to overcome this immersion into weakness. He would be strong. He could be brave. He had power and he had the treasure. These thoughts combined to call him back to the present. He left the delusions behind, summoned his strength, and slowly and carefully attempted to stand.

He began loading his pockets and bag with an assortment of coins. By focusing only on the gold and silver coins he was able to refrain from even looking towards his brother's bones hiding in the corner not very many feet away.

He carefully packed his valuables and closed the cave. He had become good at covering the entrance and hiding the opening. All required precautions would be taken to make sure he was never followed again.

As he left the site, he remained on alert and listened carefully. Overcautious would be an understatement. He stopped at irregular intervals and learned to listen to the birds. They had an uncanny way of becoming silent when intruders were present. The cacophony gave him confidence that nobody was below in the canyon, at least not now. His secret was safe for another trip.

Jesus was not afraid of bandits. He was the law and he was generally feared. As a supplemental precaution, a couple of his favorite guards were waiting for him at the base of the canyon entrance, more than two miles from his personal camp. The area was closed. They had no idea what he was up to and believed that his solo hiking with the rifle meant he was hunting for something special on Tacamonte, La Chiva, or the canyon or river areas between. They secretly laughed at his false bravado and air of superiority. They believed the cat would prevail in any struggle. They thought the Military Governor was trying to build a fearless legend, and conquering the cat was a part of the image. They understood why he would not want it known when he failed. They had no problem with his intentions or goals. He treated them well and earned their absolute loyalty over the years. Silence would be easy because nobody would ever ask.

The Military Governor had inadvertently adopted part of Lareano's family history as his own, and talked with his men about fictional childhood hunting sessions in these mountains with his own father. The men understood it to be good, for their boss was happy when he returned. His generosity extended to a small but reasonable cash bonus when they arrived back in town. He earned and purchased their silence about the failed hunting mission and many other things. They were loyal and they respected him. The pile of 8 Reale coins did not hurt. They weighed just over 3/4 of an ounce of silver, and were used from the 1820's until almost the end of the century.

Jesus was often in the company of guards so nothing appeared out of the ordinary when they rode back to his home and compound near town. He left his horse at the stable and took his rife, bags, and coat into the house. His smile was abnormally large and his good intentions were transparent. He wanted the revelations at the cave to continue. He saw hope for greater happiness and a positive influence of the treasure on his life and throughout the family.

The picture looked good to him and it turned out to be true. Jesus lived for many more years and his family grew. The grandkids gave him special joy. They helped add some component of immortality. His home was a spacious hacienda with plenty of room for everyone who desired to stay on the grounds. There was never a shortage of visitors.

This "new" version of the man seemed more accommodating and agreeable. He was lavish in his expenditures when they related to his home, family and friends. The grounds, service, and even the food were all top quality. He was extraordinarily generous to his guests. It was a joy to be present at Christmas when rare Spanish coins, allegedly from the collection of Jesus' own father, were distributed to all. Each was its own piece of treasure. Nobody knew. It was still a secret.

Often a happy and contented man has a better chance of living long. That is amplified when he has abundant love, a self-satisfying position, and the wonders of unlimited wealth. Jesus lived to an old age and was able to hike, including the Tacamonte and La Chiva areas, until the end. The customary family picnic at Tacamonte resumed and became a ritual until a couple of years before his death.

The Military Governor was one of the earliest casualties of the revolution. He died in 1910 at the age of seventy-four. Ironically, Jesus' death did not occur at the cave or on the mountain. He died at home after suffering through a week of a severe fever. But the illness was not the cause of his death. His estate was intentionally burned to the ground and he was trapped inside and killed by the fire. The arson was a strong symbolic attack by the rebels. There were no witnesses and nobody took credit for the attack. Apparently not everyone forgave him for his earlier cruelty and misdeeds.

Jesus Borella's secret about the location of the treasure died with him. Until his dying day he told nobody about the treasure. Not one person. He did not make arrangements for his succession. He wrote nothing.

The Treasure of La Chiva would sleep alone for a long time.

26. ABOARD THE *TOUCAN*

Belize – June 3, 2005

Nobody on the *Toucan* felt tired as Ellis Stevens continued with his story late into the night. The stars were a heavenly backdrop as everyone listened with earnest. His words painted pictures that were easy to follow.

Refreshments and snacks were passed quietly and we continued to sit in stunned silence. Beer tastes different in Belize. Belikin Beer.

Captain Dan's blonde hair was blowing in the breeze when he broke the silence and said, "So it seems the story died in Culiacan with the passing of the Military Governor in 1910. You said he never shared his secret with anyone, right? Are we at a dead end?"

Ellis said that is far from the truth. The next part is even better. The story does continue.

It was striking to realize that Ellis looks a lot like Mark Wahlberg, without the tattoos. Both have hazel eyes, same height and coloring. There is a strong inner strength that radiates from each.

Everyone aboard had to wait until after snorkeling and breakfast the next day for Ellis to continue. We were anxious and ready. Fortunately, nobody was going anywhere.

∾ ∾ ∾

PART III – THE SEARCHERS

27. EPIMINEO CORRALES

Culiacan – 1920's

Not everyone in the Culiacan area believed the search for hidden relics of the past should be abandoned. To one, the Treasure of La Chiva would be a lifetime goal. There was a burning fire of curiosity in the youngest of the seven grandchildren of the former Military Governor. Epimineo Corrales was the baby of the group, and enjoyed special privileges as such. The others were not afforded such experiences because of caution, but even the shrewd Jesus Borella found no threat in this young child. He opened his special box and often entertained his youngest scion with beautiful coins and jewels. They played on the floor together with these relics, creating the seeds to our direct link with the treasure.

Epimineo had memories of some activities with his grandfather when he was very small. The boy remembered them clearly, or at least he thought that he did. He was sitting on the floor in his grandfather's lap. They were playing with small boxes and bags, handfuls of shining coins and colorful stones. The images were vivid in his mind.

Over the years, doubt caused him to vacillate whether they were actual memories or mental pictures created from stories heard after his grandfather's death. He thought he remembered. The words of doubt were never his. Negativity had the hidden power to cancel direct observations. He had many questions, a direction, and just a bit more.

For years after the death of his grandfather, Epimineo's father talked openly about his unequivocal belief in the existence of the treasure and his conclusion that his own father was one of its secret custodians. His thesis was detailed and conclusive.

Epimineo remembered numerous family stories and jokes relating to the Tacamonte camping excursions. They all ended with coins, every time. The stories of the treasure fertilized Epimineo's memory and, over the years, he became focused on finding his grandfather's hideout. He could easily visualize a selected outpost filled with beauty and wealth somewhere near the big mountain. The only problem was where.

Epimineo had his grandfather's stubborn streak, especially when he believed himself to be correct, which was almost all of the time. He demonstrated an inner strength and conviction that overcame most obstacles. The mountain itself, La Chiva, tested every aspect of this. His belief that his grandfather came down the path from La Chiva seemed more real as each year passed and he was convinced the treasure was there. Epimineo was tireless in his dedication and efforts, spending all of his free time during his teenage and early adult years on this endeavor. He became obsessed with claiming his "inheritance" from his grandfather. He was driven with the image of success.

Epimineo began his exploration around the accessible base areas of La Chiva. He began at the bottom and around the most level places. In time he expanded his search and transitioned through the numerous zones that make up the region. Hundreds of hours of hiking over and around La Chiva proved futile. The terrain was steep, the footing was difficult, and not a sign was evident of anything valuable or extraordinary. In spite of these setbacks, Epimineo maintained a persistent quality to his search. Each day of failure would encourage him to believe that he was that much closer to the goal. Nothing would sidetrack his fierce determination. He had a permanent case of treasure fever. It would be an understatement to say he was obsessed. It took on the qualities of possessed. He would not stop looking until he found it.

The countless days on the mountain consumed all of his spare time. He continued to live and breathe the uncovering of the treasure. The persistent rumors amplified by family stories of the Treasure of La Chiva would help refill his tanks with motivation. They remembered the coins. The fact that most outsiders believed it to be a myth was of no consequence. Any mention of the subject by his family would be psychic fuel to his energy field.

Over the years Epimineo found himself to be the only person up on the mountain. His visits seemed lonely and isolated. People were afraid to go there. Bad news always travels fast and far, and the continuing legend of El Tigre became an overriding concern. Some claimed the cat represented the soul of the bandit and it stood guard over his lost treasure. Epimineo, like his grandfather, Jesus Borella, took a contrarian view and believed the cat story was his protector. It kept most of the others from searching La Chiva for its secret.

The mountain acquired a death-like quality. The vegetation was less visible and the animals were no longer abundant. People in the valley below knew that to be the work of the cat. It was not a good feeling. Epimineo did not agree.

His father and two oldest brothers were positive that grand-father came from the direction of La Chiva every time, and even pointed out the crosses on the fence posts that mark the beginning of the path. He was not on Tacamonte. He didn't come from the direction of the river either. They were adamant that he wasn't in the canyon. La Chiva was the sole focus for exploration and investigation. On that fact they were of one viewpoint.

Epimineo became so accustomed to the mountain that he began to gather additional energy when he was there. He believed La Chiva was feeding him and driving him onward. He noticed it was easier to walk uphill than downhill on this strange surface. That was contrary to every experience he had previously. It made him think his eyes were not working properly. He declared himself to be the one chosen to release La Chiva of its burden buried deep within. His mission was steadfast. He had lots of practice.

Things continued as they were until a chilly afternoon in the fall of 1932.

28. SEARCHING

La Chiva – March, 1932

It was Epimineo's twenty-fourth year, with more than ten years of experiences in searching for the treasure on La Chiva, when the status quo changed without warning. Although unknown to Epimineo, this was his date with destiny and an answer to his dedicated quest. It was time for the mountain to reveal one of its secrets. Unfortunately, one cannot prepare for an unscheduled appointment. Fate works in such strange ways.

The treasure was not an object of discussion on that day, or any other day. He had not spoken with many of his friends about his decade-long search for his grandfather's legacy. The last discussion with family members about his search was years earlier. By that point he knew all that they could remember about this portion of their family history. There was no doubt that grandfather had valuables hidden on La Chiva. He was able to isolate which initial path, but that was all.

He spent an extraordinary amount of time walking up, over and around the canyons, ridges and faces of the proud mountain. He was always secretly looking for anything unusual, including landmarks, noteworthy structures, small monuments, or other guideposts to his goal. He was looking for a sign. He believed an unusual landmark or a marker of sorts would guide him to the secret treasure. His grandfather must have used some means of identifying the site. According to family lore he was more of a city man than a hunter and adventure type. His physique was inconsistent with a mountain man.

There had to be some visible exterior clues. They had to be discernible, obvious, and impervious to time. The most lasting thing was the mountain itself. He questioned if the sight or locator was made of stone. Was it a distance or direction from some permanent point? Perhaps it was even a unique planting or type of vegetation? Could it be a post or other wooden object that deteriorated long ago?

On the pivotal day in 1932, Epimineo went to the mountain with his current best friend, Arturo, and a couple of young ladies to drink and have fun. That day his mind was on things other than his dedicated search for the treasure. He had a special interest in one of the girls, and the romantic possibilities preoccupied his thinking as they started to ascend one of his favorite paths on the mountain.

To Epimineo, each of the trails had a different designation and meaning. These personal identifiers were all secretly named for local wildlife. This particular one he called "the snake" because it undulated back and forth as it went up the mountain. The snake trail had the most switchbacks and was far from the easiest of all to ascend. Epimineo believed this narrow trail was created and used by the larger animals, and maybe even hunters with pack animals. After hearing a strange sound he began to wonder if the large cat, El Tigre, traversed this very path.

The group was having a great time frolicking on the mountainside. As usual, Epimineo's eyes were scanning the surrounding surfaces for signs of anything out of the ordinary. He had years ago given up trying to evaluate what he was looking for. He was just watching for anything unusual. It would be subtle, if noticeable at all. He let his consciousness float and prayed for a sign. There had to be some guide, marker or signpost of sorts making it easier to identify the hiding place. Was it an unusually shaped tree? Or perhaps a unique rock formation? Or was it a sighting taken from the triangulation between existing landmarks? Even more simply, was it a fixed direction and distance from any one specific identifiable object at the base or elsewhere on the mountain? How about a combination? He had gone over the possibilities for years. Did it have anything to do with the sun and shadow patterns? How about the stars? Or points on a compass? The possibilities were endless.

His mind returned to his friends. He was impressed with the ability of the females to scale this difficult path. They climbed with the grace of cats. It became obvious who was stronger and more agile. The more the group drank, the more easy they found the ascent. The impact of the tequila was becoming noticeable. They were getting louder and giddy. Sometimes spontaneous laughter would erupt over nothing at all. It was a great relief to be on the mountain with friends just having fun.

The girls had never been in that area and were impressed with the views as the climb continued. They wanted to see if they could reach a height where the town of Culiacan would be visible in the distance. That had been the original goal of the outing and climb. They went up and up. Everyone felt like birds as they looked down to the canyon below and the desert in the distance. They sat and took another break. This time Epimineo removed some food items from his pack bag and they enjoyed a leisurely breather with refreshments.

They almost jumped in unison with the first loud boom of thunder. As they looked around they noticed a buildup of cumulus clouds just becoming visible over the top of the peak. The speed of the movement combined with the rapid buildup caused Arturo to ask if Epimineo thought it would rain. He was concerned because they did not have any type of protection against adverse weather.

The group's main focus of attention shifted to watching the beautiful cloud movements. They seemed to twist and expand upwards at they came into view. The contrast between the sheer white face at the top of La Chiva and the darkening gray clouds was like a monochromatic portrait of nature. It was stark, powerful, and suddenly alarming. Nobody in the group was prepared for a major thunderstorm and there was not enough time to descend safely.

They decided to locate temporary cover and make the best out of it. A little water never hurt anyone. It went well with the tequila.

The sky darkened and Epimineo began a short sobering discussion of the dangers. They had to avoid lightning. Also, the damage from flash flooding was evident all over the mountain face and small sloping canyon areas. They needed to find a dry place and wait out the storm. Epimineo knew that the whole natural process from the dark cloud buildup to rain would take less than half an hour. Storms matured quickly around the mountain. It had happened to him before. All they had to do was find some form of shelter, but he bore a pessimistic attitude because of his history in this area. Epimineo knew there were few places for them to seek protection from the impending thunderstorm. The few trees would not provide adequate cover because the foliage at this elevation was not thick. Epimineo had never found any structures or lean-tos in his searches and he did not believe any existed in the vicinity.

The solution had to be under some rock outcroppings. He quickly scouted around a ten-minute perimeter of where they rested and found a large fallen boulder slide destined to protect them from the rain and the prevailing winds. He gathered his friends and returned to that site. It was easy to find again because of three narrow trees that grew from the west-facing side.

They all climbed under the largest rock and marveled at the building cloud formations. The sense of adventure permeated them and it made the mating urge even stronger in the males. In spite of their intense inner feelings they knew this would not be the time or place. The clouds became solid and dark. The storm was maturing rapidly. The winds began to gust in many directions at once. It was a glorious display of the developing power of nature. It matured more quickly than anticipated and more ferocious on the mountain than ever experienced in the town or valley.

Huddled together with their backs supported against the rocks, they enjoyed the snacks and alcohol. The rumble of thunder vibrated the ground beneath them and everything shook. The lightning cracked, emptying the clouds as if on cue. The deluge was unbelievable.

Epimineo realized he had misjudged the direction of the rain as he was soon pelted with hail. The overhang was capable of sheltering only three of them. Conversation was impossible. It was too loud for anyone to hear each other. He motioned for his friends to stay and he ran off to seek protection at a spot that he remembered from a recent scouting. His goal was near a singular Mapa tree apparently overlooking a deep canyon below. The earth made a formation like a small wall to one side. He pulled tightly on his hat and began running to that site. He was getting soaked because it was further than he thought. He became disoriented a couple of times but found it in less than ten uncomfortable minutes, dove under the shelter of the rock, and brushed off the freezing hail stuck to his clothing. He was soaking wet, cold, and disgusted.

La Chiva was making even a bigger fool of him. After years of combing the area with steadfast optimism and uplifting thoughts, he was depressed, huddled under a rock overhang attempting to stay dry. Besides being cold and uncomfortable, he was isolated and miserable. This visit was not in search of the treasure, yet he blamed his current predicament on his obsession with La Chiva and his years of searching for his grandfather's gold and silver storage site.

The earth shook in response to the deep bass notes of thunder. With a bolt of lightning his life flashed before him and he knew it was time to give up on his fruitless search. Too many years had been spent without one positive sign. He realized it was time for him to stop chasing his obsession and to settle down, acquire a trade or skill, and attempt to live a normal life.

Great balls of hail began to fall again. The temperature suddenly dropped more than fifteen degrees and Epimineo became aware of the bitter cold. The hailstorm seemed to last forever. He lost concept of time and purpose, which only added to his frustration and resolve.

The hail changed to rain and Epimineo's discomfort continued to increase. His friends were at least a few hundred meters further down the ridgeline huddled close together and having fun, while he was sitting here soaking wet, alone, lonely, and feeling like a total fool. They had the food, beverages, and each other. He had nothing. He turned his head downward and closed his eyes. He thoughts went inward as he listened to the rain. It was a perfect time for reflection. He found no justification for his countless years of scouting the area. He felt like a dreamer while reality was staring him in the face. His inner conflict was great, and there was no solution at hand. He would sit out the storm, rejoin his friends, and see what could be done to develop a relationship with the dark-eyed beauty named Sonja.

He resolved to make every possible effort to forget about the mountain and its buried secret. There must be better things in Culiacan than dreaming about hidden treasure. His obsession with finding his grandfather's hiding place was becoming too costly. He had spent valuable years in that search, and it was time to admit his failure and develop new goals and objectives. Times had changed and Epimineo knew he should change with them.

The resolution restored hope and he declared his intention to take a new direction and live a more meaningful life.

His sessions on the mountain were declared to be over. He knew he was done. Once down he would never climb the mountain again. He was through with La Chiva and welcomed the forthcoming freedom. The burden of searching for more than a decade was almost released.

Resolutions or realizations are often tested. That would instantly be the case for Epimineo Corrales. He was at an inflection point in his life, and the decision fathered by his own years of frustration and serious doubt would be instantly withdrawn. It happened that quickly.

Without warning, the storm punctuated the moment with the exploding sound of thunder. It was so loud that it alarmed Epimineo, causing him to open his eyes in immediate alertness. The rain intensified with the cloudburst, and he lightly gazed upward with gratitude for the protection from the elements provided by the large flat rock overhead.

His eyes were staring and he couldn't believe what he saw. His lower extremities went numb and he felt paralyzed. He was looking at his most sacred of all symbols, the cross. Somebody had carved a small cross in the stone above his head to mark this very spot. Shaking with excitement he automatically brought up his hand, also in the same sign.

Had his prayers been answered? He was sitting under a cross. This was an auspicious sign, and he began to cry with happiness. He felt relieved. It meant something serious and he knew it. Some possibilities flashed through his mind as he was overwhelmed with waves of excitement. His most optimistic thoughts centered on the legendary treasure. His negative moments engulfed everything else. Maybe it marked a burial spot? Perhaps somebody else sought protection from the elements in the very same place, and carved the cross in appreciation. Maybe that person was running from El Tigre. He could not discount the fact that he found it while seeking protection during a storm. Was it the hand of God that pushed him there? Was it a marker?

He was alone yet his friends were not too far away. He was protected from their view, and the distance he actually traveled was
greater than he thought. The nature of the ridgeline, the major
rocks, crevices, the smaller outcroppings, as well as the punctua-
tion of trees, sharp brush, and animal paths made the whole scene
quite protected. The only place to see him would be from certain
isolated spots on the opposite ridge and with extremely good eyes.

He was alone and yet he felt great company. His heart was beating too rapidly, his blood was gushing with excitement, and yet he
experienced an inner calm, a feeling of knowing. He believed he
was within the target zone, where he wanted to be, and it was good.

When the rain stopped he scouted the immediate area. With all
of his experience around the lower to middle realms of La Chiva,
he never came upon this site before. It was uniquely protected. It
had access from two directions, but was invisible from the path.
There were few distinguishing features, and the spot blended
into its greater surroundings. It was by a steep edge. It would take
almost a leap of faith to uncover it. Epimineo knew that immediately as he looked straight down.

He also knew that his grandfather would never hide anything
at that location. In the house was a painting of his grandfather
wearing the full dress uniform of the Military Governor. The man
was too large to ever carry anything up to this place. Epimineo
questioned his own rationale and lost hope as he returned to the
protected overhang with the cross. There was nothing there. It was
too remote, too dangerous, and impossible to ever move anything
of substance around the immediate terrain. But, that argument
was immediately defeated when one adds in the possibility of pack
animals or mules. It could be done.

The weather took center stage again with the unloading of a
very dark cloud hanging directly above. It began raining so hard
that the drops were bouncing up off of the rocks and running
downhill in small streams. Epimineo returned to his protected
sanctuary, dove under the stone ledge, and watched the down-
burst. He knew his friends would await his return so he decided to
utilize the time to his advantage. He wondered what he should do.

He decided to take the most positive step of assuming he was
at or near his grandfather's secret spot. The cross in the rock was

an excellent symbol for that. After all, the family posture at the local cathedral was noteworthy and went back for as long as he could remember. The benefits of this rich history were lost upon Epimineo as he was approaching manhood. He had never taken a wife and was not a man of regular practice of anything. Like the bandit, he was not on speaking terms with organized religion.

He could not understand the significance of the surroundings. He sat on the ground and stared upwards at the cross. He spoke out loud and calmly asked, "Grandfather, what should I do?"

One particular thing happened to him and he knew what to do. Has it ever happened to you where you almost "hear" a faint voice inside your own head? Is your mind talking to you? Is anyone else? Does it seem that it only speaks once? You can do it or not, but the soft voice only says it once. Do you remember? And hasn't that voice been right almost all of the time? Well this was one of those moments, a time of good medicine.

With a momentary flash of reason Epimineo understood what he was to do. Epimineo looked up at a huge rock shelf. To his back and sides were large boulders and solid rocks. There was evidence of sticks and brush at the deepest point, but they were as illogical as the placement of the cross. They did not grow under the rock overhang and they were all dead. Perhaps somebody placed the brush there to disguise the spot. Or, maybe the wind just blew it all there.

If the site marked anything at all, it was beneath him. That was the only real possibility. Either that, or the carver of the cross was just wasting time. He would know soon. He took one of the larger sticks and began prying into the dirt. It was surprisingly soft. He used his hands to help move the loose sand, gravel, and brush away from beneath the overhang. Epimineo laughed at himself. Here he was, digging with a stick chasing his old dream. Hadn't he resolved to forget about it less than an hour ago?

After fifteen minutes of using sticks and flat stones as tools, Epimineo stopped and looked at his hands. They were sore and scraped, and hurt from this unnatural activity. Man was not designed to dig with his hands. Resourcefulness is one of the birthrights of the human mind. His tools were rudimentary but progress was being made. He had a hunch that fit into his dream.

He worked quietly. His pace was quickening every few minutes. Something was driving him forward and his hopes were at a new high. Epimineo heard two conflicting sounds almost simultaneously. The first was the faint voice of his friend calling out for him. It brought him back to reality in a flash. The louder was the sound made when his stick hit something that sounded like metal. There was a slight echo as if the ground was hollow. He hit it repeatedly and was convinced that it was not natural to the site. It was not the sound of stone or sand. It sounded like metal. He wanted to dig deeper but was afraid to go further with his friends nearby.

He wondered how much time had elapsed since the rain stopped. Whatever the answer, it was clearly time to return to the group. He removed a small ax from his holster and chipped away the old marker, the cross, left by either the bandit or his grandfather long ago. At no time did he foresee a problem. There was no doubt in his mind. He was convinced that he would find the spot again now that he had been there. He hastily kicked the dirt and rock rubble and threw some of the sticks and available brush back where they had been.

With deep regret he proceeded back up to the ridgeline to find his friends. He had drifted much further than he thought. Once he was up a few hundred more feet it was easy to hear them laughing and joking. Their sounds were melodic and playful, in stark contrast to the seriousness of his mindset. He was dreaming of gold as he followed their sounds. He did not know how to resolve his inner conflict, and decided to play it safe. He would have to return soon.

Epimineo Corrales trudged back to his friends. It was far steeper than he remembered. The landmarks were confusing and something was definitely wrong. At that moment nothing felt right. He was suddenly disoriented. He could hear his friends, but the sound echoed off of the various angular canyon walls below and above him. He suddenly lost faith in his ability to find them. He felt strange and very alone. Abruptly he changed his course to a more lateral path rather than vertical ascent, feeling as if a hand had gently turned him in that direction. Not doing too well on his own, he decided to go with this touch of guidance. The climb was less difficult; the direction was towards town and away from the face of the great mountain. As he topped a minor ridge he saw something familiar and was able to ascend to the place where he thought he left his friends. They were not there.

Panic began to overtake him. He felt weak and confused. He believed he heard voices somewhere further below. He began to descend and ultimately reached one of the narrow animal paths that might lead to the canyon below. The voices became louder. He was very close to his friends now and relief overcame him. He felt energized and encouraged again. His outlook was renewed.

The highs and lows of the day had been noteworthy. He had more questions than answers. More investigation would be needed. He began making plans as he came upon his friends. When he looked at them he realized that they had not moved at all, and that it was he who had become lost. Once again he was amazed at the impact of the mountain. He had traversed it for years and he was still getting lost. These thoughts were replaced with the joy of seeing his friends.

Epimineo did not discuss his strange findings. This was his secret and it was not to be shared, at least not now. He quickly restored his blood alcohol level and enjoyed the balance of the day with his companions. The mystery of the mountain drifted out of his present thought and into his memory. There would be plenty of time to deal with that. Right now he was going to enjoy the food that they saved for him and the beauty of friendship. The tug of love overcame him and the dreams of treasure withdrew to a safe place in his mind.

Circumstances beyond his control made it impossible to get back to the mountain for more than two years. He became busy with the new love in his life, and suffered through an eye infection that would have made a trip up the mountain most difficult. After that he broke his wrist and had to wait until it healed properly. He often thought about the carved cross in the rock and the possibility that he was at the secret entrance to the rumored treasure. He tried to visualize the relationship between the potential metal object and a logical opening for an underground storage vault. It all began to make sense to him.

Over time his old friends, doubt and denial, took control. His mind began playing tricks on him. Life can be cruel, with truth able to overcome fiction in scope and severity. There is not always the perfect equilibrium between the two.

Bad luck has no rules. It plays where it wants, independent of the game at hand. It can interfere with a life and impact generations in the future with a simple flutter of its independent and evil ways. Bad luck sucks you into a virtual mental whirlpool. It makes you talk to things that are not there. What is worse, you feel that they are talking back, telling you of all the ways you do not deserve success in your project or immediate goal. Fortune is what gets blamed when you are at the crossroads and make the wrong choice. It is more complex than thought, and you know it.

Epimineo's story over the years became hopeless. His friends thought he was a dreamer. Nobody believed his tales of family gold and treasure. And the few who maintained some sliver of hope could not comprehend his inability to return to a place where he had allegedly been. Nobody could understand and he felt humiliated. He may have come close to great riches and lost the opportunity.

29. THE TREASURE HUNTERS

Central California – 1971

Epimineo Corrales was no longer a young man and he had clearly lost the spring in his steps. He suffered from glaucoma and was losing his vision. His inner sight of the treasure, his memory from that fulfilling but not successful day on the mountain of his destiny, drove him onward in spite of his failing eyes. Over the years he continued to climb La Chiva countless times but never again located the site of his earlier success.

Epimineo needed help. His options were decreasing and he was losing hope. He was desperate and willing to disclose his secret of the treasure and bring in partners to ensure his success. Through a series of confident introductions and strong referrals, three American treasure hunters were recommended to help fulfill his dreams. These men had a good name for chasing various dreams and legends of hidden treasure in the mountains of California, Arizona, New Mexico, and around some of the border regions in northern Mexico. They had a favorable reputation and appeared to be trustworthy. People liked them. They were a critical link and brought knowledge and contact to other people in California and New Mexico. These three successful men shared the same exciting fascination and hobby, the eternal search for buried treasure. It was much more than passion; it was their obsession. It took almost a month for Epimineo to make the connection.

These hunters were more outspoken about their passion. When they heard about Epimineo's tale they quickly gained interest. They were on it. They collectively had a feeling that it had been a case of bad luck that kept Epimineo from returning to the treasure site.

Bob Klein was a farmer, Ben Richardson had his own dental practice, and the third, Ed Burkett, was a charter pilot. Their strong friendship had roots in their childhood. The trio thought and acted as one. They were much more than desert rats: they were self-proclaimed treasure hunters.

All had been born and raised in Bakersfield, California. If you have never been there it could easily be said that you missed nothing. The lack of adequate stimulus caused the three young boys to venture out into the surroundings and learn many of the tricks and lore that later defined their passion. They loved nature and spent countless vacations camping in the barren valley as well as the nearby southern part of the Sierra Nevada range. They did everything from desert camping to mountain and wilderness excursions. They had a fascination with nature and, as young men, honed their survival skills. They were equally at home in the arid desert areas near their homes as they were in the steep canyons and towering cliffs of the Sierras. Neither the terrain nor the climate were their adversaries. They enjoyed the challenge of extreme conditions and varied temperatures.

These gentlemen often fantasized about making a noteworthy discovery. They were young enough, strong, and energetic. When they visited the California ghost town of Bodi the seeds for a fascination with gold were developed. Whenever possible they planned tours of the paths of the Mother Lode towns and dreamed of the realities of miners of early California and the Gold Rush which began in 1848.

After a visit to Sutter's Fort in Coloma, near Sacramento, their destiny was set. They wanted to be like James Marshall and other local discoverers. They were going to be treasure hunters. This dream did not abandon them as they completed their respective educations. The fascination with legends, lore, books, rumors, and anything related to undiscovered gold, minerals, or treasure continued. It was their usual topic of conversation. The passion was deep and the time together only intensified their individual and collective commitments to make a discovery. The extent of Epimineo's treasure would be more like outer space than within the realm of their visualization. They still had work to do.

Over the years they chased their childhood dreams. They followed rumors, hunches, and stories in search of lost or buried anything. Magazines, newspaper accounts, and every form of barbershop story were taken seriously. They maintained the big dream and believed destiny would reward those who persevered.

The results were not so positive. Lost mines in Arizona ended up as dry holes. Secret sites in the desert revealed nothing but old cans, bottles and debris from previous parties in pursuit of the same or similar dreams.

Spare cash was spent on new camping equipment, metal detectors, and more trips and adventures. Ultimately they married and their wives would laugh, but the trio became more steadfast that their time was coming. They had chased more rainbows than Don Quixote, and became strangely confident that the next project would deliver the big payday. They believed they were due. Tireless were their attempts, fruitless were the results.

The effort bore its own reward, as there is universally something good about the doing. They experienced places not even on the map, including desert oasis, old camping sites, ghost towns, and vacant homesteads which still echoed the dreams of their long-departed occupants. They explored mines, caves, rivers and lakes. They followed a story wherever they could.

In time their exploration included trips into the states of Nevada, Montana, and New Mexico. Ultimately they tried their luck in Mexico, the breadbasket of treasure lore. These excursions yielded the same lack of results, nothing but a great experience together. Nevertheless, the trio felt enriched and amply rewarded by their travels. They loved the scenery, companionship and adventure, but not in that order. No failure was scarring. Each new outing promised the long-awaited result. It was a matter of numbers and they knew after each dead end they were closer to knocking on the door of a large success.

The treasure hunters developed a reputation in northern Mexico. The gringos were friendly and brought fresh hope into many wasted areas. They paid in cash and were usually quite generous to their guides and other chartered staff. Their ability to inject optimism and joy were motivating features for the others, transforming hard work into fun. Each day brought the enthusiasm that it would be "the day".

Out of sheer good fortune the positive reputation of the trio intersected with the needs of Epimineo Corrales. The aging and visually challenged grandson of the famed Military Governor was elated when he learned of the trio. Perhaps they were the answer to his prayers. The relationship appeared to be reciprocal.

After a couple of telephone conversations it was decided to fly Epimineo to San Francisco to meet and share his complete story. A prepaid round trip ticket was in the mail hours after their last conversation.

There were many big components to the expedition and they understood the risk. After some research into the history of the treasure lore, topographic maps, general soils data, old stories, Culiacan history and Epimineo's own life, a plan was conceived by the treasure hunters. They had plenty of experience with being on the losing end. Their plan for this unique situation was brilliant in its simplicity.

They met in a local hotel room paid for by the dentist, Ben. His wife was a travel agent and she had the ability to facilitate inexpensive travel plans. This was well before the Internet and the era of online everything. The meeting began almost immediately after Epimineo's arrival. They were excited, impatient, and had no time to waste. A cassette tape recorder with a portable microphone ran throughout the session and a Super 8mm movie camera on a tripod ran intermittently to document the historic meeting.

What they heard caused them to believe this was the bonanza they had been seeking since childhood. It appeared that their ship had arrived. The point of abstract reality developed into an experience of overcoming clarity. It was the deliverance from above.

After almost twenty-five years of on and off searching, they were about to become involved in the best story yet. The Treasure of La Chiva was believed to be the largest of all of the old legends of treasure in Mexico.

Epimineo shared his story in his native tongue. His less than perfect command of the English language made this necessary. Two of the men understood relatively good Spanish and they would translate for the third. Epimineo spoke slowly with very clear pronunciation. His controlled pace was well within the ability of the two.

Now in his 60's, Epimineo was a large man with a commanding presence. His voice was deep and seemed to rumble forth from his extended belly. Although none of the men wanted to visually indict him, they all silently wondered how in the world Epimineo would be able to climb any hill or mountain. Each was afraid to vocalize his concern about Epimineo's poor eyesight and heavy weight.

Unlike the trio, Epimineo was subdued. His years of defeat at the hands of the mountain gods had humbled his personality and frustrated his life. He spoke with hope and anticipation, but his words were filled with doubt. He lacked the positive excitement that was shared by his three new friends. It was a study in contrasts. He was calm and deliberate, while they were animated, excited, and fidgety.

Epimineo easily convinced them about the existence of the treasure. The facts sounded true. The gentlemen were almost immediately sure that this would be the one they were looking for, and the fulfillment of their lifelong dreams. It was real and they could feel it.

Epimineo took an hour to talk about the legend of the Lareanos, a band almost as large as that of the famed Pancho Villa. There were obvious marketing parallels and personal clichés that would be beneficial if the men were successful and the legend was harvested. Both of the famed bandits had a classic leadership style and a stature larger than life itself. Lareano rode his trademark brown stallion, while Pancho Villa had Siete Lagunas. The life stories of the two major bandits had different endings. They were two men with opposite levels of fame. That would change if the combined efforts of Epimineo's new team were successful. The "if" was large and presumptuous at this time.

The meeting went on for endless hours. Epimineo talked around some of the key areas of his life, and appeared to resent interruptions or piercing questions, being reluctant to take responsibility for his personal trials. The men were perceptive of this trait and exhibited great patience as they listened to him ramble and labor through the story of his life, upbringing, family, country, and tradition.

The attention level increased when Epimineo Corrales spoke about the history of Lareano Garcia and his band, goals, community respect, and deeds. The details helped backfill the attributes, tenacity, and sheer nerve of this bold regional hero. The story of the Lareanos has percolated, grown, expanded, and later shrunk over the last hundred years. The lack of tangible evidence of the fortune mitigated the potential for truth. Time can erode even great mountains. The church never acknowledged the theft. The bandit had been publicly buried almost a century ago. The men made a note to check for his gravestone when they visited. Their list of questions and tasks was growing.

No part of Lareano's reported treasure was ever discovered, or even formally acknowledged. The story appeared to be a dead end to the general public, one of hundreds of Mexican treasure stories. Every town had a number of their own local tales. Epimineo knew differently. His conviction was contagious. His conclusions were obvious. The history of his own family was illustrative of so much. His grandfather's wealth was known and acknowledged, his family position was solid and intact. His father had never been prone to exaggeration, and the descriptions of the infamous family trips were vividly engrained in his heritage. To all of that could be added Epimineo's own visit to the area outside of the cache.

The story took an intense turn when Epimineo talked about the mountain, La Chiva. The men were not sure if he was describing it as a friend or foe. His emotional state was shaky on this subject. His admiration was evident, but this respect bordered upon fear. His voice was crackly and his demeanor was noticeably different. His eyes widened when he spoke about the middle and upper layers or elevations, the zone of the cat. El Tigre was not a metaphor for Epimineo; it was alive and very real. The cat was more than a symbol. It was a living, breathing, terrifying animal intent upon protecting its sacred hunting grounds and all that lies within his domain. To Epimineo, the big cat bore the qualities of a protective spirit. It was on the prowl and kept all life, both human and animal, away from its home.

Epimineo was talking at his own pace and on his own agenda. Nobody bothered to interrupt or question him. The men wondered how this cat could live so long. They made a note to check on the life span of the local predator cat species with the hopes that their research could obliterate their own developing concerns. They also wanted to learn if the legendary felines could have progeny nearby, especially if they appear to be alone.

The men jumped in unison when there was a loud knock on the door. It was room service bringing the sandwiches and beverages ordered hours before and scheduled for delivery at this hour. One of the men looked at his watch and was shocked to see how much time had elapsed. The hours merged into minutes for the trio whenever treasure was discussed. This story was more real than ever before.

Epimineo was famished and devoured his plate. He also consumed three full cups of coffee with cream and heavy doses of sugar before the taping resumed. The flow of caffeine prepared him for the late evening to follow.

When they formally resumed Epimineo talked in depth about his many sojourns to the fabled mountain. The men understood his story of frustration and the rebuke by La Chiva. It bore a parallel with their history. Though from different cultures the men had a common set of experiences. They all had been searching for their entire adult lives. They all spoke in terms of survivorship rather than victory. It was a time for a change in their luck.

The description of the hot, dry, endless trips to La Chiva made Epimineo's story more credible. He was dedicated and indefatigable. Only father time was having his way.

The men observed Epimineo had become animated yet emotional when he talked about his accidental discovery of the old treasury as the thunderstorm exploded around him. He disclosed the specific details of the discovery of the carved cross and his decision to postpone entry into the hidden chamber. As he spoke, the men saw the glimmer of light on gold coins and other objects in their mind's eye. They were transported into Lareano's secret lair with the utterance of every word. Eureka!

For years Epimineo had not trusted his friends and companions with his obsession for the treasure. Now, time was not on his side. He had made the decision to tell his story to literal strangers because life had forced him to change his ways. He was aging and going blind. These men appeared to be worthy of his trust. More important, he accepted that he had no choice.

The treasure hunters were pleased to hear of Epimineo's search for the ideal partners and felt honored to be selected to help. The goodwill developed on their trips to Mexico was paying dividends in their credibility. Fortunately, their reputation was known and positive, especially since they had no results. On the treasure ledger they were losers.

One by one they quietly interrupted the story and interjected questions about what he saw at the site. They wanted to know more and more specifics, as if additional words would teleport them to the doorway to the Treasure of La Chiva.

Epimineo shared their excitement and devoted sufficient time to describe, in more detail, all that he saw and experienced on that rainy day. He felt good as he bathed in the mental victory of that single occasion. They were disappointed that Epimineo did not have any direct knowledge or experience of the interior layout, access, or dimensions. He did not know what was inside other than by speculating and expanding upon the gifts his grandfather had generously and frequently bestowed upon the family. Without having visited the site it became clear that the men could not comprehend how or why Epimineo was unsuccessful in finding the exact location on his many returns to La Chiva. It was a fundamental truth that once discovered, the second sighting of almost anything could be more easily made.

At the next break Ed went to his adjoining room and telephoned a respected friend. He had a burning question and could not wait for an answer. After pleasantries and an overview he made his position clear.

The question for Blaine Court was simple and direct, and was the threshold to their approach. "Is it possible for somebody to develop a deep psychological block and find himself physically unable to return to the place where they incurred the specific psychological trauma or injury?"

Blaine was not exactly happy with the late hour of the call and asked what was wrong with his friend. Were they onto something or merely at the affect of an excessive quantity of alcohol? After a brief recap of the events, including a discussion of the bandit, the storm, and the cat, Blaine found himself better able to understand the context, circumstances, and depth of the true inquiry.

Blaine was ready for the real question, which was asked second-arily. "Is it possible for someone with a deep fear to return to the site of the incipient event under hypnosis and regain full memory of the site?"

The answer was an unqualified and simple word, "Yes."

Blaine Court began packing within the hour. He intended to drive to the hotel near the San Francisco International Airport (SFO) very early the next morning to meet Epimineo.

It was after midnight when the recorder was turned off and the 8 mm movie camera shut down. Epimineo was drained and three new friends were equally tired. It had been a long day and much ground had been covered. By this point Epimineo had described in detail his frustration at the hand (or foot) of La Chiva and the impact of his wasted life's efforts. He hoped his new friends, Ed, Ben and Bob, could help him recover his grandfather's treasure and thereby validate his own lifelong process.

The subjective benefits of sleep were lost that evening on the men. They were collectively too excited about the potential adventure ahead. By breakfast they had agreed upon a plan and couldn't wait to present their proposal to Epimineo. Their concept was simple. An easier plan has a higher percentage of success. Although that philosophy had never yielded results, they had a unanimous belief that as complexity increases the results decrease. Not one of the three ever found the irony in the clash between their beliefs and their absolute absence of results. Man has a way of overlooking numerous slips to always focus on the goal ahead. It was a healthy component of an optimist's tool chest and an indicator of a healthy state of mind.

30. HOTEL LOS TRES RIOS

Culiacan – 1972

Epimineo joined his American friends at a small hotel located at the junction of three rivers towards the south end of town. The men rose in unison as Epimineo entered the dining room. Almost five months had passed since their first gathering near San Francisco and the men had been busy. They began by meeting with Blaine Court six days after Epimineo flew home, at which time they gave him a transcript of the tapes and selected strips from the filming. The trio had retained a pair of professional stenographers to transcribe the tapes and paid overtime for the quick results.

Blaine was known to the trio for many years and stood in a position of trust and respect. They were not concerned with his ability to maintain their secret. Blaine was an editor of a small newspaper in his hometown and always protected his sources. Among his other talents, Blaine was a gifted hypnotherapist, creative writer, and new age thinker. He was Spartan in his appearance and Athenian in his diversity and breadth of knowledge.

Blaine was the perfect person to add to this adventure. He joined the group with the intended role of putting Epimineo in a hypnotized state, thereby removing the personal psychological and emotional blocks incurred on the mountain and permitting him to return to the place he had been before, the perfectly hidden entrance to the treasure. It sounded simple and easy. After all, Epimineo had been there before.

While the trio had been purchasing the required tools and supplies, Blaine had prepared a personal profile on Epimineo Corrales along with a timeline of events and a list of repeated terms and phrases from his taped discourse. By graphing the frequency of Epimineo's words and phrases, Blaine believed he had found the hot buttons or touchy spots beyond which Epimineo was afraid to proceed. It was his belief that these impediments were part of the barrier to success.

Blaine's objective was to hypnotize Epimineo at the start of the trail and hope for a hypnotic mental state free of family issues, criticism, betrayal, unworthiness, generalized apprehension, fear of the cat, and his health issues and limitations. The hypothesis was centered upon the belief that the isolation of these huge barriers could permit Epimineo's subconscious mind to retrace his own footsteps and proceed directly to the source of the treasure.

Blaine was a firm believer and vocal advocate of positive intention and the power of the subconscious mind. He often voiced his personal philosophy, "We create our own reality." He wanted to help Epimineo relax and permit him to return to his hidden goal. That was the theory.

Epimineo was happy to see Blaine again. He was comforted by this unique American and remembered feeling that way when they first met at the hotel in California. It was something about his silver gray beard, strong jagged features, beautiful blue eyes, calming voice, and the turquoise arrowhead he wore around his neck. It was a reassuring package that inspired most everyone he met.

Epimineo had been able to instantly perceive the trust and respect that his new American friends felt in Blaine. The confidence was contagious. Epimineo understood that this kind man was going to talk to him in some strange manner, relax him, and put him into a trance state. After that occurred, Blaine intended to take him back to the thunderstorm day when he found the opening to the cave.

Nothing is more powerful than an idea that is right in its time. For Epimineo Corrales it was his magic moment. Tomorrow was the day and they were ready. Tomorrow he would climb the perilous mountain up to the site of the hidden treasure, find the secret entrance, and realize his dreams. Tomorrow he would honor his father and grandfather, as well as restore the family legacy. Tomorrow he would be healed from the mountains of guilt he carried following years of failure. Tomorrow his neighbors and friends would stop laughing at him and mocking his failures. Tomorrow he would become well again, and very rich too.

31. TIME HAS COME TODAY

Culiacan - 1972

Blaine heard three small knocks on his door and couldn't believe he had overslept. He never used or even needed an alarm clock. He was always able to set a time in his mind to awaken. What made this more unusual was the fact that he never wore a watch. Time was a relative phenomenon to him. He lived in what he called "the now" and was capable of responsibly conforming to the needs of others. Today was an exception, and the knocks brought him out of a deep, dreamy sleep.

He opened the door to realize that he had not overslept. Ed, the charter pilot, had a question. Epimineo had called and wanted to bring a friend named Oscar along. He claimed it was a matter of comfort to him. Ed questioned the concept and wondered if the presence of Oscar would interfere with the posthypnotic suggestion or the innocent pursuit of the goal. After all, the friends and family had been a source of Epimineo's pressure for the previous two decades. They might just be scapegoats for his inner failures, but the impact was worthy of discussion.

Blaine saw nothing wrong with the addition of the sixth member of their party, and noted that the rental van had the right number of comfortable seats. He dismissed the unusual change in behavior as a matter of fact. True, Epimineo had committed his whole life to keeping knowledge of the treasure from most of his friends, but bringing one along at his moment of personal triumph was not extraordinary. Now was now, and nothing should be deduced from this apparent change. Blaine quickly returned to sleep and the rest of the night passed uninterrupted.

The excited treasure hunters gathered at the appointed hour. The van was already loaded and a tarp concealed the provisions in the rear cargo area. Their secret mission was unobservable to the casual onlooker.

Blaine approached from the hotel at the exact same time as Epimineo and his friend, Oscar. Introductions proceeded, greetings were exchanged, and the hexamerous team boarded the van with a unified vision of good fortune. They collectively believed that their lives would be changed before nightfall.

It was almost instantaneously realized by the treasure hunters that Oscar was joining the group at the request of Epimineo without any knowledge of their goal. He bore a clear distaste for the Americans and had an openly hostile and distrusting attitude. He was merely along for the ride and unaware of the destination. Blaine wondered why he was invited at the last moment.

Oscar spoke not a word. His dark eyes maintained a downward gaze and his face bore a frown. His worn brown boots were his visual focus rather than the other men or the surroundings. The trio was concerned about the obvious negativity and antisocial behavior. The ride out of town was silent but for the occasional sound of rocks from the road bouncing up against the undercarriage of the Ford van.

The driver, Bob, had topo maps and local road maps. This was before GPS and portable personal direction devices. The roads were adequately marked and he had committed his initial course to memory. The silent ride continued as they left town. The anxiety level increased. The air became thick and tense. Oscar sat in the center back seat with Epimineo to his left and Blaine to his right. Epimineo also looked downward with an unreadable expression as they proceeded onward.

After about thirty minutes outside of Culiacan, Blaine made a comment in Spanish that broke the silence and put a smile on the faces of Epimineo and Oscar. "Mucho trabajo, poco dinero."

Their stiff demeanor softened and the change was noticeable. The trio appreciated Blaine's perceptive good humor and welcomed the change in attitude. "Lots of work, little money."

Bob followed this break by turning on the radio to a local station and humming along with pop tunes, sounding somewhat like Michael Jackson in Spanish. The mood became more jovial the further they were from Culiacan. The difference was so noticeable that Blaine thought he misread the initial reaction, at least for now.

There were no further surprises as they proceeded toward their destination. Nobody else was on the road so the group was confident that they were not being followed.

The excitement grew as Epimineo pointed out Tacamonte towering out of the right side of the van. As they proceeded further into the canyon area they could see La Chiva to the left. La Chiva was strong, sheer, and forbidding. The sun had yet to rise over its crest.

It was only with La Chiva in sight that Epimineo explained the mission to his friend. They were going to climb part of the way up La Chiva and find his grandfather's treasure. Oscar's services were needed to help carry things and he was promised generous wages for his efforts. Attitudes improved and again the group appeared to be of united purpose.

Epimineo directed Bob to the best place to park. The Americans stared in awe as they got out of the van. The scale was greater than anticipated. The mountain was large and complex in formation. Ridges, cuts, and elevated plateaus added to the depth and complexity of the task. There were few identifying features above the tree line. Below it was thick, dark, and mysterious. From their vantage point, it appeared that they would be looking for a needle in the haystack.

Some of the enthusiasm was lost as the scope of the ascent was silently calculated by each of the Americans. It looked like a tough day ahead. That sucker was steep. Of course, none of them expected the treasure to be at or even near the peak.

Epimineo was having a "deliverance" form of experience. He possessed a high degree of confidence in his American partners and his current best friend was at his side. At the present moment he exhibited neither fear nor apprehension. His mind was filled with glorious excitement and a renewed sense of self-confidence.

The brief explanation of the mission ignited Oscar in a unique manner. He became another person entirely. He was excited, animated, talkative, and full of life. His realization that he was a participating member rather than an observer increased his involvement and heightened his awareness. He transformed from acting isolated and withdrawn into being one of the group. He offered to help the others unload the truck and was quick to volunteer and carry some of the heaviest gear. On a selfish level, he realized that he could quit his horrible job if they were success-ful. He was converted into a partner, a player, and a future rich man. He felt lucky and grateful. These Americans were becoming his best friends for the moment.

The liberating impact on Oscar's personality was easy to observe. He was part of a new team and he was happy. He shifted to being cooperative, involved, and even supportive. He was the youngest member of the group and wanted to carry the heaviest pack. That one contained the crowbars, short-handled shovels, and other heavy tools.

Epimineo led the group across the flats of Tacamonte Canyon, over the stream, and to the gap between the two fence posts that bore faintly carved crosses. Epimineo pointed out the carvings to all of them. When convinced of the fact that they were gathered at the first known and verified marker, Blaine and Epimineo went off by themselves to begin the hypnosis procedure.

Epimineo was an ideal subject and had a pre-determined posi-tive predilection towards the process. He trusted Blaine and was confident of their goal. Blaine removed the turquoise arrowhead from his neck and began the process. His voice remained soft, calming and gentle. Epimineo underwent the suggestion easily, seemed to act younger and stronger, and bounded off with the other five men following quickly behind.

Epimineo traversed the base, chose a specific course or direc-tion, and began the ascent with manifest confidence in every step. At times he would stop, survey the terrain, and point to a clump of bushes blocking an unseen path. It was as if he could see things that the others could not. He was functioning from an altered state of consciousness.

Blaine believed Epimineo was following an invisible marker in his mind. It was going easier than anticipated and everyone was as positive as could be under the circumstances. It was a per-fect day for uncovering the treasure. The temperature was rising quickly and the air was already hot, dry and still. It promised to be a scorcher. Fortunately, their path was still in the shade. Their foot-steps made crackling sounds on the loose pebbles and dry brush as they silently continued their ascent. All was well at the moment.

Epimineo led the ascent on the narrow path in single file, with Oscar following Blaine and the trio trailing behind. While not superstitious, the group was clearly cautious. They did not want to distract Epimineo. Not a sound was uttered for fear that it would change their good luck.

After fifteen minutes or so, Epimineo stopped at an upright elongated rock perhaps three feet high and pointed to the rear about a foot above the ground. A small cross was clearly visible. The men smiled in unison as they connected to the history and the landmarks Epimineo had disclosed in the Bay Area hotel room. Oscar did not understand the significance of the marker, but observed the positive reactions of the others and took it to be a good sign.

Six men were climbing silently in single file and not a word was spoken. Epimineo was still leading the way in a blissful trance, followed by Oscar at least ten yards behind, then the trio of adventurers, with Blaine now bringing up the rear. Blaine let the others pass because he wanted to take in the whole scene. The fact that he was the oldest may have also been a factor. The man in the rear could go as slow as he wanted.

The happy party continued up the hill. For some reason Blaine began sensing a problem in the making. A hidden knowing overtook his awareness and a silent alarm was going off. Blaine didn't know what could be wrong, but he had an inner knowing, an intuitive instinct. It was a feeling that he usually trusted to be accurate. His senses told him all was not well in the kingdom. They were in danger. This was not a usual state for Blaine, who viewed his experiences through a positive frame of mind and an ever-youthful spirit. He was the oldest in years of the group hiking up the almost invisible trail yet he was concurrently the most youthful and open.

It was often said by his friends that Blaine was unique in the entire world. He spoke with a higher power and tapped into a true altered reality. Simply stated, Blaine was alive, awake, and aware of everything around him and was not clouded by his personal objectives, wishes or desires. He could sense something unusual.

Blaine remained alert and observant as the team tracked onward towards their secret destination. His scan included the five men ahead of him. Footsteps on the pounded earth were muffled and smooth, a percussion of twelve feet marching to one drummer.

The air was still and silent. The day was becoming hot and the atmosphere felt dense. The men were all sweating profusely but continued climbing without complaint. There were neither sounds of birds nor animal life. It was doubted if many humans ventured into the area. The animals, rodents, and whatever else lived at the lower levels of the mountain were safely tucked into their holes, nests, or hiding places. It was too uncomfortable outside.

The trail could even be considered hostile. The brush was thick, dry and thorny. The browns had a hue of gray and the greens were dull and dusty. Nature was not happy at the base of this mountain and the benefits of the annual rains had long since been erased.

The muted sounds of footsteps created a rhythm of their own. The tone was one of toil. The men continued slowly onward and upward, each deep within his own thought process. Not one was brave enough to break the silence. All were developing some percentage of negativity and doubt about their own strength and ability to complete the difficult ascent. It was worse than expected, and the heat did not help.

The sun cleared the top of La Chiva and the men marched into the sunshine. The rise in temperature was noticeable and the trio reached for their canteens almost simultaneously, as if responding in unison to some hidden signal or cue. It was dusty and hot.

After ten more grueling minutes they reached the true base of the main face of La Chiva and Epimineo suddenly stopped for a break. This was a welcome relief for all as they sat together and made small talk. The break in the silence brought comfort and everyone spoke of the steep angle of ascent and the heat. In spite of the rising mercury it was all smiles on the outside.

Blaine looked at the seemingly contented group and began to doubt his earlier feelings of alarm and warning. He wondered if it was mere apprehension or nervous anxiety, or an attempt at balancing the optimistic joy he anticipated when they would be finding the treasure spot later that very day. It was a case of mitigating the excitement, or so he thought. He sought balance and maintained inner control.

The men resumed their ascent on no specific signal. Epimineo was suddenly ready and he rose and continued again with the others in hot pursuit. He demonstrated the energy of a man ten to fifteen years his junior. The rest break was apparently beneficial to all of them. They climbed with a renewed vigor and sense of confidence in their strides. Oscar backed off and walked in the rear with Blaine. He seemed to feel more at ease with this man. That experience was not out of the ordinary for Blaine. He just had a naturally disarming way with people.

They made eye contact, smiled, and then nodded to each other in a way that acknowledged their mutual delight with the adventure at hand. They were hiking towards a treasure that had been secreted away and buried well over a century before. They were climbing towards a new history. The impact of opening Epimineo's legendary family treasure would change the lives of generations to come for all of their families, their communities, and more.

Oscar was quick to realize that his part in the discovery of the treasure would bring him instant recognition, fame and fortune. He was a simple man with ordinary roots and little motivation. Nothing special had ever happened to either Oscar or anyone in his family. All would change today thanks to the generosity of his friend, Epimineo, and the secret he had been hiding within for most of his life. It was a pleasant surprise.

Occasionally Epimineo would stop and canvas the area. His eyes would scan from the left to the right and back again a few times like a windshield wiper in slow motion. After that he would select a direction and continue as if guided by an inertial device deep within his brain. His eyes were glazed and his demeanor was distant. He was clearly on automatic drive. As before, not a word was spoken. He was a homing pigeon going back to a place in his personal history. He was functioning on autopilot.

The treasure hunters were not of like mind at this moment. Ed was thinking about the treasure and was mentally counting his wealth. He clearly had his cart before the horse. He thought about what he would do with his portion of the treasure and how he would spend the money. He visualized the end to his history of personal financial struggle. His children were in college and the economic drain had created friction at home. His childhood dreams were about to be realized. They were going to open their first treasure today.

The dentist's focus was in another place. Ben was having a pure out-of-body experience that labored towards their secret fulfillment. The treasure was very real to him. His personality was such that each failure, every dry hole, only served to strengthen his resolve and prepare him for the next. He had the optimism of a salesman and the resilience of a wrestler. He was a treasure hunter, whether successful or not. This day was of extreme importance because it was the day of revelation, the day when his childhood dreams and fantasies would be finally fulfilled. In his mind's eye he could already see the area around the trap door opening to Lareano's cave as described at the hotel by Epimineo. He saw the images through Epimineo's failing eyes and he knew the vision was true. He felt joy for Epimineo, his friends, and especially the people of the region. Their discovery would bring hope and a renewed sense of strength to the locals. Each could again believe that a dream could be true. It was a Walt Disney moment. He felt elation for the bandit too, understanding the liberation of the treasure would revitalize his story and renew the tired legend. Lareano Garcia would move from an old forgotten myth to his rightful status of major local hero.

His mind went to his college buddy, Blaine, who was walking behind. Blaine had been a serious student of the school of ancient mysteries and believed that every myth, legend, and allegory was very real. He was a full-grown child. His vigorous support was ever-present and Blaine never laughed at any of the stories of the next dream. Blaine offered true and unconditional support. Blaine rarely blamed, criticized, or judged. He thought about the irony of that fact since Blaine's surname was Court. True friendship was accessed and acknowledged. It was wonderful having him here for this personal moment of triumph. It was a milestone, a graduation, and an initiation to a higher purpose.

Things kept changing for the third American. The farmer, Bob, was a contrast of almost simultaneous highs and lows. He was excited about the prospects before them, enjoying the adventure with his friends, yet struggling physically with the ascent. He was in the worst shape of the trio, greatly overweight, and not mentally

prepared for the difficulty of the climb. La Chiva was already getting to him, and they had yet to reach the major part of the ascent.
He was becoming angry. He was hot, tiring quickly, getting rude
and impatient. Thoughts of failure were beginning to creep into
his mind and he was becoming irritated with the heat, stickiness,
and occasional flying critter. He was out of condition and running
low on energy. His discomfort was gnawing at him and he tried
to fight back all doubt and negative thoughts as they followed
Epimineo up to their dream-fulfilling destination.

He was wondering how in the world they could extricate anything from this site. The logistics were complicated. He looked
up to the imposing rocky white face of La Chiva towering above
them and wondered how far they would have to go. With every
few steps he gained greater clarity of how Epimineo Corrales
could traverse this mountain for years without knowing where he
was and then, after stumbling upon the site in adverse weather
conditions, being unable to return. Things were just that strange
up here.

Epimineo stopped abruptly in front of a very large rock and
looked left and right a few times. He seemed stumped and decided
to sit and rest. Epimineo was breathing heavily and had a look on
his face that could be described as troubled or confused. As the
men caught up with him they summoned Blaine forth to assess
the situation. Although not a doctor, Blaine believed fatigue was
the only problem. Epimineo was in a mental state similar to thirty-
nine years previous, but physically Father Time had clearly taken
his toll on the body. Epimineo appeared to be happy, alert, and
still deeply connected with the goal. The intense heat could easily
be a contributing problem. They would just need to hydrate more
often and expand their rest periods.

Blaine had a dual role that was neither assigned nor acknowledged by the others. When he began reviewing the tapes he
decided to take notes about the key visual points in Epimineo's testimony, if you would call it that. He wanted to utilize the transcript
and tapes as a reality check to ensure the alleged purity of the
process and increase the chances for success. After all, he didn't
want to find himself chasing Epimineo and his new friends all over
some blasted mountain in Mexico, especially not at his age.

Blaine was the oldest of the Americans, but his exact age remained his secret. He hid behind his youthful looks and bubbling inner spirit. To Blaine, age was just a number, nothing more. His knees were starting to disagree and his heart was raising its own objections too.

Blaine had experimented with hypnotherapy for many years. It was a glorified hobby and part of his study of consciousness and altered states. He was not a treasure hunter and his personal philosophy was that life in and of itself is a true miracle. He had never been involved in a project of this nature. His experience with hypnosis had been limited to helping friends and associates stop smoking, lose weight, relax before exams or important job interviews, and other life experiences of that genre. He had also used hypnosis as part of past life regression therapies popular in California and New York during the 1960's and early 1970's. Although he had advised his friends that their objectives were sound with this regression of Epimineo, he had zero history with this modality of therapy. He was winging it based upon intuition and some reading. His confidence made up for his lack of expertise.

Blaine had made a bold representation and was charting in unknown personal territory. His research had revealed numerous papers claiming the very objective as a potentiality for hypnotherapy, but success here would be its own reward. Others had performed similar services, and Blaine did not consider failure as an option. It all seemed to make sense to him. He trusted his instincts and the group was climbing La Chiva at that moment because of his faith in the process.

Though he never traveled with the trio on their quests before, he was with them in story and spirit many times. He had vicariously joined his friends on many of their wild ventures. He shared their failures and would always add a positive spin to keep them motivated for the next opportunity. The rewards were in the doing.

This was a very special extension of the friendship, because Blaine had been invited along to co-experience their earth-shaking achievement. He had been living the possibilities since his early morning encounter with Epimineo in California. Now they were in Mexico and this was that special day chosen for the realization of their fantasy.

Oscar looked at the group sitting together. He felt like an out-sider and had nothing in common with the others. He was isolated by language and somewhat distrustful of the Americans. He had neither sunglasses nor a hat. He was overheating and the sun was almost blinding him.

The break ended quickly as Epimineo again rose without notice and resumed his slow but steady ascent. From this point he aimed the party around the huge rock with the pointed face and up to the right along something resembling an animal path. It looked like they were on a deer path, though they doubted the existence of deer in that area. To their perception the land did not appear to support large animal life. It was unusually warm and dry. The only living things they had witnessed in the area were small chipmunk-like rodents, until one saw the snake.

It happened in a second. A medium sized diamondback rattler crossed the path between the second and third treasure hunter. Blaine watched in shock as the third man, Bob, instinctively reached back into his pack, extracted a revolver, and shot at the snake. It happened in an instant and it was over. The snake was safe but the expedition was not.

The magnitude of the exploding bullet was exaggerated by the echo off of the mountain, surrounding hills, and the canyon below. It sounded even louder to each of the hikers because of the contrast. The most noticeable sounds up to that point were those of heavy deep breaths and shuffling feet. That changed in a brief instant, as did the outcome of their undertaking.

The blast of the exploding bullet reverberated throughout time and space. It shocked Epimineo out of his blissful trance. It also provoked the worst possible reaction from Oscar. At that moment his fear and distrust of the foreigners reached its apex. He had already felt outnumbered in the classical sense. Now he was out-armed too. It was too much for Oscar. He could not figure out why one of the Americans had a gun, and he let his wandering mind and negative attitude assume the worse. Epimineo's friend lost all logic and reason, and took things to an impossible new low. It turned out to be past the point of no return.

Oscar was the most reactive one in the group. His behavior bor-dered on out of control. It had nothing to do with the poisonous

snake. His reaction was to the gringos bearing guns. Oscar was pro-
testing loudly to Epimineo. His voice was animated and his body
language was extreme. The presence of the handgun frightened
him. He wrongly concluded that there were more. He wondered
why the men had guns and could not think of any rational reason
to bring a firearm on a treasure hunt. He ascribed evil intentions
to the Americans. His illogical conclusion was communicated to
Epimineo. Oscar was sure the visitors intended to double-cross
Epimineo and kill both Epimineo and Oscar on the spot once the
treasure was uncovered. Oscar was convinced they would never
live to leave the mountain. The Americans were going to kill them.

Their conversation occurred out of the hearing range of the
Americans, whom had all rushed to where Bob was standing with
the pistol held limply in his right hand. They were interrupting
each other with questions about what happened and why. His two
original partners were surprised to know that a gun was brought.
It had never been discussed. They questioned whether or not the
snake was any form of threat. The lack of Bob's judgment was
forcefully criticized. Unfortunately, the bell could not be un-rung
and some serious damage had been done. They did not realize the
severity at that moment, but it was irreparable.

Blaine was thoroughly frustrated with the whole situation. All
of their efforts were thwarted with the stupid gunshot. He had yet
to consider the consequences if the firearm had been detected by
customs upon entering the country. Epimineo was already known
to be strongly in fear avoidance and capable of superstitious influences and suggestions. The problem was compounded by various
factors including the alarming breach of the silence and the sub-
sequent anxiety amplified by Oscar's rant.

The fragile situation had been thrown into chaos with the loud
discharge of the handgun. The human constitution is strongly
programmed for survival. Anything that challenges our protective
instincts has an alarming and jarring impact. If the harsh blast
of the echoing firearm exploding in close proximity was not bad
enough, the excitement and Oscar's words combined to destroy
the objectives of the day.

The alarming situation had the impact of overriding the hypnotic suggestion. Epimineo had the "off" switch working. It was

easy to see. Epimineo and Oscar continued to talk while the Americans got louder and began to argue. A conspiracy of silence was reached based upon their new mutual fear of the Americans. A quick plan was concocted. They were bonded and united. Oscar said they would be safe if the mission was unsuccessful. That would be easy to achieve. When the group reunited they would walk about aimlessly as if Epimineo had lost the scent of the trail. In reality, it was true.

Unknown to Epimineo, he would no longer be able to find the precise location again even if he tried. The cumulative stress and prior fears about the mountain had now combined and been magnified. The fear of immediate death by the armed Americans was a stress of greater magnitude than the fear of the cat, feelings of unworthiness, and years of ridicule following more than thirty years of searching for the same goal. They were now dealing with an impossible mission.

After sharing a collective piece of their mind with Bob, Ed and Ben asked Blaine about the apparent impact of the startling shot upon the hypnotic suggestion and the agenda of the day. They could see Epimineo and Oscar involved in an animated conversation twenty or more yards up the trail. The articulated body language, head and hand motions revealed great agitation. It was not hard to understand. Words were not needed.

The scene was the direct opposite of the calmness and quiet of only a few minutes before. A serious problem had been created and the extent and impact had to be discovered. The six men regrouped and took a canteen break. Small talk began but the issue at hand was too uncomfortable to deal with. It was another failure. The matter was complex, and not one of these men had the ability to honestly confront and discuss their deeper feelings. Ignoring the issues was easy. Failing to deal with them was disastrous.

Blaine was the most upset of all. He felt betrayed. His personal philosophy was to avoid any situation where guns were involved or needed. It would always have to end with communicating, so why not start at the beginning? He had a great point with that.

The men acted like only old friends could, picked themselves up, ignored the present dilemma, and continued onward. No one permitted himself to inquire into the extent of the damage. The meager explanation about the alleged snake was obviously insufficient. Incidentally, the snake was not seen by any of the others, and the shot had apparently missed the target.

The Americans tried to apologize and explain what happened. Whether or not the snake story was real had not one centavo of relevance to Epimineo or Oscar. It was another seed of distrust. Epimineo did not have to fake anything. He was in another mental state and nothing that Blaine said or did could change it. The mission was a failure and the group decided to abort and return to the hotel.

The journey back down the hill was silent. Not a word was said on either the descent of La Chiva or the return to the van. If possible, it was even quieter on the ride back to town. One of the men had an Elvis cassette tape and played it to break the thick atmosphere in the van on the way back to their hotel in Culiacan. There is something soothing about the King of Rock 'n' Roll.

Blaine slept on the ride back to Hotel Los Tres Rios. He was frustrated beyond belief with his friends. The trio knew his feelings about guns. Nothing good ever happens when guns are involved. Absolutely nothing. He considered it to be a significant breach of mutual trust, and did not want to be involved further with this project.

He secretly believed that their failures could have been reversed so easily. This was the mother lode for them and it was lost for nothing. Blaine trusted Epimineo and believed the man was honest and sincere. He saw something special in Epimineo's aging eyes, and the story struck him as true. Each and every detail was believable. The sad chain of events had a degree of tragic plausibility. All was lost because of the possession and inappropriate discharge of the firearm.

The group disbanded at the hotel and, despite promises to meet soon, never united again. A few messages to Epimineo were either not received or never sufficient to elicit a response. Contact was lost.

Epimineo and Oscar went up to the mountain a few more times together during the next eight months without any luck. Oscar gave up hope and decided the story was a pure fabrication by Epimineo and an attempt to gain attention. Oscar went to his grave without sharing the story. He was too embarrassed, thinking that others would laugh at him for believing and acting on the words of Epimineo. This was Epimineo's folly and Oscar did not want to paint himself with the same brush. He would not acknowledge his personal trips to La Chiva in search of some sign. He thought he would know. He was wrong. He gave up quickly.

The trip to Mexico in 1972 was the last for the trio. A lifetime of chasing fantasy and dreams was too much. The economic, spiritual, and emotional baggage from so many years of searching without results was the demise of the treasure hunting club. They remained close friends but never ventured out together again. The story of La Chiva would die with them. At least that was what they believed.

32. SILENT QUESTIONS

Placencia, Belize – June 4, 2005

The *Toucan* was still anchored inside the reef about ten miles north of Placencia. The plan had called for sailing to Laughing Bird Caye but the impact of Ellis Stevens' story kept us fixed in place. The boat had not moved for two full days and yet we felt like we had traveled hundreds of miles through time and space.

The crew gathered again for breakfast after a late night of treasure talk. We ate in absolute silence and nobody said a word to Ellis once he joined us. Our smiles said it all. Our minds were filled with questions but our lips did not want to move.

There was a good chance that the treasure would never be found again. We would learn more when Ellis Stevens resumed the story.

First we were going snorkeling, followed by breakfast and time to relax. I had a few hours to wonder. It still looked like the secret access died with the murder of Epimineo's grandfather in 1910.

Was this a hoax?

33. BLAINE COURT

Monterey County, CA – 1978

Little was said of Blaine for the next few years. He kept busy writing, traveling, and coordinating a few real estate transactions. Some time later he realized that he was in avoidance. It was a bad case of denial. He had a gnawing feeling that a great opportunity was lost and felt betrayed by the senseless conduct of a former team member. Blaine was having deep and depressing thoughts about the experience on the mountain in Mexico. It was eating at him. His mind was becoming filled with the story of Epimineo, his grandfather, and Lareano Garcia. He found himself daydreaming about the treasure. He was suffering through a relapse of treasure fever.

Finally, Blaine called the leader of the trio, Ben Richardson. He knew he should have checked in long ago. He had numerous questions about the status of their additional attempts in Mexico and hoped for an update. Had contact ever been reinitiated with Epimineo? Was he still alive?

Blaine's call was enthusiastically received and he quickly learned that the trio had retired from the treasure business. Not one more moment of their lives would be spent chasing dreams of treasure. They had mentally released the treasure back to the mountain and had no desire to return. It was time for them to feel satisfied and move on. They had some wonderful travels and that era was over. Their respective careers in dentistry, light air aviation, and farming all felt more comfortable to each of the three close friends.

Blaine confessed his renewed interest in the treasure. He received the approval to continue and permission to use the tapes, notes, maps, transcripts, photos, and the film footage in his possession. Though not specifically discussed, it was clearly understood that they would appreciate his generosity in the terms of a finder's fee or other gratuity if Blaine succeeded. They had invested considerable sums in searching for Epimineo's treasure and the first trip to Culiacan and to the mountain. As the direct link to Blaine's introduction to the treasure, compensating the trio would be appropriate.

Blaine was grateful for their blessing, promised to include them in the success story, if ever realized, as well as the bounty, if any. With this consent and handoff, the future of the treasure was now entrusted to Blaine Court. That was late 1978, six years after their aborted expedition.

The thoughts of the treasure permeated Blaine's days and nights. To Blaine it was a given that the treasure remained unopened and untouched. It was beckoning. He could almost hear the call in his sleep. It didn't occur to Blaine that Epimineo would try to return to La Chiva and locate the secret opening. He considered the chances to be very slight, bordering on the impossible. Even if Epimineo returned to the mountain the additional stress from the last trip would only compound his problems. History was against him again.

As time passed he became progressively more obsessed with the treasure. Like Epimineo, Blaine was suffering from an incurable case of treasure fever as he fell under its spell. He would invest his time, money, and energy in revealing its secret.

Blaine was an entrepreneur and representative of the Northern California "free spirit" movement. He believed everything was real, both seen and unseen. He possessed a faith in science and the spiritual dimensions simultaneously. He was an editor of one of the local Carmel alternative newspapers and was a regular on the old-timers weekend radio talk shows. Blaine was perfect in that role, bringing a calming influence and fresh perspective to even the most complex issues raised by the panelists or callers.

Blaine presented a dynamic example of the power of positive thinking. He saw great health as a virtue and every day presented a unique opportunity for growth and enjoyment. He always enjoyed a challenge. He was a throwback to the hippie time yet respectable because of his stature in the community. Blaine was known to coordinate and host parties for political causes and yet there was talk that he never voted.

Blaine's home was located high on a cliff and consisted of a series of former water tanks. The round structures were joined at the midpoints, and may have looked like a large hamster habitat from above. The terrific crash of the Pacific Ocean three hundred feet below made visitors wonder about the certainty of their footing. I was surprised this gentle and peaceful man had the strength to live on the edge of the earth so close to windy Hurricane Point. The name itself reveals everything one needs to know about this portion of the California coastline.

Hurricane Point is intense during a storm. Gale force winds join pelleting rain, hitting the windows with such impact it sounds like a series of machine gun shots. With the pressure of a fire hose the wind and rain shake the place until you wonder: Nature's pressure wash? How safe was this place? Could it withstand the tremendous blasts of the elements? Will the old foundation hold? Did Blaine ever have doubts here?

I remember the night I was invited to join the project. It was 1981. Blaine was convinced the time had come to return to Culiacan. He had been assembling a team to help verify the achievement, fortify the legend, and honor his vision of the project, which was the improvement of the region's educational system. He was convinced that he maintained this directive on behalf of Lareano himself. He envisioned new classrooms, teachers, books and supplies. Blaine never spoke of his own education or the personal basis for this focus.

The Government of Mexico would be the largest benefactor of the discovery. Like many sovereign nations, Mexico had enacted confiscatory laws making all treasure found within its physical geographical borders and coastal territorial waters the property of the government. Blaine had his own ideas and developed an alternate plan that he considered to be fair and equitable. Of course he had his own plan! Why not?

For the people of the Culiacan area, Blaine saw the treasure as a reaffirmation of their roots, a validation of their traditions, and a potential release of some economic suffering. He saw a great need, and the treasure could fulfill many aspects.

For Lareano Garcia, to whom credit must be given for the treasure itself, it would honor his memory as a true revolutionary, a spirited leader, one of the boldest rebels against the control of the church and state, and one of the most brazen bandits in the colorful history of Mexico.

For history buffs and dreamers everywhere, it was a true bonanza. It would renew faith and hope for the small guy.

It was a different story for the church. It was another black eye during a time that the church was under attack in America and in other parts of the world for having stolen so much from so many. Part of the noble history of the church was tarnished with shame.

For the students of the area it was a literal gold mine, a lifting of the burdens obstructing education for one and all. There would be plenty of money for schools for a long, long time to come.

For the new age buffs, a major, if not tangible validation on the world stage of the value and truth of intuition, channeling and other metaphysical realities. That is because Blaine had a plan to provide clear and convincing evidence that knowledge was structured in consciousness and truth could be accessed by very strange means. Blaine ensured that forces were at work, which were part of the paranormal.

For Epimineo, the unearthing of the treasure would provide vindication, release, fame, and financial gain. His honor would be restored and he would be considered a current-day folk hero.

For grandfather, Jesus Borella, it would not present a desired outcome. He would never want anyone to find it. The treasure was his and would remain so as long as it was never discovered and touched.

The burning passion of the treasure became a full time endeavor for Blaine. He neglected his regular duties and became consumed with solving its riddle. Blaine read and studied the transcripts from Epimineo's visit to the California hotel. He paid special attention to the descriptions of landmarks and looked for similarities and patterns. He repeated the tapes so often that he was close to memorizing portions of the content. He was developing a clear picture.

34. IN SEARCH

Sayulita – 1979

Blaine needed additional information to continue after the hand-off. He needed to know if Epimineo was still alive and available to help him. After hours of investigation and dozens of telephone calls, Blaine learned that Epimineo had moved from Culiacan to Los Mochis, and ultimately to Sayulita, in the state of Nayarit. A trip to Mexico was required, and plans were made for a visit to the only known living person who had allegedly been at the secret opening to the treasure. Now in his early seventies and with his vision failing, Blaine clung to the desperate hope that Epimineo could still describe the surroundings to the treasure site. Were there features of note in the rocks? Trees? Shapes? How close to the edge? How large or small was the overhang? How high up the mountain? How far from the main face? The questions could be endless.

Blaine took an American Airlines flight from San Francisco to Puerto Vallarta with the hope of finding and meeting with Epimineo. After clearing customs, he hired a driver for the short fifty-minute ride north to Sayulita. Blaine fell in love with this small seaside fishing village before he even finished the short descent into town. The bay was colorful, a beautiful mix of the hillside jungle forest tapering down to the Pacific Ocean below. Sayulita reminded him of the Northern California town of Sausalito, with the hillside land sloping down to the water's edge. The similarity was also noted with the name of the adjoining town being San Francisco for both.

Like most of the towns and cities associated with this adventure, Sayulita bore the classic mix of traditional heritage, entropy, and an attempt at modernization. It exhibited the shell of a third world community emerging into modern times. The contrasts were evident wherever one looked. Old and new.

Blaine gave the address to the taxi driver and then tried to contain his anxiety as they made their journey to Epimineo's last known forwarding address. His head was filled with questions and there was only one person who could help. Blaine prayed that Epimineo was in decent health and still at that location. Otherwise the trail would be cold and the adventure terminated without results. Epimineo was once again critical to proceeding.

Blaine felt at ease as the cab stopped in front of a very small traditional house. The bright yellow structure was trimmed in royal blue. Epimineo was sitting alone outside on the porch. Blaine's heart swelled and waves of excitement overcame him as he approached. There was still hope. The only surviving person who had actually been to the Treasure of La Chiva was sitting in a rocking chair before him. Any stress or difficulty associated with finding Epimineo dissolved away as a new chapter of the treasure story was about to begin. Blaine was elated to see Epimineo.

It was apparent that Epimineo's vision was failing. He could not identify the stranger as he came through the gate. Epimineo's look was questioning. When Blaine spoke to Epimineo and introduced himself a big smile formed on his face. It was his good friend from America, Mr. Blaine.

Epimineo felt instantly at ease and invited Blaine to come forth and join him. His friend had come a long way to find him, and there must be news of interest. He did not have a phone and rarely had visitors.

Their reunion became a happy moment for both. After a beautiful exchange of greetings the men sat on the porch and talked for hours, interacting like old friends. Their experiences together starting in California and then on La Chiva bound them for life. Neither would be the same because of knowing the other. Sometimes things work that way.

Blaine commenced the discussion by asking Epimineo about his health and eyesight. Epimineo shared the stories about his cataract surgery and other medical woes. His vision was worse but he could still see out of one eye. Glaucoma had taken the other and his health was failing. He had gained weight and was suffering from a type of diabetes. He was taking medicine and it was helping.

The subject of the treasure quickly came into focus. It was the common bond. Epimineo had plenty of time to reflect on their last day together and expressed deep regret that Oscar had been

invited to join the venture. Nothing good became of anything following that day on the mountain.

In order to prove his position, Epimineo revealed that he had
returned to the mountain without positive results. He seemed to
lose track of his location while still on the lower section of the mountain. The climb was too difficult, and his distorted vision made any
reference to prior landmarks useless. Things had changed.

He shared with Blaine the fact that his anxiety level was too
high to ever return to La Chiva. At his age he was finally able to
accept the notion that he had been looking for a needle in a haystack. He had been lucky once and squandered the opportunity. It
was clearly not his to find again. He couldn't do it.

Blaine asked if anything that had transpired up to that moment
caused Epimineo to change his belief about the reality of the treasure. This was the time to come clean. He breathed a sigh of relief
when Epimineo told him that he was more convinced than ever
that the treasure was there. He had years to reflect upon his life
and the mysterious events relating to the treasure.

Time opened his eyes and he wanted to talk about it. He had
not hallucinated anything in his younger years. He did not have
alcoholic projections. His family members had remembrances of
the gold coins and jewels that his grandfather had dispensed. He
was not fabricating any event for self-glory. He had been at the
treasure site and he was sure of that. He even carved away the
marker cross.

He knew it was there and he understood that its powerful influences would never benefit his life. It was in a cavern and protected
by a metal cover. He could hear the sound in his mind still. He
abandoned his dream of returning to La Chiva years before his
bearded American friend appeared at his doorstep.

Blaine told Epimineo of his interest in returning to the mountain again to search for the treasure site. Epimineo did not hesi-
tate with his response; he wanted Blaine to succeed. Success would
booster his mental health, restore his reputation back home, and
fortify his assets and lifestyle for the remaining short duration of
his life.

The men talked for hours and Blaine gained significant new
insights into his plan. He walked away confident that he would

succeed. He was given a drawing Epimineo had made of the approach to the site. It was surprisingly clear with a split-screen view of the orientation. Epimineo cautioned that it was in concept only and not close to scale.

Equipped with Epimineo's blessing, additional descriptions of the markers and route, the drawing, and information from their hours of discussion, Blaine reassured Epimineo that any success would be shared with him as it would have been had the men been successful in 1972.

Once again Blaine apologized for the unfortunate events of that day which led to the abrupt end of the search. He gave Epimineo his word that he knew nothing about the gun and was positive that the trio had no evil intent. Blaine explained it was absolutely inconsistent with everything the men stood for and was not within any realm of reality.

Epimineo provided an update and laughed when he confirmed Blaine's suspicions. He had returned to La Chiva a few more times after the disastrous climb with Oscar and was more confused than ever. He confessed that he could not locate any of his familiar markers and that everything looked different. He was more lost than before. All of the trips were wasted efforts.

35. ELLIS STEVENS

Phoenix – Summer, 1981

I vividly remember my first meeting with Blaine Court. At that time we both lived in Monterey County, California, but we intersected in the summer of 1981 in Phoenix, Arizona. We shared a common interest in higher laws of reality and self-empowerment in a metaphysical sense. We were both optimistic enough to believe that we created our own reality. We had a common friend, a writer who brought us together.

He approached me at the end of the first day of a conference and invited me to join him for dinner at a local Thai restaurant. Blaine's friendly, open nature and easy-going demeanor warmed me to him immediately. We were two Californians meeting on a hot desert evening in Phoenix, Arizona, enjoying Thai food, an unlikely start to a relationship that would lead to Culiacan, Mexico, and the story of the Treasure of La Chiva.

I still remember his eyes, a shade of blue reminiscent of a Caribbean sky. They were clear and bright, and reflected a life of learning. His long hair and full beard were silver gray. Youth had left him many years previous. A turquoise arrowhead hung from a braided leather lanyard around his neck. His presence was uplifting. He spoke with a sense of joy for life and attention to the miracles in even the smallest of things.

He was a generous host and a wonderful storyteller. His respect for those that passed before us was genuine. We would soon begin our tradition of saying "All my relations" when we were together. Blaine believed the origins of this custom to be from the Native Americans. It felt good and came off of our tongues easily.

Soon enough Blaine began to talk about his latest passion, the search for a buried treasure in Mexico. That was how it all started. I share this in his footsteps because he did not live to the end of this story.

The name was so powerful; Treasure of La Chiva. It was unique, easy to remember, and caused quite a stirring within me. In a surprising short time I found myself agreeing to share his passion.

My approach to life contained room for an appreciation and excitement of the unknown. That attribute had allowed me to walk into situations where common sense may have dictated a more cautious approach. Some of the greatest photographs I have taken were single shot opportunities. You either got it or you didn't.

One I missed was the grizzly bear at Glacier National Park. I turned a corner and saw the huge animal standing before me on the path, forgetting that I even had a camera around my neck! Being prepared with my equipment and alert for the shot was my ideal. I would try to have the most effective lens selected for the circumstances. Anticipation helps, but best intentions are not always the same as perfect practice.

Treasure hunting attracts a unique breed of dreamer. The odds are slight and the frustrations are obvious. Blaine's group was no different. Each was a specialist of his own creation. There was no school for treasure hunting dreamers. No test had been written to select team members for a project of this magnitude. Attitude was a key ingredient, and Blaine selected each after thorough investigation and scrutiny.

Blaine's patience in working towards a single goal was admirable. While the treasure was the main focus, the common thread that wove all of us together was the mutual appreciation for his efforts and the desire to be part of this amazing story.

The dreamer always has an option, another possibility, when the forces of life add their own cruel seasoning. It is harder to dream when the dragon of reality is breathing its hot-fired breath upon you and melting your concept of existence. We were at the culminating stage of his dream. The interaction of fantasy and reality wove a tapestry of magical proportions. The anticipation had a mild suffocating effect. The excitement in the air was so thick that at times I found it hard to breathe.

I always wanted to be a photojournalist. I have worked around books, papers, photographs, and words all of my life. They have manifested themselves in many forms. From this perspective they have all been but tiny steps on the road leading to the now. Each has been a momentary resting spot for my feet as I traveled on the path of life. Perhaps nothing more significant can be gleaned than that. Friendship, loyalty, and family are all words that have different meaning to me now. I listen to the distant voices hoping to hear a song that I can recognize. It will take time until I can unmask the illusion and arrive at pure truth. Until then I must shoot the photos and share my vision.

At my first workshop we were told to wait and listen to the voice, the key to capturing the moment. The problem for me was instantly obvious. There are too many voices. They all want to scream out and tell their story, their version of life as it presently exists. Everything is part of a changing story. The camera never lies. It freezes a split second of time and permits a thorough dissection of the visual components. Yet that is only a picture's worth of skin-deep examination, a micro slice of time. The essence is the soul. To capture the kernel of life out of every situation is the goal of the exercise.

Photo-documentation has served us well since the creation of silver halide film in the late 1880's. Of course we are now in the digital age, with the ability to totally change the photographic image. One can no longer trust any picture. While they still may be worth a thousand words, they may present a visual lie. A picture is not always an accurate representation anymore. We can "fix" anything by the manipulation of pixels, and yield a more detailed and yet inaccurate image in the process.

A picture is now art of a different form. The creativity reveals much more including the digital artist's touch and influence. The story is no longer always the truth, or at a minimum, it may not reflect what the lens initially captured. It becomes a composition and reflects a different art form.

My awards for photojournalism preceded the digital age. They came at a time when people trusted the eye of the photographer and the accuracy of his media. Success is a relative term. It usually applies to your neighbors or friends who have more than you. Success is sometimes out there. Often it is an illusory line in the sand always slipping a little further away.

Life is tough in the commercial world. The competition is stiff and their numbers are great. To reach the top requires sacrifice and perseverance. Time spent on the goal is the easiest way to manifest the desired results. It takes hard work and trust. Then, of course, comes the element of luck. But first comes preparation and dedication.

To begin the journey requires listening to your inner voice. What do you really want? How strong are your desires? What does it take to achieve the goal? Is it worth the effort? Without the correct answers the actions will only be efforts. With the right attitude, the joy along the path will also ensure the correct results, or a more meaningful means of obtaining a new reality.

My father introduced me to photography when I was very young. The camera was a Kodak, a Brownie Hawkeye I believe, with black and white print film, of course. After reaching fame as a photojournalist, my photographs and stories gained a level of credibility far in excess of the commercial media.

Blaine understood my reputation and affirmed my role to record the newsworthy achievement. He wanted to gain the attention of the international press when we had successfully completed our task. My resume, history, and alleged credibility combined to be my entry ticket into the adventure, with a front row seat. I felt like a very lucky man. This story would be a knockout.

Move over Geraldo Rivera. I was going to be present when the Bandit King's buried treasure was opened, holding a camera, and solely responsible for shooting and reproducing the film.

36. AIRBORNE

Mexican Airspace – 1982

The charter flight had been airborne for half an hour or so when the meal service began. It is amazing how the smell of food can quickly bring one back to the present time. I was on the adventure of a lifetime and not one of my family or friends even knew where I was, let alone the purpose. The joke was on me, because I did not anticipate the apparent danger that accompanied all that was going to be attempted in Mexico.

The absurdity of using a chartered airplane was not lost upon me. The Federal Aviation Administration watched all chartered flights across international borders even more closely than scheduled commercial flights. All I knew for sure was something did not make sense. I was naive enough to overcome my internal reaction that this was not going to be as easy as was explained, anticipated, and even expected. Looking back, I wonder why danger had never entered the equation. All of the signs were there from the start of my knowledge and involvement with the project.

I was dreaming, thinking, babbling, and building with excitement as I heard the landing gear drop and the wheels lock down. I had many years as a pilot of single engine aircraft, and the familiar sounds came back to me. No matter how many flights I took I couldn't forget the GUMPS check when I sensed the pilot going into his landing preparations checklist. That was the acronym for:

Gas selector on both tanks;

Undercarriage down and set;

Mixture or fuel adjusted to rich;

Propellers fixed or set; and

Seat belts on.

We landed in Hermacillo, a mandatory stop to clear customs. No problem. This group was clean. Blaine was a careful man and personally interviewed and selected all of us. The hatch door opened and the customs officer boarded the plane. The guards walking around the airplane were carrying machine guns, and they meant business. I hoped their wives were nice to them this morning.

After examining the pilot's records and logs, everything was declared to be in order on the plane and we were asked to exit and proceed to immigration. The bladder stop was the first major sign that we were out of the USA. The ripe smell identified the location of El Bano. The open windows did not help.

We entered the customs area and presented our ID's to the agents. There is some intangible about customs that makes the experience nerve-wracking and I was understandably anxious. Past incidents kept me on alert.

The customs officer looked up from his computer screen, smiled, and quietly said, "Welcome."

I took a deep breath and whispered a heart-felt "Thank You" in sincere acknowledgement to all of my relations.

Next stop was Aeropuerto Internacional de Culiacan. A quick glance at my map showed the city to be on the Panamerican Highway that ran north to the United States and south to Guadalajara and Mexico City. It was a great location for moving commerce, both now and then. The topography dictated a natural junction for the various lines of rail that intersected the area. The city as it was now configured had nine bridges, six of which crossed the Tamazula River, two on the Humaya River, with the longest crossing the Culiacan River. On arrival in Culiacan, our destination was Hotel Los Tres Rios. It meant "three rivers," and that was precisely where it was located.

I had done my research in advance of this journey to Mexico and I was prepared to see a mixture of old and new when we reached Culiacan. Many of the old colonial style buildings were preserved, along with the old street near the cathedral. Every tourist book talked about the cathedral. The most preserved old street, Calle Rosales, connects Rosales Square with the cathedral. It was an area of heavy traffic, yet the streets were considered safe and tourism was encouraged. It helped mask one of the most profitable business lines in history, drugs. But that is part of the recent history, and not relevant to the time of the origins of this story.

During the flight to Culiacan my mind sifted through a pano-
rama of images, bits and pieces that created my mosaic of this journey. I loved the story, from the legendary bandit, to the discovery
of the map, to this moment. The various means used by Blaine to
get to this point were utterly phenomenal, from old libraries, legends and storytellers, hypnosis, channels, spirit guides, resonant
crystals, and direct testimony from countless interviews with residents and descendants.

Blaine has worked on this phase for about four years. Now
we were going to find and open the bandit's door, an ironic
statement which should turn out to exhibit ingenuity and adapt-
ability. The protective qualities of the chosen method cannot be
overlooked.

The Treasure of La Chiva, through a century and a half of history, had become a power of its own, an entity with radiance and
energy. It has been protected on the spirit plane since the commandments of Lareano, who was as much a shaman as a thief. Can
we judge him in a negative light when it appears he unselfishly
took care of everyone?

I opened my notes and refreshed my understanding of the timeline. Blaine felt his efforts and unusual investigation techniques,
especially the results from the use of psychics, healers, channels,
and Tarot cards, had important appeal because it proved the spiritual elements were woven through the material plane. There are
many levels of existence, and they relate and work together to
make the complex whole.

The Legend of La Chiva was an enduring myth in Culiacan,
Mexico, a city of over one million people. The focus, or birthplace
of it all, the cathedral, was still standing and I couldn't wait to see
it. Photographs of the entry doors as well as the main chapel were
needed for the record.

Many within Jesus Borella's family thought that he was up to
something suspicious at the mountain. A number of the grandchildren had witnessed their grandfather coming back down from
the mountain while they were playing near the camp. A seed was
planted in them that would take many years to sprout. Their parents, who also witnessed more than one such return from the same
area, verified the stories.

Speculation centered upon variations of the theme that he had something hidden that was illegal or improper, or worse. The abundance of generous gifts always followed his trips to the mountain and became highly suspect. Jesus Borella was a changed man after he was through with the stress of the bandit episode. Grandfather relied on the tale of his inheritance to substantiate the generous gifts, yet this idea had worn thin and inconsistencies became more evident as the years passed. The younger family members believed his generosity had something to do with the raids by the legendary Lareanos. Didn't grandfather have the responsibility for the bandit gang when they were captured? Wasn't the bandit locked up and kept under his control? Didn't he have personal access to Lareano? Wasn't grandfather one of the last men to see the bandit alive? Did the bandit ultimately share the secret of his treasure?

They knew Jesus was ruthless and persevering. Collectively, they would bet on grandfather over the bandit. The discussion continued for years, fueled by the realization that Jesus Borella was not the beneficiary of great riches from his own father. The generous gifts of coins and jewels were the rewards from other undisclosed activities, but what?

The inescapable conclusion was reached that grandfather had discovered the bandit's gold, and it was hidden somewhere near the old gathering spot in the Tacamonte Canyon. Rumors began quietly like smoldering embers, but once fanned with conversation and belief, ultimately gathered a life of their own. The stories of the Lareanos, coupled with the life and deeds of Jesus Borella, combined to create an inspiring quality to the Borella family history.

Rumors of treasure were spreading and many of the townspeople came to the twin peaks to challenge their luck and tempt their fate. Decades passed and nobody found even a trace of the treasure on either Tacamonte or La Chiva. The stories shared the same fate as many others.

It was easy to conclude that the treasure was merely a myth. The Treasure of La Chiva became yet another treasure rumor with colorful anecdotes but lacking in substantiation. The passage of time without its discovery dictated no reasonable alternative. It was a virtual dry hole.

At different times the rumors of the treasure reached far beyond the City of Culiacan and the state of Sinaloa. The local and national governments also became involved in the search. Teams of soldiers were brought to verify the findings. They found nothing, not a trace, and the matter was again reduced to speculation. The area was rich in a tradition of legends, and this was no different. No further time would be wasted chasing that rainbow of dreams. The bandit's loot, the alleged Treasure of La Chiva, was classified as a myth.

As with many other areas of Mexico, the stories of buried gold or other treasures were unfounded. These myths had a value, for they represented hope. These stories would join the countless others that permeated the oral and written history of this young and growing nation. Decisions were made to abandon the search for the rumored hideouts. It was time to move forward towards progress and ignore the speculation of bygone times. Plus, laws had been enacted giving the government rights to all treasures found within its boundaries. The government would take no further action other than to wait.

37. SHAMAN & MONEY MAN

Tacamonte Canyon

There was a time when it became evident that there was something else happening with this story. It was a validation, on a grand scale, of the principles attendant in the schools of ancient mysteries, secret societies, and even the church itself.

Lareano knew that the treasure had significance far beyond the monetary value. The so called "power objects" were something he gradually understood and greatly respected. They held secrets of an era lost to mankind. They were reputed to contain pure magical power. That can sound preposterous at first. The Aztec Empire was famous for gold, which they used in religious artifacts.

During periods of hiding in the mountains, Lareano and Camacho had encountered an encampment of native medicine men, or shamans, who lived totally outside the confines of society. They were a throwback to an earlier time, when man lived more in touch with the laws of nature. Their life was almost symbiotic with the earth. They lived in the rocks and trees not far from the base of La Chiva but never climbed above a certain height or elevation. Superstition helped build an invisible fence that kept them from considering climbing beyond the barrier. They had a name for this point, but that name has not endured.

I thought about the bandit and his acquired skills. I wonder how much was accomplished through his experiences on this mountain. What did he learn from that indigenous culture? Is this why he had that special understanding? Was he open to energies unknown to the others?

My mind was gushing with questions. Images and pictures are the curse of the photographer. I was always wondering about the why or facts behind every picture.

The story started with a central character who was not dedicated to good and who was disrespectful to the authority of his time. Following the rules did not appear to be his style. He was an outlaw, a criminal, and a thief by all norms of society. But when considering the times, life, and what he represented, then the viewpoint softens and shifts. The context usually matters. At times it looked like a war between virtue and mischief. Was it in equilibrium or was one factor more dominant? Could there be a victor? The policies of the powerful ultimately blurred the value and judgment line for the masses.

I came to appreciate his boldness, strength, and ability to influence the lives of thousands. We have no photographs or paintings evidencing his physical appearance. There are few notes and descriptions in old periodicals. Lareano Garcia planted a mystery that took on a life of its own. It seemed so incredible and yet real. We believed it. Blaine had made a commitment to continue the dividends of the bandit's gold by using the treasure for the good of the people of Mexico.

I thought about our living link to the treasure story, Epimineo, the last person to discover the location of the entry to Lareano's cave. He had met with Blaine a few times and had shared the stories of his paternal grandfather as they relate to the bandit and the treasure. Our success was Epimineo's last hope. It could justify his life's efforts, but never really help him. He was old, immobile, and losing his sight. His vision was beyond repair. His aged knees could no longer carry him up the mountain. There was no chance for him to ever enter the cave.

Epimineo would share in our success, but never again experience the sights, smells, or sounds. He would also forego the heat, bugs, and the climb itself that we knew would be tough. He spent years experiencing that truth. He won't get near La Chiva. But vindication would be sweet and he could enjoy a deep level of fulfillment if we succeeded. He was weak, but was it a metaphor?

The truth of the whole endeavor had a major nexus through this man. Was he credible? One could easily wonder. The success of the entire venture rested in his veracity. My experiences in life made me always wonder: where was the line between truth and exaggeration? How much of the story was reliable?

The turn of events that occurred for Epimineo was disappointing from every perspective. Fears and doubts ultimately blocked him from his goal. The fear implanted by the spirits was very real to him. He had run away more than once.

I came to enjoy the team and felt like a participating member of the group at this point. They were all welcoming and focused. We each had our assignment and area of expertise. For me, it was a photographer's dream. This was all before we went to the mountain. There was more than I ever anticipated.

I don't remember when I first heard his name, or even why, but it is only whispered in our presence. We are not supposed to know. His name was unique. Was it a single letter, or the friendlier version? Was it D or Dee? Or did it just represent the first initial of his first name? My mind played tricks on me, and I thought of Blaine's games. Could it be the first letter of his last name, like they use in Vegas-speak, Mr. D? It was clear that we would never know his identify. I'll call him Dee, and leave it at that.

It would have taken big bucks to finance this operation. Who paid for this private jet? Why the special accommodations?

Again I found myself wondering if something bad could happen on the mountain. It was a caution sign. Everything had been so easy. Could we have been sold out, our intentions misused for publicity and control purposes? Were we vulnerable in a situation where unreasonable was more like the norm? Danger was a weak description. D as in danger? These thoughts were a caution sign and I was becoming paranoid.

Suddenly, my mood began to sweep back and forth like a pendulum. Within an hour I felt warm and uncomfortable. An inner feeling, a knowing, began to creep into my awareness. Were we treading on a dark and dangerous secret? Were we crossing into forbidden territory? How about the curse? Had I ignored the more dangerous stories and representations? The tiger? There was something gnawing on me, an inner irritation. I didn't want to share it with anyone yet. I knew I should, but as the last comrade to join Blaine's brigade, I did not want to appear afraid. This was not about fear. It was worse than that. I was filled with overpowering premonitions. My heart was racing, my body was hot and perspiring, and I had the creepiest feeling about being watched.

38. WATCHED

La Chiva - 1982

I never understood what Blaine did for a living or how he could pay for all of the expenses of searching for a buried treasure. He had no noticeable source of income, no apparent revenue stream, yet he covered all of the costs of the search expedition, including the airfare, gear, supplies, food and lodging. Did he have a Money Man? Are there any other secrets? The negative aspects of our adventure made their appearance once we were on Mexican soil. I began to share Blaine's paranoia.

Not everyone on the mountain was on Blaine's team. Soon enough we would discover that three independent sentries were on the mountain, in secure hiding places with excellent vistas of the area below. These sentries, maybe they were guards, maintained their hidden vigil on Tacamonte and one of the foothills of La Chiva in small, well-supplied bunkers. Each was firmly entrenched in his position with sufficient food, water, and other necessities so that movement would be unnecessary. They had tarps, blankets, and anti-glare shielding on the reflective surfaces.

These men were equipped with various items of mid-level technology including high-powered binoculars, two-way radios, and a film camera with a large telephoto lens. More important, they were also heavily armed. Fortunately, they did not have night-vision optics.

Why were they here? What were they protecting?

39. MISDIRECTION

Culiacan – 1982

The words are not unique, but the saying fits: "Don't bring a knife to a gunfight." The sights and smells of Mexico are original and unique, combining the mix of dust, sweat, exhaust, and aromatic spices with the images of a country on the move. The people appear to be in a hurry in this historical town. They have gone through changes parallel to the country since the founding of the city. Yet the old church stands today as a landmark like it did a few centuries before.

Although areas of Culiacan were preserved to maintain the cultural and architectural heritage, the city had grown to almost a million inhabitants. It bore no resemblance to the small town of Lareano's time. A major exception was the cathedral.

Built in the early 1800's, the cathedral still stood. The very same church from the 19th Century that spawned the career and life goals of the young Lareano sat proud and erect on its original site. It had outlasted time, weather and the elements, bandits, scandals, and even the revolution and a couple of changes of governments. It stood as a monument to the strength and enduring power of the Catholic Church.

The city government had taken great pains to preserve certain streets and buildings. There were perfect reminders of its architectural and cultural past. Preservation districts have their value, and a journey into the past is as simple as walking around one of these special areas. The cathedral is the center of one such site. It was the launch point of a unique career. It gave me chills to think the same building is still standing.

I wonder if anyone in the cathedral even knows about the church articles removed long ago to the bandit's mountain cave. Too much time has passed. Too many people are gone.

The Lareanos visited their personal havoc upon the states of
Sonora, Chihuahua, Durango, and Sinaloa. The proof of their
existence rests entirely in local folklore and the wondrous treasure resting peacefully in the bandit's brilliant hiding spot. At first
I had great difficulty in understanding how it remained unopened
for so long. It wouldn't matter where it was hidden. Many have
looked for a very long time. I was about to learn the obvious reasons why. Protecting spirits with unusual powers? Hidden in plain
sight, but off the beaten path?

Lareano was not discreet with his pilferage, for he took almost
everything in sight. This we learned from the "channels" that
Blaine consulted a few years earlier. The spiritual channels were
an important part of the evidence-gathering process undertaken
by Blaine. It was a big thing then, and a new source of vital information. Many thought it was rubbish but that was fine with him. It
doesn't require belief or agreement for this story.

Blaine would usually begin his inquiry with various qualifiers.
He used these questions to test the strength of the channel and
the veracity of the "tune-in" or ability to "see." After feeling somewhat confident with their connection to spirit, or discarnate entities, guides, or whatever, he would usually say, "Tell me about the
Treasure of La Chiva."

On one such occasion he was told one simple thing, "There is
no treasure."

When that was the response, he would then ask questions such
as "Tell me about Lareano Garcia, the bandit," or "Let me speak
to grandfather, Jesus Borella, the Military Governor of Culiacan at
the end of the 19th Century."

Often the channel would actually shift in his or her seat, perk
up, and begin rattling off information about specific individu-
als associated with this story and even certain items within the
treasure. It was through this means that Blaine learned about the
Military Governor's brother, Gerardo, being the skeletal remains
within the cave.

In time the repeated inquiry would lead to concurrent and
similar observations, such as the initial "D" on the boxes of coins,
the ancient objects hidden deeper in the cave behind the minted
coinage, the piles of colored stones, and the vault door.

There was a landmark event that preceded my recruitment by a couple of years. After significant inquiry Blaine found talented teachers who believed they were able to channel the spirit, Cheryl, who was protecting the treasure. Cheryl was the coagulation of unhappiness, frustration, pain and darkness.

For the sake of accuracy, we used the name Cheryl out of convenience. It was actually an out-of-this-world arrangement of syllables, beginning with a guttural "shush." And it goes on from there in a way that you almost strangle yourself when you repeat it. Please trust and accept the shorthand, Cheryl.

Cheryl was stronger than thought and nastier than our most evil moments. I sensed her from another dimension. She cannot be busted. All of the "ghost-buster techniques" are mere appetizers for her voracious diet. She eats thought form energy. She radiates from the deepest point within the cave, in the back and up on a ledge. She is bizarre. Her range easily reached Blaine's home in California, and she often gave visual images to Blaine that were of a holographic quality. They were a mountain lion, bat, and rattlesnake. Ironically these were the very totems of the local shaman. She could morph each into the other, and back again, right before your inner eyes. Since it was only light energy, the transition was quick and frightening.

The entity known as Cheryl was brutal and never showed mercy. When you locked on you had to be prepared to ride out the entire experience. She works with packets of energy that have a half-life of six to eight minutes. That's six to eight minutes of a nightmare, an overtaking physical and mental sensation totally out of control of any level of normal sanity. It can involve intense headaches, the sensation of burning in fire, sounds of a volume level that could break glass, or pure pain. She was ugly and, as I said, brutal. No mercy. She had been guarding the treasure for well over a century and had acquired unusual talents over that period. She liked her gold.

The spirits of La Chiva made her job much easier. The mountain was home to some out-of-this-world life forms, all of which fed on the treasure and protected it into various realms of existence. It was a unique equilibrium.

The whole image was a carnival of death. She was the personification of the curse uttered by Lareano Garcia almost a century before. She is a descendant of the negative portion of the thought form power of the bandit leader. The impact was being reverberated out from the chorus lead by his love for his grandmother. Everything was amplified by the ancient power objects hidden behind the gold.

I could feel her presence. She was the wall, the doorkeeper, and the secret unspoken. One could never find the treasure without her consent. She protected the treasure at all costs, and the thought of penetrating her defenses was useless without her cooperation. She was a guardian spirit wrapped in a protection powered by the treasure itself. She understood the energy created by the physical items amplified by the power objects hidden in the cave. You could say she was armed.

There is a human skeleton lying against them too. At least that is what the psychics had said, which fits with the mysterious disappearance of the Military Governor's brother, Gerardo. A pile of bones is a sad memorial. Greetings to Gerardo Borella. The cave has been his resting place since the accident in 1893. He died because he followed his brother one day and discovered his secret. Accident or murder?

Reality lends its own cruel touch to life. It is hard to dream when the dragon of reality is breathing its hot-fired breath upon you and melting your concept of existence. I did not envision being involved in some multi-dimensional cosmic game with unseen forces possessing powers beyond imagination. I would settle now for the days of the voodoo fire-breathers on the Caribbean island nations of St Lucia and Saint Vincent. Interesting that we were with Captain Dan Powers there too.

I was trapped in a mindset mixed with equal parts excitement, confusion, and pure fear. I was operating on faith, conviction, and curiosity. Blaine's paranoia was not funny to me anymore. He had been involved with the project for years, and had probably experienced and overcome many facets of denial.

There would be no way to predict the behavior of the force that is controlled by Cheryl. Trying to match such a wild and overpowering opponent was meaningless. Cooperation would be required. Everything had to be capable of being answered with one word, "Yes."

My mouth still gets dry and my eyes almost hurt when I reflect back upon those times. They were chilling in scope. The energies were beyond verbal description. Can you believe that? Belief is not required here. Experience changes the mindset forever. An experience of expanded vision of unbounded awareness was not expected to be associated with the treasure story and was a byproduct of the many ways that the story influenced me. Life is a great teaching tool. Everything is real. Yes, everything.

Each of the participants underwent a serious of independent training sessions coordinated by Blaine. We all had our own "homework" in a manner of speaking. The physical demands of the trip favored a well-conditioned body and an alert mindset. In addition to exercises and physical training to deal with the climbing environment, some of my time was spent studying the history of coinage from the time and potential items within the confines of the treasure. Museum collections were helpful too.

We studied the system of money in general use around the time of the creation of the treasure. This included information about the various mints, coinage in Mexico, Spain and America. We learned about why the coins were created in Mexico and also about the ones minted in Spain. There was information about sunken treasure, coinage in the American colonies, and the need for a standardized means of trade.

Although nobody to our knowledge had been within the treasure cave for many decades, we had a strong expectancy of what was behind the trap door. A carryover in the local lore was independently "seen" by the psychics. There had been confirmation from various sources, none of which are highly credible. It was the total mosaic, the composite of the various little secrets and clues that made our adventure ahead both over-the-top exciting and also transformative at the level of the soul.

There were layers of this story that kept unfolding. The depth of the experience was expanding almost exponentially when the realization hit me that we were being watched. Oh Blaine. I'm so sorry that I doubted you. My overzealous optimism had clouded my thinking. Of course we were being watched. The question was by whom? Or what?

"Could you instantly understand when you are overcome in an energetic way?"

"Would you put your faith in me if we were confronted with this situation, together?"

Those two questions were only a few of the strange things that I heard from Blaine after being chosen to join the team. The understanding of the history enhanced my perspective and was part of the training. Blaine's team was not the first to make an attempt to find and open the treasure. We wanted to be the last, the victors in a cosmic puzzle.

We finally arrived in Culiacan, unloaded the gear and equipment from the plane, and headed to Hotel Los Tres Rios located at the edge of the city. Later that evening we joined up for dinner in the dining room at the hotel and enjoyed the most amazing tortilla soup you could ever imagine. It was superbly flavored with local spices and true Mexican cheese. I doubt if it would taste the same back home. I finally felt we were here in Culiacan, Mexico, in place and ready to begin our adventure. My whole body tingled with excitement. Little did I know, enjoying this lovely meal, of just what an adventure it would be!

My assignment included documenting the arrival and ascent in both black and white and color film. I carried a pair of Nikon 35 mm cameras with multiple interchangeable lenses. There were fresh batteries in the motor drives and the flash units had been charged and tested. I had more film than would ever be necessary.

I usually carried a hand held cassette voice recorder, which was small by standards of the time. It was often quicker to use than a notepad for retaining photo information. Time and f-stops used to be important. It is only history to the current photographer. I also carried a composition notebook. It was my journal, notepad, and reminder, a habit that started with my first college chemistry class.

My equipment bag contained nylon boat line, duct tape, and my favorite knife, a hand-made ornate blade that I purchased at the Nepenthe store in Big Sur. It was allegedly made by a local craftsman who drank only natural brew. An Indian Head Buffalo Nickel is the top of the clasp on the sheath, modified to a domed shape by some blunt instrument. The effect was impressive. I also carried my classic Swiss Army Knife, a gift from my grandfather who never went to Switzerland.

Blaine's instructions were clearly followed. There were no notes about the community, treasure, or our goals. Absolutely no clues existed in our homes, rooms, bags, or on our persons. We exhibited no familiarity greater than a relationship of a professional or business nature.

The story at check-in centered around Blaine as a land man from Monterey County looking at property for potential agricultural development outside of Culiacan. The rest of us comprised his professional team of advisers. My photography equipment made sense in the context.

Everything we needed to know was previously committed to memory. We had what I called "Blaine's Homework Packages" arrive while we waited back home. I always found Blaine's collection of resources to be interesting. One pack included old photographs, drawings, and some old coins. Holding the old coins, I wondered about life in Mexico way back then. My favorite was the primer on gold and silver coins. The treasure allegedly contained boxes of minted coins from Mexico and bags of old coins from Spain. Blaine knew the difference in value between many of the alternatives and wanted us to be able to make the most efficient choices with the limited amount of time in the cave.

It was my understanding that mints in Mexico used local silver to provide the coins for the entire area. Millions of silver pesos were minted over more than a century. Because of the scarcity of the British currency, Colonial America used the peso as a standard. They represented one dollar at that time.

The power objects, Incan plates, shaman crystals, scepters, wands and other tempting objects of interest were beckoning. Blaine hoped to secret away a number of the ancient artifacts to help prove the veracity and accuracy of the psychics, channels, and other spiritual communicators.

Blaine felt that their revelation of the treasure was an independent validation of spiritual truths. This was in direct contrast to the schism that was developing about spiritual and material matters on one hand, and the control and dogma of the church on the other. On this point I would find conflict with the alleged non-intervention of philosophy in contrast to the Catholic Church. To me Blaine had an agenda that was neither subtle nor indirect.

For my part, my personal experiences with crystals, meditation, and developing interpersonal thought somehow shielded me from the normal cynicism that most people would feel upon hearing the initial story. The floodgates of negativity would open whenever I shared in personal confidence even a small portion of the theoretical story. Friends and colleagues became skeptical when they learned about the strange publisher from Carmel whom I had met at a conference in Phoenix. No one really believed he was underwriting the entire costs of the expedition and doubted that my role was free and without control. There was skepticism whether I would actually have the right to produce the story, the photographs, and document the recovery.

It was arcane in concept and probably too stereotypical to be believed. Some didn't buy the fact that Blaine consulted with and relied upon spiritual mediums, channels, and psychics. This actually was the key to unlock the secrets hidden for so many years.

When I would explain the basic history of the treasure, as I have to you so far, my friends and family would often change their position and ask if there was another seat on the plane! Did we need a cook, quartermaster, or strong person to help carry out our share? Did we need anybody or anything?

The possibility of success would overshadow all logic, reason, or skepticism. The smell of adventure was that sweet. Such is the continuous magic associated with the words "buried treasure." Denial was no longer within reason. This had all of the elements of a real, not imaginary, story. It was time to find out.

40. On The Road Again

Culiacan, Mexico – 1982

Awake? I was finally awake. We were in a van passing through a suc-culent-filled landscape. I was witnessing a kaleidoscope of colors and wondering what the hell happened. I had vague memories of walking back to my room at Hotel Los Tres Rios after an evening feast of local food and fine tequila. Too much tequila is not soon forgotten. No wonder they call it "To Kill Ya." The rhythmic bounc-ing of the van had lulled me into a state of altered slumber as the Culiacan landscape passed by my closed eyes.

It was a dry hot morning. Extreme heat was never my favorite. My skin felt creepy and my lips were too dry. To make matters worse, I awoke thirsty beyond belief. Was it too much alcohol? Did we drink that much? The rest of my group's eyes were closed and their heads were bobbing. It made more sense to close my eyes again, relax, and await the next part of the adventure.

A sudden lurch surprised us into wakefulness. We were all awakened when the driver hit the brakes a little too hard. A scan through the front window explained why. We collectively gasped as a checkpoint was upon us. It came out of nowhere and was strategically located after the road crested and began a small descent.

I could not tell from the uniforms whether these armed guards were of the military or police persuasion. They looked very young yet they exuded excessive power, force and control. What was obvi-ous was the convincing display of aggressive firepower held by each of the guards nearby. Their high profile presence ensured compli-ance with the demand to stop. Running this roadblock would be fatal.

The automatic weapons hung on long straps close to their sides. I would not take the gamble that the rifles weren't loaded. This was a sobering moment for me. I did not want to lift my cam-era and shoot photos of these men; I desperately wanted to forget about them quickly. I prayed that the images they left imprinted in my mind's eye would not be there for long.

After we passed through the driver explained they were searching for guns being delivered to a rebellious group more than 100 miles further down the road. The guards appeared to be surprised with the number of gringos in the van, and after a very brief check motioned to pass through.

It was hotter than hell in the van. There was no air. I was going absolutely crazy inside. My skin was crawling, my head was spinning, and my inner thermometer was clearly running on hot. This was not good. Feeling nauseous, I fought to keep my mouth shut. I did not want to experience breakfast again.

I was in trouble, spinning, and losing it. This was becoming a habit on this trip and I was not happy. I was usually strong and resilient. This was an obnoxious start to one of the most potentially exciting days of my life. My attitude was anything other than positive. It was my own fault. I should have seen and reacted to the signs. Was this the beginning of a trip to hell? All aboard!

I believed we would be leaving the flat desert valley and reaching the foothills within half an hour. I wanted to feel clear for my first sight of Tacamonte. After driving into the canyon the mighty La Chiva would reveal itself.

I began to recap my historical view of the treasure. It was a sequential approach, as if I had graphed it in my mind for the first time. It was a linear reality, a timeline view. We were nothing but a speck in time on its long chart, a wave upon the great history of this treasure. For more time than not its secrets have been protected.

The treasure must have been perfectly concealed. Its doors have remained closed for a long time now. It was rumored to be protected by an extremely sophisticated location, a legend, time, snakes, a curse, a mountain lion, devas, a spirit witch with a chorus of friends, and probably much more.

For moments I had doubts as to whether or not we would be successful in locating and getting inside the treasure. It was as if a voice was speaking to me. But the word "speaking" itself was incorrect, because it was more like another's thought or series of thoughts entering my mind from the back of my neck. Has that happened to you? It was a shame that I could not share it with anyone at the time. I wondered if I was even sharing it with myself. Was it real? What is?

The timeline came back into focus and appeared as if written on a sheet of ancient parchment with a quill and ink. I wondered if it was from the time that Spanish galleons sailed the area. Even Coronado landed in this region of Mexico prior to venturing north to New Mexico and California.

The timeline started with the year 1836 standing proud and alone. From there we begin because it is the first potentially significant date in this story. It is the year of the birth of Jesus Borella, the Military Governor. His long tenure as the second steward of the treasure may have protected it for us. Without his role the treasure may not have been perpetuated. He defused all rumors with the mere passage of time and solely monopolized the treasure until his death in 1910.

1857 was the birth year for both Lareano Garcia and his partner, Camacho. The synthesizing event for Lareano occurred ten years later, in 1867, when he attended his grandmother's funeral and had his crystalline image of relieving the church of its excess wealth and accumulations. It took a few years for the boys to grow up and the essence of the gang to be created, but the spark was verifiable.

The bandit's treasure was accumulated from 1876 until his capture in late 1890. Camacho was executed in early 1891, and Lareano was double-crossed and murdered on May 1st of the same year. With their deaths, the accumulation phase for the treasure was over. Thereafter, it was subject to regular withdrawal by the Military Governor for years. The secret was shared for only a few minutes with his brother on one chance and fatal encounter. It was his grandson, Epimineo Corrales, who is our major source for this story and primary link to its veracity.

Jesus Borella died in 1910 at age seventy-four, and Epimineo did not find the stone cross until the rainy day in 1932 following seemingly endless hours over more than a decade of obsessing and searching for his family truth. And of all the bad luck, he never found it again despite numerous attempts.

On one such attempt, he had a total panic attack upon hearing the scream of a wild animal, perhaps a cat. When his eyesight started failing he reappeared on the mountain a few more times before giving up on his lifelong dream. For him, lightning was not going to strike twice. He resolved to end his longtime quest for the treasure with the resignation that he was unworthy of the rewards.

41. AWAKENING

La Chiva - 1982

Being unsure about what had happened makes me hesitant to share about this point. I was sitting at the base of a mountain, under the shade of a large rock facing a strange landscape. It towered above me. My awareness was cloudy and my vision was not yet in focus. I didn't know why I was here, how I got here, or where I was. There was no sense of time or space. Nothing connected me to any recent event. Was I lost and alone?

As my consciousness began to clear I felt deep pain in my body, and I hurt everywhere. My hands were caked with dry blood and dirt. My pants and shirt were torn with more than a casual amount of blood on them. A personal inventory was taken and nothing seemed broken, just scraped and sore. I felt a connection with my limbs but I was not convinced that I could move.

I shouted out, "What is going on?" At least I thought I was shouting, but not a sound came out of my mouth.

"Oh shit," I tried to say. I realized I was in some serious trouble.

I looked around my immediate area, scanning left and right. I could find nothing to identify the time or place. It seemed odd that a camera was not nearby for I almost always carry a camera. My wrists, arms, hands, feet and knees were aching terribly. There were small scrapes and scratches everywhere. I was a mess and I was disoriented. It felt like I fell a great distance, and perhaps rolled some too. I was a mess.

I still couldn't remember where I was, much less why. I was hot, tired, sore and confused. The whole situation sucked bad. The blood was not a good sign. My equilibrium was shot so I remained seated to gather my senses, the few that seemed operable. Nothing seemed right.

Fortunately, I sat still and waited almost motionless. As my breathing slowed a clarity overcame me and I began to think more calmly, remember more, and began to understand my circumstances. With each inhale more images returned, and with each corresponding exhale I consciously tried to forget what I had just remembered. It was a tug of war between an ugly reality and my very survival.

Images of bloody events began to form. People had been killed. All of the people. All of the group except me! Why? By whom?

A floodgate of increasingly ugly and vile impressions rammed my mind as full awareness returned. My memory was from a real-life horror movie.

As reality dawned, I knew the day was going to get much worse. Oh yes, much worse. It was a tidal wave of terror.

42. Drop the Ball

La Chiva – 1982

The ambush or premature attack by the snipers was initiated by the youngest of the group. His name was Chris Painter but they called him "CP" or "The Greek." His excitement overtook his ability to reason. He lost control and destroyed the mission. Hell would be paid if they did not succeed. That would come on another day, and probably within twenty-four hours after their return to the states. A fatal accident could easily be envisioned while still in Mexico. Time was not his luxury anymore.

His failure to stand down appears to have cost his benefactor countless millions of dollars. He had already been told by Dick, "You will have to explain this mess to Mr. D yourself. I hope I am miles away when you do."

The instructions were written and not ambiguous. The assignment was to watch Blaine's treasure party from a remote distance, remain hidden, and secure the exact location of the treasure after everyone left. Violence was not condoned. Their employer was generous as well as being an outspoken man of peace. They were sent as an insurance policy to protect his investment, and they became the cause of the claim. It was a rotten turn of events and the buck stopped with them.

"What the hell were you thinking?" Dick asked CP quickly.

Their orders were clear and they blew it bad. They were to watch and protect, not act as bandits themselves and try to hijack the goods. Human error and misunderstanding would be no excuse. With twenty-twenty hindsight they began the blame game about initiating the attack. Waiting until Blaine's group was inside the cave was their secret plan.

Chris Painter waited quietly as Dick continued, "You are going to have such hell to pay for this. We have no way out."

They breached the protocol, lost their cool, and would suffer for the rest of their lives, however short, for this mistake. They represented themselves to be professionals, were paid commensurate with their resumes, and yet acted like intoxicated college boys on one of their first outings away from school.

There was something strange about the mountain that had taken them out of autopilot and released a bizarre enactment of pure rage. It was sparked by simple greed and exploded out of control. They acted like cowardly thieves and had lost any air of dignity that came with their prior military and law enforcement training. It was a fool's game and they became the perpetrators and the victims.

Not one of the men felt comfortable with the available alternatives. They were in a creative gap and could not envision any way out of the trap that they caused for themselves. The hunters did not succeed. Simple greed had taken away their brains. Nobody took control.

43. STAYING ALIVE

La Chiva – 1982

Nothing at the moment gave me any glimmer of hope other than the fact that I was still alive. Believe me, that is always a positive event, but today was going to cast a long shadow for me. It would take more than positive attitude and optimistic reflection to see my way out of this potentially life-ending predicament.

I was beginning to debate with my inner voice about my surroundings. One thing I knew for sure, I was in deep shit, alone, and desperate.

The questions began to run quickly.

"Where was I?"

"How did I get here?"

"When did I get here?"

Even simple inquiries became meaningful. I heard myself ask, "Am I even here?"

"Why do I hurt so much?"

To be beaten on the mountain was tiring and troublesome. To come this far and lose everything? I felt drained and frustrated.

The story was about to be lost without ever being told. The legend was in the process of going underground, and Blaine's lofty intentions were going to be replaced by malevolent ideals. Many lives were lost without reason, including possibly my own. There couldn't be a positive spin on this experience.

I refused to feel sorry for myself and could not conceive of giving up. The odds were horrendous but I was still alive. When there is a will there is hope.

Staying alive was the task for the day. That was going to be a tough assignment. Tomorrow would take care of itself if I were alive at the end of today. These simple words brought neither comfort nor resolution.

The order of the moment was remaining undetected. I had no intention of giving up. I had taken too much care of my body to end up as carrion feed. It was time to stop and listen.

I was being hunted like an animal on a hostile mountain in a foreign country. I spoke more than a few words of the language, but had neither surviving friends nor reliable assistance, and no means of gaining any help. I was the absolute image of alone. Being without identification, money, or companions in a foreign country was a hurdle that I couldn't comprehend. It was more like a barrier, an impenetrable wall.

The distance from civilization compounded my fate. The lack of transportation and no proper direction were great frustrations. But the worst thing of all at this point was the heat. It was becoming unbearable. If I saw Robert Frost I would now vote for ice.

My normal sensitivity to bright sunlight was accentuated by the strong glare off of the rock and mineral surfaces. Fortunately my sunglasses and canteen were still with me. I sought cover as soon as my wits were gathered. I had no way to do anything, and it was futile to run because there was no place to go. It was time to test my faith and belief. My survival depended upon this success.

I became invisible more than once in my life. A time-out is valuable in much more than sports. The easiest thing would be to hide in plain sight. I meditated scrunched under a rock overhang and used the sutra for protection. I knew what I had to do but was unsure about the means to achieve this. I understood that they would come looking for me and running would create the worse odds for survival.

As I calmed down I thought about my most immediate surroundings. My mind wandered further and further in each direction without much hope. I was worse than Heinlein's stranger in a strange land. I was a fugitive gringo in the mountains outside of Culiacan, Mexico, without a means of finding my way home.

My lack of contact with the outside world was an advantage for the moment. I knew nothing about the true predicament or the story being told, if any. It seemed like I was being hunted unless they believed me to be dead. If not, there was no way out and no visible means of survival. They could easily wait at the bottom of the canyon and catch me as I attempted to leave the area. That would be the lazy man's way. Use gravity as the net. Do nothing and catch any of the survivors.

Surprise. I was not going to be that easy. I had a plan and it could work. The environs of Culiacan sported another form of bandito. The modern outlaw had a product to sell: drugs. Culiacan had a long history of narcotics trade. It was a center for opium grown for the United States government during World War II and the conflicts that followed. The business was legal and sanctioned for a long time. There were also wildcat farmers who dealt with that commodity. Another drug that grew plentiful in the area was marijuana. The pot fields had once been protected with governmental immunity, an unspoken pass to help the local economy.

The location of Culiacan put it at a crossroads for transport in all directions, especially north to America. This was my hope. I decided to go uphill, away from Tacamonte and the predictable canyon trap below. The idea was so stupid that it bore its own shade of brilliance. Was it my fatigue, lack of alternatives, or the clarity of a good plan? Time would tell. For now it seemed like the only thing to try.

I elected to stay put, gather my strength, and listen. I had to make sure I was alone on the mountain before I began the ascent. I could remain under cover of the vegetation and terrain, but the sounds could amplify by the rocks, echo off of the canyons, and betray my existence if not my position.

Patience would be the watchword. I would wait and listen. With luck an answer would come. Guidance works that way, and I still had a surplus of confidence and faith. I really wanted to be right about this one. Rest felt good, if that was possible. My body was whacked because of the overflow of adrenaline. My veins must have been like rivers of the stuff.

44. PROTECTION

La Chiva – 1982

My mind played tricks on me while I waited for the cover of the dark. Blaine said there were numerous protectors or barriers to the treasure and it amused me to consider the list. It would serve as an excellent diversion and aid in the resolution of my personal mystery. This was the making of a major life crisis. The fact that it favored a terminal result was no encouragement.

Here I was, ready or not. Do less and accomplish more. I hoped to have a long day ahead to think. I did not want to make any unnecessary sound, the consequences of which could easily accelerate my doom.

I knew how to meditate and I could easily rest in place. My mind drifted through chapters and pages lying on top of the inner filing cabinet. Hello Siddhartha.

The most obvious barrier or protector was simply the element of time. Time was a benefit to the sanctity of the treasure itself and an incredible factor to overcome. Even Sir Isaac Newton saw inertia as one of the most powerful components of nature. So here I sat, waiting.

The heat was another force that had worked to help protect the treasure. The mountain did not appear to be friendly or conducive to life. The afternoon sun was brutal, and the reflection off of the white stone face of La Chiva had the effect of magnifying the intense rays of sunlight. Every time I thought about how hot I was my skin began to crawl. It promised to be a very long afternoon.

The dryness of the area was noteworthy. It was reflected wherever I looked. The brush was desiccated and the trees were without many leaves. The vegetation was brown and did not radiate the life-fulfilling chlorophyll of the springtime. The actual parched feeling made the floating dust and dirt even more obnoxious. The rocks were so brittle that they broke off into chips and slices. Everything was in a state of change.

I had to conserve my available fluids. The absence of additional water made me afraid. Dehydration would only complicate my problems if I could not ultimately find water. The heat would zap my strength and the lack of sufficient water supply would make an escape more tiresome. I reflected upon this problem for some time, and ultimately came to peace with some alternatives.

The original story was replete with spirits and entities from other dimensions. It did not matter whether or not I concurred with Blaine's openness with this subject. It was not a matter about personal belief or verifiable values. The spirit world was clearly part of the history. This dated back to Lareano's unique personal powers, the curse at the time of his betrayal, the strange events and sounds associated with his funeral procession, the death of Gerardo, the Military Governor's brother, the involvement with shamans, and the use by Blaine of channels and spirit mediums who proved instrumental in keeping the dream of the treasure alive to this point.

I have always enjoyed watching birds. Their majestic skills were a form of visual poetry. They were able to scale great heights and travel far with the greatest of ease. Today they became a motivating force for me. My airborne friends showed me where to escape.

I had hours until I would implement my plan and I tried to rest without moving much or changing my location. I did not know if I was being watched but waves of paranoia washed over me. I knew to stay put. Logic dictated taking the safest approach and making the personal assumption that I was not alone on the mountain. Patience and paranoia would combine to be a recipe for survival.

Any movement could instantly enhance detection if I was not alone. It could easily initiate another sudden and deadly event. Time to continue waiting.

The hours passed slowly and my mind drifted in and out. I tried to stretch and relax whenever possible. Although I was without any form of weapon there were things on the mountain that could be used for defensive purposes. The most plentiful of these was barbed wire. I remember encountering broken strands and long runs further down towards the base of the mountain. There were also some rudimentary hand tools that Blaine had left above the stone outcropping which he called Boat Rock. The sheets of shale rock could also be used for certain functions.

I could not detect any movement or changes in my view. Other than the birds, the scene was silent and still. My survival sense told me otherwise. There was danger lurking and I was not in the mood to become bait. I chose to remain and wait.

Snakes are one of my least favorite life forms. I knew from discussions with Blaine that rattlesnakes were relatively common in the area. I prayed that I would never encounter one of those again, at least as part of this adventure. The odds were mounting against me without the intervention of poisonous snakes. Adding them to the mix would be a true test of my faith and sanity.

My mantra for the next hour was "no snakes." I repeated it over and over with the visualization that it would be true. After a number of hours of just sitting I became stiff and sore. I had some wiggle room where I was and decided to stretch in slow movements, again with the promise to be silent and avoid detection.

I remained grateful for my yoga training. Like Siddhartha, I could meditate and I could fast. Both would be significant aides to the day that was before me. The lack of food would be no problem. I could maintain my normal strength reserves and be able to implement my plan later. The ability to meditate helped calm me and avoid any foolish moves.

My attention wandered to the unheard cast of characters, from the colorful bandit, Lareano Garcia, to the Military Governor, Jesus Borella, and much later his grandson, the tragic Epimineo Corrales. I admired him for his strength and perseverance. He gave so much to the treasure yet received nothing but grief in return. I never knew any of them and yet they felt like living and breathing souls within me. We shared a common experience or dream that bound us together in an unknowing world.

I felt like a character in *The Magus*. The words of John Fowles vibrated around me. "Doing nothing: That's hard work." The images were real. Was I being observed? I thought not. Could I be observed? Something said so. The consequences of detection overrode all thoughts about running. I had a plan and I was here for the day, just in case.

Time was on my side. I intended to continue to use the day to rest, contemplate, heal, and plan my safe escape. I did not intend to be a casualty or victim on the mountain, not today and not on any other day either. I had a plan and was crazy enough to believe it would work. I had to survive to share this story.

My eyes traversed the surroundings, including the alleged home of the treasure opposite me, and I gained a new level of appreciation for the skill of the bandit in selecting the site. I thought I could see the area of the cap rock from my position across the narrow canyon or gap. There were no apparent paths in the general vicinity of the treasure site. The land was vertical and the footing appeared to be tenuous. There was also a lack of noticeable water.

The more I thought about the dryness the more my thirst magnified. I refused to tap my water supply yet. As I monitored my situation, the meter was pegged on red. No shit, I was in a bad place with no realistic option out. Back to the concept of attitude filters perception. My positive attitude blocked any realistic determination of these conditions. It was self-imposed blindness to reason.

45. INSIDE

Dreaming – 1982

Dreams are often misleading. This time it seemed like the real thing. It was not a drill or practice run, at least in my dream. Although unprepared for the enormity of the task, it was time for the experience. I was there. I could see it.

The treasure was a constant. It was an immovable force. The mountain was alive and its face was changing. That was the issue. That was also the problem. Unbelievably, it would also be the solution.

The realization that the hillside would move over time caused the perceptual shift that was needed. It was so simple that I had to try. The group had been dealing in the literal rather than the figurative. They were assuming things to remain as they were. Finding the vault door would be more of a trick than I ever expected. That would figure, based upon the years of unsuccessful searches. It had to be harder than just walking up to it. The prize was too large.

46. SMOKE

La Chiva - 1982

The watchmen were professionally trained, well paid, and excellent at their job, both individually and collectively. They had specific orders from their benefactor but lacked a thorough understanding of the goal. They knew only a little about the treasure and what was beneath the ground on the mountain below them. They were hunters and not thinkers.

The leader was Dick Harris. He supported a large muscular body on a pair of disproportionately short legs. His development was obviously steroid supported, and he looked like he spent most of his years training in a gym. Dick was part Native American and part Irish. His muscular body betrayed his sensitivities. He was in charge for a number of good reasons, and his men respected his abilities.

Every man has a weakness, and Dick had his share. Most prominent was a major disorder in the vision and awareness of himself. His training and discipline was interrupted with his love of tequila and marijuana. After a long day of sitting and becoming convinced that they were alone on the hill, Dick extracted a pipe from his ammunition bag and smoked a bowl of his favorite herb. This led to a degradation of the mission and an unforgivable breach of security.

The two other watchmen, Chris and Alex, were equally impatient. Their strict training was likewise breached when they abandoned their posts and joined Dick for a smoke. It was the movement from the man furthest up the hill that was easily detected. He saved my life.

My awareness became focused on the sounds of rocks falling. I was surprisingly alert when I noticed a small rockslide on the slope way above and to the left of the treasure area.

I scanned the area quickly and witnessed apparent motion from only one position. Was this just an illusion, or did I actually see the shape of a person's head at such a distance? I stared to see if anything else was happening.

A flash of light or reflection emanated from the same general location and the final confirmation was given. I was not alone. I was damaged goods, but the value of my stock was now rising. A big repair job was in order. The required infusion of energy had just taken place. It was spontaneous and nuclear. My awareness was instantly enhanced by the confirmation that I was not alone on the mountain. The conclusion that I was the hunted, the prey, could not be escaped, but it had a concurrent strong impact upon me. It sharpened my senses, refocused my attention, and made me stronger. I was still alive, and I intended to stay that way. I was getting pumped up about it. The challenge was on.

More than once I had suspected an uncomfortable relationship between Blaine and his finances. The man had no visible means of support and yet he was able to bankroll this very expensive expedition. He had excellent taste and was gifted at spending money. But, he did not appear to be employed and was not the type to be an investor who lived off of his stock market holdings. He was not a realtor, but claimed to profit from putting together real estate deals. He lived well, but in a temporary status. He did not own any real estate.

I could go on and on about the conflicting dichotomies, but the sole connection was to deduce the potential for the existence of an undisclosed alliance with an angel, a secret backer who provided the large cash outlay to push the expensive operation forward. That possibility of a secret financier would answer many dangling questions. It made simple sense.

One of the worst human traits is greed. The word is somewhat synonymous with avarice and has a continuous role with the treasure across the way. It appeared to be the subject on my mental table. Perhaps the backer did not share Blaine's charitable beliefs. The hidden partner may have decided that he wanted it all. That could have even been his thinking from the outset.

The history of the treasure was replete with deception. The bloody curse of the treasure continued. We were part of a double-cross, no different than the aborted agreement between the bandit and the Military Governor almost one hundred years ago.

Going back even further, the relationship of the church with the people and the means it acquired the ancient power objects and many of the other specimens buried in the cave were no different.

I was versed in the lore. The brother of the Military Governor had lost his life because he was an unwanted visitor on the mountain. The thought of the bones made me more determined than ever to save my own. I had a plan.

47. Playback

La Chiva – 1982

It has been said that in times of extreme stress one's actions, reactions and performance instinctively revert to the initial level of training. I was grateful for this understanding and the ability to discern the realities facing me.

I counted three of them sitting together in a circle passing a pipe. Rifles were propped against a nearby tree. They became careless, either because of the effect of the drug or the mistaken proposition that they were without company. This behavior would not occur if they still supported the belief that anyone was alive and still on the mountain. They thought I was either dead or gone. Their miscalculation was going to cost them the success of their mission. I intended to remain alive and get out of there. They wouldn't be able to find anything.

As part of some of the projects that I worked on internationally, I received survival training from both the State Department and a private security firm. I never disclosed these matters to either family or friends. This tool chest gave me the confidence to stay strong, think clearly, utilize my training, and try to overcome the obstacles to my survival who happened to be sitting on the hill opposite me this very moment.

I did not know if they were alone or had backup at the bottom of the hill or at the base of the canyon. I was alone and without resources that could match anything they had to offer. I lacked any negotiating position and would lose in any level of confrontation. I had neither funds nor identification to escape. Even if I got off the mountain, I would be concerned about who or what level of evil was waiting for me.

Even with that predicament my attitude was straining to remain positive because I knew where they were. Apparently they did not believe I was here in an ambulatory condition. They were just waiting to make sure.

The element of surprise is a powerful weapon, but not against the band of death. I knew their philosophy and position. I had fooled them so far. Remaining invisible was the only sensible means of escape. Time was my only partner and gravity was not my friend.

48. GUNDERSON'S LAW

La Chiva – 1982

An old friend had a set of three rules to guide his interactive behavior in business and personal dealings. They were simple, harsh, and easy to comprehend. His friends called them collectively Gunderson's Law.

Simply stated it consisted of three rules:

1. Don't mess with me;
2. Don't mess with my money; and
3. Don't mess with my family.

An accurate recap would use the "f-word" instead. To violate any of the three would justify a level of wrath sufficient to deter further misconduct, and even death if necessary. Laws of the jungle often work that way.

Two of the three tenets of Gunderson's Law were presently at issue and I was in a fever pitch of survival. Clearly outnumbered and outgunned, a defensive posture was the only sane mindset.

Always look for the good. The careless behavior of the snipers was positive evidence that they did not believe I was up here. I deduced from their casual approach that they had friends at the base of the hill and probably also at the entrance to the canyon, a safety net of sorts. There was no way out, not going down the hill and not exiting through the canyon.

The experience was one of drifting into another time and place. I maintained my same vantage point across the canyon and slightly above the treasure site. Many questions remained unanswered, including how the bandit selected the site, how he safely relocated his fortune to such a remote location, and how he protected it for so long. I tried to envision how the bandit transported his loot. The defining moment came as the hot afternoon sun hit its apex and the shadows left the face of the mountain.

I meditated on the treasure and the lives that it touched. Possessing the time to ponder its history and meaning was a luxury for the present circumstances. The clarity of the vision was breathtaking but the setting made it suspect. Not only did it illuminate the moment, it also removed me temporarily from the crisis that surrounded me. I felt light, somewhat happy in a bizarre dimension, and enriched by the experience. The fact that I was still breathing was a wonderful act in and of itself.

Beneath me and on the slope across was a trio of warriors who were convinced that the usual rules of society did not apply to them. They were paid to do a job, and their degree of conviction was directly proportionate with the magnitude of the compensation. They are unaware of the location of the cave, and their conduct acknowledged my absence as well.

Irony was everywhere. I had the ability to pay them more than anyone else if I could trust them as partners. That thought was patently stupid as I uttered it. They had malevolent intent. Bargaining with the devil would produce equal results.

It was La Chiva itself that introduced the escape route. The alternatives were few but one could be all-inclusive and outcome determinative. One was a potential ticket to freedom.

49. Guarding Nothing

La Chiva – 1982

The snipers had breached their position apparently after giving up on the possibility of survivors. The solitude bred confidence. The survivors, if any, could not escape. In case they were wrong, the area was secured with a reserve at the canyon floor. It was a win-win for them.

Might may make right under some situations, but the prevailing winds did not blow in their direction on this day. I was living proof that their reasoning was flawed.

The leader, Dick, had made a huge tactical mistake. His lack of patience betrayed his years of excellent training. He failed his own resume. Their premature attack was made when Blaine's group had stopped and taken off their packs. The snipers must have been sure the team had gathered at the opening of the treasure site. They were wrong. They mistook a break and discussion session for the final destination. They acted too soon.

After realizing their huge mistake the snipers searched extensively but did not find the opening to the treasure, nor any sign thereof. They found nothing at all, neither path, nor marker, nor trap door. There was no evidence of any cache of treasure or any place it could be in the surroundings. Nothing could be ascertained near the location.

Blaine's distrust had a benefit for the treasure itself. Nobody in Blaine's party had maps, notes, or evidence of any kind. There were shovels and lighting instruments, but nothing in the way of metal detectors, charts, photographs, or any form of equipment. The group had been moving on either Blaine's memory or instinct, but without anything tangible or visible. None of us knew specifically where we were being led.

The decision was made to rectify the problem by personally securing the treasure site. They were becoming independent businessmen. They would deal with the boss at a later time. If enough could be removed, they may even head further south and never return home. Success in reaching the goal would ameliorate the means that were employed, at least in their thinking. It took nerve to even attempt to double-cross their employer, Mr. David Andrew Davis. The consequences were huge here.

Joyous anxiety was followed by caution and later depression as they canvassed the area and concluded that the treasure could not be found. It did not look like it was anywhere in the vicinity. As they spread out further and further their initial optimism turned sour. Nothing positive could be gleaned from their predicament. They were in trouble. Either they were in the wrong place altogether or there was no treasure. Having destroyed the living links to the treasure, their alternatives were limited.

The crime scene did not even occur at the entrance to the treasure. There was going to be no easy solution. It came as a complete surprise that the treasure group was without maps, charts, or identification equipment. Even worse, they must not have been even close to the site when the ambush was initiated. It was all so stupid.

They were pretty sure that one person had escaped but doubt had eclipsed their memory. The treasure party had all been dressed in relatively similar clothes and the trail twisted and turned up the mountain. Maybe they lost count or maybe not. They disagreed about the number they had observed and whether or not the same person was counted more than once. The hats were similar and windbreakers were all the same, and a miscount could be easily explained by the fact that the path wound up the hill behind rocks and other barriers.

At no point were all of Blaine's group of treasure hunters visible together, or so they now concluded. Their belief had changed over time because of many factors including some that were self-induced. The cannabis was partly to blame.

The sun became blinding after hours of sitting in the mesmerizing heat of La Chiva. There was nobody in sight and the thought of a survivor was lost as the hours passed. Besides, he would be caught at the base of the canyon if he tried to pass the waiting van.

Their secret was safe for now. They would conclude that the whole treasure story was a hoax. Nothing could be found on the mountain. Nobody survived to tell a different story. Their misdeeds could go undetected. Dead men tell no tales. They would relax for the rest of the day, join the group at the bottom and wait for another day, and then depart for home with the revelation that their employer had been the victim of a con game, a hoax.

It was a conspiracy of silence based upon some reasonable assumptions. The secret was safe with them.

50. STILL WAITING

La Chiva – 1982

I rested as the sniper guards played on the mountain. Their behavior was actually indicative of my intended escape route. They grew louder and increasing more careless as they smoked. When they did move they hiked and climbed around their immediate surroundings in search of the opening. After regrouping they crisscrossed the area, back and forth, higher and lower, all without results.

Their actions were carefully observed from my secure position on the opposite hill. It was a human comedy being enacted by fools. I must have been nuts finding entertainment in their actions, but I had time on my side and they were functionally disabled. Although they were high they were actually too low. The treasure spot was safely above them.

The brilliance of the bandit was even more pronounced from my vantage spot. One could almost be upon the actual opening without ever seeing it. The spot was selected or created with a great understanding of the terrain and human nature. You could be within less than ten feet of the location and not even know it. Almost like something out of Indiana Jones, you would have to step around a large rock to the apparent edge of the ledge until you realized that it dropped away before you and circled under the unique outcropping. Hidden in plain site. No wonder Epimineo was unable to find it again. I wondered if I could and I was currently looking at it. I hoped I had adequate time to memorize the setting. It would look much different from the other side.

My survival had been dependent on very good luck, timing, and the unique location of the treasure itself. Before all hell broke loose, Blaine had pulled me away from the group during a so-called refreshment and rest break before the excitement level escalated. I was lucky enough to get the first look. Blaine and I climbed up and over to the site alone while the others were snacking. It was while we were at the site that the shots rang out. I'm not sure if it was paranoia or preparation, but Blaine insisted that we separate in a divide-and-conquer mindset. Blaine told me to go in one direction and he went in another. As it turned out, he went back to the group and found himself under fire. I was able to escape.

Somewhere towards the base of La Chiva were buried the remains of a wonderful friend, Blaine Court, and the others from our expedition. The trio of death found it easier to bury the bodies on La Chiva than carry them away. I watched the grisly event earlier in the day. The bastards were so lazy that they buried each of my traveling companions close to where they found them, all in unmarked graves. These villains were large men with small hearts. Fortunately, decency prevailed and they took the effort to bury the bodies rather than leave them for the carrion eaters.

I was confident that I would never return to this blasted mountain if I was able to get away alive. The prospect of success gave me strength. After all, I had a plan.

51. Jose Sanchez

El Faro, MX - 1982

The sun set quickly over the hills behind me, turning the bearded part of the face of La Chiva into a glowing alpenglow of pink and orange hues. Daylight was in short supply and darkness was coming. There was a slight moon, and the evening promised to be very dark until it came up. My patience was rewarded at dusk when the guards deserted their positions and retreated to the base. I waited an additional hour and then implemented my escape plan.

Their grand gestures and offensive behavior were exhibits of their confidence. In their way of thinking any survivor had no way out. They were wrong. Only a fool would walk into the ambush waiting below. The arrogant guards left me another avenue of escape, and that was in the opposite direction.

My plan was to go up and over the mountain, to the right of the peak and over at the mid-point of La Chiva. I didn't know what was on the other side, but it had to be a significant improvement over what I was confident would await my arrival below.

After settling into the situation, which was stressful beyond belief, a calming female voice was "heard" on a sublime level. She came to my awareness as thoughts and sounds vibrating in my being but not through my ears. She was a vibration, an inner knowing. She gave me hope and, ultimately, a key to unlock the mystery of La Chiva. I could hear her voice and see the visual impressions being transmitted to me. Inner vision overtook my sense of perception and I began a new part of the history of the treasure.

In staring at the mountain for hours, I realized that the bandit did not do the impossible and bring the treasure up from the bottom of the canyon. That was an erroneous assumption that defied the terrain, gravity, and common sense. This gave way to thinking about other approaches to the cache.

It was my belief that Lareano Garcia came over through an unseen crack to the west of the peak and dropped down to the site. It was a top-down deal, like landing a plane. That would account for many things, including the unique resting spot for the treasure. At all times it would be protected from wandering eyes, unless and only if the observer was on the vantage point that I currently enjoyed. There would be little reason for anyone to be over here on the adjoining hill; it offered nothing except a safe haven from the over-confident crazies who wanted to kill me but were too stoned to find me.

I did not suffer from any exaggerated sense of self-importance. I was not in the proposal as part of the original count. It was out of precaution, and perhaps simple vision, that they were watching for me. They should have waited. La Chiva can evoke odd behavior, and this was not unusual in the history of the treasure. Stranger things have been recorded in the mystery of the mountain. I became deluded that my deliverance was ordained.

My hours of stillness permitted a review of the stories, legends, and lore. The history was chilling. Being on the mountain and staring over to La Chiva brought everything back to life. It was like a living video. The soundtrack was missing, but the life of the treasure was revealing itself before me.

I was a witness to horrible acts, but nothing could be done to reverse that fact. The chunks of memory disturbed by the irrational behavior and unnecessary violence would have to be carefully filed away and forgotten. If successful, they would be placed in a mental file box and allowed to gather dust in the deep recesses of my mind. The story of this mountain experience and voyage into terror would remain secret with me, or at least that is what I strongly believed at that point. I just wanted it to be done.

I quietly traversed the hill, descended to a point of intermediate connection with the face of La Chiva, and then began climbing again in search of animal paths or other indicia of a potential escape route. All of the time I was careful to tread lightly, walk in such a way as to minimize sound or other impact, and stay upright in the darkness. It was no easy task.

After hours of slowly moving in the dark over the rugged terrain, I was too spent to continue. My eyes were hurting from concentration and I was suffering from lack of food and water. I sat for a momentary break and fell asleep.

Morning came with a surprise. Having slept like a dead man I was shocked to awaken and realize that this was not a dream. Confident that I was now alone on the mountain, I resumed my search with the vigor of the new day.

After aligning myself parallel to the treasure base I slowly searched for any sign of a trail. It was a foolish endeavor considering the fact that the bandit had not been there for close to ninety years, but I had a sense that something would reveal the way. Finally, a small animal path caught my attention and gave me the way to the place I saw in my meditation. It looked just like the passageway on the approach to Angel's Flight in Zion National Park. This was a long way from Utah but similar in formation. I knew what to do and I continued.

When I broke through the mountain pass I looked down at a plateau that was bright green and thickly planted. I knew it was guidance, far more than luck, which brought me to this place. It looked like an oasis. I came upon a small brook and was refreshed with the wonders of water, just water. Small joys help one take huge leaps. I drank as much as I could and filled my containers with the precious liquid.

The history of the area was full of gossip about drugs. These stories were current but also dated back to before World War II. The area was famous for opiates and marijuana, and was part of numerous reports. It did not take long until I came upon a gentleman who was tending his hidden hillside garden. We were equally startled to see the other, and my clothing and weak physical condition gave him confidence that I was not a threat. This chance meeting was part of a friendship that has continued to this day.

Jose Sanchez was his name, and I think of him as a guardian angel. He was an independent grower, a freelancer who worked far away from town and higher up the hill than the others. We had a slight language barrier, but communication was possible. He understood my need to get out of there. More likely than not he assumed that I was in trouble and worthy of saving.

Jose correctly deduced from my appearance that I was not going to care about his proclivities, and I was a potential friend rather than a foe. The blood on my clothing was like a merit badge. He offered to give me a basic meal and introduce me to a cousin who would usher me out of town. The fact that I was without funds or a passport did not seem to matter. We were close to the Highway of Sin, the nickname for the main highway that ran north and south, and I worried about passing through Culiacan and crossing the border. Issues such as those would be conquered later.

Jose had a brilliant yet dangerous idea. His solution was to broker a one-way ride in a twin-engine Cessna destined for the high desert near San Bernardino, California. It was a flight without a ticket, flight plan, or customs inspection.

I was not afraid of the DEA, U.S. Customs, or any other American bureaucracy. If I had the good fortune to find myself on the American side of the border, my resume would suffice to eventually get me free. My bloodstained clothes and lack of identification would only ensure their immediate attention. The means became irrelevant as long as I was home. I would survive it all, even if initially behind immigration bars.

I was blindfolded before being put in a vehicle and driven for what seemed like an hour. With the blindfold still securely in place, I was assisted into a small space in the airplane's crowded cargo area. I was ordered to leave the blindfold on until the pilot instructed otherwise. Compliance was easy.

I was prone on a large stack of plastic bags filled with narcotics. I was joyous once the engines started up. The ride was long, turbulent, and far from first class. I believe we flew low to avoid customs and radar. We landed twice, refueled once, and landed in California without detection.

Upon arriving in the high desert I honored my part of the deal. I made a call and had an old friend loan me $5,000 in cash for the pilot of my non-luxury transportation. Pricey considering my seating, but it felt like a bargain. No receipt was required. I hoped the pilot would share a portion with Jose. I did not think I would ever see Jose again, but that ended up differently.

I was back on California soil without a passport or identification, change of clothes, or money. I reached home a week later determined to avoid Mexico for the rest of my life. The secret of the treasure was safe with me.

52. END AROUND

Big Sur, CA - 1987

For a number of years I was successful in suppressing most thoughts of La Chiva. It was a dark part of my life due to the horrible ending and the door to those memories remained closed. I was able to survive the experience but I could not escape the toxic impact of the brutal day. In time, thoughts of revenge diminished, anger and disappointment subsided, but there is a limit for everyone and mine was clearly exceeded.

After a few years I could suppress the images for only limited periods of time. The treasure was infiltrating my awareness as thoughts and dreams systematically invaded me. I was bombarded with visuals, still pictures of scenes from the mountain, memories of Culiacan, the characters as I remembered them, the events, experiences, sounds and dreams. An optimistic endeavor ended in a terrifying day. My associates had been savagely murdered without warning or reason.

In a remote, secured storage locker were boxes, tapes, notes and photographs. Blaine's materials remained safely locked in my possession. They were miles away and yet they had the presence to come to me. As if by a time-released signal, they began calling.

I knew I could not return to La Chiva and Lareano's treasure, and yet I was overcome with an irrational drive to reach a resolution or conclusion of the real story. Could I take this story from the vaults of my memory and give it words? I've done some right; I've done some wrong. I have kept many secrets, and this one for too long. Was it time to let the secret out?

Was it safe to share it? Perhaps a universal healing could take place on the subtle soul levels of those who were involved in living this adventure as their reality. My sense of completion would not be fulfilled unless I could tell this story.

238

53. CALLING

California Dreaming – 1988

Dream consciousness is a peculiar state of mind. It takes some aspects of the real and twists them into the most bizarre mental pictures. They take on such a quality of existence that one can only question how we come up with screwy connections of random things in our sleep. This was one such event.

I was filled with excitement as the lanterns were lit and I crawled through an opening. I could not see the entrance, nor feel the surroundings. The doorway was nowhere to be seen. I thought it was a mere foot or two behind me, but it was clearly out of sight. The passageway was restrictive and tight. I couldn't turn around.

I was in a vacuum, a void that almost sucked the essence out of its own space. It was a creepy feeling. The darkness absorbed all of the light as my eyes fought to see. I waited before I moved. I was in a cave, and it was hot and musty inside. It was not comfortable. The air was thick and pungent, a smell unlike anything in my memory. It wasn't pleasant.

I heard the squeal of a bat or two. Surprisingly, I did not feel alone. The language of the bats was understood and their communication was far more complex than I would have ever conceived. It is consistent with their other items of standard equipment, like superior radar and the ability to fly, especially night flight.

The sounds increased indicating a full colony of bats. Their chorus signaled the end of the day. I had become the awareness of a bat and had been invited within. It felt crowded. They were welcoming me. The insights to the treasure involved glaring yellow light.

According to Blaine, the bat was another of the totems or protectors of either La Chiva or the specific treasure itself. With this experience I have no doubt that it was true.

I was startled into wakefulness. I was dreaming about returning to La Chiva. I was being called through the dream state of consciousness. In that arena I had no defense. I was being summoned. This was the fifth night in a month that I found myself around or inside the treasure.

I was not going back. I could not return. Culiacan was history. Flashing moments from the terrifying last day served to ensure silence and distance. I would not go back. It was out of the question.

Years passed with the secret of the treasure locked safe within me. Only occasional negative thoughts would bubble up to my consciousness. I was surprised when happier images and memories appeared, like scenes from Culiacan, views of the colorful characters that peppered its history, the smell of dried sage on the mountain, or abstract views including the bearded face of the peak.

I gradually returned to a more routine life at home, selecting my assignments carefully, and reading, cycling, and doing more yoga. It was easy to slow down after years of so much travel. Life had been good to me, and I bathed in the peace and freedom of Monterey County.

At times I thought about telling this story as fiction through my old friend, Steve, but always elected against sharing any part of my secret. He didn't know the story, none of my friends knew. It was easier that way. The secret of the Treasure of La Chiva was still safe with me.

54. THE BOX

Monterey County, CA - 2000

More years passed and the treasure story remained mostly dormant in my mind. It was the sleeping elephant that I prayed would never wake again. An inner peace accompanied its sleep state, like a hibernating bear.

Then something changed. As a spring thaw follows winter, the dreams returned. Voices began to speak to me from unknown places at night. I was besieged with memories, similes, facts and images. A dormant portion of my mental hard drive was accessed and everything came back to me. Things went into overdrive. It was an overbearing experience and a serious interruption to my self-imposed exile and forced amnesia about the treasure.

There are many times in life when we must make a difficult choice or initiate a series of decisions. Often it is at a crossroads of sorts where the road curves so the sight line does not follow the path. Logic may not even be a factor. It takes an inner knowing, a leap of faith to make the decision and to take the hard steps. I found myself at that blasted place again.

Years of avoidance forced me to the reckoning point. It was the place of departure from where one can never return. The decision point is a figurative razor's edge. The correctness is not of consequence when forced to take the step. You can easily wonder later if it was right or it was wrong. It is more a decision to act or not, to move or stand pat, to grow or to stay put.

Nighttime was not easy and it became difficult to sleep. I was facing inner demons from my experience at La Chiva combined with other things involving the treasure for the last 120 years.

After a few weeks of erratic behavior I gathered the courage to drive to my storage locker and locate the box with a small torn label reading "La Chiva." One could easily challenge my characterization as courage; it was more similar to being forced or driven. Carefully, I placed the box in my car and headed home, knowing I was about to cut loose a flood of images and emotions held tightly all these years.

I removed the cardboard box, which I knew was filled with maps, tapes, notes, photographs, receipts, etc. There were pages of quotes from Epimineo's interview and Blaine's sessions with the psychics and spiritual readers. Not everything about the treasure that I had suppressed for years could be found in the storage box. I stared at it for a few minutes, pulled out my Swiss army knife, and performed open surgery on my memory banks.

The first single stroke with the large blade announced the unanticipated beginning of another chapter in my life. Opening the box was like a visit with an old friend. As if consuming a seriously addicting drug, I was hooked within minutes. The treasure genie was let out of the box. Poof.

Facing me on the top was the smiling face of Blaine. I forgot that beautiful picture of him in Big Sur, which was the last addition to the box. I smiled at how the gorgeous blues of the ocean behind him complemented his eyes. I placed it there in honor of all that he was, and always would be, to this story. "All my relations," Blaine.

Next I removed a page with a list entitled, "Symbols." My mind was spinning as I read the list. Some of them I had forgotten and some made no sense at all. The words were printed in pencil on a piece of worn yellow notebook paper, and read as follows:

SYMBOLS

Crosses
Boat Rock
Cave
Cross cut on rock
Crosses cut into fencepost
Crosses inside
Parrots
A Tiger
Chartreuse green iguana
Bank vault door

Deep bed of ashes
Charcoal
Mountains
Goats
Rattlesnakes
Bones
Hidden Entrances
Secret Enemies
Canyons
Height – Falling

The next page was a handwritten note that had the most captivating title:

TREASURE OF LA CHIVA

Gold coins
Old Money
Doubloons
Pieces of Eight
Reales
Silver coins
Gold bullion
Silver ingots
Gold & bejeweled artifacts
Inca plates
Icicle shaped wood spears
Boxes with ropes
Old coins adorned with the Spanish King
Artifacts and cultural items
Wands
Small stones
Gold and silver Saints
Crosses
Rubies
Empowered objects
Chains

Plates
Leather bags
Cloth bags
Small decorated boxes
Ceremonial jars and objects

A folded piece of gray paper bore the dark fluid ink from a quill or fountain pen and a highly unusual script. I didn't know what it meant. Nothing triggered my memory of the site.

MAP & DRAWING ERRORS

A 3' diameter rock near a 5' or greater
tree base.
Mud and rock wall could be 5' high and
12' long.
May be gone.
Seems to grow out of the end of the wall
A tall barren tree that went up a long way before
branches.
Intertwined roots.
Landslides and accretion?
Watch for erosion.
Height issues
Scale
Angle
Perspective

There was a page dedicated to the mineral malachite with a small piece of the unique green mineral itself attached to the bottom corner.

MALACITE

The stone of transformation.

The color green has certain symbolic values that are common throughout various cultures.

In America, the early leaders created their paper currency in the tones of green.

In metaphysics the color of prosperity is referred to as green.

The heart chakra is green.

Certain ceremonial stones and crystals are green, the most notable being emeralds.

Healing lasers use the green wave.

Compare with Chrysocolla, which is associated with renewed strength and balance.

The pages that followed gave a perspective as of 1982:

TIMELINE

1531	Culiacan founded
1830's	Cathedral built
1836	Jesus Borella born (1836–1910)
1857	Lareano Garcia born (1857–1891)
1860's	Lareano in school
1867	Grandmother died (11/2/1867)
1876	The Lareanos formed
1880's	The Lareanos thrived (1876–1890)
1890	Bandit trapped
1891	Jesus Borella secured treasure (4/27/1891); Lareano died (5/1/1891)
1893	Gerardo Borella missing
1907	Epimineo Corrales born
1910	Mexican Revolution
1910	Jesus Borella died

1920's	Government appropriated church property
1932	Epimineo Corrales finds treasure
1971	Epimineo meets treasure hunters
1972	Treasure hunters expedition (12/1972)
1978	Handoff to Blaine Court
1979	Blaine meets with Epimineo in Sayulita
1980	Blaine investigates using psychics and channels
1980	Blaine assembles team
1982	Blaine Court's expedition

PEOPLE

Lareano Garcia (1857-1891)
Wife: Arlena
Daughter: Esperanza
Son: Hector
Father: Esteban
Mother: Carmen
Grandmother: Eva
Camacho Lopez (1856-1891)
The Lareanos (1876-1890)
Padre Ramone
Jesus Borella (1836-1910)
Wife: Rosa
Gerardo Borella (1840's-1893)
Epimineo Corrales (born 1909)
The Treasure Hunters:
Ben Richardson
Ed Burkett
Bob Klein
Blaine Court

The next thing neatly wrapped was an old brass spyglass in a soft leather pouch. Another mystery. There is no way of knowing if this has any connection to the Military Governor's time, but it could.

Also in the box was an old black Sony Walkman that didn't work. Hoping it was merely a power issue I changed the batteries and inserted the first of the hand-labeled cassette tapes. What a time warp. It was not hard to reflect back to the time when the Walkman was the newest musical device. I pushed the start button, and the tape wheezed into motion. It seemed plastic, clunky, and of poor sound quality. I forgot how noisy their mechanisms were.

The first cassette was an interview with Blaine from his meeting in Sayulita with Epimineo. He sounded so excited about receiving the drawing from Epimineo. I paused the tape to remove a photocopy of the drawing from the box.

I stared at the drawing with two views of the site. My attention went from the top third, being the side view from a short distance. The bottom portion was a larger view of looking from behind the cap rock. Both images show a seated human and the word "palo." A tree is the key landmark in both.

As it turned out, his scale was much too small. It was misleading and of little value unless truly understood. Holding the map helped connect me back to Blaine's excitement when he showed me the drawing. He was so optimistic about our success.

The next tape was an interview with Blaine and one of the spirit guides or so-called channels. Blaine had a lot of respect for those energies as a specialized vibration of communication and he often spoke about their unique effect through attention to inner hearing.

One told Blaine, "There is something missing here." A detailed "account" of the history of the bandit was forthcoming.

Another told him about Gerardo, the Military Governor's brother, and warned about the spirits and discarnate entities protecting the treasure.

The third told him not to go in no uncertain terms. Subtlety was not an attribute to this fountain of purported wisdom. She warned about the high level of protection surrounding the site. I wish Blaine had trusted her.

Another, Reverend Frank, also cautioned against a trip to the mountain. He predicted nothing positive happening and Blaine being denied access forever. The word "spirit" was repeated but the auditory quality was weak. These warnings had the opposite effect, making Blaine stronger and more convinced of his positive outcome.

My mind began to wander as I handled these items in the box. I found myself recalling that time, a surprising two decades ago, when I first heard about the treasure and the Culiacan area. I had so many questions. Who were these people? Why did Blaine consult with them? What was their purpose? How did they work? What could they know? How would they know?

I wondered if there was room in my personal belief system to absorb this expanded or altered view of reality. I decided to remain open and alert to the potentialities and had the faith to absorb Blaine's more expanded vision. Whether or not you believe in the truth or reliability of this subject, it is indisputable that we would never have reached the treasure without them. The communication from or through them produced important clues and undisputed validation. Upon reflection, it exhibited a sort of hippie-futuristic blending which was totally uncharacteristic for Blaine's age. He was using all levels of thought and experience available to crack the secret of the treasure.

Blaine had consulted yogis, teachers, writers and friends. He listened well, and when he spoke you wanted to pay attention. He had a warm but strong vocal quality, with a unique and friendly pace. The wisdom was always unequivocal. He was a scholar without letters; a commanding personality that served him well when he was an editor and columnist for one of the first spiritually oriented newspapers in Carmel, California.

Blaine's interest brought instant credibility to the project. No one in the group doubted the existence of Lareano's cave. Blaine would not be wasting his time, and thereby our time, chasing Don Quixote's windmill. He had proof!

As I was about to close the box and end that session something happened that changed the focus and intensity of my inquiry. A handwritten envelope was lying on its side towards the bottom of the box. It was addressed to Blaine, had no return address, and was still sealed. It was postmarked nine days before we took the charter to Mexico. I'm not sure how it got there but it may have been with the last papers that Blaine brought to me when we had lunch three days before the trip.

The envelope had not been opened in the eighteen years since it was sealed, and I was not comfortable breaching its secret even now. My anxiety calmed over the issue and I realized that nobody could complain if I read Blaine's undelivered letter. Perhaps it had nothing to do with anything about the treasure.

Ironically, the letter was not dated. Only the postmark makes the timing clear. Reading the contents changed my perspective immediately and brought that horrible massacre back to light.

Dear Blaine

Wishing good luck on the adventure of a lifetime. You will be in Culiacan in less than a week and climbing the mysterious La Chiva to our treasure of dreams. I can't wait to hear more.

I made a decision and apologize for not involving you. I know you would not agree but I view it as insurance. Since I am underwriting all costs perhaps it shouldn't matter to you, but I bet it would. I took the liberty of assigning 3 men, Dick Harris, Chris Painter and Alex White to be "available" should any need arise. These men will remain out of sight and out of your way. Their exceptional strength may be helpful after you secure the treasure. Again, this was my decision and my logic is sound.

Should you need anything, just leave a message for Dick Harris at your hotel front desk. For me he is insurance, for you he is muscle. It is a gift to our success.

David A. Davis

I closed the box and sat for at least an hour. The trio of death were supposed to be friends, not foe. So much for secrets. A jolt of understanding overcame me as I realized that Blaine was unaware of the so-called assistance being offered. He had not opened the letter.

I had the names of three people and needed to know if they were the perpetrators. I became immersed in researching the three men, Dick Harris, Chris Painter, and Alex White to determine if they were the killers. I needed time to think about what I should do, if anything.

It did not take long to learn their story. None of the three returned to the employ of Mr. David Andrew Davis. It appears that Dick Harris never returned to the United States. Everything about him turned into a dead end. He seemed to vanish around the same time as Blaine's expedition.

The other two were a different story. The first shooter, Chris Painter, had moved to the north shore of Lake Tahoe and was selling real estate in Crystal Bay. Alex White moved to Idaho and was working for a large construction company owned by his mother.

Two more years passed rather quickly.

55. FINISH WHAT YOU START

California – 2002

When the time was right I was able to acknowledge that a shift had occurred. A switch flipped in my mind and the impossible became the probable. I wanted to return to Culiacan and hike La Chiva. After vacillating over and over again in the past twenty years, I wanted to do it now.

It was such a no-brainer as soon as my perceptual viewpoint changed. I had to finish what I started, and the project would be more important now than before. Good news was scarce. The bylines were negative and stories were of the same flavor. This could be the mitigation of the darkest negative with a fantastic dose of feel-good stuff and positive press too.

I knew what to do. But I shared this secret change in attitude with nobody. That means not one single person. Nobody. The logistics would be different now. The memory of the adversaries was buried deep inside me. It was a large project to administer, but the goals were worth the effort.

If only the Military Governor had left something in writing or entrusted somebody with his secret. The treasure had not been opened since. At the present time I was probably the only living person to be thinking, talking, writing, or wanting to visit La Chiva. For years the comfort of the secret was great. Nobody was left except this friendly photojournalist with a pulsing drive to reach conclusion in one manner or another. The story had to be healed.

I previously shared my perception of Blaine's conduct and called it paranoid or fear-driven. This was noteworthy because it was totally inconsistent with his personality and his living philosophy. He wasn't a "down" kind of guy. His guidelines for daily life did not normally include acknowledging or embracing the negative. We had all been exposed to it and the subject was not an uncommon part of the grumbling when we were speaking from less than our positive selves. However, it was inconsistent and unusual for Blaine.

History shows the benefits of keeping the circle of knowledge very small. Nothing in the Culiacan literature, libraries, or newspapers had anything to feed the story. It was a dead end, and buried in another layer as things shifted to the Internet. The secret was safe, even within the growing body of information on the Web. It was amazing.

The geography was such that development did not stimulate growth. The population grew in the other directions from town, and away from the hostile hills, canyons, peaks and valleys south and southwest of the city limits. It was a different world and few ventured in that direction.

56. Have Fun, Kill the Enemy

2002

"Have fun, kill the enemy." These words rung out from deep within my memory. They were a mantra from a time of the original incarnation of this experience. They echoed from the vigilante guards while they were murdering Blaine and the rest of his expedition, and I am haunted to this day by their conduct.

"Have fun, kill the enemy" was known to be one of the favorite sayings of Blaine's financier, the mysterious Mr. David Andrew Davis, cattle rancher and land baron with major holdings in Arizona, Montana, New Mexico and Nevada. Those words were attributed to Mr. Davis in Wall Street Journal articles, and in interviews published in Barron's, Time and Business Week.

I considered Blaine's paranoia and the deadly results from my last trip to La Chiva. The attack by the guards could not have been anticipated by Blaine. I had to take every possible step to ensure my safety. Thoughts of the mysterious Mr. Davis filled my mind. Private security was probably part of his personal staff. If not, companies like Lake Waters & Associates could easily be hired to provide private "soldiers" as security for his investment. The difference between defense and offense in this context was merely one of intent. It's always about the money.

I knew about The Apollo Agency before I ever heard its name. However titled, it was a necessary element for outsourcing the logistics of a venture in a foreign country, especially this one. A cache of buried treasure would clearly fall within their expertise. The story had enough punch to earn their attention, and the magnitude and details deserved more than a second reflection.

The Apollo Agency could be a source of protection, an insurance policy of sorts. They had the resources to ensure a safe entrance, successful protection of the site, inventory and removal of the assets, and a secure exit from the country. The Apollo Agency could also be a backup; reserve forces to meet whatever needs could arise. To balance that line of thinking would be the concept of secrecy. Confidentiality is lost proportionately with the number of people involved. The larger the circle, the easier it is to create a leak. I realized the idea of The Apollo Agency had to be abandoned. The risks were too great should my return be made known.

The return to La Chiva had to be attempted with the smallest team possible. It made the most sense to plan it alone, thus the only security aspect was if I went crazy, and then it would be too late anyway.

Opportunity was knocking and I needed an overt reason to go to Mexico, a shield to my true intentions. Some calls were in order, with the first being to my agent. Shooting a feature or cover would be nice, but almost any local story would work. Even an advertising shot or publicity series would be acceptable. A special invitation would be the perfect reason. That and some extra time for sports, hiking and personal photography. It would provide a free recon shot at the site if everything went well.

The life of a diverse and published photographer was filled with opportunity. It was easy to get a freelance assignment in Mexico. The invitation and assignment came back so quickly that I had to question the forces working behind the scenes. Here comes the weird stuff again, or at least a few moments of considering the bizarre.

57. TEN TWO-LETTER WORDS

Culiacan – 2002

It took forever for morning to come. Yet it was only 6:15 am. I sat in my room at Hotel Los Tres Rios humming some of Jim Morrison's lyrics and thinking about the doors to our life. I was "waiting for the sun." It was like my own version of Aldous Huxley and the doors to perception.

I thought about my last time at this same hotel with Blaine and his crew. It was twenty years ago. I had no problem visualizing him, with his strong angular face, silver gray beard, and avuncular manner. I wondered about the genesis of his remarkable turquoise arrowhead and regretted never asking.

A senseless two years had passed since my interaction with the box of memories and the revelation that the story was still alive in me and had to proceed to its next logical step. This was it and today was the day.

I thought about Grandma's Ten Two-Letter Words, and knew that they applied to this situation as well. She was speaking at a Rotary function when she challenged the audience to provide a complete sentence consisting of ten words of two letters each that best describes a great attitude for service. We all paused and waited.

Her reply was simple and mighty, "If it is to be, it is up to me." So true, so I acted upon it.

For two weeks I had been in Mexico on assignment, photographing a feature for a travel magazine on the contrasts between the preserved old and developing new. The theme permitted great latitude in determining the museums and galleries in the old towns that blended with the goal of developing new tourism. The trip included Puerto Vallarta, Sayulita, and Culiacan on the West Coast. I had difficulty selling the addition of Culiacan, because it was not on the thriving tourist map. It was to be a two-part series, with the first featuring the Mayan Riviera on the opposite coast of the country, from the hustle and bustle of Cancun to the peacefulness of Bacalar just north of Belize.

The buildings did not have a resemblance to the Catholic Churches of Europe and were dissimilar to those in Spain too. There was only a hint of the classical European look in structures created out of materials from the new world. Stonework was replaced with adobe. Tiles covered the roofs. Old hand-hewn lumber and planking were evident everywhere. There was a beautiful blend of the old and the new, the past and the present, and the craftsmen employed in the restoration work maintained the continuity of theme. The textures and colors were complimentary and dramatic.

My visit into the cathedral carried a different mindset than when I first entered with Blaine. My perspective had grown immensely since 1982. As with the previous visit, I envisioned the opulent gold and silver artifacts, statutes, and sculptures removed by the Lareanos more than one hundred twenty-five years ago. Their replacements did not bear the same grandiosity. Apparently the church agreed that the high profile of the past was potentially irritating to some. The more understated decor was fitting with the community and its environs. It bore a historical perspective consistent with the area and congruent with the simple but noble architecture.

The darkness within the structure felt like a blanket over my spirit. It had a restrictive impact on my awareness and diminished any feeling of empowerment. I had to fight to contain my own energies and enthusiasm. To my perceptual sense there was something very dark and forbidding. I was experiencing an unusually negative space. Hopefully it was not a sign of things to come.

The contrasts between my visits were marked. My first visit was cloaked in secrecy, high drama, and a tremendous amount of collective anxiety. This adventure began without fanfare.

The last time in Culiacan began with a half dozen men. This time I was here alone.

The last time we were confident and believed ourselves to be prepared for whatever may happen. This time I knew that I was navigating on past images and totally screwed if anything went wrong.

Last time we had the illusion of safety in numbers. This attempt was closer to invisible.

Last time we were confident, while this time I am doubtful.

Last time I was innocent and excited. This time I knew much more and was scared. In spite of this, the push to return to La Chiva had overshadowed all intellect and common sense.

The darkness of the morning was different from the appearance within the cathedral. The sunlight would come within the next hour, in contrast to the perpetual darkness within the church. The stained glass windows were small and permitted little light to penetrate, and the surrounding oaks and other trees blocked most of the direct light. The impact was not dissimilar to a windowless cathedral. This had metaphorical qualities in light of the terrible revelations about the church that were exposed since my last visit.

The church was under severe attack, especially in America, for numerous issues of abuse. Our understanding was similar to the conditions in Culiacan, many of which were precipitating causes for the onslaught by Lareano many years ago.

58. Long Time Gone

Culiacan – 2002

Truly a glutton for punishment, the decision to stay at Hotel Los Tres Rios was an effort to reconnect with the past. History cannot be rewritten; it must be embraced and then released. I worked so hard to forget for so many years, and then opened the floodgates by taking it all back in quickly. It was like a change in the tides, with a slow recession over years and then a tidal wave back.

I went to the dining room at first light and ate like a pig. Not only hungry, nervous, and in need of energy, I also hoped that it was not my last meal. Everything was deja vu. Sitting at the same general window location enhanced the experience and waves of memories washed over me. The images did not stop. For a moment it seemed like time stood still, and that it was only a number of months ago that the team was sitting in the very same dining room buzzing with excitement and trying our best to sober up and act casual. Nobody even remotely considered the forthcoming danger, except perhaps Blaine. That will never be known, but I still have my suspicions.

The back and forth motion was jarring and my memory banks felt stressed from the overload. I was experiencing two overlapping spaces at almost the same time. Each part was in a different time format, permitting me to drift back and forth like a witness. The difficult part was the attention that was spent in the past. Twenty years was not sufficient time to forget. It had all the makings of being one emotionally tough day.

The wave was of tsunami proportions and I sat dazed and confused. Within minutes the sounds and mental pictures of my last trip to the mountain returned. I was overcome with the impossible task of reversing inertia and returning to the site of the carnage and the major league scariest days of my life. I felt empowered while overcoming those odds last time, but the chance to deeply reflect and absorb the experience again was disarming and humbling. I was powerless then and nothing has changed.

My mind was a battlefield of ugly images, uncomfortable feelings, and terrifying sounds of pain and suffering, all playing in mental Technicolor. I questioned why I wanted to go back. I was scared with nobody to share my fears. It was a new definition of alone for me. I had stayed away for a long time and each and every reason flashed before me. I remember all of them. Not one pleasant thought would come to the forefront. I was on the verge of returning to La Chiva and seriously questioned what I was doing.

This was nuts and I knew it. I had come to the Three Rivers and was stuck at the breakfast table. My knees were weak and my confidence was vacant. It must have taken the day off.

The weight of the treasure was on my shoulders and the magnitude of the secret was impossible to dislocate. Common sense washed over me and I felt like a victim of my own circumstances. Being unable to move, I waited with hopeless anticipation that things would change soon.

My mind crawled through the nasty tunnel of dark images and found a glimmer of hope at the other end. This was concurrent with the first rays of the sunshine coming through the window. Fortunately, I had been seated at a small window table, affording me views of the garden and the three merging rivers beyond. The sun made me smile. It will be OK.

The mountains in the distance were forbidding. The town was my own inner prison. I had to get out and go. Freedom from the past lay beyond my adventure today. The future may be able to heal part of the history, especially for Blaine's legacy and the Treasure of La Chiva. I would know soon.

Breakfast served as a confidence builder. Food had a tremendous grounding effect besides other wonderful qualities. The native culinary tastes of Mexico were especially pleasing to me. The food cured my blood sugar deficit and the coffee ran through my veins stimulating strength, power, and vigor. A transformation occurred, a burden was lifted, and my confidence returned. At last my purpose was clear, the goal was immediately ahead, and I had the strength and courage to proceed.

It would be disingenuous to take the mood swings and rapid contrasts so casually, and I did nothing of the same. It was a great cause of concern and yet nothing could be done about the situation. A great adventure waits. Walking into the warehouse of one's personal demons is never easy, and doing it alone in a foreign country is even more frightening. I know you agree. The words of Ram Das and others rang so true right now. "Be here now."

The rental car was loaded the evening before to avoid attracting any unwanted attention. Caution was the watchword. Fortunately, the city had grown immensely since my last visit and the mix of people was beneficial. Tourism was encouraged and there were many reasons for gringos to be in Culiacan other than in search of drugs or buried treasure. Real estate development was popular and the city had grown beyond its former boundaries. There was an air of prosperity and the locals were proud of their landmarks and heritage. The homogenous blend of the old and the new was inspirational.

The area had grown from third world into the twenty-first century. The massive coordinated effort deserved respect. It took hard work and a desire for change. Old horse ranches and large vacant pastures were replaced with tourist hotels, golf courses, swimming pools, and small shopping areas to exhibit the wares of the local artisans. The economy was snappy and the residents were happy. The peso was strong against the dollar and jobs were plentiful. It was a good time in Culiacan.

I drove past new buildings that reflected the essence of architectural lines of local history but utilized modern thoughts and trends. There was less use of stone and more plaster and wood. Cemex trucks seemed to be everywhere early in the morning. The concrete plant must have opened before dawn to enable such early deliveries. It looked like development and expansion were key elements of the current local economy. Prosperity abounded and change was in the air.

Within a number of kilometers the density changed noticeably. Old shacks and faded structures dotted the landscape in an alternating pattern. The dichotomy between past and present was as evident as ever. Old and new was a continued theme.

The frequency of new development and number of structures became reduced over the next few miles. They diminished in size and soon only lightly spotted the landscape. The number of trees decreased proportionately too. It did not take long for the cactus to appear, creating the look of a high desert. This was how I had remembered the environs. This continued for another fifty minutes, at which point the military-like checkpoint was still in place. This landmark was an awakening point on my first visit, being a sobering sight after a night of feast and a van ride filled with slumber.

As before, the guards were young and heavily armed. Their bulletproof vests matched their faded blue uniforms. Many bore automatic or semi-automatic rifles, bandoleros, and helmets rather than caps. Nobody could misconstrue the seriousness of their intentions to stop and inspect all traffic. To my memory, the area was more fortified than before. Illuminated warning signs appeared one hundred or so yards before the checkpoint, and a bunker was placed past the barricade should anyone be foolish enough to fail to yield or attempt to run the inspection point. The consequences would be fatal.

I slowed as I approached the guardhouse and was motioned through. Not being sure what they were looking for, it was obvious that I was not it. Not now at least. Who knows what time may bring.

The drive was uneventful and time passed quickly. My thoughts were scattered and meaningless. I was jumping around rather casually with no specific focus. Nothing profound was experienced and my expectations were staying in check as the town of Culiacan disappeared behind me and to my right the mountains arose before me. I soaked up the silence as I proceeded southeast. The sun felt like my friend but nothing else seemed familiar.

Thoughts of doubt, danger and failure began to creep into my awareness; the proximity to La Chiva setting off deeply planted fireworks in my subconsciousness.

"All my relations." Are you there Blaine?

I was on an adventure into a paradox of opposites, into the known and unknown, into the familiar and the strange, into the past and the future. The visuals before my windshield were exhibiting equally contrasting values. The desert was dissolving into strong mountains, the light sand was merging into variegated rocks, and softness was transitioning into a brittle hardness.

As I turned off the main roadway towards the canyon between the twin peaks, I ventured deep into the darkness of unworthiness. No memory exists of ever feeling more alone, no matter where I have been. This was a venture into isolation, fear, and repression. It became clear that I had stuffed a significant part of the shocking and painful memories and I was forced to see them ahead of me in living color.

I drove in silence but I was haunted by sounds from the past. First, I could hear Blaine's narration to us upon our first glimpse of Tacamonte from the van. It came with such clarity that I no longer felt alone. He was with me inside my head and was reminding me about the history and the mission ahead.

Being alone, the details were more important than my last visit in 1982. I had to stay in the lead; there was nobody to follow. I had to find the selected markers myself and reach the site alone. I had to avoid the tiger of my own creation.

Any mistake now would cause me to miss the goal. Any deviation from the path would take me far from the target. I remembered poor Epimineo and his protracted period of retracing his steps without ever reaching the entrance to his grandfather's cave again.

Waves of excitement overcame me as I parked the rental car and looked at Tacamonte, to my left, and then at the broad white face of La Chiva, to my right. The top of the peak clearly looked like the face of a goat, and the inverted triangle of almost white stone appeared to be perfectly located at the place for the beard. There was no doubt in my mind how the mountain was named.

I took my pack out of the trunk, pulled out my cameras, hat, hydration pack, and checked the gear bag. Then I locked the car, tightened my boots, and took a very slow deep breath. It was time to begin again and, if worthy, to succeed. I was ready.

59. ENCORE

La Chiva - 2002

Parking in almost the same spot as before helped with the orientation. I proceeded to the starting point with the hope and faith that Blaine was with me, in one manner or another. His explanations would sure help.

It has been said that the departed can communicate with us if we are willing to listen. They do not speak loudly, but with surprising clarity. Voices and memories became indistinguishable and I was not sure if I was hearing Blaine actually speaking in present time, or recalling sessions from the past. Either way, I felt connected.

The mountain looked much steeper and far more rugged than I remembered. The towering peak looked huge from this vantage point. I never recovered my camera from the last visit so no photos were available for my research and preparation. Most important, I did not take any photos after Blaine and I left the group and made the final ascent to the cave site. My Nikon was most likely smashed in the rocks when I fell and tumbled, and would not have been of any benefit if anyone found it. I started walking.

I had been here twenty years before and my memory was usually noteworthy. I trusted it like an insurance policy and hoped it would not fail me. I knew the markers. I had been to the area above the front door to the cave, and knelt to within three feet from the entry.

I walked almost on autopilot directly to the first entry point. I verified the marks by instinctively pulling the vines away from the posts. They had grown thick and strong over the years. Time had not stolen the markers. I was surprised that the deep crosses were still there and considered the plant materials as a protector. The crosses carved into the posts were part of a standing testimonial to the strength and durability of the local hardwood. The markers were an encouragement and a great start.

I took a few deep breaths and felt like I was meeting my destiny, simultaneously confronting the past and creating a new future. I felt energized and enlivened as my body appeared to move on autopilot and my steps felt like walking on air. The terrain shifted and I could hear but not feel the gravel beneath my feet. The experience was like floating on the ground.

I stopped quickly to listen if I was being followed. I stood frozen in place and heard nothing unusual. The birds were chirping and squawking, indicating few if any intruders. There was a light breeze blowing and the sunlight was gently bathing my face. No perceivable signs of danger were present. It was time to continue upward.

Thoughts turned back to when we were being hunted. Time turned on its axis and I went from thinking of the immediate future to expressions of pure panic from the past. It was all so horrible. Blaine pushed me in one direction with the goal of preserving the project as he turned and ran back to his demise with the others. The pressure to save his work has been subtle yet great. I would love to validate his efforts and see what comes with the project.

Memories were my demons, nothing else. Denial has the strength of its own nature. It can block a great deal of pain and obliterate elements of history and experience. The happenings on the mountain had impacted and traumatized my psyche.

By contrast, my flashes of excitement were almost incendiary. This was a journey of a lifetime. I was so lucky to be in this position. The return to the area was overwhelming and ignited my passion for the treasure and especially the story.

There is nothing like a refreshing break while hiking. Body heat moves towards or returns to normal, the pulse slows, the breath lightens, and the feet seem to cool within the boots. Water is realized to be a blessing and snacks always taste better.

I may not have remembered some of the turns, but I had confidence. I was on a guided tour for one guest towards Lareano's gold. After a number of deep cleansing breaths and a refreshing few gulps of water, I continued upward towards Boat Rock and beyond. As former UCLA basketball coach John Wooden said, "It's not so important who starts the game but who finishes it."

60. UNSEEN FRIENDS

2002

Everything felt alive as I continued to climb. La Chiva was a huge challenging living being. I talked to her like she was aware and could hear me. I was surprised with how much I had to say.

Life was pulsing in everything. The trees were part of the oxygen exchange system. The waters below all flowed downward cutting wedges into the mountain as they have done for centuries. The animal life was part of the inter-dependent feeding grounds. The bird population appeared to be a mix of locals and migratory varieties. The flowers and insects performed the same seasonal dances with each other. Harmony was aplenty.

Although I could only see evidence of their remains, the rodents were represented in full force. The snakes were the silent wanderers who made only infrequent appearances, and only if scared.

The sound of an occasional rattler would stop me in my tracks and raise every hair on my body. My distaste for poisonous snakes dates back to my experiences with Blaine hiking through the Ventana Wilderness Area in Big Sur. I have never known anyone who was hurt by a rattlesnake, and yet caution remained the watchword. I heard one in the distance that morning, representing one more than I wanted to know anything about.

Everyone thinks they know what the rattler sounds like. The sound of a rattlesnake was made known through early western films. Movies can create serious misconceptions. The rattlesnake is much louder than ever imagined, with a sound similar to a loud hiss from a very high-pressure garden hose. The volume is the surprise. Nature equipped them with a small but mighty amplifier system. Their sound creates alarm for hundreds of feet in all directions. There is absolutely nothing soft or subtle about it. In addition, there is nothing ambiguous about the sound even if it is the first time you have heard one in person. It has a corresponding bone chilling impact.

I remembered Epimineo's story about the rattlesnake as a totem. It was also the belief of the psychics that they were invited on a spirit level to guard Lareano's gold following the misdeeds of the grandfather and the blatant breach of his secret covenant with the bandit. Blaine said the rattlesnake was the enforcer of the promise and one of the unforeseen forces imposed by the bandit to protect his bounty.

There is no creepier thought than a dark space full of snakes, and there can be no worse reptile than a rattlesnake. My skin crawled with the thought. Serpent power was not a motivating force in my awareness. It was not hard to envision a cave full of snakes. The fearful image was presented to the world in one of the Indiana Jones movies: "I hate snakes!" Time has been a factor and perhaps the cave was void of the slippery devils. So many years have passed, and yet the possibility exists that they are living among the boxes of gold, the bags of various types of coins and jewels, and the piles of religious antiquities.

The undulating trail twisted and turned as I worked my way to the treasure site. At times a path was visible, and sometimes I had to create one of my own. There were so many choices and I was confused about the direction. More than once I found myself backtracking when it seemed like I was heading in the wrong direction. I trusted my instincts.

Each step took me higher up the mountain and closer to the scene of the attack. Numerous short rest breaks did not alleviate the guilt and pain associated with every step of my journey. I was experiencing all of it again. My good fortunes, and even this very breath, are due to the fact that Blaine had taken me alone up to the opening while the group remained a few hundred yards lower on the hill at the larger rest area and vista point.

My mental list of markers and landmarks were slowly being checked off. Progress was being made in spite of occasional moments of confusion. I paused at the former rest stop and said a silent prayer for my fallen comrades. The grand scenic vistas were beautiful and the terrain afforded some perfect stone perches for rest, refreshment and contemplation. It was the last reasonable resting place before the steep climb ahead. That was the principal reason why Blaine left the other members of our team at this spot while we ventured forward together. My life was saved because of this simple move. Blaine wanted some photos of the general site area before the others joined. The shots had rung out before any photographs were taken. Even if they had found my camera there would be no evidence of the exact surroundings.

Tears filled my eyes and I became both angry and weak at the same time. Simultaneous opposites were an underground and recurring theme on this trip. Duality is a strong force on La Chiva.

Above this spot the mighty La Chiva stood proud and resolute. Her white face towered over the remaining landscape and, at this time of the morning, blocked my view of the sun. The contrast between light and dark was magnificent. In the distance were many differing visual treats, including the canyons below, one of which was my apparent route the last time, the smaller hill where I sought safety across the crevasse, Tacamonte to the west, and the valley far off in the distance. Because of my escape route twenty years ago, I totally understood what was behind the hills and out of my visual horizon. It was another world.

The future would surely change if I found the treasure. The small campground below could conceivably be filled with treasure hunters and glory seekers. It could kindle a form of excitement similar to that of early California when James Marshall found gold at Sutter's Fort in 1848. It could also become filled with police or military personnel.

The manner of promulgation of the story will help determine the outcome. It could easily get out of control if not properly handled. These thoughts became humorous in a bizarre sense. This place has been out of control for 130 years if you take into account the history of stealing, death, pillage, and denial. To hope for a shift to order and reason was unrealistic.

Towering waves of grief overcame me as I walked past the area where I believed my friends had been buried. Years had not erased the intensity of that experience. While not sure of the actual gravesite locations, I had suspicions.

Blaine's quick assessment of the crisis combined with good fortune to save me. I often questioned why he sent me in one direction and backtracked from the treasure spot in the other direction to the group. Over the years I had flashes of insight that illuminated this inquiry. Blaine understood many of the forces behind the event and used his instinctive good judgment to save my life. Access to the treasure would not be gained and the story revealed without a survivor. He bet with his life on my chances of success. I did not want to fail him.

I admired Blaine's thorough immersion in all aspects of the Treasure of La Chiva. It had become part of the cut of his cloth. He tuned into the initial excitement as the history was first shared on American soil. He was present on the second day near San Francisco when the grandson, Epimineo Corrales, met with the trio of American treasure hunters. Blaine was in possession of the tapes, notes, maps, photographs, and other tangible pieces of evidence about the treasure and its lore. He was versed in the history, myth, legend, and original involvement of the church with the ancient power objects. He had lived the story long enough to vicariously feel the unsolicited anger of the bandit, Lareano Garcia, both from childhood and his double-cross at the hands of his dedicated adversary, the Military Governor.

Have you ever felt like you were being watched? Were you alone? Was it real? Are you sure? Do you know about that cold feeling you can get behind your neck or upper back?

I have heard since childhood that we are never totally alone. Whether it is faith or direct experience, many believe in hierarchies of both visible and unseen beings, things, life forms and entities. History is replete with art and stories of angels, devas, and forces of both anthropomorphic and other origins. Folklore of numerous cultures, both current and extinct, contains innumerable references to these "hidden friends." Even the fields of psychology and parapsychology have attempted a scientific level of inquiry into this topic. The Bible makes numerous references to angels and archangels as well as other components of the spirit world. Artists throughout history have attempted to memorialize man's acknowledgement and search for greater understanding of the myriad of levels of life. Modern culture has seen references in numerous songs and movies. The list goes on and on.

The lore about unseen entities associated with buried treasure goes back before the tombs of the pharaohs in ancient Egypt. The curses and their ill effects have been widely noted in Western literature, the most famous of which belong to the vicious death experienced by Lord Carnarvon following the violation and opening of King Tut's tomb by his partner, Howard Carter.

Blaine believed that the spirit world surrounding and connected with the Treasure of La Chiva needed extensive healing. He said they called out for help. He was lead to believe from his encounters with the psychics and channels that there were layers of protection maintaining the status quo at the site. Their success was their own level of dissatisfaction. Everything was stuck in place. A large number of years had passed without any visitors or change. To the world of spirit that was just a moment, depending on the frame of reference and the goal of the energies.

The last person to visit, experience, and enjoy the magnitude of the treasure was Epimineo's grandfather, the Military Governor. His last possible year to partake was 1910. Epimineo was at the treasure site in 1932, but only long enough to verify and destroy the sign carved into the rock at the entrance area. The fact that he carved away the marker for security purposes further frustrated his lifelong journey.

Epimineo's search bore qualities of some of the famous characters of Greek mythology. Was he a bit like Sisyphus, who pushed the rock up almost to the top of the hill only to have it slide down again? Or was he like Cassandra, who could foretell the future but nobody would listen?

Epimineo spent his entire life searching for something hidden. He remembered flashes from his childhood and refused to be dissuaded from what he knew to be true, remaining steadfast until the end that his family legacy was neither fabrication nor folklore. Everyone else in his life believed the treasure to be a point of folly. Epimineo withstood a lifetime of personal abuse at the hands of his friends and a few relatives for his dedicated search and faith.

Our dear Blaine had become friends with Epimineo and had agreed first to help remove a personal confidence barrier, and later to carry the torch completely. Blaine suffered similar criticism, albeit for a much shorter duration of time. His goals were altruistic in nature, hoping the treasure would be used primarily to benefit education in the local area. He gave the last years of his life in pursuit of the treasure.

A cold and dark feeling overcame me. I was poorly prepared to deal with the issues of isolation and the ill effects of the haunting memories that were unleashed on the ascent. The solitude did not help in the instant moment. To make matters worse, I sensed a presence close behind me and could almost feel its cold and angry breath. Denial was inappropriate as a coping mechanism and nothing could explain what I was starting to hear.

The oldest story was becoming true again, the hunter was actually the hunted. The searcher was being sought. The observer was the one being watched. I was scared to my bones and unable to move. I felt stalked. I was serving the role of bait for some unseen denizen of another dimension.

Trite, simple, or however else one may view it, the truth was nevertheless the same. I was miles from nowhere and yet not alone. I was powerless to protect myself, unable to provide any defense, unable to run with not one place to hide. My knees felt like lead weights. I was stuck in place as if superglued to La Chiva and overcome with fear. I was up the creek without a paddle, shaking in my seat on a mountain in Mexico. Welcome back to La Chiva, Ellis!

References can be made to unseen forces when one finds oneself thinking thoughts that are unquestionably not their own. It is easier to look elsewhere.

The lore of most treasures comes replete with references to spirit friends or foes. This treasure had its stars. The reasons could be varied and the sources almost timeless. The items collected in the treasure impact hundreds of years of time, various cultures, different philosophies, changes in forms of government, as well as the standard elementals associated with greed, gold, murder, and deception, just to name a few.

It would be the super bowl of spirit protection if you believed in that sort of thing. The question for me remained simple: friend or foe?

61. RESISTANCE

La Chiva - 2002

I was pulling myself up the hill towards the treasure site. There was no doubt that La Chiva was steep. I thought I was in excellent shape and more than adequately prepared. For me it was much more difficult than before. Hadn't Blaine explained something about an upslope vortex? The downhill would be more difficult than the ascent. Last time I was denied that experience and took the long way home.

Everything appeared to be going right but, at the same time, something was definitely wrong. The experience was a strong duality, with my mind wanting me to continue to climb and my heart dictating an immediate retreat. The fight or flight response. Yin and yang again, nothing new. Welcome back to La Chiva, the perfect hiding place and mask for sanity and balance.

The sun had cleared the top of the bearded peak and the bright golden rays were cooking everything they touched. The huge boulders and other stone surfaces were radiating the heat that had already been absorbed. The small amount of remaining vegetation was dark, dehydrated, and brittle. Flowers were scarce. The ground had heated sufficiently to make my feet uncomfortable and the day promised to be a scorcher. La Chiva was clearly a melanoma creating co-conspirator.

I trudged along, one foot after another, slowly and carefully, grateful for the protection of my hat, sunglasses, and the surplus water in my backpack. The pack felt heavy with the fluids, camera equipment, and shovel. I was sweating profusely and my back was its own river in the areas making contact with the fabric of the backpack. It was made from the new "wonder" fabric of the day that supposedly provided additional sunscreen protection. I was testing it fully and was not ready to become a shareholder in the technology after this experience. The extreme heat on La Chiva did not validate the manufacturer's representations.

The symphony of nature was usually a joy. I loved the chorus of the birds, rhythms of the wind, falling rocks, crushing leaves, and myriad of other sounds of an outdoor hike. Nature always comes with her own unique soundtrack, each place and time different than the next. It was far from silent today, but I could not enjoy the sounds. I was hearing a soundtrack from another dimension. Hello astral, the voices were back. They sang an exquisite inner chorus of doubt. I wondered if I was being warned. If I listened, I would leave while I could. I should have paid better attention.

What am I doing on the roller coaster ride of La Chiva? How did I get here? More important, why? What delusion had blocked my memory? How could I have forgotten any of this? What was I trying to prove? What was driving me onward? How did I think I could do this alone? It took madness to return, and only the successful completion would be my deliverance.

The next major problem that I faced was the fact that I was lost. Everything looked the same. I had difficulty accepting being that disoriented. Word games aplenty as the voices laughed. As dumb as it sounds, I did not have the slightest idea of where to go. Each path led to nowhere.

The face of La Chiva towered above me, looking taller and farther away with every step that I took. I could not initially accept the historical perspective. I was having a rough time, and the parallels with Epimineo's years of endless searching were buried just like the treasure.

The Greek mythologies were coming alive. I could feel the tug of the sirens upon Ulysses, and my essence was being smashed on the rocks. I was lost.

Everything is supposed to happen for a reason. Was this about me or was it the treasure? Weren't there things protecting or cursing this damn thing? Was I now part of the same cosmic play?

I picked up my pace and traced and retraced the same steps. Was I marching in an irregular circle?

The mercury continued to rise and the birds became silent. Were they conserving energy or making a pronouncement? It was now too hot, and my attitude soured to a new low. Frustration mounted with no end in sight. Anxiety and anger rose rapidly. It was a low of all lows, compounded by the years of anticipation and personal wars about the entire project. I was living a "back to the future" moment and hating every second of it.

I questioned how both the bandit and Military Governor had been able to return again and again. Then I thought about Epimineo. His lifetime of searching was rewarded by only one chance encounter. The treasure rested for almost a century and nothing looked like today would be any different.

With my energies waning the logical response was to stop and regroup. There is an old saying, "When you realize you are digging yourself into a hole, stop digging." I looked for a covered overlook to have a positive vantage point and to obtain some degree of protection from the intense sun. When I found the closest spot that met both criteria, I removed my pack, sat slowly, and considered my options.

62. TARGET OF OPPORTUNITY

La Chiva - 2002

I must have been paying with a high limit karmic credit card. It was the super gold card. What a lousy time for such a cosmic joke.

I was about to have the worst repeat performance of all time. It was the deja vu from hell. At first I could not believe my eyes. I blinked a couple of times to enhance my focus. My rushing heart sped up even more. It must have been close to redline and I was still sitting. I could not believe the only conclusion: I was being fucking followed.

There is an opening lyric in an old Jefferson Airplane song admonishing us, "If you want to get to heaven over the other shore stay out of the way of the blood stained bandit." I tried that last time and lived until today. But the wheel is round and I returned to the same nick in the cog of my life.

The energetic characters of every nightmare I ever had somehow bound themselves together and presented one united image not a half of a mile below me. I was in the front row of the theatre of the absurd again. I flashed back to my love for the writings of Herman Hesse and felt like Harry Haller from Steppenwolf. This was crazy beyond words with a high probability of announcing imminent insanity.

Was I entering Dante Alighieri's infamous Inferno? "Abandon hope all ye who enter here."

I was being followed by a familiar old face. I watched him marching up the hill all proud and strong. He was still in great shape, perhaps even better than before, and it was clear I was no match for his highly conditioned body. This was neither an apparition nor a spirit entity. It was the human killing machine after my ass. It was Dick Harris in three-dimensional living color. I was not hallucinating. Fortunately, he was alone. Unfortunately, so was I.

I wondered how this could have happened after an absence of two decades. Of course, the answer was as obvious as the question itself. The magnitude of the treasure was worth a mental marker, a signal or tripwire. The method of my detection may never be known, but that did not change the instant fact that my return had created some signal and my actual presence was clearly known. Anything from a cash bonus to hotel workers to a reward for employees of the car rental agencies would yield instant detection. Tapping the computer records of the same places would also yield successful results. For that matter, immigration records or all hotel registrations would not be a difficult assignment for a good computer snoop.

Human nature is predictable and the lure of treasure, especially Lareano's amazing heist, was beyond the ability to resist. It was a long-term bet that, if I survived, I would return some day. Maybe the only true question would be how I was able to resist the draw, contain or control the impulses, and stay away for so long. It was not long enough. My return would appear to be proof in and of itself that I knew the location of the treasure.

We were now in the computer era. I had traveled using my real name and had already been in the Culiacan area for a number of days. My name would clearly have been given to Dick at the time of the original assignment to watch Blaine's expedition. It would not be difficult to predict my return to the exact same hotel, no different than people returning like lemmings to the scene of an accident or other major traumatic event. Fire investigators often film the crowd watching the fire for a possible clue in the event that arson is suspected. The draw is too great to stay away. Investigators have scrutinized my shots of two fire scenes when they realized that I had covered and photographed the same. I don't believe they were useful. At least I was never subpoenaed to authenticate any of the prints.

At that moment I hated the fact that I was so predictable. I was always accessible and available, so my itinerary was not highly secret. I was on assignment but the feature had not been announced.

I believe I still owned the element of surprise. I had the high ground in more ways than one. I did not believe that my actual position was known, at least not yet. His stride told me he did not think I was aware of his presence. Both of these facts could be used to my advantage. He was discovered and I was not.

This was a David and Goliath redux. I wish I had a choice in the role to play but I was forced to stand pat. I was at my figurative point of no return. Should I try to stay and make a deal with him? Maybe use the treasure as collateral? Stupid idea. It would be the last deal of my life.

I was the target of opportunity on La Chiva. I ran last time. He would bet on that. This time I would have to stay and see what happens. That would be a surprise, so timing must be critical and outcome determinative.

Some friends and clients have called me the "King of Timing" because of my good luck at picking when to shoot pictures, make decisions, and do deals. Time was still on my side, but not for long. There was no room for error.

I thought about the approaching menace and the danger that he presented. His conduct last time on the mountain was a clear example. The fact that he was here today was yet another.

Once again Dick has entered from stage left at the improper time. Blaine's team had not yet reached the treasure site when something set the hidden guards into offense rage against the waiting crew. Blaine had returned to the group, definitely saving my life and all hope for the treasure. It was a massacre.

Blaine had taken me alone to the exact spot where the trap door was buried. It was not visible because of soil accretion, numerous years of weather, rains, shifting dirt and rocks. But it was there, he was convinced of it and so was I. He showed me the smudge marks on the stone cap where Epimineo removed the cross. We knelt where the vault door was supposed to be under a foot or more of dirt, decomposed granite, and debris. He said all that would be required would be some minor digging. He asked for some "before" photos of the site before everyone was there. We heard the shots before my camera was out of the gear bag.

Life is funny as things shift so quickly. Like the ebb and flow of the tides, we are often the benefactors of obstacles being placed in our way. It is always a matter of patience and perspective, two words that are often hard to swallow, both individually and collectively. A few moments earlier I was angry about my situation. I was hot, tired, and frustrated. Now I was happy that I had gotten lost. Without that time distraction, I could be digging out the entrance and broadcasting my precise location. Even worse, I would be totally unaware of my unwelcome visitor. That would have been a horrible surprise with a fatal outcome.

I hid behind a rock and looked down at the trail below. It seemed like I was alone. Was he moving or waiting? Had he stopped for a reason? Was he still alone? I knew it made no sense to make any form of deal with Dick. Any covenant would be breached as soon as the time was opportune for him. He would kill me at his convenience. Opening the treasure would be my worst move, signaling the end of the game and a fatal capitulation.

Blaine told me he had been very careful never to share the precise treasure site with anyone, and his manifest paranoia in thought, word and deed caused me to rely on this precedent and act accordingly. Even on the last visit, I was the only one he had taken up to the actual site. To add to that, I had learned that I was the only one besides Blaine with copies of the notes, tapes, and Epimineo's drawing. It was an honor to realize that I had so quickly earned that level of trust, and my very being here today was in fulfillment of Blaine's dreams. I was chosen. I was often told as a child to finish what I started. This time it just took longer.

Things were quickly becoming contaminated by the visitor below. At least I hoped he was still below. Quick reflection reminded me again that the treasure was not an available bargaining chip to be used with Dick, just a death warrant.

Even in the stress of the moment I was convinced that Dick would not act prematurely again. He was on the mountain, below me, playing the waiting game until I located the cave and navigated the opening. After all, he waited twenty years for my return. He would stay as long as was required.

This was going to be a life or death chess match, and I did not want to lose any of my pieces. The adrenaline pumping through my body could not be trusted to give the desired clarity. I needed to reason this out completely. Some meditation and breathing techniques would calm my mind, restore some energy, and help me evaluate the conditions.

Was I going to become the final victim? Should I reconsider and try to ascend the face of La Chiva to escape? I wondered about reversing the direction that the bandit had taken. Should I take the ridgeline out? Or should I try to traverse the mountain, cut across to the adjoining hill, and go over the cut to the site of Jose's farm in El Faro?

63. BURN AND RUN

La Chiva - 2002

The weather is never cold in Culiacan, yet I doubted the chills I was experiencing would ever leave me. It was hotter than proverbial hell on this mountain and I was shivering with pure terror. I cannot explain it any more clearly. Nightmares end by merely reaching or returning to the waking state. This experience was so different because it was real.

I listened and heard nothing but the usual. I looked down to the trail below and saw nothing. I tried to tune into my body and felt nothing. Scared was an understatement. Panic was not intense enough. Running started to become the most satisfying alternative. Escape again if it was possible and honor my original commitment to stay away.

Suddenly it hit me. I reached into my pack and located the copies of notes, map, and drawing in the outside pocket. A BiC lighter was in the top pocket. I quickly ignited the paperwork. Converting the materials to ash did not hinder my chances of success. It was insurance that they would not get in the wrong hands, a small victory that helped lighten my spirit momentarily.

Some new choices were then revealed as if the bandit was speaking to me. He said to act as he did. Select the venue for attack. Let the topography and circumstances work to my advantage rather than against me. This was a great concept but not clear for implementation.

Another alternative was to begin digging in the wrong spot as if I was at the hidden site. I could act surprised if peacefully overtaken and could agree to leave. That would not work if Dick decided to use me as his slave. Dead again after digging my own grave. Dumber than dumb.

I must remember whom I was dealing with and the vivid picture I saw last time. This Neanderthal would not let me leave and tell the story. Running became the only smart move and I picked up the pack, listened carefully, and quietly ascended the mountain. I had the advantage of time and a significant lead. Out of here today and live to see another day.

Not wanting to betray my location I tried to be cautious, taking small, even steps without creating much sound. As I continued upward and away from the canyon the squawking of the birds returned, covering my tracks. I looked up at the white beard of La Chiva and thought I heard the goat laugh. In the last century or more she has witnessed many men, and probably a few women also, ascend her body looking for the bandit's fabulous cave. La Chiva had time on her side. She was also aided and abetted by the elements, conditions, and spiritual forms that we now know to be associated with the treasure.

As I turned up the windy path I began to feel like I was transforming into some of the protectors. My elevated stress level caused my mind to play some tricks. That was the easiest way to explain what transpired. The first was a very grounded experience within my body. Every step became important and each breath seemed to enliven my muscular system. After a few minutes of conscious slow and rhythmic breathing it felt like my skeletal system was changing too. There was no doubt that this was merely perceptual, but I felt like I was relating to a snake. It was not just any ordinary snake, but rather a large diamondback rattler. As crazy as this sounds, please bear with me to vicariously share the experience.

To make it easier to explain, one could call it similar to a waking dream state, a hallucination, vision, or one of many other terms.

The snake is rumored to be one of the protectors of the treasure and a totem of the bandit king. I could feel why. The snake had the ability to blend into the landscape and move about silently. The snake was an equalizer and kept to itself until irritated.

It could strike with little warning and had the power to overcome and easily kill almost any local animal, no matter the size. It would rather remain hidden and watch than expose itself and fight. Its lessons were obvious to me as I moved even more silently away from the general area where Dick would eventually be climbing the mountain.

As I moved the rattler within taught me more about the mountain and its treasure. Survival was more than instinctual. There was no way I would give up now. That was not possible.

64. ONE-ON-ONE

La Chiva – 2002

My rental car was away from the road, at the base of the parking area, within one hundred yards of the empty campground. It was easy to believe that he had carefully inspected the boot tracks around the car. Did he do anything to disable the car? Maybe worse?

Dick had been patiently waiting and watching for me. Dick had high power binoculars and I could see him scanning the area forty-five degrees to the right. I was not alone, no way and no how. He's back, and too close. He was standing where I had been, and I could see him kneeling and inspecting the evidence of my passage. He probably thought I was ahead of this position, up the hill, and on the way to the fabled hidden treasure.

I imagine Dick would punish himself for the impatience and premature attack by his men against Blaine's group twenty years ago. Victory and vindication would merge into one this very day. Now one-on-one, he could wait like a cat, hiding himself at the same time.

I could see that he had a problem: his sight line wasn't right. Dick had work to do. He was forced to expose himself briefly and change his position. Upward from the base of La Chiva was an ideal vantage point. He climbed to an excellent outbreak to overview the general face of the mountain. Most of the trails peeked out through the vertical network of cuts in the hill. There was no guaranty his intended victim would be visible, but there was a chance his sounds would give him away. Waiting was not a difficult proposition at this point.

If Dick was successful he would eliminate the last witness to his horrid crime, close a life chapter, complete the cover-up, and gain access to the treasure. The man was motivated. Dick's lengthy wait would be rewarded. I had to return sooner or later. Nobody would stay away; the lure would overcome sensible thinking. The call of the treasure was too great. In time I had to come back. It was predictable.

Motive here was horrible, with all intentions being negative, even terminal and decisive. Dick had reasons to shorten the evidence chain. I was the last witness. He had not returned home since 1982 and not known that I had chosen a different path and had never gone to the authorities or anyone else. There was no statute of limitations for the criminal actions committed by Dick and his buddies in crime, Chris and Alex. I knew who they were and where they worked. I'm not a snitch and never have been.

Twenty years is a long time, but he had no realistic choice other than wait. It was easy watching me once I returned to Culiacan. The streets worked to provide their own security. My efforts with the camera became a bust. My career was easy to follow. Dick had his bases covered this time. The rental car probably had an electronic tag too. His choices were lengthy.

Dick and I could both sense the other. We were no more than a half mile apart and yet there was a scent, a silent communication, that came somewhere from destiny and informed each about the other. The distance was too great to explain any other way. No additional sensory stimulus was needed. This was a heavy focus experience.

It was the end game and we both knew how to play. We waited. I knew how to sit and wait for lighting or circumstances to change and enhance a picture. I could wait for artists, animals, athletes, models, and scheduled events. Dick was also trained to sit and watch. He was a hunter and was used to that. It was a Zen of sorts to him.

Nobody moved. It was too quiet.

65. Found

La Chiva - 2002

Dick was easy to watch and I had the comfort of knowing my position was secret, if only for a short time. He was sitting just past Boat Rock looking up at the strange formation of La Chiva, and probably contemplating the fury that was going to be unleashed just ahead. He was getting ready. It was his hunt.

An old Hermetic saying came back into my memory, "I recognize the undeviating justice in all the circumstances of my life." That saying for Key 5 in the Pattern on the Testleboard had a ring as I searched through the high-powered lens on my camera. I took a couple of shots to document his presence on the mountain. It could help if I was separated from both my camera and my life. It contained evidence that may be useful. It occupied my focus and helped calm my mind. It was like work and training, only far more intense.

Though inconceivable, Dick was lurking down below. Any escape that way along the trail would be impossible. The executioner was guarding the path. He was in a strategic position and controlled the main route down. Bummer. In the opposite direction, the towering slope behind had been proven to be hostile before. La Chiva had a record of broken dreams.

I hated what I saw. Dick had that same darn look, full beard, mirrored aviator sunglasses, jeans, blue plaid flannel shirt over a black tee shirt, and a camouflage backpack. Dick had lost nothing in size. He looked like he still possessed the strength of an elephant. To top it off, he wore a maroon and gold USC baseball hat. Still can't trust the Trojans!

His positioning was strategic. I was blocked and could not retreat successfully. I had no chance to easily retrace my steps back down the mountain undetected. It was advantage Dick. I wasted no time evaluating that alternative. The risk vs. reward ratio was horrible. Getting past him would be the primary problem.

In addition, it was unrealistic to believe he would leave the car functional.

But I had reason to believe that I had a chance. It was in my nature to be that way. This course of conduct would never surprise my friends. I always saw a positive outcome. I was resourceful, unpredictable, and did not believe I would be defeated no matter what the odds. My optimistic nature would dominate his negative personality here. Losing would not be an option, too much was riding on my success. I would not become his victim.

Neither of us moved. Dick was still watching and waiting. He could not see me and I hoped he was becoming impatient.

66. WAITING GAME

La Chiva - 2002

Moliere said, "It is not only what we do, but also what we don't do, for which we are accountable." I felt strong and motivated, clear and of heightened perception as I sat and listened, watched, and waited. I was pumped with a renewed sense of purpose. My goal was in sight too. This was not just in a metaphysical sense, but deeply psychologically stabilizing to boot. It was an initiation and I thought I understood.

The object was to remain silent, move as little as possible, and always quietly. Time would not be an enemy for either of us, nor would it be an equalizer. Patience was a practiced discipline. I believed I had the high ground along with a number of significant advantages or credits. My life was safe for the moment because I was the only one who knew where the treasure lay. In my mind was the key to the lock and the forbidden fruit of Lareano's efforts and the Military Governor's custodianship. I was the only person equipped with this information and that reality increased the pressure. Blaine trusted nobody else.

I incorrectly believed that I could outwait or outlast my pursuer. Confidence would not find an advantage here. I considered myself more intelligent and intuitive. I also had some special friends whose link came through Blaine's understanding. He often said acknowledgement is a precursor to listening. Their playbook was a slice or wedge of a different realm under specific rules and clearly defined constraints. The life force was repulsed by Dick and would do anything reasonable to assist with his defeat. They could assist but not interfere. That seemed like a paradox at the moment, but I didn't make the rules.

Balance and order would be destroyed if I was forced to bring Dick to the treasure. The only way that could happen had to involve an act of unbelievable personal submission, one totally out of character for me. I endeavored to have an angle, a way to sometimes do less and accomplish more. It was a matter of leverage. I wouldn't quit, not now and not ever.

It was heading for an energy battle between two worthy opponents. One was twice the physical size of the other with the benefit of a missing morals package, and seasoned with an extreme appreciation for violence. The treasure energies play in a larger arena. It was a battle of mind and a game of power. The warriors were equal in a cosmic sense. Each conjured up angels of protection. Totems were flying. The frequencies were shifting and a difference in the air could be noted.

He was part Native American with full warrior training, while I was an adept trained since childhood in the School of Mysteries. We were at the human horse races, animal rights aside. Tao, Zen, and some chi's too. It was the start of an amazing involvement of forces and interactions.

The treasure spirits were stirring too. They loved their precious charge just as it sat, and had helped keep all intruders away since the last approach by the Military Governor's grandson seven decades previous. A penetration of the sacred space evoked a combative quality out of the conglomeration. That word is used because of the unusual varieties of the entities present at this time. They guard the treasure and they do it with a vengeance. They are fully empowered projections of greed and avarice, some of the lower collection of behavior patterns. They are formed in part by coalesced anger. The bandit spit out nothing less powerful with his last mortal words when he cursed the Military Governor following his betrayal and poisoning. The death of his youngest brother, Gerardo, had a life altering effect on Jesus.

They are real in the same sense that many thought form projections are created. They also don't exist and cannot be approached or comprehended by a non-believer. The path to recognition was acknowledgement in this circle. Speak to them; talk to them and they will respond to you. Their toolboxes of actions, reactions, and effects were more in the realm of multi-dimensional magic. It was a combined power and responsibility.

They protected the treasure because of the contents. Their efforts were strengthened and enlivened by belief, and compounded by greed. It is a source of nourishment to them. And they were amplified by the dark and dangerous Cheryl, making it a bad cocktail. They wanted to maintain the treasure intact without further human intrusion. The goal was status quo ante.

There were also some who had no side in the battle between Dick and I, only with the potential violation of the outer door area itself. The curious blend of Aztec, Mayan, and power objects from the church enhanced the scale. The gold, jewels, and other forms of valuables and currencies strengthen their will and add to their potencies.

All sides were waiting. It was a silent balance of invisible wills. It could have been similar to the interaction intensity between Lareano Garcia and Jesus Borella. The Treasure of La Chiva was the common element. Even the spirit world loves an underdog, but my chances were ridiculously small. This was a Disney era and I felt supported and believed most wanted me to prevail over Dick, find the treasure, and share this amazing tale. Whatever can be used to psych you up is very important in this type of encounter.

67. Hanging

La Chiva – 2002

Neither side was communicating and both sat and waited. It was a hare and tortoise fighting in a new venue, Gandhi's playhouse. Slow. Wait. Breathe.

I still felt good about hanging out. I was able to rest comfortably and properly hydrate from my special spot. The manzanita interlaced into an optical barrier. I was hidden from above by a small stone shelf, a true blessing against the sunlight and a wonderful protector from the weather. It was a terrific location, and I loved La Chiva for it.

This was major league survival and I was in the worse position of all, being "It." As long as the separation was that great I would not be forced to act. The distance afforded me alternate escape routes from my present spot. I would have to chose the proper place for any encounter, should that be necessary and viable.

St. Francis of Assisi was known to love the birds. It has often been said that birds are the "little messengers of God." I would call that true in my experience and honor the advantage I gained by listening to their complaints on the mountain that day. To me they sounded agitated with something happening in the lower part of the forest. They were giving out an excited warning and the alarm signal was clear and convincing. I gathered my senses and watched carefully as the erratic behavior of some of the lower flying birds enabled me to detect some movement or activity at the edge of a clearing way below. I could only see it for a minute, but I thought I was looking directly into a small telescope or high powered spotting scope.

I could feel the chill of his eyes looking at me. I knew I was caught. No doubt, denial, or other psychological tools would work. I had the inner knowing, the sick feeling deep into my bones that he had his sights on me. It felt like it was actually into me, piercing the outer layers of my skin and trying to dive into my mind.

Evil has a freezing cold quality when in close proximity. That is akin to the feelings or premonitions that many report after ignoring the same subtle warnings and then encountering great danger headlong. This was not a pleasant realization but an accurate summation of the immediate problem. He was not going to leave. He was watching me, waiting for me, and deciding horrible things to do to me.

A sense of mission and importance can inflate the confidence and enliven the circumstances. The prey can easily become hyper alerted this way. It heightens awareness and is a natural preparation for quick reactions for avoidance and survival. It carries the rhythm of the winds sometimes. It was noticeable that all of the animals became silent within the last few minutes. The simultaneous vacuum of sound was unusual. Even the air became still. The situation was static in anticipation of a dynamic climax.

The opportunities became more vibrant and electric as the tension on the mountain began to ignite. Dick was ascending slowly, pack apparently fully laden, and his purpose closer with every step. I went through an analysis of my alternatives at almost cyber-like speed. It surprised me. It ignited like a conditioned response. I was trained and really into the Zen of this deal. I had years to work on my questions, and an openness to look at my failings as well as successes.

I found myself prepared for the challenge and ready for action. "If it is to be it is up to me."

I scooped up my belongings silently and almost effortlessly, as if in a dance, and was ready to move quickly and appropriately. I was on my way to a spot I suddenly knew well. It was the last place that I stood with Blaine, less than five feet from the opening of the treasure.

I was at the proper locale and closer than I knew. Ironic. The map Blaine had from Epimineo was the problem. The scale was wrong and misleading. The topography changed with the rains, land shifts, cuts, and fills. Of course the forces of nature would all play their combined mystery over these many years. The plant descriptions could be totally extinct. The area he was looking for could be two or three feet below. That would account for some height issues. The hill would conceivably add rock and soil from storms on the extreme exposures.

To me the illusive treasure had become more buried. It came in a daylight dream or vision and instantly made sense. I was filled with understanding and conviction. I blessed the Angels who showed me where to look. It was a merger with spirit, an initiation with the energies of nature, and a gift from the astral. I felt invited and was positive that I was being guided. I could see it in my mind's eye. It was so close.

It would involve digging, only easy excavation, and I realized where I should begin this time. It made sense and answered questions from before. To feel so calm was a sign of my conviction to the vision. Once again I was sure the treasure was within reach. I knew where to look, why it had to be there, and why they could not find it before. There was something on the drawing, Epimineo's gift to Blaine from a few decades ago. It helped.

I knew. It had that look. There was an added light, a confidence, a true radiant knowing. I was just a few feet from here with Blaine when the shots echoed everywhere on that terrifying day.

Straight down. Right here. I was confident when I had marked the predicted spot for entry below. I had a fix. This was the spot.

I could feel the treasure pulse beneath me. It felt like the earth had a heartbeat. I sat cross-legged over the opening and said a silent prayer for my friend, Blaine, and then the Bandit, Grandfather, the Spirits of the Treasure, and "All My Relations." I tried to soak up the significance, and then complete my plan.

Years before I had established credibility with Jose Sanchez through the cut and over the double ridge. The under-the-radar return had been by a trusty friend or relative who was a reliable and skilled bush pilot. It worked well for me last time when San Bernardino was the drop-off. This time would be by a commercial airliner and a destination outside of the United States. I would have to stay away for a while.

No return to the hotel was required. I had my passport, identification, credit cards and sufficient cash, camera and gear. I just had to get out of here.

68. OPPORTUNITIES

La Chiva - 2002

The apparition was dark, deep, and instant. My eyes saw it before my mind could grasp what I was seeing. The system needed to process before it reacted. Then I was ready, as if shot with caffeine at the perfect moment.

The biggest bummer possible came in the form of Dick, probably more than a hundred yards above me, on a rock with a medium sized rifle in his arms. Dick came up like a cat. I never heard a thing. I had previously acknowledged that Dick was good, real good. He didn't make a sound. He didn't wake the birds or the animals in the trees and brush. Dick just climbed through the area unnoticed. Only he missed. He sure miscalculated the path. It was a horrible error. I was effectively lost to him. I was invisible from his sight and he was moving further away. Embarrassing, but still even. I had to think fast, and I did.

I stepped back suddenly. My movements appeared to be organized from deep within my core, the hard-wired automatic stuff. I was there and then gone. Back. Gone. Done. It was time to be out of there with the speed of the lion. That was true.

I became one with the spirit of the lion that allegedly guarded the treasure at the time of Epimineo's search. The strength of the lion pulsed through me and I felt overtaken with the speed, mass, valor, and intensive aggressive instincts of the animal. These were alien feelings within me yet the communication from my amplified body to my brain was still reliable. As with the snake, the transformation process was magical and profound. Many may disbelieve this. It still happened.

Dick continued to climb upward and around the hillside for hours before he accepted the possibility that I had actually escaped. The most reasonable was the unthinkable. Only a fool would think he would quit. It would just take him longer to find me.

There were no signs and nothing unusual anywhere he climbed. He rested his laurels and placed his life wager on my return, preferably sooner. My apparent escape again after so many years was unforgivable. He was feeling angry. He was clearly the wrong man to confront when alarmed.

Could I continue to evade him, escape down the hill, and make it back to the car? Did I get around in the same way as Dick had approached? Turnaround was fair play. No answer would be forthcoming regarding the mystery of my disappearance. I escaped again and there would be no opening of the treasure, at least not today.

69. THE LION

Tacamonte Canyon – 2002

There was an increase in strange reports of mountain lion sightings around La Chiva, Tacamonte, and the surrounding hills over the last month. Hunters, campers, hikers, and visitors reported various independent encounters. The locals were afraid to talk. It sounded like more than one cat to them, and that was unusual. They were known to be solitary hunters.

The newspapers reported only one death by lion attack. Apparently a freelance American security consultant who had been residing in Culiacan for the last twenty years was surprised by a mountain lion when climbing La Chiva in the afternoon. According to the report, a bystander said the man was an American who often used the mountains for training hikes. He was said to be in pristine physical shape but others said his eyes told of his age. From the looks of the site he must not have noticed the lion when it was jumping down upon him from a ledge above. There was no time to react.

According to the paper, the attack was so vicious that it was difficult to identify the victim. Fortunately, there was an eyewitness who turned and saw the overhead attack while shooting photographs from La Chiva to Culiacan. He was not able to capture the event on film.

Police made a positive identification from some clothing, a wallet, and the inscription on the back of a watch. It was a bloody story, and the authorities are reminding the visiting public that the attack was unusual in the area. It was only the second such recorded in more than twenty years.

70. AeroMexico

Culiacan – 2002

The flight out of Culiacan International was a relief. I enjoyed the quality of the new airplane and the comfort of the cabin. I chuckled when I thought of my position upon the bags of illicit cargo around twenty years earlier. These seats were leather, the exterior was washed and shiny, and the airplane operation was legitimate. The pilots were flying on a scheduled flight plan and were using international clearances. Nobody was worried about being tracked or followed, other than electronically by air traffic controllers.

The fare was much less than it was the last time I left the area and a meal and drinks were also served. I never felt more value received when the flight crossed through turbulent air into United States airspace last time. This time I had a smooth flight to a different destination.

I pulled out my digital camera and began to scan the very small images on the back screen. The photos looked sepia-toned because of the reflection of the light off of the piles of gold bars, coins, and other metal objects. The lack of natural light also added to the impact. I was confident that the images captured by my Nikon 35 mm, evidenced by the undeveloped rolls of film in my gear bag would be unbelievable. I hope the flash was powerful enough to fight through the thick darkness.

The entry was made as dusk was approaching. The old door had been difficult to dig out and then lift. It was narrow and deeper than I expected. The top of the cave had been dynamited into place by the bandit to enclose an original open-ended area. It was much larger than I anticipated. That was a splendid surprise.

That construction technique would have been highly innovative in the times of the bandit. He filled his space well. The engineering was more significant than ever anticipated. The bandit, Lareano Garcia, had certain innate understanding of mining and physics that permitted the nature of the secure and permanent enclosure.

The shots of the piles of coins included delightful gold and silver coins, pieces of eight, doubloons, pesos, Spanish coinage, and local substitutes for cash. The photographs did not reveal the depth of the storage piles. There was incalculable value stored in the cave.

There was no evidence of Gerardo's skeleton. Time had removed that evidence. Dust to dust.

From the photos, the Mayan artifacts were more rustic than envisioned and expected. They were often carved out of wood or stone, and had a more primitive level of craftsmanship and detail.

The Aztec series showed a time of more material exploration. The boxes of currency bore the brand of the local mint. The legends were true. The nature of the treasure items verified and validated the stories.

Many on the Internet challenged the authenticity of my La Chiva photo series. Critics were convinced the shots had been faked. The treasure could not be so vast. Speculation has been raised that the photo setup was shot in a warehouse near downtown San Francisco using elaborate and carefully made props. They called it a wonderful publicity hoax.

I stand behind the veracity of my story and the existence of the Treasure of La Chiva.

EPILOGUE

Belize – June 6, 2005

The composition of the people on the *Toucan* in 2005 was no accident. Captain Dan Powers was trying to organize a return expedition to La Chiva. Like Jesus Borella, the Military Governor, Ellis Stevens would not share the exact location with anyone. He had plans of his own and was waiting to be invited.

Negotiations are underway, but a third trip to the mountain is a difficult assignment. I now had a personal interest and could easily be a participant if the parties came to terms.

I am not being permitted to give out any more names or information than is contained above. But I have one special mental photo that will keep me interested. I still can see the brown leather bag that Ellis was holding when he finished the story. When he opened it a large number of old Reales fell out onto the table. All of them were dated 1858.

∾ ∾ ∾

Author's Note

This is a novel. The characters and events in this book are fictitious, or should be treated as such. The author intends no similarity to real persons. With that said, the names and events are my best recollection of the sessions with Ellis Stevens, Captain Dan, and a few others on the *Toucan* in early June of 2005.

ACKNOWLEDGEMENTS

Thank you Moire for your love, support and patience. Thank you Shannon and Jon for your understanding, Juliet and Dan for your loyalty, Lisa and Chris for your encouragement, Jeff and Shelly for your confidence, Bryce and Heather for your energy, Sophia and Bo for your wonder, Bradyn for your joy, and Scarlett for what never will be. Thank you George and Gloria for everything, Dennis for the memories, and Mike for being there. Thank you Harry and Joyce for being the last, Grandma for being the oldest, Marlene and Joe for sharing, and Jennifer and Peter for the love. Thank you Evy for not laughing at the 15-year-old boy who said he would write a novel one day.

Thank you Blaine Court for the opportunity and experience, Captain Dan Powers for your hospitality, and Christian Cummings for your clear insight and constructive criticism. Thanks Danielle for the look and opinions, and all of those who encouraged me throughout this project, including my family, friends at the Bay Club Marin, and everyone else who ever listened.

Thank you Ellis Stevens for your trust and candid openness as I took so long to experience, write, and edit your living journey.

Made in the USA
Charleston, SC
03 February 2012